MW00973970

To Mary Ann & George —
May your fun include a lot of wickedness!
Have fun!
Lucia Bruels

Little Bit Wicked

by

Lucia Bruels

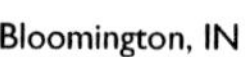

Milton Keynes, UK

AuthorHouse™
1663 Liberty Drive, Suite 200
Bloomington, IN 47403
www.authorhouse.com
Phone: 1-800-839-8640

AuthorHouse™ UK Ltd.
500 Avebury Boulevard
Central Milton Keynes, MK9 2BE
www.authorhouse.co.uk
Phone: 08001974150

This book is a work of fiction. People, places, events, and situations are the product of the author's imagination. Any resemblance to actual persons, living or dead, or historical events, is purely coincidental.

First published by AuthorHouse 01/03/06

ISBN: 1-4208-9259-2 (sc)

Printed in the United States of America
Bloomington, Indiana

This book is printed on acid-free paper.

- Other Books by Lucia Bruels -

UNBREAK MY HEART

AH, BEAUTY

MAN ENOUGH

PURE AS SIN

IT'S ME, LUV

CHAPTER ONE
Tuscany, 1770

"Bloody hell!" The words escaped Geoffrey's mouth as he crested the hill. He'd promised, hadn't he? Leave the skirts alone until his engagement was certain. Well, at least his choice was certain although the lady was not yet approached. He ran the tip of his tongue over his lower lip as he breathed in the scene below him. He'd ridden through a maze of flowering thickets following a path not meant for a horseman. Boredom and curiosity had kept his eyes glued to the trail and then this!

He shaded his eyes; no one anywhere near; just the girl, a feast laid out before him. From here he could see she'd removed her shoes and stockings and was preparing to wade in the small lake. No, perhaps bathe. As he watched, the vision unlaced her gown and stepped out of it. He grinned in anticipation. With quick decision, he dismounted and let the reins drop. His mount was well trained, content to graze.

Who was she, out here all alone? Circling the slope he picked his way toward the protection of weeping willows to hide his approach. Perhaps they could pass the afternoon in idle play. Hell, even lively conversation would be appreciated. He was weary of the stress of courtship, proper protocol, what passed for civilized gentry in this country. Naples had been wicked and exciting. Northern Italy was peaceful, too peaceful.

His red-gold hair was beginning to curl about his neck in the heat as he made his way between the trees. Thick gold lashes almost hid the deep blue of his eyes as they narrowed in the dappled sunlight. He'd lost sight of her there in the trees. Now he stepped into the clearing where several broad rocks bordered the water and stopped short.

Her back was to him; a perfect back that narrowed to a slim waist flaring to womanly hips. Her arms were raised as she pulled her short chemise over her head. The heart shape of firm buttocks invited his touch and his mouth went dry.

The lovely form bent forward and dived into the lake with barely a splash. Alarm came close to causing him to run to her aid before he realized the girl was stroking out with her arms as gracefully as a swan. Perfectly nude, she moved through the clear water.

Dazed, Geoffrey stepped back into the shadows and watched, his heart beating a rapid tattoo. Barely an hour earlier he'd been whispering sweet nothings into the ear of Margery Omar-DuBois, his choice of bride-to-be. Tomorrow night the announcement would be made of their engagement if her parents agreed. And he was sure they would. After all, he was a catch. The eldest of the St.James boys, he'd inherit his father's earldom with all its privileges and wealth.

Their grandparents had been friends forever although his were British and theirs French, more or less. The lines intertwined several generations back and this match had been discussed for years. It was a good thing Margery was beautiful and intelligent. She was just so damn predictable.

He moved nearer a thick tree as he realized the nymph was rising from the water and walking directly toward him. The crooked grin split his face once again, eagerness running rampant.

She was perfect. Drops of water centered his attention on the tips of her breasts, slipped downward to glisten on the dark gold at the apex of her legs. The vision leaned forward, those ivory globes swinging into offerings for his enjoyment. She wrung water from her long hair, then sat upon a spread quilt while her fingers threaded through the strands. Now supported by braced arms, she tipped her face up to the sun and closed her eyes.

Geoffrey's shaft pushed painfully against his tight trousers. His fingers itched to touch her, kiss those full lips, cradle his erection between those perfect hips. He shed his jacket and loosened his shirt at the throat, stepping into the sunlight as he did so.

For a moment she was unaware of him; her thoughts far away on a dream. Then his shadow touched her and the spiky lashes flew open. Neither of them spoke.

Had she conjured up this perfect male? Tall, masculine in a sinful way, he stood over her. Long muscled legs snug in tight pants seemed to reach to the sky. Their smooth stretch marred only by the large bulge, more exciting than defect. His face was hidden in the glare of the sun but his hair curled about his neck in red-gold lengths. Her glaze slid to his shoulders; shoulders wide and powerful. He had on a white shirt with full sleeves. She saw him reach toward her.

Before she could react, he took her hand and pulled her upward and against him. One hand cupped the round of her bottom, the other caught the nape of her neck, guiding her mouth to his. The fabric of his shirt scraped her tender breasts and they tingled. She was nude and she was in the arms of this man, this stranger – and her entire body reacted as though he had every right -.

Jillian was so shocked she allowed the invasion of his tongue as he skillfully pressed against the seam of her lips. They opened and he pressed home the advantage, tangling, teasing, plunging. Somehow she couldn't breathe, only the breath he allowed her, his breath. His mouth moved, slanted, took once again. His teeth nibbled when she tried to speak, then enticed further.

All the while his other hand was massaging her, pressing her into him. She could feel his hard shape against her belly. It did strange things to her, weakening her knees, causing an ache to begin low inside.

The hand that had held her head steady lowered to squeeze a breast, the thumb roughing her nipple. Somehow her entire breast was cupped in his large hand, swelling to fill it, begging more.

She squirmed, pushing against him but his arms tightened, his mouth moving over her face and throat, his tongue in her ear. Her arm circled his neck, tangled in his red-gold hair without conscious thought.

Still no word had been spoken. They were both gasping, Jillian in panic at the need he was generating within her. He held her about the waist as one hand slid between them and tangled in the silk of her private place. She felt the slick of it, his hand grinding against her, just as he insinuated a finger deep inside.

Her legs buckled. Keeping his hand in place he caught her and laid her down on the quilt, following her body with his own. His finger continued its magic while his mouth mimicked the rhythm in her mouth.

Jillian had never been kissed but by relatives. She knew about mating. After all, she'd been brought up watching the stallions on her father's stud farm. Wild she was but never had it occurred to her that she was in any danger here on their own property. No one ever came to this lake. It was hidden. It was hers, her sanctuary.

His blue eyes opened and one brow quirked in question as his finger pleasured her. He pushed a knee between her legs to spread them, releasing her long enough to unfasten his trousers.

Her grey eyes widened, the thick lashes now dry in the summer heat. Color washed over the perfect skin. Jillian turned her head from his gorgeous lips so she could breath.

"Stop! You must stop. There'll be no end of trouble." She turned her head back so she could gaze into his blue eyes, eyes that had deepened in color to be almost navy. "Please." Without thought she'd spoken in French but he'd understood her. She drank in his gorgeous face, the high cheekbones, the chiseled nose, the full lips that gave such pleasure. Oh, she wanted him to teach her, anything, everything.

Geoffrey took a deep breath, then another. He removed his finger, his hand, from between her legs but so slowly as to be an enticement. He smiled as she caught her breath.

"Are you sure? I won't get you with child. There are ways – and we can both enjoy it."

He debated kissing her again. She would weaken. He was sure of it. But then, the chase made the conquest more intense, didn't it? She wanted him. He had another day. He could wait.

She shook her head wildly, tears beginning to gleam in her eyes. His accent was British. She knew who he was now and that made it worse. What in the world had possessed her to let him go so far? Even to let him touch her?

She stared at him as he rose from between her legs. He was so handsome, so big and masculine. It was the first time she'd ever been attracted to a man in that way and she'd had no shame. What had gotten into her?

Geoffrey watched as she stood and slipped the short chemise over her head, smoothing it over her hips. It clung to every curve, every indentation. The damp cotton was worse than nothing at all. He throbbed with wanting her. He gnawed at the corner of his lip. He should not have stopped. She would have enjoyed it. He'd never had any complaints.

"Do you live around here?" When she glanced at him but continued her dressing without answering he turned grumpy. He fastened his shirt, ran his hand over his cock to ease the pressure. "Will you be here tomorrow? I'll bring you a present, a real present." He bit the inside of his jaw, considering throwing her back down and burying himself between her legs. She did look very young for all her womanly curves. Perhaps she was a virgin.

"How old are you, oh lady of the lake?" He touched one nipple with the tip of his finger and watched the bud peak, her shiver of response. "I didn't mean to frighten you, you know. There you were, all spread out like a banquet, and here I was, starving." He grinned at her and she smiled back.

His French was perfect, she noted, but his accent was British. She switched to English to be sure. Her parents had been expecting English guests. Her mother had been excited, match-making for her older sister.

"I should not have been here – or should not have shed my chemise. Papa caught me once and threatened to spank me if I swam alone again." She cut her eyes up at him, more confident now she was clothed. She sat down and began to pull her stockings into place. "It just gets so boring out here and the water feels so nice against one's skin."

In truth, she'd been on her way home. She'd run away from the sequested school where her parents had left her for the past year; punishment by her mother for unladylike behavior. The lake had been just too tempting.

Geoffrey licked at his dry lips as she tied the garter in place. Didn't the girl have any pity? And spanking? He'd like to spank her rosy butt. "How about tomorrow then? You didn't answer me."

Jillian shook her head. “I don’t think so. I’ve heard the gentry at the villa have a lot of company and a party tomorrow. You’re one of them, aren’t you?” She smiled in mischief. She knew exactly who he was now – the match made in heaven, as her mother said. Her sister’s letter had sizzled with excitement.

“And what if I am? Doesn’t mean you and I can’t have a bit of fun, now does it?” When she looked down at her feet, he caught her chin and lifted her head.

His lips took hers and this time she felt it to the bottom of her being. Oh, damn Margery. He should be hers, hers. She leaned into him and he gently squeezed her breast.

“Do you care very much for the lady of the house - the red-haired one? I thought you might be her suitor.” Her heart was in her eyes, the full lips parted.

Geoffrey breathed in her scent, the freshness. Desire hit him again like a hammer to the gut, for this young girl, not the settled Margery. “The lady Margery? She doesn’t hold a candle to you.” He brushed her lips with his. “Tell me your name. Give me a name for my dreams.”

It was on the tip of her tongue but he pressed his hardness against her belly again and she lost her direction. It was just as well. She couldn’t tell him who she was. He must never know. He was probably going to be her brother-in-law.

“I must be getting home. It’s getting late and they’ll be worried. Perhaps tomorrow if I can get away.”

He released her, nodding, “Tomorrow morning then. I’ll have you a surprise.” He gave her the crooked grin that always charmed the ladies.

Jillian had started toward her mount, a dappled grey and white mare with no saddle. She turned, nibbling on her lower lip, observing him. Her first love, and he was so beautiful. She wouldn't be here tomorrow. It was impossible. On impulse, she ran back to him, threw her arms about his neck and pulled his mouth within reach. One last taste, she wanted just one taste of him.

This time her lips took his, the intiative all hers. He opened and she kissed him with every bit of expertise he'd just taught her. She had to pull from his tightening arms but now she didn't look back.

Geoffrey watched her ride in a direction away from the large villa up on the side of the mountain. So, she wasn't one of the upper servants. Who was she? He would savor today as he made all the proper overtures tonight. Until the morning, until he could figure out how to have his cake and eat it too as the saying goes. Yes, he could wait until morning. He remembered the feel of her long legs, the satin skin cool from the lake. For this girl beneath him he could wait as long as it took – or as long as he had. That was the trouble. He and his brother would be leaving for England after his engagement was announced.

In bemusement, Geoffrey wove his way back. Smiling to himself he reviewed every detail of his newfound lady. She was different from anyone he'd ever known. He could still picture the golden waves of her hair as it dried in the sun, the tawny tone of her perfect skin, the soft mews when he pleasured her.

Who was she? She spoke at least two languages, and with an educated tongue. Her hands were dainty, flawless, that of a lady. He grinned to himself and had to shift in the saddle for comfort. A lady he could court, a lady he could marry rather than offer for the prim and proper Margery, if only he knew her name, her family. Then again, no lady behaved as she had. No, she was someone's mistress, had to be. And he intended to steal her away. He'd never been so taken with a female, so enchanted.

CHAPTER TWO

Jillian made her way up the back stairs undetected. She threw herself across the sprigged green and white comforter on her bed and kicked her slippers onto the polished floor. She licked her bruised lips, tasting again the wonder of the Englishman. Her hands cupped her aching breasts, her thumbs rubbing over the taut nipples.

"Oh, damn. Why couldn't it be me? Why does Margery have to be the first to marry?" She sat up and pommeled the soft pillows with her fists. Then a thought struck and she hugged the object of her fury to her breast. "And I allowed him to have sex with me – with me – soon to be his sister-in-law." She wailed, angry tears running down her cheeks.

Jillian wasn't sure about the sex thing. She'd only observed the stallions once or twice and both times her mother had made her come back to the house before the act was completed. But he'd been between her legs, hadn't he? And his hands, his fingers, ohhhh, the wonder of it. She closed her eyes and her body flushed with pleasure. Damn, damn, damn. Now what to do?

....

Geoffrey rubbed the gold locket between his thumb and forefinger. The delicate chain would drop it to hang just between those young breasts, just right. He would fasten it about her neck, allow his hand to follow the links downward, caress – ah, he felt his shaft harden as his palms remembered the feel of her.

Of course, he had bought the locket for Margery but she'd never know that. Thank goodness he'd not had the time to have it engraved. Shame he couldn't combine the two women. Margery would make the perfect wife, his future duchess. She was elegant, beautiful, and so damn sensible. Make that boring.

She would never ride bareback, swim naked in a lake, spread her beauty out in the sun for all to enjoy. This girl, his lady of the lake, was everything enticing. Her eyes had an air of innocence, changeable with every emotion. Those long lashes curled onto high cheekbones, dark, much darker than the silk of her hair. It was a shame she hadn't Margery's auburn locks but the girl's pale brown was almost gold, curling, and her skin touched with the sun. He liked that. He had enough of the milk-white skin in England.

He thought a minute. Now, Margery's was more cream, a pretty enough shade. But then he pictured the girl's again; burnished by the sun, the tip of her nose and cheeks rosy from the heat, and smiled. The warm feeling spread until he could almost feel her satin skin as he stroked her.

He jumped with guilt as the door was flung open. He dropped the locket into his coat pocket as his younger brother strode across the room and opened the cupboard.

"I need to borrow the navy jacket. Mine seems to need a bit of mending." Stephen noticed the expression on his brother's face. "Don't you look smitten? Is it to be a love match, then?" He laughed, a laugh identical to his brother's.

Geoffrey's answering grin was noncommittal. "You read me wrong. She's a lovely girl, of course, but love match? Not bloody likely. Anyway, I'll save you from a like fate and produce the required little heir."

"Well, you could have fooled me. What were you comtemplating when I came in? Nothing innocent, I'd wager." Stephen's dark brow rose.

His coloring was unlike his brother's although their features were from the same mold. Stephen's hair was dark brown but had the slight curl also. His eyes were long-lashed and a soft chocolate color that could darken with emotion to almost black. They were of a height though and often wore each other's clothing.

Geoffrey shrugged, watching his brother don the navy jacket. "You'd look better in the tan. Her little sister will be there tonight, perhaps. I hear there is one although she must be hideous or she would've been presented before now. Probably too tame for your taste but might as well keep it in the family." He dodged as Stephen struck out at him.

"Not interested, big brother. One marriage every ten years would suit me fine. You're lucky I even accompanied you up from the coast. Now, where were you earlier? Thought you wanted to stretch those muscles. Many more hours in a coach and I'll turn into an old man."

"Sorry I didn't wait for you. Saw you cornered in the library and I just had to escape." Tongue in cheek, he punched Stephen on the shoulder. "Actually, I'm not sorry. I met the most fascinating bit of skirt. You won't believe how my siren and I whiled away the time; and I'm to meet her again tomorrow."

That got Stephen's attention. He sprawled in the oversize leather chair by the hearth and regarded his gleeful brother. He'd never seen him quite like this.

"Do you think that wise? I mean, after all, you're to announce your betrothal tonight. I take it she's some servant?"

Geoffrey shook his head, his fingers rubbing the hidden locket. "I don't know who she is; an escaped governess perhaps." He ran his fingers through his thick hair and licked his lower lip. "She 's the most perfect thing that's ever happened to me and I don't even know her name.."

"A governess? Isn't that a bit far-fetched?"

"Well, she speaks with intelligence; when I allowed her speech, that is." He grinned crookedly. "And she rides barebacked but the mare was a good one. And she swims! Really and truly swims. I watched as she shed her clothes, piece by lovely piece, and dove into the lake. Enough to hypnotize a man."

Stephen had straightened up in the chair and was leaning forward, elbows on his knees. "Naked, you say? Around here?"

Geoffrey adjusted his pants for comfort and his brother smirked. "When she exited the water she took her time, stretching in the sunshine, wringing water from her hair. Then she half-lay, half-sat upon a quilt, still nude, and waited for me. Just waited." His voice took on a dream-like tone.

Stephen's brow rose. "And you're sure you didn't just dream this up? Were you drinking?"

"Not a drop. She's real, young, beautiful, everything a man could want. She seemed surprised when I took her in my arms but then when I began kissing her she was all fire. Lord, but she was good!" He looked down at his polished boots. "I might ask her if she'd consider returning to England with me – as a mistress, of course."

Stephen jumped to his feet. "Are you crazy? Two women when you didn't even want the one? And a mistress before you've even sampled your future wife? No bit of fluff is that good! Think, man!"

Geoffrey let out the breath he'd been holding. "I know you think I'm bewitched but wait until you meet her. Just remember, she's mine. I don't share this one, even with my beloved brother." He grimaced. "We'd better get below. There'll be dancing on a small scale so that means being partners with these country females and tromped toes. I'll be glad when this night is over."

....

Meghan Omar-DuBois followed her husband to his study, closing the doors and turning the lock. Storm looked up from the papers on the dowry he'd meant to review, a frown of puzzlement on his brow.

"What is the trouble, Kitten? I thought everything was going as you wished. Margery has made a perfect match. Geoffrey St.James is what you always wanted for our girl and a future earl of England besides." He crossed the room and gathered his wife in his arms.

Meghan's blue eyes glistened with tears but she was angry. She took a deep breath, brushed her husband's lips with hers, and pulled away so she could speak without his distraction.

"Jillian is home. She ran away and has been riding all over the countryside, alone. It's a wonder that girl has not been ravished, or murdered. She's upstairs. I forbid her to show herself until I had talked with you." Her voice began to waver and a tear fell. "She'll ruin Margery's engagement party. You know she will."

Storm forced the smile from his face. Jillian was his favourite, wild and sensuous, innocent and much too intelligent. Margery in all her sedate beauty was no competition. When the two girls entered a room every male eye gravitated to the younger girl. He loved Margery but he loved Jillian to distraction. Her behavior was, in large part, his fault.

He took his wife in his arms again, one hand making small circles on her back. "Now, now, Kitten. Jillian will always be Jillian. She doesn't do anything on purpose, you know. When I agreed for her to enter that school I never meant to desert her there for this long. You know how confinement, even within attractive walls, spurs her on to escape, to have her own way."

He chuckled in spite of himself and received a furious look from his wife. "I'll speak to her. Perhaps it's best she is home. I would've sent for her once our guests had gone anyway. You know, it won't do any harm for her to meet the young men. That younger brother, Stephen, is a handsome rascal. He should deter her from distracting Margery's beau."

"Oh, you know it is unintentional. She just is - ." Meghan sighed. Her daughters were so different. "I suppose Margery should be able to hold him if he cares for her at all. But you will insist Jillian dress in something suitable to a young girl, will you not?"

Meghan left to lie down for an hour or so. Storm climbed the stairs to his daughter's room, anticipation at seeing her hurrying his steps.

He knocked, then entered. Jillian was standing before the window, brushing her long hair. He smiled at her and she ran into his arms.

"Oh, Papa, I couldn't stay away any longer. I forgot this was Margery's weekend but do not worry. I intend to stay upstairs in my room until everyone leaves. I know how Mother thinks and I don't need an old party right now anyway. I just needed to see you and be home and free."

She looked up at him and kissed his cheek. She wanted to tell him about her wonderful afternoon but some things she could not share. It was the problem with growing up. She would be seventeen in six months, two years behind her sister Margery.

"You know I would've come for you at the end of the school year. I only agreed to hush your mother. Then again, you did need some polishing, you know. I've let you run wild too long, my sweet. The lads were beginning to hover like bees to honey."

"Oh, Papa." A light blush tinged her high cheeks. "You know I never paid the slightest attention to those silly boys."

"Ah, but boys grow up. It's time you think before you act." He set her from him. "Let me look at you. Hmm, my girl is prettier than ever. You've filled out. Now, I suppose, it'll be the young men and not the boys." He laughed.

Jillian gnawed at her bottom lip. "I do feel a bit ill after my long ride from school – and tired, so tired." The half-curve of a smile escaped. "It will please Mother."

"Hmph. You do whatever you wish, Princess. I'll be up to check on you later." He turned to the door, then looked back over his shoulder. "I would rather you come downstairs; in fact, I'd be delighted. There are two brothers, your sister's intended and a younger brother. Also several Navy friends of theirs are here for the party. You might enjoy the young men. Just do wear something that will not out-shine your sister. Keep your mother happy." He winked at her and was gone.

Jillian sighed. She'd remain upstairs. Her mother was already angry enough. One of the guests had to be her lover from the lake. Perhaps it was not Margery's beau but she couldn't risk it. Her body flushed with heat as she remembered his long fingers, his hot mouth devouring her. No, she couldn't face him.

If he wasn't to be her brother-in-law perhaps she could meet him in the morning. She'd see tonight which one of the visitors was her dream lover. She knew just where to hide and spy on the guests.

....

Jillian shoved the hot water bottle to the foot of the bed as she heard the door open. Her father's dark head appeared. She smiled in delight then remembered she was sick and tried to look depressed.

"Princess, your mother told me you wouldn't be coming to the party tonight. Have you a fever or is this to please her?" His rough hand caressed her hot forehead before he bent to kiss her cheek. "I'm so sorry. I wanted you to meet St. James' younger brother, Stephen. I believe he's more to your taste than the future earl."

"I'm sorry too, Papa. I have a confession. I stopped at the lake on the way home. The water was especially cold today. I know I shouldn't have and I didn't dare tell Mother." She hoped he didn't notice the flush of her cheeks as the memory flooded her senses. "I don't want a beau just yet anyway. Let Margery be the center of attention. She deserves that." But she doesn't deserve first choice Jillian thought with resentment. She smiled weakly at her father as he took his leave.

She had remained out there in the country, locked away at that old school, while her parents had taken her sister to meet the ship from Naples. It had always been so. Her mother's insistence overruled her father's adoration and Margery was her mother's favourite. They had all just returned and now she would not get to meet the two young Englishmen. That is, she'd not officially meet them. She was almost sure her lover from the lake was the elder St.James, Geoffrey. His description fit her sister's recitation of his attributes down to the last detail. Oh, why had she not thought before she acted – melted against his hard body – allowed him to kiss her breathless?

Jillian giggled. Well, who was thinking? But she couldn't very well meet him now, if indeed it was he. She would just have to remain ill and out of sight until they left. Surely, she could fake a fever for a day or so. Her mother had insisted the choice of suitors was Margery's so until she was settled Jillian didn't stand a chance.

Was it her fault if the neighboring young men preferred to dance with her rather than with her sedate sister? She'd never felt the least attraction for any of them but that didn't matter. Always the receipient of the 'after the party' lecture, as Jillian called it, she still did not know what she was doing that made the men think she could be other than proper.

Even Papa smiled at her in a knowing way and assured her that one day her sensuous nature would bring her joy but that for now she must learn to act more demure. Well, today it had brought her joy, whatever the cause. If only she'd dared allow him more – just to see how it was. She nibbled on her lip. Perhaps she could just watch the dancing tonight, just see him. Her young breasts seemed to fill and ache with the thought.

....

Stephen frowned at the spoilt lace at his cuff. The wine stain hadn't been his fault but the chubby young lady had been saved from the spill, at least. He climbed the broad stairs to his chamber, hoping his other white shirt would be suitable beneath the dress jacket.

His assigned room was at the very end of the long hall, near the balcony that overlooked the formal rooms below. As his hand closed on the doorknob he saw a flash of movement among the draperies and plants on the balcony - one of the maids? He opened and closed the door but remained in the hall. Curious, he slipped to the far side and observed a young girl kneeling very near the railing. A long plait hung almost to her waist. She wore a wrapped robe and no slippers. She was peering between some potted plants at the dancing below.

"If you lean any further you may fall." His voice was soft but still she jumped up in alarm, her fingers to her lips.

"Shhh. They'll hear you." The light was dim but there was enough from below to see that he was a stranger. "What are you doing up here?" Jillian's heart was pounding. She had been caught. There were quite a few guests in the house that she didn't know but this one was young and handsome, much like her lover. She narrowed her eyes at him. "The retiring rooms are below."

"I wasn't hunting the retiring room. My chamber is just there." Stephen motioned toward his door. He kept his voice a mere whisper. "Do you always spy on the gentry?"

"I do not spy." She drew herself up to her full height. "I'm -." She stopped. It wouldn't do to let this stranger know who she was. Perhaps he was the other Englishman, his accent was not so strong but even in the dim light he reminded her of him. Still – his coloring was all wrong. This one was dark, not the golden looks of her man. "I do like the dancing. I'm not hurting anyone by watching." She tucked her head shyly so he wouldn't get a good look at her face.

Stephen chuckled softly. The music for a waltz had just started up. He nodded to the orchestra below. This dance was considered decadent by many but if they were playing it here, then -. "Do you know how to dance?"

Before she could answer Jillian felt a strong arm circle her waist as his other hand clasped hers. She was swept out into the hall to the rhythm of the waltz as elegantly as any debutante. She gasped, laughing, and matched his steps with perfection.

Stephen's brow lifted in surprise. He'd thought to delight a timid maid, perhaps a guest too young to be below. The girl in his arms was old enough to provide soft curves for his embrace and her dance steps were graceful and light. He tightened the arm at her waist and realized she wore nothing beneath the robe or at least nothing of any consequence. He'd never waltzed with an uncorseted woman. No wonder they considered the dance decadent. He could feel the flow of her body with each movement, the soft curve of her breast, the long thigh as it brushed his.

He grinned down at her, his eyes crinkling at the corners in delight. "You've done this before?"

She smiled back, even white teeth appearing between full lips. "Not like this, Monsieur." Now, why had she done that?

"Oh, French, are you? A French maid, perhaps?" He proceeded to address her in that language. No British accent ruined his pronunciation, and his Italian had been perfect also. She was impressed.

Jillian answered in kind. After all, her parents were a mixture of English and French and she 'd lived in Italy with her grandparents for years also. Then she became aware of the slight shift of his hips, his body pressed closer, his long leg tangling in her robe. She stopped in mid-swing and stepped back from his arms.

"I think that is enough for tonight, Monsieur. Thank you for the dance." She glanced down the hallway to her room but thought better of it. She turned as he bowed, smiling, and fled up the servants' stairs.

Stephen stood watching as her bare feet disappeared. Her lingering scent was that of apple blossoms. He smiled to himself. This house was full of surprises. He inhaled again as he turned to his room. Best he change shirts and go back to the party.

....

Geoffrey stretched his legs out to the seat next to his brother. Thank God that was over with and they were on their way home. He'd been allowed two hours to the exact minute alone with Margery in the garden.

Her breasts were fuller than his dream lady and she was a bit shorter. Her eyes were a clear green with a slight slant at the corners. Her thick auburn hair had paler red-gold streaks as though she'd been in the sun. In the sun, as his lady of the lake. perhaps? He snorted. Not bloody likely. Still, she'd been warm enough when he'd held her; relaxing against him.

She'd offered no resistance to his kiss either. It wasn't his fault he couldn't put any fire into it. All he could think about was the lass he'd wanted for his mistress. No, Margery Omar-DuBois would be his perfect duchess when he came into the title, but never his passion.

He closed his eyes and tried to remember every touch, every detail, of his short encounter with his lady of the lake. His shaft hardened in response and he shifted in his seat, waking his brother.

Stephen's brow rose in question, a smile playing about his full lips. "Dreams, brother? You're warming up to your future lady wife?"

"Hmph. I'm thinking I will have to imagine her naked beside a lake, naked with her sex glistening with need, her breasts less full, tipped with tight buds – maybe then I can get her with child. Why isn't it a perfect world?"

"You ask too much. You always were a spoiled brat. You have a beautiful woman, a rich woman, one that pleases Father. And she's not pure English, therefore there's hope she won't be dull."

Stephen closed his eyes then opened them again. "I take it the redeavous did not go well this morning?"

Geoffrey grunted. "She wasn't there. I don't even know her name or how to find her. Damn it. I should have followed her that day." He closed his eyes to feign sleep.

He'd left the locket on a spread piece of velvet where he'd last been with her. It was gold with open work and he'd left a scrawled note inside when she hadn't appeared. Would she find it? Foolish - foolish of him to be so taken by the girl. He grinned. She was a little bit wicked though, wasn't she?

Before they had left he'd cornered the friendly upstairs maid and inquired about some gossip he'd heard. Was there a young blond mistress of some gentleman living nearby? Well, near blond, pale brown with blond streaks, more telling of time spent in the sun. Or perhaps a governess, a daughter of an artist? He'd be willing to pay for her name, information as to where she resided. He'd described her as best he could but the maid had pulled away from him, shaking her head, insisting she knew no one that fit that description. She had fled in panic and he was forced to leave none the wiser.

CHAPTER THREE

Meghan covered her eyes with the cool cloth. She seldom had the severe headaches now. The guests had gone and her Margery's future was secure. She tried to relax but Jillian's sensuous face with those changeable eyes kept floating before her.

She suppressed a sob. It wasn't the girl's fault. She tried to love them both equally, she did. But every time she was around her youngest daughter the nighmares returned.

Storm's family was delighted with the girl, insisting she was the image of his grandmother, the deceased Angelise. Well, except her hair was much lighter and perhaps curlier. The looks though, the blue-green-grey eyes; those long-lashed eyes that changed with each emotion, that fascinated the male sex. She was sure they were his eyes. Her skin was tawny, like Storm's, her lashes black, her lips full and sensuous. It was the hair that did it. His hair – no matter what they said.

Logically, she knew she'd already carried Storm's child when he'd had her but his face, his handsome face, and those blond curls haunted her. And Jillian had been born late and with curls of gold. Curls that had darkened somewhat to a pale brown except when the sun touched her head - but still gold, the gold of the Dutch overseer. And the girl was wild, sensuous, like the man. Never mind that her husband also fit that description. Her emotions fastened again and again on that day – the day he took her.

They'd spent the first year and a half of their marriage with Storm's parents, first in Italy, then in Marseille. Then had come the extended visit to London, to the St.James', a distant relative. Storm had monies invested there and stashed away in the Bank of England; funds he'd earned the hard way, trapping for fur and working for the British government in Quebec.

With Gill St.James' advice and introductions, her husband had made his start in their shipping company and plans were laid to return to the French held Louisiana. Storm had inherited over a thousand acres upriver and fully intended to establish a plantation to offset any losses his shipping might incur. They had set out together to see if Meghan would consider living there, first making a stop to leave their small daughter, Margery, and son, Andre, with his parents.

Storm's uncle, the Comte Michel DuBois, had once resided in Louisiana but had sold his interests to his partner and overseer and had had no contacts since. The land that was now Storm's was deeded from the King to Michel's father, Andre. The will of the deceased Comte Andre DuBois had left it to Storm, his favourite grandson.

At the time no one in the family had been to New Orleans in over ten years. The town had grown and prospered since Michel's departure. Meghan could still see the whole episode in her mind – she and her husband side by side – excited to make their future here. She closed her eyes, remembering.

They stood close together on the deck of Storm's ship as they surveyed the bustling wharves. Meghan's memory of it was as clear as though it all happened yesterday.

"I need to file my claim and settle the inheritance first thing. Would you like me to find a room at a hotel for you, Meghan?" He knew she was weary of shipboard and would like a good bath in a large tub for a change.

"Would you? I'll be fresh and ready to explore by the time you get back. It'll be so good to be on land again." She ran a finger down Storm's chest where his shirt hung loosely. "Then we can enjoy the other comforts of the city together."

He kissed her with lingering sweetness. "I'm looking forward to a large bed, myself. Not that I have any complaints of the cramped space we've enjoyed. Perhaps the fruits of our labors will be born in Louisiana, a true Creole." He raised one black brow, his mouth curved in a crooked grin.

She laughed, drawing his hand to splay upon her stomach. "Shame, Monsieur, when I'm barely certain of it myself. Do not shout my demise from the decks for all to hear. Are you truly glad?"

"I promised you four, didn't I? We've one yet to go after this present. And yes, I'm happy, the happiest man alive. I have you, a fine son, a lovely daughter, and a bairn on the way." He rubbed her belly, still smiling. "It doesn't show yet. Are you sure?"

"Hmm, I feel pregnant. But I've only missed one time. Still – we haven't missed a night, have we?" She stuck her tongue out at him, then ran it about her lower lip slowly.

"Keep that up and we won't make our appointment, Kitten. Come on." And he tugged her behind him as he headed for the boat being lowered.

....

The hotel manager fingered his black mustache as he observed the auburn-haired woman. Some nerve to come here as though she had every right. He'd never seen Delia this close but any man would know that hair. His dark eyes snapped back to the stranger with her.

"I don't know how long we'll be staying." Storm laid payment on the counter. "This should cover a week."

The man behind the counter suppressed a snort. A week, indeed, a night with Delia would be enough if gossip were correct. 'Course , if Monsieur DuBois found out she was stepping out on his time -. He turned the ledger to look at the newcomer's name. His breath caught and he swallowed convulsively.

Storm frowned. "Are you all right, Monsieur?"

"Of course, of course, I have a condition; yes, a bit of a condition." He cleared his throat. "From that three-master in the harbour, are you? Haven't seen you around."

"Yes, we're just arrived from London." He smiled but the smile didn't reach his eyes. There was something odd going on here. "Don't worry, though, we are of French nationality. Name's DuBois, Storm Omar-DuBois, and this is my wife." He nodded and glanced to the cubbyholes containing keys. "Do you mind? We're rather tired and my wife would like hot water sent up for a bath as soon as we're settled."

"Of course, of course, a bath – the copper tub, then." He spoke to someone in the room behind him then handed Storm a key. "The boy will take your luggage up, Monsieur."

The clerk stared until they were out of sight. Only one small satchel; but then he hadn't expected the woman to have extra clothing, had he? Left the rest aboard ship, the gentleman had said. Now, where had he met up with Delia?

He called to his wife to take over the counter. "I have to run an important errand. See the new occupants are kept happy – perhaps dinner in their room later – you can ask." He hurried away toward the stables.

……………………………………………………………

Rene Louis DuBois scratched his black beard. The hotel manager had just left, well paid for his information. Of course, the woman in town couldn't be his Delia. He knew because Delia had been upstairs in his bed for the last several days. Not that he'd told his weasel of an informant that fact.

It had happened at last. The DuBois family had come to claim their land. He chuckled. Well, let them try. He was well established as the owner, had been for some years now. A pillar of the community, he'd built this fine house, purchased several hundred slaves, cleared land, planted cane. He twisted the ornate ring on his little finger. Why, he even had the DuBois family ring, a gift from his 'grandfather'.

Let this newcomer dare claim what he'd taken. He'd almost come to believe the lie himself. This Storm Omar-DuBois, if memory served him correctly, was the husband of the redhead he'd kidnapped in Paris. The muscle worked in his clenched jaw. Justice at last, payment for his brother's fiery death.

Of course, it wasn't Storm that was his enemy. It was his uncle, Comte Michel DuBois, but he would take what vengeance he could get. It was all in the family, wasn't it? And they'd never prove a thing. They were strangers here.

When his band of stragglers had attacked that coach in the French countryside he'd never suspected it would cause his brother's death. They'd been hungry and desperate, angry at the rich with too much money and too much food. They hadn't intended to kill the old man and his wife; it'd just happened. How were they to know he was a count? Or that his entire family followed close behind – close enough to discover the bodies and the destruction of the coach – close enough to hunt them down and kill his entire band of men?

Rene's nostrils flared in anger and his fist slammed against the desktop. They would pay. What was his now he would keep. The night he'd broken into Michel DuBois' home and stolen the papers and the ropes of pearls had given him a future, a life in this raw land. He'd sold the pearls, a few at a time, to finance his way. His fingers beat a tattoo on the desk as he thought.

He sent for his overseer, his right-arm. Phillip had been a pirate, had tried his hand at planting, and failed. But he was a jewel in the rough. Here, as overseer, the man had his own house, a share of the profits. He followed orders without question.

The heavily muscled man paused at the open door. His blond hair fell in slight waves to his shoulders when it wasn't caught back at the neck as it was now. Perspiration beaded his brow and he wiped his arm across his forehead before entering the room. Eyes that reflected the sky, eyes surrounded with dark lashes, surveyed the room as he took a chair before his employer.

"You sent for me, Monsieur?" His words were more polite than his sprawled posture. "I saw your man leaving. Trouble?"

"A hint of excitement to come, perhaps. I want you to keep Delia out of sight for a while, down in one of the cabins should do."

"She won't like that." Phillip's sensuous lips quirked upward.

"I don't care what she likes. Be sure no one knows she's there." Rene crossed to the decanter and raised a brow in Phillip's direction, then poured. "See she's happy but quiet."

Rene's tongue rolled the liquor before he swallowed. "There's a woman in town, a woman with auburn hair, looks like my Delia. She's staying at the hotel with a man named Storm Omar-Dubois. She claims to be his wife." He turned from the table to face his overseer, watching his reaction.

Phillip's grin widened. "Wife? This DuBois claiming to be some kin of yours?" He'd always had his suspicions about his employer. The man's French was not the most polished for one thing nor did he seem fond of his homeland.

Rene nodded, tongue in cheek. "Well, we both know a slave can't be anyone's wife. Especially when she belongs to me, and always has. Of course, letting Delia set up housekeeping in town might have given her ideas. Perhaps she got ideas about paying me back when she heard this man's name."

The blond head nodded. He took a deep drink. "That's so. Women do get ideas. Up to us to straighten them out. How would you like it done?" He finished his drink and set the glass down so abruptly that Rene jumped.

CHAPTER FOUR

Storm returned to the room just before dark. Meghan ran across the room to throw her arms around his neck. She was shaking and he had to pull her loose so he could look at her.

"What is it, Kitten?"

"Oh, why are you late? I was so afraid. They all treat me so strangely here. No one will speak to me. They brought the bath water and then later removed it without saying a word. And it's almost dark and - ." She raised tear-filled eyes to him.

He kissed her nose, her eyes, her lips. His hands caressed her back, then splayed over her tummy. "Is it the baby? Are you feeling well? You remember the last time you were breeding you imagined everything wrong and cried at naught." He held her head against his chest as she cuddled.

"It's been a confusing day and I'm sorry I'm so late. It seems there is already a member of the DuBois family working the land that I am claiming. They seem to think I am trying to swindle him. I rode out to the land that Michel once owned – the land deeded over to his partner. No luck there. The man is suffering from a fever and is no help; his son doesn't know the family."

Meghan pulled from his arms. "Oh, Storm, I'm sorry I'm such a baby lately. May I help in some way? Perhaps if I described Marie and William to them they would be remembered – or something?" Marie and William had created quite a stir when they were here after Michel left.

Storm shook his head. "I've filed papers with the court. I'll ride out to visit this DuBois tomorrow, perhaps with one of my ship's officers. It's too much property to turn over to an imposter. Michel would have known if even a distant member of the family was living on the land."

He turned at the knock at the door. "I've ordered a good meal sent up. The manager suggested it since it was so late I didn't think you'd want to dine downstairs. You can go shopping tomorrow while I'm gone. It appears to be a bustling little city, not Paris exactly, but you should be amused. I'll leave you money." He caught her bottom and pulled her against him hard.

Meghan laughed and kissed him just as the door opened. The maid, a fat woman as black as sin, pursed her lips and shook her head. Meghan's eyebrows lifted in question. Whatever was the matter with everyone? Couldn't she kiss her own husband in thier own room?

....

Meghan strolled down the bustling street. Which shop to try next? After all, she had all day and she'd only purchased a new bonnet so far. She turned to stare at two rough men coming toward her. Everyone seemed to be clearing a path for them and she instinctively moved closer to the shop front to allow them passage.

"You there, nigger!" Meghan's eyes widened as she looked around. Everyone had disappeared into the shops but herself. She took a step backward toward the nearest door but a beefy fist closed about her arm.

Attempting to jerk away, she slapped at him. It was a mistake. The back of his hand caught her face so hard her head snapped back, ears ringing. Her mouth opened in a scream for help but no sound came out.

Together the two men dragged her down the street. Once around the corner they stopped, surveying her. She was gasping for breath, disbelief in her eyes.

"So you're Delia. Heard you're a beauty, near white. No wonder Monsieur DuBois was so upset at your sneaking off. You're gonna catch it now, girl."

"I'm not this Delia. I'm Meghan Omar-DuBois. My husband is even now -." She squealed as his hand closed over one breast and squeezed.

"Sure, Delia, sure. You're married now." The two of them laughed and pushed her ahead of them to an old building near the Cabillo. The door closed behind them.

A stern man looked up from the desk. The blond giant propped on its corner straightened and pulled her closer.

"Fast work. DuBois will be pleased. Should be something extra in it for you. Put up much of a fight?"

Meghan stared at him, open-mouthed. This wasn't happening, couldn't be happening. "I demand you release me this instant. My husband will have your hide."

Amused, the blond man leaned closer, his mouth near touching hers. "And? Come now, Delia, the game is up. Your owner is waiting for you and he's not pleased at your latest escapade." Catching her arm, he headed for the door.

"Glad to of been of help I'll finish up the paperwork. He gonna let it go again or do you want her branded this time? Fire stays hot." He nodded to the back room.

"Monsieur is forgiving again. After all, she'd have been brought back sooner or later. She has his mark. Merci." Meghan dug her heels in as the door closed and the man stopped.

"Why are you doing this?" Tears hovered in her large blue eyes.

Philip pushed away the touch of sympathy he felt. After all, if her husband did as bid then she would be free again.

His voice was gruff when he spoke. "We have one more stop to make."

The next stop took longer. Meghan was let into a small dingy room and told to change into the clothes there. She looked at the simple cotton dress with dismay. The voice through the door spurred her into action.

"Either you change or I'll do it for you; your choice. Take everything off."

Shivering with fright and confusion Meghan stripped. There were no underthings, just the dress. It was full-skirted and had a sash to hold it in to fit. The material was soft enough and clean. There were no shoes and she had begun to slip her laced boots back on when the door opened.

"No, no, that won't be necessary. Leave them and come with me." The blond man motioned with his head and entered another room.

She was told to sit upon a high stool. The other occupant of the room pulled another, lower, stool up beside hers and placed a tray with color pots and needles on the table nearby. He nodded to her captor.

The man caught her hands in his beefy ones and held them tight. The old man lifted her skirt to expose her upper thigh and tucked it between her legs. Held as she was with her legs between the blond man's thighs and her wrists secure, she couldn't move.

Meghan screamed, only a little scream. He was sticking her with needles. What were they doing to her leg? The sound died as the blond's mouth closed over hers. She struggled for breath as the kiss – if that is what it was – deepened.

The pricking had continued. Yet the blond man kept kissing her, almost a welcome distraction. Her upper thigh felt numb to the small pain now. She tried to twist and see what was happening but could not. And then it was over.

"See that it is blurred somewhat. Monsieur wishes that the tattoo does not appear recently done." He nodded as something was rubbed into her leg. At least her mouth was free but she no longer had the desire or the will to fight back

……………………………………………………..…

It seemed like time had stopped. They had been driving for hours into the dense forest, then past fields and fields of waving cane. A turn into a gateway and a beautiful two-story house came into view. Its front faced the river but this side was imposing. Geese scattered in alarm and the door opened, someone looked out, then disappeared. Their buggy continued around to the side.

Meghan sat mute. Whatever had happened, Storm would find her and everything would be all right. This was all a mistake. They thought her someone else, that was all. She watched as a tall, dark, man crossed the yard . He was smiling. Thank goodness. He would know she was not this Delia.

She scrambled down from the buggy. Her bare toes curled at the unaccustomed feel of the prickly lawn.

"Philip, good work! Amazing resemblance, isn't it?" The well-dressed man, arms akimbo, was accessing Meghan from the top of her head to the tip of her toes. "Yes, she could pass for my Delia. And the other?"

"I took care of it, Monsieur DuBois." He caught Meghan by the waist and lifted her skirt to expose the tattoo on her upper thigh. "Looks like she's your property for sure." He laughed and released her as Meghan dug an elbow into his ribs. "Fiesty just like Delia, too."

Meghan stared at the man. He was familiar somehow. Where had she seen him? His clothing was the latest style and expensive. He had black hair that curled slightly, like the DuBois family, but his eyes were dark brown.

"You're not a DuBois."

"Am I not, Sweetheart? Well, that's to see, isn't it?" He raised a bushy eyebrow. "Have I introduced my overseer, Philip? You'd best be good to him. You have just been registered as a runaway slave, belonging to me. Of course, my Delia has fled before but I'm a patient man. This time I had Philip complete the paperwork so it's a matter of record. And you bear my mark. By tomorrow it'll age so no one will know it hasn't been there for years."

"I don't look like a negro. I'm not a mulatto and I'm not yours. Why are you doing this? What have I done to you?" She twisted but Philip still held her with wrists pinned behind her back.

"Ever heard of a quadroon, Sweetheart? Just a drop of nigger blood but you're still nigger and you're still a slave. Now my Delia's skin is as light as yours, same hair, eyes a different color but no one will remember that. I never let another man close enough to that piece of prime ass to notice."

"If she gives you any trouble, Philip, you know what to do. Just no permanent marks, you understand. We may be forced to sell her if her husband doesn't agree to my terms. Wouldn't want to damage the value."

Meghan slumped against Philip in shock. She couldn't think. This was worst than her kidnapping in Paris, worst than – she stared at the dark man.

"You! In Paris – you're the one – ." Her breathing ragged, she struggled with the words. "You filth! Storm will kill you this time. He will!"

She was still screaming at him when Philip dragged her down the path that led to the slave cabins.

....

Meghan sat on the stool in shock as the big black woman worked around her, humming. She closed her eyes so not to see the auburn locks that fell in a rain about the stool. Her beautiful hair, reaching below her waist, had not been cut in years. Storm had loved to see it down, to brush it, to make love to her as it made a canopy of fire over their twined bodies. Silly, silly to cry over hair when she had worst problems right now.

The snipping stopped. Meghan opened her eyes. The round black face was beaming. Plump fingers plucked at her hair, fluffing, the scissors still open for use.

"There now, Missy. He say make your hair like Celia's, all curly. This be best curly you get." She squished her fingers through the shortened locks.

Meghan felt of her lightened head. Her hair was in varying lengths, the longest of which came just below her shoulders, the shortest just a few inches long. It was still wet but beginning to curl, each to its own length. She shook her head in dismay. Her long hair had kept almost straight, just a bit of a wave. It would be forever before she was her old self.

"Now you ready. Master say come with us to garden. Don't think you much use but garden not so bad as the fields."

Meghan followed sullenly around the house to the kitchen garden. She noticed several black girls, very young, hoeing weeds. She was handed a hoe and pointed to a plot of herbs. She stood perfectly still. Darn if she'd work like a slave.

A big black woman twice her size descended on her from the kitchen door, wielding a large paddle. The paddle cracked against Meghan's bottom, toppling her into the dirt. Her mouth opened in indignation and the paddle hit again, harder.

"Get up, girl. Ain't got all day. That patch is yours. Don't think I won't watch you from the window, either. Lazy trash. Don't know why he send me such as you. Get!"

Meghan scrambled away as the paddle swung again, grabbed the hoe , and began to hack at the row of plants. She shrank away as the shriek heralded another whack of the paddle through her thin skirt.

"Not those! Don't you know weeds from the good ones?"

And so it went – all day – until the sun set. Meghan's back ached, her skin itched from the unaccustomed sun, her hands blistered – and her hair curled into a mass of ringlets from the heat and perspiration.

The other girls had disappeared but she didn't know where to go. Her bare feet squished in the muddy earth as she watered the plants of her labours. They were still tender, unused to being without slippers. At least the ground was soft in the garden, she thought. She looked up as a shadow loomed over her.

The blond man again. Arms akimbo, he watched her. Her loose blouse had slipped low on her shoulders and she hastened to pull the string tighter when she saw where his eyes rested. She set the watering pot down, wiping her hands on her skirts. He smiled and motioned for her to follow him.

Meghan looked around but there was no one else about. Swallowing a lump in her throat she trailed behind him down the little path to the cabins.

"Why am I here, Monsieur? You know my husband will come after me. You'll be sorry for all this." She bit her lip. He hadn't said a word.

Phillip stopped at a small cabin set away from the others and pushed open the door. "There's water to wash. Someone will bring you supper. I wouldn't try to leave if I was you. There's 'gators in the water, all kinds of wild animals in the woods – and some of these blacks really like a taste of someone with skin as light as yours." He waited for her to squeeze by him then shut and barred the door.

Meghan sat down on the pallet spread on the floor. Silent tears rolled down her blistered cheeks. She was so tired. She lay back and fell asleep as her head touched the quilt.

CHAPTER FIVE

Storm and Raoul, his second in command, had planned to pay a visit to the DuBois plantation early but when they'd asked directions they'd been told that Monsieur DuBois was away quite a bit and would be in town at his office later that afternoon. It seemed he'd had a runaway slave and wanted to pay her captors a reward for work well done. The city was obviously addicted to gossip.

Storm had stopped by the hotel to pick up Meghan but she was out shopping. The city had grown and was filled with narrow streets and tiny shops. Believing his wife to be content with her foray into the city he and Raoul retired to a local brasserie to pass the time and enjoy food and drink.

At two DuBois had not shown up at his office. The two men stopped by the hotel to inform Meghan of the day's events. It appeared they would have to ride out to the plantation after all.

Meghan was not in the room. Storm stopped by the counter downstairs and rang the bell. "My wife, have you seen her?"

The man fidgeted, shifting from one foot to the other. At last he pulled a wrapped package from under the counter and pushed it toward the men.

"This was left by the catchers. Said you'd understand they had no part in her trying to rob you, Monsieur. The money she had left is all there." He tsked with his tongue against his teeth. "Delia, she's caused trouble before, sorry to say. I thought as much when she came in, all hanging on your arm that way. Our apologies for the lapse in our hospitality. Monsieur DuBois sent word you should see him if you wanted anything, anything at all. Thought maybe you were a distant cousin."

Storm's face paled. He grabbed the man's shirt and pulled him off his feet. "What the hell are you talking about? Where is my wife?"

The man's voice quavered. "That's what I'm trying to tell you, Monsieur. She's no wife. She's Delia, a quadroon belonging to Rene DuBois, upriver. He just sent the catchers to fetch her back this morning. She should never have posed as a free woman, she -."

He never finished. Storm dropped him to the floor like a sack of flour. He shook off Raoul's restraining hand and ripped the package open. Inside were a few coins and Meghan's clothes. He cursed, flinging them off the counter and across the room.

He caught the little man again before he could make his escape. "Where is my wife? I'll ask you just once again." He slammed the man against the wall dislodging a large painting which fell to the floor with a splintering crash.

"Don't know, Monsieur. I swear I don't know. Up at the DuBois place, I'd imagine. I didn't do nothing, anything."

....

Storm and Raoul lost no more time. The ride out in the humid air soon had both men perspiring heavily. They stopped only once, to shed their jackets and give the horses a breather, then continued through the jungled countryside. The sun was setting when the DuBois place came into sight.

The windows of the mansion were all abaze with light yet it seemed deserted. The men threw their reins to the boy that came forward and Storm climbed the front stairs, motioning for his friend to remain there. His fist was poised to bang for entrance when the wide door opened.

A cheroot in one hand, the man was dressed in impeccable taste. His head nodded in a slight bow but his dark eyes bored into Storm's.

"Storm Omar-Dubois? Would you like to come in for a drink, Monsieur? I believe we have business to discuss." He turned and led the way across the polished dark floor without waiting for a reply.

Storm glanced over his shoulder at Raoul, his gaze scanning the yard, and followed. The heavy doors closed behind them. His anger cooled somewhat. The house was ornate, lavish. Surely there was some mistake. Could this be some distant relative?

"Monsieur Rene DuBois at your service. I was informed you were in town. You're a relative, I presume?" He waved the hand holding his glass to indicate the lush furnishings. The DuBois signet ring flashed in the light. "Like it? I've done well here; a pillor of the community one might say. Word has it that you think you have some claim to my land. I assure you I hold the deed to the entire thousand acreas."

Storm's jaw tightened, the pulse in his temple throbbing. Only the head of the family wore the DuBois ring, his murdered grandfather and now his cousin Michel. That ring had been stolen, in Paris, and the man had not the look of the DuBois family – nor the polish. He shook his head at the proffered drink; first things first. He must find Meghan.

"I understand my wife may be here – some misunderstanding. Her given name is Meghan and she has auburn hair. She was seen in the company of your overseer in town today. I'm here to take her back to town." His hand tightened on the hilt of his sword.

The door opened and a brawny blond man appeared. He wore no jacket and his shirt was open at the throat, his skin tanned bronze by the sun. His light eyes crinkled at the corners in multiple small creases. A coiled whip was held close to his hip.

Without turning Storm's host smiled. "My overseer, Phillip. I believe it was he that retrieved Delia for me today. My apologies if she played on your sympathy, pretending to be a free woman. We don't know of any lady named Meghan, do we Phillip?" His lip curled in a sneer as he spoke. He half-turned as Storm's sword cleared its sheath.

With a crack it was snatched into the air by the whip's tip. Storm caught his fingers, stinging from the blow, and stared in amazement. Philllip was re-coiling the weapon with a satisfied smirk.

"Would you care to follow me outside, Monsieur? I'm sure we can straighten out this mistaken identity. Philip will return your sword as you leave. Oh, yes, I will need you to sign some papers first."

Storm's temper was blinding him. He snarled, "What papers?"

"I don't want any trouble with you younger DuBois'." Rene picked up several pages from his desk and indicated a quill and ink. "This is a disclaimer. You admit you have no legal right to my land nor will you pursue it in the future. In exchange I will sell you the girl, Delia, or whatever you wish to call her. I believe she's been asking for you."

Storm's fist caught the man's chin, snapping it backward as he fell against the desk. The lamp crashed to the floor, the oil soaking into the rich carpet. A second's pause as they all visioned fire but the flame extinguished itself. Storm's hand fisted. Before he could follow with another blow the whip lashed out, wrapping about his throat, pulling him backward.

Storm's hands clawed at it as he lost his breath but it tightened like a live thing. He kicked out at the blond man's knee and the rawhide loosened. Gasping, Storm turned but the whip lashed out again, catching about his waist, drawing a bloody line across his chest. He danced out of the way, crashing into furniture, searching for his sword. Again and again, his shirt half ripped away, the whip toyed with his flesh, cutting deep. He attempted to grasp the torturing tails as it bit into him but Phillip was too fast.

The nightmare of his flogging when he was a youth flashed before his eyes. Not again, he couldn't take it again. He fell to his knees, shamed, and felt the whip wrap his shoulders once more before Rene DuBois called a halt.

He looked up into the muzzle of a pistol, panting. Phillip stood, legs spread, the whip like a live thing snarling at his side.

"Now, Monsieur Omar, we talk." The black eyes were cold.

When they opened the front door Raoul jumped up from the bench under the old oak where he had been seated. Seeing Storm half-stagger toward him he reached for his sword.

"I wouldn't if I were you. Call off your man, Monsieur Omar." He watched, amused, as Storm shook his head at Raoul. "Come back tomorrow when you've had time to think. The sooner this is settled the better." He ran a hand through thick black hair. "Oh, and bring payment for the quadroon if you still want her. She's a bargain at any price."

By now they were joined by another rough looking man with a whip and five or six large black men, slaves apparently, but all there to reinforce their overseer. Storm mounted and motioned for Raoul to do the same. He guided his horse to the steps where his host stood posed above him.

"I'll be back. If you harm one hair on my wife's head you're a dead man, you and your cohorts."

Black soil flew as they rode across the carefully tended plantings.to the drive. Storm ignored Raoul's questioning looks until they were almost back to New Orleans.

Without explanation he rode first to the Cabillo but was denied entry or information. Exhausted, Storm turned to his friend.

"Go back to watch the ship, Raoul. She's there. I know she's there. He wouldn't dare harm her. He wants clear title to the land he squats on. I'll go to the authorities first thing tomorrow and get their escort out to the house." He nodded to his friend as he turned toward the hotel. "Guard the ship well."

Storm ignored the stares in the lobby. "Send hot water for a bath and supper afterwards. Have there been any messages?" At the clerk's mumbled answer he climbed the stairs to his room. Would they had stayed in Italy, or England. This country was nothing but trouble.

He was up at dawn. His sleep had been plagued by nightmares, his stripped body hoisted aloft while the first mate tested the cat-'o-nine-tails before administrating his sentence. Only this time he knew Meghan was watching him as he twisted, biting through his lip to keep from crying out.

He'd been no more than a raw youth but he'd not made a sound. He woke, sweating, flexing his shoulders. He'd almost died. The scars still roughened his back and shoulders. Meghan was the only woman he'd ever allowed to see him without a shirt. But then she was different. She loved him.

He buried his face in his hands as he sat upon the side of the bed. "Ah, Kitten, what would I do without you? Know that I'll come for you. Whatever it takes, you come first in my life." He brushed moisture from his cheeks. Had he lost his manhood? What was the matter with him? He crossed to the pitcher and splashed cold water over his head.

But the wheels of authority move slowly, especially when the person of concern is a friend of the Commandant and a wealthy citizen of the city. By the time Storm was interviewed by several distinguished men and had proven time and time again just who he was it was afternoon. Then they insisted on dining and waiting for the air to cool before they undertook their mission, a mission they obviously believed to be a waste of time.

Little was said on the ride out of town. Storm had insisted a carriage be brought along for Meghan's return trip. He ignored the raised eyebrows. At least they had agreed that his own deed appeared to be authentic. Now if he could only find someone who knew Michel DuBois, who remembered him. He and Michel looked enough alike to be brothers.

At Storm's insistance a squad of armed men attended them. The commandant dismounted beside Storm as Rene DuBois came forward to meet his friend and his "relative". He was all politeness. After his invitation into the house was refused he strolled into the shade of the old oak, followed by the two men.

"Well, Monsieur Omar-DuBois, I presume you have decided to agree to my terms. Did you bring the Commodant as witness?"

Storm remained polite, his tone giving nothing away. " I have brought the Commodant to reinforce my request that my wife be returned to me – immediately. She is here, you agree."

"Well, now, the woman you have called your wife is here. I believe you wished to see her prior to purchase. Phillip is bringing her up to the house. She's a valuable piece, you understand." Rene turned to his friend. "You know I've enjoyed Celia for several years now."

The Commandant nodded, smiling. "Something we all would have liked to take part in, Monsieur, if you had been more sharing." He stopped as the blond overseer came into view on the path from the slave cabins. Walking behind him one could see the skirts of a woman.

When they got closer Phillip held the girl by the arm, pulling her along. She stumbled somewhat as though her feet hurt, her eyes turned downward watching the ground. The sun glinted from auburn hair, touched gold streaks, curled about the wild lengths.

Storm's stomach knotted, hard. He swallowed, staring. Where were the long tresses? Her hair was a mass of curls of every length, the longest just below her shoulders. She wore a cotton skirt and blouse, the neck scooped low and tied together with a drawstring. Her feet were bare and dirty, her arms scratched. Her face was rosy from the sun but her skin was dusky, maybe tanned a bit. Blue, blue eyes stared wide at him in disbelief. He must have hesitated for just a minute, a minute too long.

The Commandant observed his reaction with raised brow. He exchanged a look with Rene DuBois.

Then Meghan burst from her shock and ran into Storm's arms. He lifted her, his arms holding her close, while she kissed his face and neck, murmering her love. Storm grinned, trying to keep from laughing. She looked so different- wild somehow!

"Kitten, it's all right. I'm here now. I'm here." He kissed her, trying to pull her arms away from his neck so they could finish their business and leave.

Meghan desisted at last, breathing hard, a smile curving her mouth. She nibbled at her bottom lip to keep from laughing in her happiness. But then she caught the other men's expressions – amusement, disbelief.

The Commandant drew hiimself up to his full height. "So, Monsieur, this is the woman you claim as your wife?" His mouth twisted into a sneer. "Truly, Monsieur, your taste defies reason. Cellia would make an exceptional mistress, with the right clothes, a bit of polish - ."

"Indeed, Commandant, this is my wife, Meghan Omar-DuBois." Storm's face had become a harsh mask. "We would like your escort to town now."

"Not so fast." Rene stepped forward and Meghan instinctively backed. This is my property and I expect to be paid for her in full before she leaves the premises. "Phillip, show our friend my proof of ownership."

He turned to face Storm as Phillip pulled Meghan to his side. When Storm's hand moved to his pistol, he was immediately surrounded by the Commandant's men, weapons drawn. He watched helplessly as the overseer's hand gathered her skirt up to her thigh, twisting her hip to face the audience of men.

The mark of ownership was unmistakable. Rene reached out to squeeze the tattoo into relief as the Commandant leaned closer.

"It seems to have been there a while – as one would expect." The Commandant's eyes met Storms and he shrugged. It would appear the woman is the quadroon called Celia and the property of Monsieur Rene DuBois as stated. Do you wish to purchase the woman?"

A shriek pierced the silence. Meghan twisted away from the overseer's grasp and attempted to fling herself back into Storm's arms. "He's no DuBois, Storm. He's my kidnapper; the man in Paris, the man who murdered your grandfather. See, he even has the ring. Oh, do not leave me here, I beg you."

But even as she spoke the men had bound Storm's wrists fast, a pistol jammed against his ribs. He was outnumbered by the very men he'd insisted accompany them to protect Meghan. Cursing, he submitted.

"My apologies, Monsieur, but we do not wish trouble. You and Monsieur DuBois may meet on the grounds of honour and settle your differences at a later date or you may make arrangements to meet his price for the quadroon. I will escort you back to town and then I will no longer consider this to be my problem."

He watched Phillip drag the screaming woman away. "I trust her punishment is not too harsh. It would be a shame to mar such beauty."

Rene smiled, shaking his head. "I rather enjoy her temper. It will be a shame to lose such a challenge. Still, if the price is met -." He cocked a brow up at Storm where he had been forced onto his mount, his arms bound tightly. A trickle of blood marred Storm's temple where he'd been struck but he was so furious he hadn't noticed.

....

Before the Commandant's party had reached New Orleans a message was on its way to Storm Omar-DuBois from Meghan's "owner". Rene would give him time to raise the gold needed for her purchase, two days hence. He, himself, would accompany her to town that morning. Storm could meet him in his office there on the square if he had made his choice. When the papers were signed dissolving all future claims against the DuBois land and the purchase price met for the woman their business would be complete. The meeting was set for eleven o'clock. Any attempt to contact the woman in the meantime would result in a forfeit of their agreement. She would be sold at market elsewhere.

Rene chuckled as he pressed the DuBois signet ring into the hot wax. This was better revenge than the Paris kidnapping. Perhaps it wasn't the Comte himself, Michel DuBois, the killer of his brother, but it was sweet. He'd set the meeting for two days hence to give Storm Omar time to be miserable, to imagine what his woman was enduring. And there was nothing he could do about it. The Commandant would keep a close watch on him until the meeting. Rene doubted not that Storm would scald his cousin's ears when he fled home with his tail between his legs. His own brother must be laughing in hell, or wherever he was.

CHAPTER SIX

Meghan was awakened early the morning of her freedom. By the time the door was unbarred she had splashed cold water over her face and was ready to leave. Both the so-called Rene DuBois and the man Phillip were outside. Hovering under the edge of the trees was the big black she'd seen watching her for the past days.

DuBois tipped his hat to her with a gentlemanly smile. "It seems we both get what we want, hmm, Madam?" He turned away as she hesitated on the doorstep. "Just one more item of business remains. Phillip will see to it, won't you, Phillip?" He began walking up the path toward the big house. "We leave in an hour or less."

Meghan siddled past the overseer but he caught her skirt and pulled her back, motioning to the cabin. He stepped inside after her. The black man had moved closer and propped against the doorway, blocking it. She looked from one to the other. Her hands trembled and her knees felt weak.

"Are we not leaving? We are to meet my husband this morning. I'm free. You heard him." She backed away.

"You hear what you want to hear. First I have a gift, a keepsake, for you." Phillip nodded toward the large man behind him. "Do you know why we call him Bull?" He laughed deep in his throat. "He's at stud all the time. Biggest damn cock this side of the river."

He turned to the big negro. "Ever had a white woman, Bull? You can pretend she's that hot little quadroon, Celia. Everybody knows you pant after her ass." He laughed again as Bull shook his head.

"Don't think that be a good thing, Master Phillip. Nigger get hung for such round here. Don't mind the riding but don't want no hanging." He eyed Meghan where she'd backed into a corner. "Not that I wouldn't do a good job, mind."

Phillip crossed the small space so fast Meghan didn't move. One hand closed on her waist as he pulled her against him. "Your choice, Madam, me or him. Either way you're getting fucked." His fingers pulled the drawstring of her blouse and the cotton fell open, catching on the tips of her breasts where they pressed against him. "Which? I enjoy watching Bull perform."

Her eyes wide, unfocused, she could only shake her head. Phillip's hand closed over a breast as he backed her against the wall, his mouth taking hers. Bull had stepped outside but she didn't notice. Her legs wouldn't seem to hold her anymore. Somehow she was on the pallet with the overseer on top of her, his knee pushing her legs apart.

"Never liked an unwilling woman. Be nice and I'll send that big black on his way." His blond hair loosened from its fastening as she struggled. His changeable, pale, eyes were grey today – grey and cold as ice. Only his mouth smiled as he moved over her.

His teeth nipped and tugged at her breasts until they peaked for him and she moaned. His fingers played deep in the tawny curls as his swollen cock lay heavy against her thigh. He laughed as he spread her legs further before filling her, his beefy hands digging into her soft thighs.

Meghan stared at the ceiling. The sun played on the dust motes through the tiny window. It touched his gold curls with a halo as he at last had mercy and took his pleasure It made prisms of color where the tears lay on her cheeks.

Phillip collasped atop her, sated, but still sporatically grinding against her. He leaned forward and kissed the tears, licked at them with the tip of his tongue. He took a deep breath then breathed out against her mouth. In disgust she turned her head away and he settled deeper in her even though he was beginning to slip.

"Not yet satisfied, Madam? I give you my best and you cry for more." He rolled from her and fastened his trousers. "Up! On your hands and knees." His foot caught her hip to roll her over.

Sobbing, Meghan did as she was told. What did it matter anymore? They'd never let her go now. Her breasts ached where his teeth and hands had used her, her woman's place was still swollen with need. She didn't even move when he bellowed for Bull and she heard heavy footsteps. Her eyes were squeezed tight.

"See you finish the job. There'll be a bonus in it for you. A little white ass will do you good." Laughing, Phillip left, calling for someone to fetch the wagon to the big house.

Meghan never heard him return. Large rough hands covered her buttocks, gentle hands. Soothing murmerings in some language she did not know were whispered in her ear as the hands massaged. Her sobs lessened as he stroked her back and slid around to her breasts, spread over her stomach. Tender fingers trailed over her belly, all the while the soft sounds filled her ears. The trembling began to subside, her body waiting, waiting, for him.

Frantically she thought about the baby within her. They didn't know, did they? She was already carrying Storm's child. She had to be. She'd been late with her monthly bleeding that once. No matter how many times they took her – she was already pregnant – they couldn't hurt her if she didn't lose Storm's baby.

The hands caught her upper thighs, lifted her hips, spreading her. Meghan's flesh quivered and the soothing words began again. Her eyes still tightly closed she was mesmerized by the stroking, the feel of the pulsing organ thrust between her legs, seeking but not entering. Her hips shifted. Like a cat in heat they sought his entry. She was almost panting as the big black's penis pushed forward in acknowledgement, inch by inch. Gentled, like a breed mare, she responded. She tightened, thrusting backward and up as the buck's huge shaft sank deep. Oh, God, so deep. She'd never felt anything like it. She moaned, whether in pleasure or pain, she knew not which. Again, so slowly, so deep – the slide seemed to last forever – each filling her so completely she couldn't get her breath.

The roughened hands moved to her breasts, using them to pull her back until he was seated just so, his balls pressed as far as they could go, moving, moving. She exploded as his shaft throbbed and pulsed, crying out, shamed and uncontrolled.

He withdrew, turning her upon her back, and thrust to the hilt, again and again. A deep panting – was it hers? - and she felt his hot seed spreading. Stars exploded in her head once again, rippling through her body, sucking at him. And still he pumped, her sheath milking his offering, pulling it deep, deeper. Her mons ground against him, hips raised, fire spreading. So full, so complete – she moaned as he withdrew, her body in dismay at the loss.

She looked up into dark eyes, a forehead creased in worried lines. But then his large mouth split in a wide grin, white teeth gleaming. He bent her knees upward, tilting her to hold his seed.

"Best do this right. I have reputation. You happy now?"

Meghan wanted to laugh but couldn't quite. She nodded at him, why she didn't know. Happy? The world was turned upside down. The big man was the devil himself and no man should be hung like that. Her eyes traveled to where his shaft lay in rest. It was still huge. He followed her stare and his grin grew larger.

"Madam want more? Be ready in few minutes." His hand continued to move over her belly as he held her legs.

"No, no, thank you."

Still grinning with big white teeth his hand traveled down to her buttocks, patting, stroking her inner thighs. Her flesh quivered in response.

"Don't you worry none, Madam. Bull make beautiful bebe – skin like you, maybe little brown, hair like you, like sunset. Boy bebe hung like me, prince in my own land. Girl-child a little bit wicked, like me." He chuckled deep in his throat. "Bull never fail."

Meghan laughed before she caught herself. She was hysterical. She felt like a fool – and the biggest sinner ever. She'd just been raped by two men and she was still panting over this one – and him a slave. May God forgive her. Stunned, she realized he'd lowered her legs and was pulling her clothing into place.

"I carry you up to wagon. Master Phillip say so."

He scooped her into his arms as though she were a small child and proceeded to trudge up the hill toward the big house. Her cheeks scarlet, she noticed that the overseer had been standing outside and was now walking up the path ahead of them.

Deposited in a prone position on a bundle of quilts in the back of the wagon she tried to collect her wits. Phillip climbed onto the wagon and took up the reins. Monsieur DuBois came down the steps and glanced at her then cocked a brow at his overseer.

"Well? Is it taken care of?" His lips twisted as he pulled on his cheroot.

"Just as you wished. The little bitch is a hot one. She enjoyed every inch." He twisted on the seat to smirk at Meghan in the back but she wouldn't look at him.

Rene DuBois came back to stand beside her. "Shame I won't be around in nine months to see the DuBois family's reaction. The black kinky head of a slave on the newest DuBois heir?" He patted her belly. "Perhaps I can find a way to hear the gossip."

Meghan's face had lost all color. What if she wasn't already with child? She most certainly was now. And whose? She wanted to spit in his face but her mouth was so dry she couldn't even speak. She stared at the overseer's back. So, perhaps DuBois didn't know he'd raped her. He'd only meant to breed her to the slave. She memorized the blond curls of his hair, the cold changeable eyes. God forbid she'd conceived his child – though Storm might overlook a blond white baby. Her mother had light hair or at least a lighter red than her own. She bit her lip. Damn men! All of them!

Rene climbed into his carriage and the procession headed for the city. He chuckled as he thought of the "quadroon" he was selling. Well, if the husband wouldn't deal he'd make a tidy profit when it was known she was breeding – and with Bull's seed. And there wasn't a thing Storm DuBois could do about it.

CHAPTER SEVEN

The gold exchanged hands. Meghan, pale and shaky, now belonged to Storm Omar-DuBois. The papers were signed to disclaim the land. Just to make sure Storm drew up freedom papers for his "slave" and made sure the witnesses were reliable. He wanted no future trouble where Meghan was concerned. Her full description and name, both Meghan and Celia, were listed. He didn't know this Celia but he wanted to be sure.

When he walked into the hotel there was dead silence. The desk clerk choked, surveying the female held close to his client's side. He sputtered in protest as Storm asked for the room key but quickly stopped when Storm withdrew a pistol and placed in on the counter.

"There will be a copper tub full of hot water immediately. Followed in one hour by a hot meal, your best. Any disrespect and this hotel will rue the day it came into being. Is that understood?" His mouth twisted in a snarl as the clerk quivered and hastened to call for service. "We will be checking out after we finish eating.

I prefer my wife reside in safe surroundings from now on."

Holding Meghan's hand, he crossed the lobby of staring people, her bare feet leaving dusty prints on the polished floor. At the foot of the stairs he lifted her into his arms. "I love you, Kitten. I won't fail you again."

He waited in the sitting room at her request while she bathed. Meghan was afraid he would see the multiple bruises that were beginning to show on her breasts and thighs. If only the overseer had been as gentle as the big black. Storm must never know what happened, or not until they were far away. They'd kill him if he went back to that house. That's what they really wanted – for her to tell him they had taken her.

She hadn't counted on how exhausted she was. The warm water lulled her, soothing the aches and the memories. She hadn't slept the night before and had eaten very little. Storm had insisted she have wine before she bathed to help her relax.

When he was not called, Storm stepped into the room. The lamps were low but he could tell she had fallen asleep, her head resting on the edge of the copper tub. He stood looking down at her. The bubbles had long ago dissolved and he felt his usual hardening as he gazed at her beauty. He dipped a finger into the water. It was cool. She would catch cold. He stroked her cheek but she didn't awaken.

He looked around and found the toweling. Rolling up his sleeves, he lifted her from the bath and sat her on his knee meaning to dry her as she awoke.

Meghan's eyes opened with slow ease. She felt so good, so clean, so safe. She snuggled into her husband's arms, tilting her face upward for a kiss.

Storm was staring at her breasts. He stood, dumping her to her feet before him. His honey eyes darkened as they dropped to the marks on her thighs. He turned her. There were angry handprints on her buttocks, scrape marks down her throat. He cupped one breast. Distinct teeth marks circled its nipple.

His gut knotted, twisted, as the truth sank in. His voice a mere croak, his hands tightened on her shoulders.

"Why? Why didn't you tell me? Who did this to you? You were raped? That bastard who calls himself DuBois did this? When?" He realized he was shaking her and stopped abruptly, gathering her in his arms, stroking the wet curls that dripped in wild disarray about her shoulders. "Oh, Kitten, I'm so sorry, so sorry. Tell me how to help you. I've failed you again." He buried his face in her neck, his arms clasped about her.

Meghan stood numbly trying to think. When his grasp loosened she picked up the toweling and wrapped it about her to hide the evidence. Storm sank into a chair and she climbed onto his lap, her head on his shoulder.

"I love you, Kitten, no matter what happened. You know that, don't you? I just want to know who to - ."

Her lips sought his, teasing until they responded. He returned her offering with desperation, his hands buried in her wet tresses. At last he calmed somewhat and began to rub the toweling about to dry her. She handed him the smaller piece and he wrapped it about her hair.

The maid with their supper interrupted any more discussion for a few minutes. When the table was spread and Meghan had swallowed a few bites she began to explain as best she could.

"I was hoping you wouldn't find out. He will kill you. He wants you to challenge them. And it wasn't DuBois directly, only his orders, I think." She paused for breath, trying to read Storm's expression. "I love you and nothing they did will ever change that. Can we not just leave – just sail away from this place?"

"Who was the man, Meghan? You owe me that much- unless you wish me to kill every last male on the place." He thought a minute then reached across the small table and cupped her chin with his fingertips. "Did you lose our baby? Are you still pregnant?"

A smile touched her full lips, lips now bruised with other men's kisses. "Our son – or daughter – is safe. They didn't know. They were trying to – they wanted to present you with a bastard. It was his final revenge."

"Who but Rene DuBois then? The overseer? That Phillip that struts about with the coiled whip?" He saw her expression. "It was the overseer, wasn't it?" His jaw tightened as he recalled the shame of his whipping that first night. "Did he touch you more than once? I'll cut off a piece of him for every time he touched you starting with his balls." He looked up to see her reddened face. "I'm sorry, Kitten. I've lost all sense of decency it would seem. Don't worry, it's just my temper. I'll file charges against the man. He's no gentleman and it would be useless to challenge him. We're going home."

He shrugged, his mask in place. There was no need for her to know what he planned. “Let’s finish our hot meal and you can dress. I’ll take you out to the ship where you’ll be safe until we can sail. I’ll see to the last of the cargo tomorrow. No reason why we can’t make a bit of profit with a full hold. Raoul will stay with you while I attend to thc last details.”

Meghan watched as her husband seemed to relax. Would he truly let it go? He was chewing on a bite of beef and buttering a hot roll. She took a long sip of wine and her head quit its spinning. They were going home.

He looked up, his attitude casual. “What were you doing in your captivity? You seem to have been out in the sun. I didn’t know you liked the land – the outdoors.”

“The land was important to you, not me. I’m sorry you had to use it to free me, Storm. I – I worked in the kitchen garden while I was there. I hoed and pulled weeds, watered plants – wiggled my bare toes in the mud.” A smile spread slowly. “I guess the outdoors itself is not so bad.” Then she shivered and the smile disappeared. “It wasn’t bad until this morning.”

....

New Orleans was growing but it was still full of gossip and everyone who mattered knew everyone else. By the next morning the entire story, with embellishments, had reached the plantation where Michael DuBois had once lived. The old man, Michael’s former partner, had been in bed with the recurring fever that plagued the area. His son, Gerard, had not informed him of Michael’s kin, Storm Omar-DuBois', arrival, nor of his request in proving his identity.

The old man, furious at being sequested in his sick bed, now ordered his carriage brought around. He was carried out by his manservant and placed within as his son protested that it would be the death of him.

He met with the Commodant and word was sent out to the ship for Storm's attendance. Storm was at last located down at the wharf. When he arrived at the Cabillo, Gerard was standing beside his father and the Commodant wore an apologetic expression. He was, however, dressed in full uniform; his dignity intact.

Cautious, Storm accepted the excuses for the misunderstanding. The old man had met the man claiming to be Rene DuBois when he first arrived, at a gathering. He hadn't liked the man then and didn't now. It hadn't occurred to him that he was an imposter. He was more than ready to stand by Storm's side. The young man was the image of his uncle, even his mannerisms brought back memories.

Both he and the Commandant would write to the Comte to straighten out the claims on the land. Storm's signature as disclaimer would mean little under the circumstances. However, nothing could be done until Michel responded.

The meeting dissolved into dinner and drinks while Storm tried to extract himself from their well-meaning grasps. He wanted only to challenge Rene DuBois, to make him pay for his wife's ordeal. As far as he was concerned the duel would be to the death. The man directly responsible for her rape would be dealt with on a more personal level. He couldn't give a damn whether the law santioned his approach or not. Nor did he care about the land at the moment.

…………………………………………......……………

It was late afternoon before Storm was able to saddle up for the long ride out to the DuBois land. The cargo was loaded; the ship ready to sail on the morning tide. By then he would have rid the world of two men. Raoul was ordered to sail without him if he wasn't back by daybreak. He wanted Meghan safely away if he were arrested – or killed.

He hadn't counted on his wife's interference. A half hour after he'd left she'd wheedled the plan from Raoul. Threatening to jump overboard and swim ashore if he didn't help her she was soon being rowed to land.

Trailed by a disgruntled Raoul she marched into the Commandant's presence. Startled, he didn't recognize the lady demanding his attention. At last she leaned across his desk and into his face. His gaze fastened on the lush view, flesh tinged with sunburn, she came into focus.

"My apologies Madame DuBois, on all you have gone through. If I can be of any assistance, anything at all." He had jumped to his feet and attempted to kiss her hand but she would have none of it.

Raoul hastily explained that they needed an escort to the Rene DuBois'; that Storm DuBois was on his way to challenge the man.

"We need witnesses, Monsieur, reliable witnesses, to be sure that all is fair. They will kill my husband. It will not be a fair match, this duel. You must do something." Meghan leaned across the desk again, her blue eyes flashing, her breasts threatening to spill from the low-cut of her bodice at any moment.

His eyes glued to her breasts, the Commondant tried to think what to do. It was hard to believe this lady had appeared only the day before to be a slave. Shame she wasn't the quadroon, Celia. His nostrils flared as his mind saw again the shapely leg with the DuBois mark riveting their attention to her soft thigh, corrupting a man's rational thoughts.

"Well?" Her voice dripped honey but her eyes narrowed, her lips a flat line. Her hands flicked upward in exasperation and she spun on her heel. "Come, Raoul, he is no man."

Left staring after the two, the Commandant picked up a cheroot and slowly lit the end. A deep draw, another, to soothe his errant imagination. Then he bellowed for the captain of his garrison.

....

There were no side-saddles in the stable but two horses were hired. Her skirts hiked to ride astride, the two of them rode for Michael's old plantation. Surely they would help, the old man, Gerard, someone. They would kill Storm. There would be no duel. They were not honorable. Meghan fought back angry tears. This was no time to be thinking what they'd done to her. This was about Storm, his life, the only man she'd ever love.

....

Storm dismounted. He'd taken his time on his ride here. He'd needed to think things through. Now he cut his eyes to where the big black was rubbing down a sleek stallion under the spreading oak. It looked as if it had been ridden hard, sweat gleaming on its withers. The slave looked up and stopped what he was doing. Their eyes met and he seemed to pass some message, some warning.

Too late; Storm heard the crunch of boots and turned to face Rene DuBois, riding whip still in hand. His jacket over his arm, the man wiped perspiration from his brow with his sleeve. His mouth twisted in a crooked smile.

"So, we meet again. What is it you want?" His black eyes narrowed.

Storm took his time as he reached for the immaculate white gloves tucked into his waistband. He stepped forward and slapped them across Rene's face. One brow raised in question, he waited for the expected response.

Rene threw back his head and laughed. "You dare challenge me? Do you know how many duels I've fought?" When Storm said nothing he continued, "I suppose this is about your wife. Or is it the land? What's more important to a true Frenchman, a hot tail or black earth?"

Storm snapped. He lunged for the man's throat. They rolled in the grass, evenly matched, fists flying. Storm was astride Rene when he felt the cold hard muzzle of a pistol against the back of his head.

"Well, now, we were hoping you'd show up." Phillip motioned for Storm to release his employer as he backed away. "Such a temper; almost as bad as that redheaded wife of yours. 'Course a man can overlook a temper when her legs are spread for him." Phillip glanced at Rene to see how he took this last statement but his boss didn't seem too surprised.

A red haze blinded Storm. He was choking. He couldn't think. He didn't even notice when the pistol was pocketed and the whip uncoiled. It snapped with a crack and Storm's head came up. The flayed tips curled around him jerking him off his feet. He clammered upright again, backing, and it struck full on his lower body, where a man is most vulnerable. Half crouching in pain, the next stroke caught him about the chest. A trickle of blood oozed onto his immaculate white shirt.

The next lash caught his ankles and brought him to his knees. He stared at the big black's broad feet, inches from his head. The horse neighed, sidestepped, but held. Did he imagine it or was the slave talking to him? Quietly urging him to get up?

The leather bit into his shoulders, twice again. White shreds of once crisp linen clung to bloody slashes. The pain in his genitals fading, he held to the slave's leg and pulled himself up. The big black hadn't moved but he was sure he heard the words, "Fight. She want you to fight."

The stallion took that moment to take fright, rearing and pawing the air.

"Get that animal out of here!"

Rene's shout sent Bull hurrying away just as the overseer's arm flicked back for another blow. Storm lunged. He caught the rawhide in midair, wrapping it about his wrist and yanking it forward. Off balance, Phillip stumbled and lost his weapon.

He snarled and came up, crouching, a long-bladed knife in his hand. Storm's face split in a grin. This was more his style. His right hand slid to his boot for the hidden blade kept there.

The two men circled, momentarily distracted by the sounds of horses riding fast. Determined to end this before he was stopped, Storm feinted toward the man's abdomen. A thin line of blood appeared but no real damage had been done.

Growling, Phillip slashed at his opponent's left arm but was blocked before the blade did more than tear the sleeve. His blade was longer than Storm's by several inches, wider, and wicked. But Storm knew how to use a knife. His days on the frontier were paying off.

"Finish him. Now!" Rene had recognized the uniforms. Damned if he wanted witnesses when this business was over.

Storm had allowed Phillip to back him into the stand of trees; the man was now staring into the lowering sun. Both men lunged and it became a battle of muscle as the blades hovered, deadly flashes of light being held at bay.

The overseer's biceps bulged as he forced Storm's right arm back. His shorter stature had proved to be an asset after all. His head against the tree, Storm strained to stop the ascending blade from gutting him.

At the last moment he rolled to the side and Phillip's knife sank deep into the tree trunk. The man was struggling with the hilt but it would not budge. Disgusted, he whirled to face Storm, weaponless.

Storm rocked on his heels, ready to deliver the death blow. He half-crouched, circling. He concentrated on Phillip's hands, still lethal weapons if he overreached. He met the man's eyes. Sheer hate, fear of dying – what?

Disgusted, he remembered his oath to beat the man to death; this filth who had raped his helpless wife. Nostrils flaring, he straightened, aiming his own knife at the roots of a tree deeper into the stand of woods. His hands fisted, he watched the man's expression change from cowardly fear to cruel delight.

By now the Commandant and the two soldiers he had brought with him had dismounted and were avidly watching the fight. Not what he'd expected to see but he had no quarrel with a man defending himself any way he saw fit. He said not a word to Rene DuBois who was also watching with fascination.

The two opponents would have been evenly matched but for Storm's whipping. Even so, fists connected amid grunts and kicks. Storm's feet were lethal, an art learned in the Far East, but his current clothing was restraining. Rolling, the men grappled against the trees, the slendar trunks defining the arena.

Storm felt a sharp pain pierce his side, slash into his left bicep. Stumbling back he realized the man had somehow obtained another knife, a stiletto, small but deadly. He remembered his hand at his left boot. Damn his stupidity. Storm made a dive under the attacking arm and into the trees. Where was his own knife? He'd thrown it about here -.

Before his fingers could close about its hilt, Phillip was on him. His head hit a hard root or a rock, he didn't know which, but for a moment he was dizzy, his eyes blurred. It was a moment too long. The man straddled him, his hand reversed on the hilt so that the slender blade now pointed directly down at his throat. With every beat of his pulse it threatened death.

Phillip's mouth twisted in triumph. He was breathing hard. One eye was swelling shut, his lip was bleeding, his ribs ached. But he'd won. Yes, he'd won and he'd gloat before he killed the bastard.

Between gasps, the stiletto pricking deeper but not yet deadly, he leaned into Storm's face. "She cried as I took her, you know. She carries my brat. She fought like a wild cat but she loved it in the end. I had her again and again while she screamed for you to come." The blade drew a drop of red. "DuBois will sell her now. His friend, the Commandant, is here. He'll fix everything just like it was. She's breeding for sure. Red-haired half-breeds are worth a lot of money. Those Creoles line up to fuck their almost white asses."

A string of curses blistered the air. Storm's wounded arm screeched as he reached for the man's balls, determined to cause the most damage even as he died. Their audience couldn't see them in the stand of trees but he could hear them stomping through the woods. It would be too late. He twisted and Phillip screamed, the scream ending in a gurgle. The man seemed to lose his grip on the knife. He fell to one side, blood gushing from his throat.

Dazed, Storm stared up into the big black's round face. He still held Storm's knife and one hand gripped the overseer's hair on the top of his head. The slave dropped the knife in reach of Storm's outstretched fingers, turned, and faded into the woods.

"Why, damned if he didn't lick your man, Rene!" The Commandant was the first to see the scene. He finished rolling the overseer's body off of Storm's legs and gave him a hand up. "Too bad. Good overseers are hard to find."

He watched while Storm inspected himself for damages. The victor wiped his blade clean on the thick moss near the pool of the overseer's blood. Storm still could barely believe what had happened. What had possessed the black to help him? Death was the penalty for killing a white man, for so much as looking cross-eyed at one.

He stretched, his muscles complaining. "I'm not quite finished here, Monsieur. If you'd be so good as to be my second -."

"Now? You wish to fight a duel now?" The Commondant looked from Storm to Rene in disbelief.

"Did you not accept my challenge, Monsieur DuBois? Just before this interference, I believe." Storm's eyes narrowed. He wouldn't dare refuse before these witnesses.

"Anytime you are ready, Monsieur, the sooner the better." Rene almost purred. He was confident of his skills but his opponent was obviously at a disadvantage after the whipping and the fight.

Storm nodded, his crooked smile opening the wound in his lip. His tongue quickly flicked at the blood. "Perhaps a basin of cool water to wash with first, if you don't mind, and linen to wrap my arm."

"Of course, Monsieur. As they say, you who are about to die - ." Rene smiled, all charm.

The Commandant continued to offer mild objections to the coming contest. "We will need more light. The moon's not yet up and no man can expect to fight what he cannot see."

"There is not a problem." Rene DuBois issued orders and by the time Storm was ready, a dozen slaves had formed an extended circle, each with a large torch. At his signal they were set aflame, casting a bewitching light on the scene.

....

Meghan, Raoul, and Gerard rode ahead of the buggy with Gerard's father. They reached the drive to the big house at dusk. Flares had been lighted around the front lawn and in the glow two men faced each other, swords drawn.

Meghan slid from her mount without aid but Raoul caught her before she could run toward the ensuring duel. One arm encircled her waist, his other hand closing over her mouth, as Gerard moved closer to bear witness.

"No, Lady, do not cry out. They are already engaged. Do you wish to be the cause of your husband's death?" Raoul waited until she quit fighting him. "Walk peacefully with me. Do you promise?" When she nodded he released her, taking her arm as she hurried across the expanse of grass.

Storm heard the disturbance but did not look away from his opponent. New arrivals? Would he be murdered yet when this was over?

His left arm, though bandaged, throbbed like a toothache. He ignored it and concentrated on the deadly steel that licked at him. His swordsmanship was excellent although he was a bit out of practice. Confident, he stalked his prey, waiting for an opening.

Though still hot, the wind was rising, and clouds skidded across the sky. Sweat streaked the men's faces in the humid night and mosquitoes added their torment whenever the wind faded. Storm's queue had come undone and his black hair clung annoyingly about his neck and face in damp curling strands.

Rene kept a smile plastered across his dark face. In the flickering light he seemed to be facing the devil himself. He'd counted on his own superior talents with the blade but it seemed he'd met his match. He'd killed three men in duels and wounded three others before word had spread. No longer challenged by the local gentry, still he spent the rising hour of each day polishing his fencing skills.

The silence was broken only by the clash of blades, the stomp of a man's foot as he lunged, an occasional scurry of brush as the wind caught it, lifting it into the fray. Torches flicked casting long fingers of light into the darkness.

A quickly muffled cry as steel met flesh. Rene's teeth gleamed in the meager light. But his blade had struck bone – a rib? His second of lost concentration cost him. He staggered as the devil's sword cut a deep swarth across his upper thigh.

Storm was on him in a flash but he was met by Rene's answering sword. He barely managed to block the next thrust, their weapons locked at the hilts. Both men forced them free and stepped back for the next foray.

Blood was oozing onto Storm's shirtfront just over his heart. A minor wound but he looked like the walking dead. The two men circled and a gasp broke the silence. From the corner of his eye he saw the glint of red hair.

Meghan! How the hell had she gotten here? Distracted, he barely managed to parry Rene's next move. Or did he? He felt the slide of cold steel, visceral, smooth. No pain, just shock, that it could come so easy.

Storm stared into his enemy's cold eyes; so close, so full of hatred. His teeth gritted, his jaw clenching with the effort, he raised his blade to the side as the man stepped back.

"It's not over." His words spat into the face of the imposter as Storm's sword sank into the man's exposed armpit in an upward thrust. He saw the mouth lose its smile, gape in astonishment. Both men tumbled to the ground.

"Oh, God, I've killed him!" Meghan twisted from Raoul's grip and ran to her husband. She took his head in her lap, tears spashing onto his closed eyes.

Raoul and the Commandant pulled her away, applied linen compresses to his wound to stop the bleeding. Storm's eyes opened and he smiled, though it was more of a grimace.

"I did it, didn't I?" He tried to lift his head, looking for Meghan.

Then she was there, laughing, petting him, smoothing the damp curls away from his temples. "I love you, I love you, you crazy fool. Don't ever scare me that way. I'll never interfere again. I'll do anything you want, live anywhere you want. I'm so sorry, so sorry." She kissed his swollen lip, licking at the cut, tears still bathing his face.

Someone had checked Rene DuBois when he'd fallen but the wound was a deathblow and everyone knew it. Now he gasped a last request and they hastened to comply. He was carried up the stairs to the broad verandah of the big house and laid out before the open windows. One of the torches was brought and thrust into a potted plant beside him so he would not die in the dark.

"Now leave me. Get off my property! I'll die in peace." His strength was seeping away with his life-blood. Even now red bubbled from his lips; the lungs were filling up. He glared at them as they returned to the yard, hovering around his enemy. He'd almost won, almost. He stared into the flames of the torch. Would he see his brother in hell? Well, then it couldn't be all bad, could it?

With his last strength he grasped the torch and toppled it through the open, floor-length window. The billowing curtains went up in a blaze as the rising wind whipped licking flames further into the house.

"Fire! Fire!" Everyone scrambled in different directions. Storm was lifted to a safer location, the horses moved away as they shied in fright. Torches were dropped as their holders stared at the conflagration.

Only the big black seemed to come to life. He ran for the front steps and disappeared.

Minutes crawled as the house was engulfed. As with many of the country homes, there were outside stairs descending to one end of the verandah as well as the ornate inside stairway. On these stairs, where the fire had not yet reached, movement appeared.

Bull, carrying a wrapped bundle, staggered into the yard. He unrolled the linens and the woman inside jumped to her feet, flinging her arms about the big man. Pulling her arms from his neck, he turned her to face his audience.

"My woman, Celia."

He stood before Storm Omar-DuBois, whose head lay in Meghan's lap. He waited but no one spoke, just stared at the lovely girl.

Hair identical to Meghan's but with more of a curl, hung to her shoulders. Her dusky skin covered a delicate form; that form shaped beautifully. The full lips were pouty, the dark lashes of her eyes curling and thick. It was hard to tell the color of her eyes although they would later prove to be golden, not Meghan's deep blue.

At last Storm came to his senses. "Celia? No wonder it was so easy to believe -." He looked up into Meghan's face.

The Commandant cocked a brow at him. "Well, now. It seems you're the new owner – the only DuBois around with papers left to prove it. Two Celia's – I could take one of them off your hands if you like."

The expression on Bull's usually stoic face was pure panic. His eyes flickered from Storm to his wife, Meghan. He'd paid his debt; he'd saved the man's life, hadn't he? But his new master's wife was likely carrying his baby. Had she told him? No, no she hadn't. He would've killed him outright.

Meghan met the dark eyes, read the panic. She licked her dry lips. Storm must never know what had passed between them. If she birthed a dark baby they would be far away from this place, wouldn't they?

She broke the connection as her thoughts threatened to betray her. The vision of his dark body hovering over her, soothing, possessing, - the long, slow, slide as he filled her to perfection. She felt the answering moisture between her legs, the tightening of her breasts. Disgust at herself threatened her calm. She loved her husband with all her heart. He'd almost died and now they could be happy together.

"Give them their freedom." The words were out of her mouth without thought, echoing in the night.

Storm blinked. "What? What did you say?" His eyes focused on the stoic face of the big man. "Do you know this slave?"

Meghan shook her head. "It's just that – he was kind to me while I was a prisoner here. Some good should come of this night."

Storm grunted in answer. His various wounds of the night were beginning to pain him. Then he remembered. The big black had offered encouragement, saved his life. How had he forgotten? He must be more tired than he thought. Why? Why had he done so?

He motioned for the man to stoop lower. His voice a whisper, Storm croaked out, "Why did you help me? Why do I owe you?"

The slave called Bull hesitated. He didn't dare say, "Because I took your wife, because my purpose on this land is to breed the slave women." His eyes tortured, he dropped his voice so only the white man could hear.

"Sometimes a man owes another man. Here they take my woman and I could do nothing. They take your woman and you could do nothing." He swallowed, his Adam's apple bobbing convulsively. "Slave or free, I ask we be together, Master." His black eyes met Storm's golden ones, for a moment on equal terms.

Storm lay back, exhausted. "Se la vie. You and your Celia will stay together as you wish. What do they call you?"

"I be called Bull, Master, but my name be Jean."

"Bull, huh? Strange name -." He glanced at the Commandant.

The man grinned and spoke up. "He's hung like – um, pardon me, Madame. He's used for breeding the women, when he not black-smithing."

Storm laughed, quickly catching his side. "Damn, that hurts." He looked up at the discouraged slave. "Well, Jean, or Bull, I'll see that freedom papers are drawn up for both you and your Celia. It may be the last thing I do in this God-forsaken place."

Storm turned to Raoul. "Do me a favour. When you can, retrieve my family's signet ring from what's left of that bastard."

....

The big house had burned to the ground but no one seemed to mind. Arrangements were made for the old man's middle son to act as share-owner for the plantation until other plans could be determined. He would live in the overseer's dwelling. It was much better than many of the river houses.

Feeling generous in the glow of his wife's love, the impending birth of their child, and his recovery, Storm deeded a small furnished house and the shop backing up to it to the two freed slaves. The shop would make a perfect setting for a blacksmith shop and the Commandant promised their overflow business to the new freedman.

Anxious to leave, they had sailed for Marseille while Storm was still recovering. Meghan suffered with mal de mer for the entire voyage; or perhaps it was this pregnancy. She was miserable.

The little girl, Jillian, was born in Marseille, in the leased house near that of her grandparents. It was adoration at first sight for Storm. Not so for Meghan.

Exhausted, she stroked the fair skin of her daughter with the tip of her finger. At least she was not of the slave, Bull. Or was she? In the months and years to come she wondered if more than one man could father a child. The young girl she was to become was more than a little bit wicked, just as the big black had said.

The baby was not blessed with Storm's dimple – that singular dimple all his offspring, legitimate and illegitimate, had. Her mass of golden curls, present at birth, brought the overseer's cruel face to mind every time she looked at her.

As Jillian grew, her hair darkened a bit to pale wheat, but her eyes – they were never the same color twice. Sometimes grey, or almost gold, they would reflect the blue or green or turquoise of her costume. The little girl's skin was dusky, a lovely darkened cream. Meghan fretted. Perhaps it was possible to conceive a child from two men, - or three. She had no idea nor did she dare ask and the child was her father's – Storm's – darling.

Wicked – Bull had said if she birthed a daughter the child would be a little bit wicked, like himself. And he had grinned at her with those big, white teeth, assuring her he could take her to heaven again if she wished. Flushed, Meghan couldn't quit thinking about the feel of him. Every time she looked into Jillian's mischievious eyes or saw the glow of the child's dusky skin, she felt guilty. Yet Storm saw none of this. He loved the little girl beyond belief. He assumed her aversion to Jillian was due to her bad pregnancy.

And so the child had grown to young womanhood. There had been the birth of another son two years later; a son with her husband's dimple. No one thought Jillian's lack odd, no one but herself.

Meghan no longer thought of the big man who had soothed her terror, who had taken her to heaven with his mastery, who might be the father of her daughter. She was happy with her husband, content to let the past stay buried. Only – only – when she looked at Jillian, only then did her fantasies and her fear come back to haunt her.

CHAPTER EIGHT

It had been a long engagement; a bit more than two years, a lifetime when one is young. Margery hugged her sister goodbye, so excited she couldn't sit still.

"At last my Geoffrey has sent for me, little sister! Oh, I was beginning to think he'd changed his mind and I'd be on the shelf. I'm to reside in London while my wardrobe is completed and my wedding dress ordered. I cannot understand why you do not wish to come with me? What could be more exciting?"

Margery danced around her bemused sister before taking her hands in hers and stopping, breathless. "I'm sure Mother will order new dresses for you also. Just think of all the young men you can meet."

Her mother swept into the room crinkling a list in her hand. "I don't know what's gotten into you, Margery. Why, you're as scatterbrained as Jillian of late." She dropped the crumpled paper on the little desk. "This must be redone. The colors are all wrong. You must remember 'sedate', beautiful but aloof is the image until after you are wed. With your hair, you should not wear bold colors. Do you wish your fiance to think you are 'fast'?"

Jillian burst into a fit of laughter. "No one would ever think Margery was 'fast', Mother."

Meghan frowned at her daughter. "This is your last chance to change your mind. Do you wish to accompany us or come later with your father? I have your measurements but your gowns will be done here so they can be easily fitted unless you 're coming to London. Of course, the exception is the gown to be worn to the wedding and ball itself. It will be fitted the final time after you arrive."

Jillian shook her head. She didn't dare show herself too soon to Margery's bridegroom. If he didn't see her until after the wedding it would be too soon. What if he recognized her? Surely it was a mortal sin to dream of the golden man who had loved her beside the lake, knowing now that he was her sister's promised?

"I'll be glad to stay here and keep Father company. That way I won't interfere with Margery's introduction to the ton. We'll be in London in time for the balls and the wedding supper."

She could almost see the relief in her mother's blue eyes. Her mouth turned up with mischief. Now was the time to ask, wasn't it?

"You will allow me to choose the color and material for my ballgown this time, won't you, Mother? After all, I am almost nineteen now, and we wouldn't want all of London to think I'm on the shelf, would we? Just because I didn't 'come out' like all those simpering females -." Jillian allowed her voice to trail off.

Meghan nibbled at her lip. It was true she'd ignored her second daughter. She'd been so involved in Margery's future marriage and it wasn't as if Jillian seemed to care. If the girl didn't wear white or pastel to the ball it would seem she had been presented elsewhere, had had offers.

"All right. You may choose your colors - but nothing too daring, mind." She turned her attention back to Margery. "And stop that prancing about before you trip on those frilled petticoats. I told you to remove that last ruffle of lace."

Margery stopped in mid-twirl, staring down at her lace-covered ankles. "Oh, but, Geoffrey would like the lace, I think." Her cheeks blushed a becoming rose.

"After you're married, dear, not before." Her mother left the room.

The girls' eyes met and they hugged. Jillian smoothed her sister's dress over the forbidden lace.

"Don't you worry, Margery. I think Geoffrey is a man that will appreciate lace, on or off."

Margery's face reddened more, clashing with her auburn hair. "Oh, Jillian, Mother is right. You are wicked."

....

Geoffrey drew himself up to full height before the long mirror. He did cut a magnificent figure, didn't he? And now he was to be shackled in his prime, wed to a cold-natured beauty, just for the sake of an heir. He blew his breath out in disgust and waved a hand for the tailor to remove the jacket.

At least the wedding would bring his brother home for a visit. Stephen was resigning his commission in the navy at the end of the month. He had made quite a name for himself but wished to command his own ship. He now owned several fine vessels and traded in teas and spices.

The newest, still in the shipyard, would be his prize. Fully armed in this time of uncertainty, she could outrun or outshoot anything that sailed barring a British man-o-war. Geoffrey thought this strange since his brother professed to be in trade but he shrugged off the feeling. Stephen always did the unexpected and cared less for others' opinions.

At that moment, Stephen was bowing his way from the Royal chambers. In his hand he carried the papers making it legal to sail as a privateer for the King. Along with others he would harass the shipping lanes feeding the American colonies. Prizes were divided with the Royal coffers but the profits were astounding.

He couldn't keep the grin from his face. Wait 'til he told Geoffrey. Not that this would, or should, be general knowledge, but he and his brother shared everything.

Only Geoffrey knew the truth of his capture years before by the pirates. Those sons of dogs had taken their British ship off the coast of Naples, held the officers for ransom. He'd lived through hell for eight months, more a slave than a prisoner. His naturally dusky skin was still darkened from the sun, the forced exposure as he suffered their amusements in near-naked state. In the proper attire he could pass for one of them easily.

It did not increase his popularity in the ton. Were it not for his extremely handsome physique and his family's connections he would have remained on the fringes of society. Of course, the air of danger did wonders for his reputation with the women. Behind their doors and in their beds they coveted him, vied for his attention, then often snubbed him in public. Stephen found them amusing, their moans as he gave them what they wanted salved his conscience. They meant nothing to him, no woman did. The heathens had done their damage.

CHAPTER NINE

Stephen tossed the brandy to the back of his throat and swallowed, almost choking. He grinned at his brother, waiting.

"That's a disgusting way to ruin a perfectly good - ." Geoffrey's eyes focused on the vision just admitted through the side garden doors. Sunbeams flooded in behind the female dressed in pale yellow voile, sprigged with embroidered butterflies. He blinked. Was she real?

Stephen turned to see what had his brother so entranced. The liquor must be doing strange things to his imagination. Did the girl not wear petticoats? The distinct curve of female hips, the defining of long legs – he stared. Then one of the servants closed the door leading to the garden and in the muted light the vision became more normal as she approached.

Her straw hat, broad-brimmed, hung by a ribbon from her neck. One arm circled through the basket handle wherein lay a variety of fresh flowers. Scissors dangled from a sash of rose about her waist. She'd stopped.

Both men raised eyes, eyes bemused by still-defined long limbs, when the soft fabric had ceased to move. This was definitely not Margery DuBois.

Jillian's mouth curved upward in a delighted smile. She couldn't help it. She'd stayed all but hidden for the week she'd been in London, dreading this meeting. Now here it was. Gregory stood before her with another gentleman. And it was not so awkward, was it? He looked a bit shocked though. She swept into the room, depositing the basket beside the doorway.

"Perhaps you were expecting my sister? I'm Jillian DuBois, her younger sister. I did arrive in time for the wedding, as promised." She extended her hand to Geoffrey. "I'm to be your new sister-in-law, I believe."

Geoffrey recovered, brushing his lips across her offered hand. "Geoffrey St.James at your service, Madeimoselle." He didn't know why he'd used the French address but somehow her accent was almost French. She didn't even speak like Margery.But his fiancee's family hailed from Tuscany and Marseille, didn't they? He still held her fingers. "And this is my younger brother, Stephen."

He was fascinated. He knew her, every sensuous inch of her. But how? The blondish curls were caught to one side and her exposed ear – a most dainty ear, he noticed – wore a tiny gold hoop; Italian, most definitely Italian. His eyes dropped lower and fastened on the gold locket nestled between her cleavage. He almost choked.

"By God, you're -." At her startled expression, he dropped her hand, bowing slightly. "My apologies. For a moment I thought -."

Stephen rescued him. "I've only arrived myself, for the wedding and the festivities. Perhaps you could show me the gardens while my brother awaits his fiancee?" He unleashed his devilish smile. He could almost feel her reaction as her long lashes lowered then fluttered open to meet his dark eyes with a twinkle.

"That is a delightful idea, Sir – what shall I call you?"

"Stephen, after all, we shall soon be near kin. No need to be formal here." He tucked her hand under his arm. She was enchanting. Whatever was wrong with Geoffrey he'd discover later. He looked back over his shoulder to see his brother staring after them, a stricken look on his face.

They circled the graveled walkway, stopping here and there, speaking of small things. Jillian watched him when she could. He was not like his brother, her Geoffrey. He was dark, mysterious. His full lips made her think of things better left unsaid. His lower lip curled and she wanted to bite it, pull it within her mouth, sucking. Gad, what thoughts the man generated. He made her want to be a woman, to be taken, possessed, taught once and for all what desire was like. Geoffrey had only stirred the pot and left it simmering.

The faint scent of apple blossoms drifted with them. Stephen leaned closer, pretending attention to her soft chatter. The girl herself carried the scent, sweet, inviting; and it brought back a memory of a darkened hallway, music, soft curves that fit his arms -. He swallowed. It couldn't be, could it?

"Do you enjoy waltzing, Madeimoselle? On balconies?" His question was asked in French. He'd stopped and she stopped with him. The buzzing of honey bees made music in the background, not quite a waltz, but -.

Her eyes full of mischief, she nibbled on her lower lip, teasing it with the tip of her tongue before she spoke. She answered also in French.

"A darkened balcony, Monsieur? And not properly dressed, perhaps?" She laughed and he laughed with her. "So, I am found out, hmm?" She shrugged and his eyes were drawn to her soft shoulders.

"It was the apple blossoms – you smell of apple blossoms, as you did that night." He was looking down into her grey eyes, eyes ringed in gold; such beautiful eyes. His head lowered, his lips hovered an inch from hers before reason returned. Was he bewitched? Disgusted with himself he straightened and cleared his throat. He hadn't been the pursurer of a female since his return from captivity. Always the pursured, they'd honed his skills, passed the time.

"Perhaps we should go back inside. I did wish to meet your sister again before the round of balls and suppers began; less awkward that way." He willed his reaction to her to subside.

Confused, Jillian moved ahead of him on the path. Damned if she would cling to his arm like some helpless twit. For a moment there she'd thought he would kiss her. And she'd wanted him to. For the first time since

Geoffrey had spoiled her innocence, she'd wanted a man's kiss. But then, they'd just met, hadn't they?

Margery and Geoffrey were sitting primly on the sofa having tea. Her sister looked up as they entered from the garden.

"Oh, so you've met? I'm sorry I was engaged upstairs." Margery smiled over the rim of her cup at Jillian, her eyes dancing. She'd been trying on her new undergarments, all lace and silk.

Jillian swept into the room and settled on a comfortable chair. She was aware of Geoffrey's eyes following her every move. He excused himself, put down the dainty cup, and met his brother at the decanter on the far table.

"My lady of the lake; her sister is my lady of the lake." Geoffrey's whispered words stung at Stephen's ear. "For God's sake, what am I to do? How will I break the betrothal at this late date?"

Through clenched teeth, Stephen muttered, "Are you insane? You can't do such a thing. Think of the disgrace – to her – to the family. The little sister wouldn't have you under such circumstances. What makes you think she even remembers you?"

For some reason Stephen's heart was racing, his gut knotting. So, his brother had had her. She wasn't the innocent she appeared. And he'd almost kissed those soft lips, damn her. He closed his eyes, recalling his brother's tryst with the lovely nymph – naked, laid out for his taking, he'd said. His jaw clenched. What the bloody hell difference should it make to him anyway? He took a deep breath.

"Don't ruin this marriage. Margery will be the perfect wife. She's everything a man could want, lovely, rich, intelligent. Grow up, big brother. Go back over there and do your duty."

With a grunt Geoffrey returned to the two ladies. His easy charm soon had them fawning over him as Stephen watched, disgusted.

An hour later and they were on their way home. Morose, Geoffrey hadn't spoken since they'd left. Now he turned in the saddle, his smile spreading.

"I've but to speak with her, touch her. Tonight they'll be a crowd. If you'll keep Margery distracted I'll talk with Jillian." He tilted his head as though listening to an inner voice. "Yes, that's it. Just give me thrity minutes alone with her. Do this one thing for me, Stephen. I've got to know if she's still as I remember. If she still feels as I do."

"Are you sure she even recognized you? Perhaps you've whipped the incident into more fantasy than truth."

"She wears the locket; the locket I left her as a gift. Would she do that if she didn't still want me?" He chuckled. "Just the look of her – enough to make a man remember that satin skin glowing in the sun, those legs spread. And this time -." He broke off at his brother's expression.

Under his breath, he continued, "There's other ways to have her. I've but to think on it."

CHAPTER TEN

Jillian had worn the locket on purpose. Better to get it out in the open, to make sure he knew who she was. He'd made no move so it must be all right. Yes, everything would be all right now. Margery would be married and she could go about her life.

It was a shame that the dark stranger had turned out to be his brother. He was different and she could like him. Then again, what was that almost kiss in the garden? Was he a tease? A seducer? He couldn't know about Geoffrey, could he?

Well, tonight she could be herself; except that she knew no one. Even her sister's fiance had made no acknowledgement of their brief whatever it was. Angry, she blinked back the threatening tears. She would enjoy herself tonight. She would not think about her blond dream-man's touch ever again. It was over.

Her mother had left earlier with Margery for the ball. She had waited for her father's escort. Storm Omar-DuBois had been tied up with business, much to her mother's irritation. Now, proud of the handsome man beside her, Jillian paused at the steps before descending into the ballroom.

Pairs of eyes glanced her way, lingered on her escort, then moved away. She saw her sister on the dance floor with an elderly gentleman, laughing happily. Her father led her down the two descending steps to her hostess, introducing her to the St.James', Gill and Catherine.

"I can see where Geoffrey gets his good-looks." Jillian smiled into Catherine's blue eyes. Her hair reflected her son's red-gold coloring. The lady smiled back, introducing her husband.

"And Stephen is a reflection of my husband, more French than British, I'm afraid. Of course, all the ladies are fascinated by the dark devil." Catherine laughed showing even, white, teeth. "There he is now." She waved a hand at him and Stephen made his way across to their side.

"I believe you've met Margery's sister, Jillian. See you're a proper host and introduce her around, dear."

With a bow to his mother, Stephen kissed Jillian's fingertips. Did they tremble just a little? He was attuned to such female reactions and met her eyes as he kept her fingers in his grasp, his mouth curving into a smile. His lips grazed at her hand once again, feeling her resistance.

"Stephen! Sorry my dear, he may be my son but he is more devil than gentleman." She shooed at them with her fan. "Be off. Dance or something." Catherine was exasperated with him. The look on his face was pure challenge. She watched from behind her fan as he led the blond girl across the dance floor. They did make a fine couple.

Jillian waited for him to swing her into the dance but he didn't. Instead, with his hand at her back, he directed her to the far side of the floor, near the open doors. He turned to face her at last, his back to the room.

"My brother wants a private word with you. He'll meet you in the library at the end of the hall in half an hour. He's been watching for you."

He seemed annoyed. Jillian bit the corner of her lip. There seemed no reason to play coy. "Suppose I don't want to see him?"

Stephen's expression darkened. "A little late for that, don't you think? You wore the locket. What did you expect, oh lady of the lake?"

Red tinged her cheeks but it only made her more attractive. He glanced down. She didn't wear the locket now. There was no distraction to the path his eyes took. Nestled in lace her femininity rose and fell, begging for his touch, his tongue. From his greater height, the vague outline of darker rose tips could be discerned, - or was it his imagination? He felt the definite beginning of arousal.

"That damn bodice is too low for a lady your age." His voice was a growl and she took a deep breath in offense. He was standing too close, way too close. Her lace brushed the starched lace of his shirt. That did it. The dusky nipples edged into view for a fraction of a second, pointed tips taut, and he groaned before he caught himself.

Jillian gasped as his long fingers pulled the crumpled lace upward, covering the offending beauty. Her flesh tingled with sensation. Her lips parted to protest but he no longer touched her. She snapped her fan open but it offered no protection.

What the hell had just happened? Stephen dropped his hand as though burnt; and indeed it felt singed. He focused on her parted lips but that was worst. His voice hoarse, he growled, "Twenty minutes. See that you're there." He turned on his heel and retreated.

His shoulder jarred Geoffrey as he fled the room. With a glare he nodded to the corner where he'd left Jillian. "I took care of your little message."

Geoffrey met his dream's eyes from across the room; noted the spots of color on her cheeks. Had his brother insulted her? He moved around the floor of dancers in her direction.

"Jillian? Would you care to dance? We can meet later." Before she could object he had swept her onto the floor. After all, he should partner his future sister-in-law at least once, shouldn't he?

Geoffrey's hand was cool to the touch, his posture that of a perfect gentleman. Only his eyes betrayed his thoughts, his eyes and his wicked tongue. Every opportunity for private speech was used to entice her.

The dance over, he led her to the edge of the room. "Would you like some punch?" The shake of the blond curls dismissed the idea but her eyes seemed alive with the memories he'd envoked. "The library is on the left, last door. I'll slip out after you."

Jillian waited until he left her side then glanced around before leaving the ballroom. No one noticed her. She didn't even see Stephen. Her heart beating so fast she couldn't breathe, she lifted her skirts above her ankles as she fled down the long marble hallway.

She had to do this. She had to clear the air; make him understand that she was glad to have him in the family but that was all she would be to him – a sister. The way he'd looked at her she wasn't sure this would be easy.

Stephen, fuming, had gone into the courtyard for fresh air. Pacing, he watched the glow from the library. The glass doors were thrown open but with the air misty no one was outside. Unable to resist, he made his way to the terrace where he could observe the tryst.

They were both there and seemed to be arguing. He could only catch a word or two but was afraid to move closer. His brother's hands were on her shoulders, they caressed bare flesh as he pushed the dropped bodice of her gown lower. Her hands rested against his chest but not in protest.

The gold head dipped, his lips kissing her throat, her shoulder. The girl's head was back, her lips parted. She seemed to be pushing him away, or trying to. Geoffrey's hand cupped her face. He was murmuring softly, words Stephen could not hear, gently kissing the corners of her mouth.

She was shaking her head but not struggling from his arms. Stephen's gut knotted, twisted. Why did he care? But he did; he wanted her. If only for a night, for a tumble, he wanted her. And she was going to ruin his brother's marriage. Dared he interfere? He took a step forward and ground to a stop.

Jillian's arms were about his neck, one hand pulling his head downward. Geoffrey's hand lowered to her bottom, pulling her closer, between his hips.

Stephen cursed under his breath. His brother's mouth took what she offered, devouring the tenderness, grinding her to the shape of his hard body. Stephen felt sick. He took a step closer but it was too late.

She had pulled back, catching at his hands, pulling them from her. She was trembling and shaking her head. Geoffrey seemed to be arguring but she stepped backward against the little table.

His brother's voice rose angrily. "So be it, then. But I'll find a way. You'll be with me one way or another, sweet Jillian." He turned to leave but with his hand on the doorknob he looked back at her. "If you'd had the sense to tell me who you were that day none of this would have happened. You would be my bride. I would have chosen you." He took several deep breaths. "Now I must work some other means."

She shook her head and Stephen saw the glistening of tears on her cheek. "No, no, you will do nothing. It's over. She loves you. Why, I hardly know you."

But now she was speaking to the door. Geoffrey had fled the room. Stephen frowned, watching her. Had she told him nay, then? But she wanted him; that was plain. And his brother was a fool. He'd dreamed of his fantasy lady for two years. He'd not give up easily.

Clutching the sofa back, Jillian forced the tears to cease. Foolish, foolish, dreams; they only caused trouble. Why had she met him at all? She must keep him from telling Margery. Is that what he was planning?

Her fingers touched her lips. Never, she should never have kissed him. But he'd been pleading, and so persuading. She'd wanted to, hadn't she? Just one more time; after all, it would be her last taste of him, her dream knight. Her body still throbbed with the hard feel of him, the old memories freshened anew.

What if she never wed, never fully knew a man? What if Geoffrey St.James was the only man fate had for her? She focused on the vision of his brother, Stephen. So dark where Geoffrey was so fair; the younger brother was mysterious and dangerous. But Stephen hated her; he knew about the lady of the lake and he hated her for what she'd done.

The night air was a mist, almost a fog. She pushed the glass doors full open and stepped out onto the terrace. She never noticed the figure in the shadows. Only then did she realize the shoulders of her gown had dropped lower and she pulled them back into place, smoothing her hands over the bodice.

Her eyes closed, she tilted her head upward. Her breasts ached; felt full and taut. Cupping each with a hand, she tried to ease them but it was no use. She turned back to the library. She would send word to her mother that she was ill. She was leaving the ball.

In the shadows Stephen watched her every move. He should speak but he didn't. If he said anything his voice would betray him. His erection jutted against his tight pants. He pulled the long jacket into place to hide his condition until he could calm.

CHAPTER ELEVEN

One week more, only one, and it would be too late for any trap to be laid. Stephen began to relax. He'd watched his brother like a hawk. He'd acted as the sister's escort to the theatre, to musicals, to dinners. He'd done anything and everything to be with Geoffrey and Margery; to encourage the union.

What Stephen didn't admit to himself was that he'd enjoyed every moment with Jillian. He'd kept his distance, or tried to; yet the girl had gotten under his skin. Geoffrey, noticing, had even warned him off. He chuckled. Now that would take the cake, wouldn't it, if he stole her away from his older brother? Not that it was possible. He couldn't help but notice the looks that passed between the two of them.

The day was perfect for an outing in the park. Geoffrey manuevered his horse beside his brother's, allowing the two ladies to ride ahead on the bridle path. He was unusually smug today.

"I've done it. I've made the arrangements. It will happen at the house party tomorrow night. All my problems will be over once I set everything in motion." Geoffrey broke into a large grin. "I can't wait to have her all to myself."

A chill ran down Stephen's spine. "Margery? You're speaking of Margery, I take it? Looking forward at last to the bridal bed?" His hand clenched on the reins and his mount side-stepped. He corrected, bringing the stallion again beside his brother's mare.

His brother laughed, blue eyes crinkling at the corners. "I've arranged to be caught in the act. My love doesn't seem to give a fig for propriety but it'll definitely be a surprise. And I'll make it right with her. After all, marrying the future Earl of -."

Stephen halted his horse abruptly. "What are you talking about? At the Marquis' weekend?"

Geoffrey nodded, also halting his mount. The ladies, unaware, moved ahead. "You know some of the ton's biggest gossips will be there. I've arranged for several couples to come upon us in a state of – umm – bliss, one might say. Jillian won't like it but with her sensuous nature she can be managed. And voila! The wedding will be called off. Margery and her mother will be outraged. Her father, and mine, will insist I do the right thing and wed the fallen Jillian. She'll have no say in the matter." Tongue in cheek he waited for his brother's approval.

Stephen barely managed to keep from assaulting him. "You wouldn't! You will destroy two innocent women – well, one innocent, anyway. Think, man!"

"I have. There's no other way. I've talked to Jillian until there's nothing else to do. I told her I would allow Margery to call off the wedding, to wait until gossip died down. I even asked Jillian to be my mistress after I wed Margery but she would have none of it." He grunted. "Made her a fine damn offer, in fact." He clicked his tongue at his mount. "I can't breathe without thinking about her, Stephen. The girl is a part of me. I'm going to do this."

Slowly Stephen followed his brother as they caught up to the ladies. He felt nauseated. This was worse than war. War could be handled. He couldn't let it happen. Should he warn Jillian? He glanced over at her and she smiled, her tongue flicking over her bottom lip. No, she was probably in on it. He watched the play of sunshine and shadows over her face, her soft curves. She tempted a man, that's what she did. How could she be innocent? And his brother was obsessed with her. So Geoffrey had taken her maidenhead, so what? He was sure she wasn't the first virgin his brother had despoiled. One fuck and the man was behaving like a complete fool.

………………………………………………………………

The house party was at the Marquis' private estate just outside the bounds of London. As the select guests began to arrive, Stephen watched their faces closely. Whom had Geoffrey chosen to trigger the scenario to secure his freedom? The men appeared guileless, flirting with the ladies as was their individual style; the ladies fluttering their fans, returning the oft unspoken flatteries. Then it dawned on him. The attendees weren't in on the plot. They probably would be asked to participate in a game of charades, or some other pasttime; anything to assure their arrival at the convenient moment, to be witnesses.

The weekend was to begin with an elaborate dinner and entertainment so the guests arrived dressed for the event. The next day there would be a fox hunt followed by a picnic upon the grounds. Most guests would leave for London after the picnic since.the wedding was the following day, in the city.

Ah, the arrival of the guest of honour. Margery came into the room on her father's arm. She was lovely with her auburn hair piled high and cascading in loose curls over one shoulder. Her gown was a deep emerald green with cream lace dripping from the sleeves and an insert of lace ruffles down the front of the skirt. Her left hand sported the emerald ring Geoffrey had given her and matching emeralds dangled from her ears.

Geoffrey stepped forward, kissing her hand, tucking it under his arm. He turned to face the group and a few of the ladies clapped. Everyone was laughing and teasing the couple of the coming nuptual. Behind them appeared another attractive redhead, her mother, Meghan DuBois. Her husband offered his arm and she moved into the room.

A pause in conversation marked the next entrance. Stephen caught his breath, then glanced at his brother, hoping Geoffrey had enough sense not to show any reaction. Geoffrey had a frozen smile in place but his eyes were heated.

Jillian DuBois swept into view in a rush of skirts. She had caught her hem on the coach step and had fallen behind her mother's entrance. Breathless, she stopped. Why was everyone staring? She looked down at her gown but it seemed to be in place. She nibbled at her bottom lip and dropped them a low curtsy, her beautiful skirts sweeping the floor. Eyes sparkling, she rose to see the Marquis himself offering his hand, heavy with rings.

The Marquis, William Shanksbury, waited for the girl to accept. His eyes twinkled with merriment as she placed delicate fingers into his palm. The glow of many candles touched her hair with gold. Beautiful! He admired beautiful things; he collected beautiful things. He patted her hand as he led her further into the room.

Stephen gaped at the girl's action. Once again, she had stolen everyone's attention. Her gown was of some changeable color, now green, now blue shading to turquoise. Extremely full and of some gossamer fabric, it swirled about her like the sea, a tropic sea. Her eyes matched the colors to perfection. Her dark lashes, thick and curling, made half-moons on her high cheekbones as she lowered her eyes in acceptance of the Marquis' attendance.

Conversation began again but eyes drifted repeatedly to Jillian and the Marquis. A confirmed batchelor, he was in his late forties. Still young enough, wealthy, and titled, he was much sought after by mothers with marriageable daughters. It was said he would never marry but now he seemed smitten and kept her by his side until dinner was served.

"I regret I cannot rearrange our seating but I must attend our guests of honour. You will ride with me to hounds tomorrow?" A dark brow quirked in question as he stopped before her designated chair.

Jillian could see Geoffrey's glare over his shoulder but she nodded. The man was thin, wiry, but vaguely attractive. And anyway, how did one refuse a Marquis?

"I would be delighted, My Lord." She smiled into his eyes, excitement brimming over. "I've never ridden to hounds but I ride well. I'll not embarrass you."

"I'm sure you won't, my dear. You wouldn't dare." He touched the side of her cheek with two long fingers as though assessing a prize piece. "After supper I can show you my art collection." He started to move away then leaned back down to her ear. "And you may call me William when we're in private."

Jillian tilted her face up to hear these last words, almost brushing his lips. Embarrassed, she tucked her chin down quickly, surveying her plate. What a strange man. He was moving too fast and he had no appeal at all for her. How on earth was she to discourage him within his own realm and remain polite?

At dinner her seating was across from Stephen. The table was long and narrow but with candles and flowers along the center, the position made it next to impossible for him to hold a conversation with her.

He watched as the men seated on either side vied for her attention. She was able to eat little but the gentlemen constantly plied her with drink as there was toast after toast to the happy couple.

His were not the only eyes observing Jillian. Geoffrey, brimming with jealousy, watched helplessly as her dinner companions fawned over her. Much to Stephen's amusement, his glare shifted between them and the Marquis.

Their host appeared not to notice. After all, Geoffrey St.James was to be married in a few days to the lovely Margery, was he not? Nervous, aloof, the auburn-haired young lady drank and ate little. She stole little glances at her soon-to-be husband, her eyes adoring. He didn't respond except when yet another toast was made and it was necessary to acknowledge her.

The meal over at last the guests split into smaller groups, some exiting to the card room. Stephen saw the Marquis moving toward Jillian and strolled in that direction to observe. Perhaps this would solve the problem? The man separated her from the group neatly and Stephen smiled as the couple moved away, chatting.

Geoffrey cut through the corner of the room into the back hall to appear in their path without seeming to interfere. He'd heard the earlier reference to the art collection. There was no way he would allow the man, Marquis or no, to be alone with his Jillian tonight. He had plans.

"Ah, just the man I wished to see. You are going in the direction of your fine collection. May I join you?" He ignored the look of annoyance from his host. Jillian looked surprised as he moved to the other side of her.

The tour ended – and nothing gained by either man – Jillian was escorted back to the main party. For the next two hours everyone joined in various amusements. Ever shy, Margery refused to play charades but Jillian joined in wholeheartedly. She was the first pick on every team chosen, keeping them all laughing at her antics as the puzzles were solved.

People had begun to drift to their assigned quarters. The hunt, for those attending, would require an early rising. Jillian excused herself and climbed the elegant stairs to her room.

Her maid hovered, sleepy, waiting to unfasten the elegant gown. There was a knock and Geoffrey St.James marched in. He waved at the shocked maid, dismissing her. She flew the scene. Jillian stood transfixed.

"Why are you here?" Her heart was pounding. His expression was furious.

"You practically threw yourself at the Marquis. Did you expect me to just sit there and watch?" He pulled her into his arms and his mouth took hers, his tongue playing havoc with her senses.

Jillian pulled away, coming to her senses. "This must be over, Geoffrey. I told you. It's over between us. What makes you think I want this?"

His hand circled her throat. He kissed her again, knowing his power over her. He broke it at last, one thumb stroking at her pulse, still about her throat. "You know you want me. It'll be over soon. We'll be together. I'll make you happy, so happy." He buried his face in her hair.

In shock, Jillian stroked his shoulder. What was he talking about? She no longer dreamed of this man. He belonged to her sister. She shook her head, trying to extricate herself from his arms.

He caught her hair, holding her, and again kissed her, his mouth moving over her with all the passion he'd held in check. He slipped her gown off one shoulder, reached about her back, beginning to unfasten the hooks.

The heavy door crashed open. Geoffrey stared into Stephen's angry dark eyes. He released Jillian, who almost fell as she staggered back.

"What the bloody hell are you doing here?"

Stephen's jaw was clenched so tight it hurt but he snarled between his teeth, "Get downstairs! Your fiancee has fallen on the steps. She's calling for you. I'll take care of this. Go!" He caught his brother's shoulder.

Dazed with emotion, Geoffrey glanced at Jillian. "I'll be back." He brushed past his brother, running for the stairs.

Stephen crossed the open space, taking in the scene set by Geoffrey. Her eyes were wide with passion, or was it disbelief? Her gown was half off one shoulder, pins from her hair scattered over the floor. He would have to hurry.

He opened his arms wide, in seeming comfort, and she came into them, trembling. He murmured against her ear, stroking her back. Nimble fingers released the back fastenings down to her waist as he seemed to console her.

It was all too much for the inexperienced Jillian. First Geoffrey's advances then the handsome Stephen's. Her heart racing, she tried to think what they were about but her senses overpowered her.

He murmered her name over and over, his mouth beginning to move over her eyes, her ears, against her cheeks. "Do you know how long I've wanted you, alone like this? You're so beautiful, so soft, so perfect." He interspersed his soft words with kisses, at last taking her mouth, tenderly. Nipping at her lower lip, sucking, darting with his tongue, he felt her begin to succumb.

"I want you, sweetheart, like no one else could ever want you."

She moaned when his head dipped, nuzzling into the lace until he could suck her aching breast. "Oh, do not, I cannot think."

He pulled at the taut nipple, his teeth teasing, while backing her to the plush chaise lounge. He ignored her feeble attempts to push him away. He heard footsteps in the hall, laughing conversation. How long did he have? This had to look real.

"Stephen, you mustn't -." Her words were blocked by his tongue as he kissed her deeply. His hand slid up her silk-clad leg to stroke the bare flesh above her garter.

Her hips moved against him, an unconscious enticement, and he felt his shaft harden yet again, ready, insistent. With one hand he unfastened his breeches, pushing them open, pulling his shirt out of the way. His mouth kept her unaware of his actions. He could scent her arousal and concentrated on keeping her confused.

Lord, but they'd better hurry – his witnesses. He wasn't immune to this foreplay. Much longer and he'd take her for real. He heard his own groan of admission as her knee bent to allow his access. His palm cupped her wet curls, opening her legs. He was kneeling on one knee beside her spread body when the exclamations exploded.

"Lud, what have we here?" The Boswicks, the biggest gossips in all of London, pushed their way through the half-open door. Behind them two other guests followed. Soon one of the younger bachelors stood staring. More footsteps rang on the wood floor.

"You could at least close the door." - This last from Boswick himself. - The young buck snickered, enjoying himself. He licked his lip, his nostrils flaring. One hand adjusted his tight pants.

Just as they'd entered the edge of Stephen's hand slid into her clit then palmed the soft thigh as he forced his hand away. One last touch of heaven; this was harder than he'd thought.

His lips against her ear, he murmured, "I'm sorry." In seeming panic he jumped to his feet, making sure they saw his own state of arousal, the open breeches. He'd lowered her skirt in the process of rising but they'd seen enough.

He faced them, his witnesses, then turned back to the girl on the lounge. Jillian seemed dazed, her lips parted, her skin flushd. She struggled to sit up, one hand covering the exposed breast. He reached down, adjusting the bodice, his arm beneath her as he half-lifted her to her feet. She had to catch the gown to keep it from falling to the floor.

Her lips were bruised from his kisses, swollen, plump. His evening whiskers had reddened her throat and the tops of her breasts with scrapes. The evidence of his passion darkened in a spot just over the pulse in her neck. Shame filled him, shame and remorse. But this had to be done, didn't it? If not him, his brother would have set this trap. The marriage would be off, this chit forcing Geoffrey's wedding to herself.

The audience parted as the Marquis himself pushed to the front. He took in the scene in silence, no expression reflecting his thoughts. He motioned the voyeurs to leave. “They’ll be nothing said of this until it’s straightened out. Please go to your rooms.” He waited until they left before speaking again.

“I thought it was your brother that was the danger here.” He’d no sooner spoken then Geoffrey appeared in the doorway.

“I couldn’t find Margery. She’s not -.” He ran a hand through his tousled hair and crossed to take Jillian in his arms. She backed away and Stephen pulled her behind him.

“What have you done?” Geoffrey’s fist caught Stephen’s jaw, knocking him against the far wall. “What the hell have you done?”

Stephen stood, his lip split and bleeding. He wiped at it with the back of his hand. “I figured one brother was much like another where she was concerned.”

This time Geoffrey’s fist was to his abdomen, followed by another to Stephen’s jaw. His brother took his punishment without fighting back.

“Enough.” The Marquis’ firm voice stopped them. He looked with regret at the trembling girl. Just how much was she to blame for all this he wondered? He re-focused on the brothers.

His dark eyess fixed on Geoffrey. “You’re to be married within days. You will behave accordingly.” He stepped forward, turned Jillian’s back, and proceeded to refasten her dress in the silence that followed.

Stephen had recovered his nonchalance. He gave Jillian a crooked grin, the one that melted all the females he’d ever known. “I’ll do the right thing – marry you – of course.”

Jillian had finally come to life, her wits returning. She stared at the smirking Stephen. His dark hair had loosened and fell into his face. She had the awful urge to kiss the hurt away from his split lip. By all that was holy, she was in love with the scoundrel. When had it happened? Just now?

She wanted him with every inch of her body; and she'd be a fool to let it happen. His words came back to her – words just spoken.

"One brother is much like another to me? Is that what you think? Either of you will do? Perhaps any man will do?"

She ignored Geoffrey and positioned herself before Stephen. She was so close her body cried out to melt against him. Then her hand connected against his tanned face, snapping his head to one side. She didn't see the surprise in his eyes as she turned away.

"I wouldn't marry either of you if you were the last males on this earth." She took several deep breaths, willing the threatened tears away. "Please leave my bedroom. I seem to be very tired."

Jillian fell onto the chaise lounge as the brothers left, both still glaring at each other. She was wearing only one shoe. She wiggled her stockinged foot, looking for the other.

The Marquis retrieved the shoe from beneath the seat cushion. He knelt and replaced her slipper, his hands gentle. He saw the glisten of moisture in the clear eyes but she wouldn't look at him so he said nothing. He stood up and left her to comtemplate her fate.

CHAPTER TWELVE

They were mounting up when William saw her. Wearing a navy blue riding habit, her hat sporting a cocky feather, Jillian approached the group. He couldn't believe his eyes. She had dared show up this morning.

Chin high, she marched to his side. "I hope you have a spirited mare saddled for me, My Lord. After all, I promised to demonstrate my skills this morning."

Amusement twisted his thin lips. "I wasn't expecting to see you after your recent experience, Madeimoselle. My apologies for the delay." He called to the stable master to see to her horse. Admiration for her spunk lifted his spirits and he laughed. Several heads turned. The Marquis wasn't known for joviality.

The hunt was a success, at least for the Marquis. He didn't know when he'd enjoyed himself quite so much. The St.James brothers kept their distance although they seemed to have made peace. He overheard the darker one making some excuse for his split lip and bruised jaw.

....

Upon returning to the house the guests scattered to change for the picnic. Stephen, now in more casual attire, paced in the library awaiting Storm DuBois, Jillian's father. He would leave for London after the requested meeting. He would probably have to.

Storm entered, his face doing justice to his name. He closed the door behind him. He took a seat before the large window and motioned for the young man to do the same.

"I've been appraised on some strange happenings last night – of some concern to myself and my youngest daughter. Our host came to me before the hunt to be sure I was not caught off guard by certain gossip. Then I received your note requesting I meet you here." Storm rose, pouring himself a brandy. He offered the young man nothing and resumed his seat.

Stephen shifted on the edge of his chair. "Sir, I regret that the Marquis took it upon himself to inform you, before I could ask, that is -." His mouth was dry. He felt like a schoolboy before the headmaster. He stood up.

"I would like to ask for your daughter, Jillian, to be my wife. I understand the circumstances might seem."

Before he could continue, Storm's full lips spread in a smile – more an evil grin in Stephen's opinion. "No need to say more. You have not the means nor the financial position to marry my favourite daughter; and she has refused you."

"But – but – I only this moment asked." He knew he sounded stupid, undignified. He couldn't seem to help it. She wouldn't have him? Her reputation was ruined in British society. No one would offer for her. He'd thought to wed her even if he left her to do whatever she liked while he enjoyed his sailing career.

"She will not have you, Sir. Nor will I." Storm swirled the brandy, took a sip, leaned back in the deep chair. "I believe matters did not go so far as to – create life – therefore another offer will be considered." Tongue in cheek he waited for the young man's reaction.

Stephen's jaw clenched. Damn the girl. All he'd meant to do was foil Geoffrey's plan to wed her and not the sister. Now all he could think about was her, the feel of her, the taste of her, the scent that was her. He'd itched to touch her all morning during the hunt, forced to keep his distance as she laughed at the excitement of each jump, each new experience.

"What offer, Sir, if I may ask? I am apologizing for any damage done last night but the fault was mine and I intend to make it right."

Storm stood, placing his snifter on the table with care. "As soon as Margery's wedding to your brother has been celebrated, the announcement will be made. Jillian is to wed our host, the Marquis, William Shanksbury."

....

Jillian sat alone in the wood swing overlooking the small lake. Guests were beginning to climb into the variious vehicles to be taken to the picnic site. Behind her she could hear the chatter and laughter. She smoothed the skirts of the white dress, following an embroidered daisy with her fingertip. She should be happy, shouldn't she? She was to marry a marquis. Her reputation would be saved.

Tears welled in her eyes. Her life would be over. William was so considerate, and so unexciting. He had spoken with her father, explained the night's happenings, and made everything right – just like that – a few words – power. She shook her head and a tear splashed onto her hand. What was it she wanted, anyway?

She heard the footsteps behind her but did not turn. Strong fingers stroked her shoulders and she knew. The feel of him, that special male scent of him – Stephen St.James. One hand cupped her cheek. She couldn't resist and for a minute he laid her head back against him before recovering her senses. His hands disappeared. Still she didn't turn. He mustn't see the tears. He was feeling guilty. He cared nothing for her.

"I came to say goodbye, Jillian. I'll be leaving immediately after the wedding." He waited for some sign that she cared. "Best wishes on your coming marriage."

She heard his footsteps disappearing. Sobs shook her shoulders and she buried her face in her hands.

Gentle hands lifted her to her feet, fingers tilted her chin upward. William frowned at her. "A man would think you weren't happy, my dear. You did accept my offer of marriage of your own will, did you not?"

She nodded, catching at her breath, trying to stop the tears. "Oh, yes, My Lord. It was so kind of you. There has just been so much happening. I am so sorry."

"William, you must call me William from now on, Jillian. Marriage is not the end of the world, you know; not even the end of pleasurable pursuits. I'll see that you have anything your heart desires and you will be my hostess, my jewel to display at my side. Fair enough?" He admired the trembling lips, the glitter of tears hovering on long lashes. Beautiful, she was beautiful. She would be the prize of his collection.

Jillian smiled through the tears. He really was trying to please her. What did she have to complain about? She felt his hands at her waist, large hands, with long tapering fingers. They seemed to be taking her measure as they slid down her hips and upward again. No passion there, just assessment.

Well, perhaps he needed encouragement. She'd heard he was seldom seen in the company of a lady. She nibbled at the corner of her lip. She could change that. She'd be a good wife. If only she could get the dark devilment of Stephen St.James out of her mind's eye.

CHAPTER THIRTEEN
One Month Later

Geoffrey watched lazily from the large bed as his new wife modeled the black corset for him. Her pale skin emphasized the lace concoction. It pushed the white breasts outward, the rosy nipples tight buds. He licked his lips and she laughed, turning her back and placing one leg on a stool. Giving him a good view of an enticing bottom, she proceeded to slowly don the black silk stockings and tie off the satin garter. By the time she'd finished the other leg he was rock-hard. She turned, a saucy smile on her full mouth.

"Come here." His fingers wiggled. "You're going to be the death of me."

Laughing, Margery climbed into bed between his spread legs. She squealed as his large hands caught her buttocks and brought her down atop his hard body.

"You'll ruin my stockings. Just wait and I'll - ." She got no further.

Her husband lifted her, his ready cock seeking her hot core. Legs spread wider, Margery's dainty hand guided him as she settled with a satisfied purr.

She'd never been so happy; never even dreamed marriage could be like this. She moved, tightening about his invasion and her husband groaned, thrusting upward, before he rolled her beneath him.

Together they met heaven. It didn't take long but then they'd been out of the bedroom only twice in the last three days. Their wedding trip to the peaceful countryside had lasted the planned two weeks. The surprise was that neither of them wanted it to end. And so it was extended two more weeks, then another. They had moved to the coast; a rented house from which they could watch the waves crash against the rocks, view the sea birds as they called to each other, and be totally alone except for a few servants that came with the house.

Geoffrey's hand played with her soft bottom, kneading, caressing. He nuzzled his face into her dark red hair and nibbled her earlobe.

"I love you." And strangely enough, he did.

He breaathed in the scent of her. Life was full of the unexpected. His aloof fiancee had become everything a man could want once he had initiated her.

Margery laughed deep in her throat, one hand threading through his red-gold hair. She moved her legs, already entwined with his, so that she fit against him perfectly.

"You sound as if you don't believe me." Geoffrey kissed her swollen lips with tender care. "I surprise myself even. I never thought you would be so perfect

– that we'd be so perfect together. I'm a very lucky man."

She took a deep breath. "My sister won't believe me when I tell her how happy I am." She felt him tense and drew back to look into his eyes. "What is wrong? Do you not like Jillian?"

Geoffrey had not thought of Jillian since the first bedding of his new wife. A stab of guilt tried to take root but a soft kiss from Margery and it vanished. "Of course I like her. It's just that she – she's not you, Sweet."

"I hope she'll find a man as wonderful as you, Geoffrey. Well, or a close second. Sometimes I think she's a little bit wicked."

"Perhaps -." His first love's slim body spread before him in the sun assaulted his vision. He propped up on one elbow and swept his eyes down Margery's beautiful body. "I have all I'll ever want or need right before my eyes. I married the right sister." He sucked one nipple into his mouth and she moaned, her breasts reaching for more. "I'm a lucky, lucky, man."

CHAPTER FOURTEEN

Storm Omar-DuBois watched his wife as she brushed her long hair. He'd always enjoyed this ritual. He set aside the glass he held in his hand.

"One daughter settled and another soon will be. We may have a peaceful old age yet. Sons are so much easier. Andre is the perfect eldest son. He tells me he likes the shipping business but that he intends to invest in the spice trade. He has a wise head for one so young. He enjoys having his younger brother with him. It establishes a pattern of family, don't you think?"

He took the brush from Meghan's hand and continued the long strokes. "So, why the worried expression, Kitten?" He watched her face in the mirror. He'd seen that cloud before, usually when Jillian was mentioned.

Meghan met his eyes in the glass. Would she ever have peace without a confession? Was Jillian even her husband's child? She nibbled on her lower lip, a habit her daughter also used to gain time.

"Do you ever wonder about Jillian, Storm? She is so unlike me, like any of us. And – and – she has not your dimple. All your offspring have the single dimple, all except Jillian." There, she'd said it. But it was like breaking a dam and she could not stop. "Her eyes change color like none of us and - what if I conceived her in New Orleans – that man -."

Her eyes swam with unshed tears. Her voice so soft he barely heard, she murmured, "She is so wild sometimes. I've tried to punish her, to stop it. He said his child would be a little bit wicked, he said -."

Her husband laid the brush down with slow care. The grey streaks in his thick hair only added to her heartache. She had put those streaks there. That dreadful episode in New Orleans had done that. The silver had appeared within weeks of their departure from that place. Her heart brimmed with love and she caught his hands, clasping them about her breasts. Her head bowed, she kissed the roughened knuckles.

Storm watched her, his lovely wife's reflection, in dismay. This is why she'd always rejected Jillian? There was no question in his mind as to the girl's paternity. But how was he to convince his wife?

He kissed the top of her head, then lifted her and turned her into his arms. "I think a visit is long overdue. You've never been to the DuBois' estates in the north of France, have you? It's where my grandfather spent much of his time, he and his wife, Angelise. There's something there you must see."

…………………………………………………………..........

The visit to France would have to wait until after Jillian's marriage. The Marquis had insisted the wedding take place as soon as Geoffrey and Margery's honeymoon was over. The date had been set for the week after and every available seemstress in fashionable London was busy with the wedding gown and trousseau, most of it at the Marquis' expense.

When the couple sent word that they would not be returning as soon as planned it was decided that the wedding would proceed on schedule. After all, invitations had been sent out and everything was in place by then.

The marriage was the talk of London. Gossip of Jillian's disgrace filled the parlours of the ton yet every repetition had a different version. In the latest, it was the Marquis himself that had been caught with the beauty. William did not deny any of the tales. He merely smiled and assured them he was marrying his choice of ladies. No one dared openly snub Jillian DuBois. After all, she was to wed one of the most powerful men in England, and one of the wealthiest. His father was already ancient and at his death William would become a duke. He already wielded his father's influence and power.

……………………………………………....……………….....

The ceremony had been extravagant but in good taste. The dinner afterward had grated on Jillian's nerves. The ladies of the ton were icily polite, at least in her new husband's presence. In the receiving line several of the gentlemen made joking remarks, whispered in her ear; most she didn't understand.

Her mother seemed distracted and clung to her father's side. They were traveling to France by way of

Amsterdam in two days and it was all Meghan could think about. Storm himself, was jovial; convinced his little girl had made a grand match.

If only her sister had returned before the wedding. She had so many questions. Margery had always been the one to ask advice. Now the tables were turned.

She closed her eyes tight. No, no, that man was not Stephen St.James. It had only been three weeks. Had he even been invited? Or had he left the country? Every dark head made her heart race. This had to stop. She smiled at her husband seated beside her but her dread grew.

William bent over her. "You seem nervous, Jillian. No need. Why don't you make your excuses and go upstairs. Maids are waiting to undress you for the bridal bed."

Jillian's face reddened as she realized the tablefull of guests were watching her. Bed, with this stranger, how was she going to pretend she cared? She nodded dutifully and her new husband stood, helping her from her chair. Her hand in his, he led her to the foot of the stairs amid many jovial remarks.

One drunken lord's voice rang out above the rest. "No problem tonight, eh, William? An early dipping saves the satin sheets." This was followed by loud whoops. Even the bridegroom's frown didn't diminish the laughing.

………………………………………...…………………....

It was some three hours later when the door leading into William's chambers opened and he entered. He'd been drinking and his face was flushed. He stopped just inside the room, looking first at the turned down bed, then at his new bride.

Jillian had been waiting for him curled up in a large chair. She'd fallen asleep at last but his entrance startled her into awareness. She rose to her feet, waiting for his next move. She wet her lips.

He had removed his ornate jacket and loosened his shirt. He was a well-built man for his age, trim and narrow-hipped. He continued to unbutton the ruffled shirt, taking immense care with each tiny button. He spread it open, displaying a muscular chest devoid of hair.

Jillian made a move to climb upon the large bed. She was stopped by a soft command and turned, puzzled.

Her husband was standing, arms akimbo, slightly swaying. "I want to look at you. Stay as you are." He walked around her, seating himself at last in the large chair, stretching out his long legs.

"Turn about, slowly, so I can see you. Remove your robe."

His eyes, his face, were in shadow in the depths of the wing-chair. Jillian dropped the satin robe to the floor, took a step closer, then turned. She heard him take a deep breath.

"I wish to see what I've purchased. Remove that abomnable piece of cloth." He waved his hand at her.

Jillian didn't know whether to be annoyed or amused. Her nightclothes had cost a fortune. This one was of silk and clung seductively to her curves. She loosened the ties and let it fall in a poof of softness about her ankles.

He said nothing, just stared at her body. His eyes raked from her curling hair to her toes. She turned, beginning to feel rather like a doll on a music box. Her hair tickled her bottom and she had the awful urge to scratch but didn't dare. Instead she swung it to one side, looking flirtatiously over one shoulder.

As he stood, she smiled up at him, then glanced at the bed, hoping to ease the next step. She wanted to get this over with as quickly as possible. But he made no further move, just seemed to memorize her with his eyes.

"Exquisite. You are worth every penny." He turned on his heel and exited to his chambers. The door closed firmly behind him.

Jillian stood in shock. That was it? Her wedding night was over? She stared at the lovely silk on the floor and realized she was shivering. She ran, stark naked, for the bed with its' warming pan. If he returned she was ready for him.

……………………………………...………………....

But William came no more to her bedroom. He was an entertaining escort to musicals, poetry readings, and dinners. She was introduced at court with all its pomp and ceremony. Anything her heart desired was instantly produced. She began to feel like a spoiled child, constantly on display.

This morning was different. The day had turned cold and bleak, wind howling against the long windows. Moping about the house, Jillian was busy planning how to entice her husband to her bed. After all she was not ugly, was she? Had he not said she was beautiful? Then what was wrong with her?

A gust of wind and the subject of her thoughts blew into the marble hallway. He handed the butler his hat and cloak and began to slowly pull off his snug gloves before he noticed her. He stopped, dismissing the man with a curt nod, and strode to her side.

His hands, still encased in the soft doeskin, cupped her face, moved down her throat. He caught her earlobe, rubbing. Jillian's cashmere shawl slipped to the floor unnoticed. Would he kiss her now? She tilted her head up, her lips parted.

He chuckled, actually chuckled. His thumbs still moved across her skin. "You like that, do you? You're like a little cat, waiting to be petted."

He removed his hands, peeling off the gloves. Sparks of anger flashed in her green eyes. He noticed, in fact appreciated the fire that banked beneath her cool exterior, but he chose to pretend otherwise. His eyes moved over her dark green dress. He retrieved her shawl and placed it about her shoulders.

"The color does wonders for your eyes. You must wear green more often, Jillian. Umm, perhaps tonight, the green velvet. We're going out."

"Out? On such a night? Why would we go out?" She was angry and not sure why.

"Didn't I tell you? Your sister is back in town with her new husband. We're invited to dinner; just a small party, I believe. I was sure you'd want to see them." He saw the panic in her eyes. Yes, it was going to be an amusing affair.

....

Margery hugged her sister, all blushes and happiness. She seemed to glow and when she looked at Geoffrey no one else existed for her.

"We're so sorry we missed your wedding, Jillian, but how were we to know? I'm so happy for you. Just think, you are married to one of the most powerful men in England – and he's not that old." She caught her breath. "I didn't mean he's old, it's just that, well, I pictured you with someone more like Stephen."

Jillian's felt a pain deep inside. Didn't her sister have any sense? How could she –? She bit back her retort and smiled. "You seem happy yourself. Perhaps your husband does like the lace both on and off, hmm?" She laughed, trying to make it sound genuine.

Margery caught an answering laugh before it escaped. She lowered her voice. "Just you wait until I tell you how perfect he is. We were so selfish after that first time; we wanted to stay away forever. Oh, Jillian, I'm so lucky! And all those things Mother used to worry about us doing – well, we've done them."

"Ladies, are you going to whisper all night or will you join the rest of us?" Geoffrey's voice rang out across the room.

Margery took her sister's hand, pulling her to her husband's side and into his arms. "There, now, a hug for your new brother-in-law. I want you two to be the best of friends."

She didn't notice the panic on Jillian's face but William did. He extricated her from Geoffrey's bearhug, tucked her hand beneath his elbow, and straightened to his full height.

"Unhand my wife, Sir."

Everyone laughed good-naturedly and Jillian blushed. The talk turned to other topics.

It was after dinner when William asked to see Geoffrey alone. The two men moved to the library, the others settling about the crackling fire to nibble on little cakes. Jillian excused herself to find the retiring chamber before her husband rejoined the group.

As she was returning she passed the library and noticed the door was ajar. Gnawing at her lip she conquered her guilt and slipped closer. It wasn't as though they had any secrets, after all. Their voices weren't loud but were easily heard from where she stood.

"So, you understand my position." She recognized her husband's voice. "I wish to keep her contented without -." This sentence wasn't completed and she assumed some gesture explained it.

Geoffrey cleared his throat. "The situation has changed. Yes, I did stage that night. Your assessment is correct. I fully intended for us to be caught together. It was the perfect plan to allow Margery to withdraw from the betrothal. I would have been forced to do the right thing, marry Jillian, and have the wife I thought I wanted."

The other voice broke in, "But your brother decided to interfere. He made rather a mess of things, did he not?"

"Stephen has a tendency to butt in where he's not wanted. He somehow discovered my plans and made his move. He'd have married Jilllian if it came to that rather than allow me to jilt her sister."

"Very noble of him, I'm sure. Still – he seemed very involved. Perhaps there was more to his feelings than -."

"Stephen? My brother? He uses women. He has no taste for any one of them. Maybe some day he'll find his match." His voice lowered. "As I've found mine."

"Well, I'm disappointed that you're not interested. It would have been the perfect solution, her marriage to me. I believe I heard you say that your second option had to do with making her your mistress while marrying her sister."

Jillian could hear the scrape of a chair as they rose but she couldn't seem to move. Her throat closed, her chest hurt. Her legs seemed not to support her.

"I told you that idea, that whole situation has changed. Margery may be carrying my child now. I love her very much. You'll have to find some other pigeon."

Jillian shrank back behind an ornate cabinet as William exited the room and walked briskly back toward the others. Her brother-in-law did not appear and she started down the hall just as the door opened wider.

Geoffrey's expression did not change. "How long have you been there, Jillian?" He stepped closer but did not touch her. "Nothing said here will reach Margery's ears, do you understand?"

Jillian shook her head. "No, no, of course not. She knows you love her now anyway. After all, we're both married and content, are we not?"

His eyes narrowed for a moment. So, she had not heard all that was said. Good; the less she knew the better. Surely William would manage.

She motioned toward the end of the hall. "I was just going to – umm, and when I passed, the door was open." She nibbled at her full lip.

Geoffrey followed her action, a wave of nostalgia drawing him closer. He caught himself in time. "Well, I imagine she's wondering where I am about now." With a nod he left her standing there.

....

The next days were a blur of activity. Jillian tried not to think about what she'd overheard and if she stayed busy that was easy. It was the nights that haunted her.

What had been said earlier in their discussion? Geoffrey had looked so worried. Surely he knew she'd never hurt Margery. She had said she would not be with him again even before that fateful night. She tried to remember what Stephen had said but his image was swamped with emotion. All she could remember were the hateful statements that either brother would do; that she only wanted one of the St.James' males.

Just thinking of his liquid brown eyes made her melt, the way they devoured her, his hands urging her body to blend with his – she felt the ache begin low in her belly, the moisture between her legs. Oh, it wasn't fair that he could do this to her and it mean nothing to him. Were all men like that? Her nails bit into the palms of her hands.

No, no they were not. Her husband was not. He was good to her but he did not even attempt to seduce her. What was wrong? Was he ill with some disease? Was this his way of protecting her? She'd heard of the awful things a man could get from sleeping with cheap women; perhaps that was the problem.

She had been shopping with her sister earlier and she was tired. William had gone to one of his clubs and she had eaten alone, then soaked in the large copper tub. Tonight she had plans. She smiled as she slipped the silk chemise over her head, tying it at each shoulder. It had come from the Paris shoppe of one of the DuBois relatives and was very simple but very risque.

Standing before the mirror she smoothed the clinging fabric over her stomach, down her hips. It was caught up under her breasts with a tiny ribbon and a petite bow, then hugged her form as it dropped to the floor. It was the same shade as her flesh and so sheer one could see the distinct darker curls at the apex of her legs, the rose hue of her nipples. Her satin slippers matched, their tiny heels padded both for comfort and silence.

She pinched her cheeks to make them rosy, wet her lips, and took a deep breath. It was time. She'd heard him come in and given him time to undress. Never before had she dared enter his room.

Jillian turned the knob and pushed the door wide. Two candelabras lit the massive bed, one from each side. Satin sheets were rumpled, tumbling near to the floor. She blinked at the bank of light.

Her husband bent over a white form, his hand caressing a long thigh. His shaft was at full mast and in full display. Both occupants were nude; both were male, very male.

A sob caught in her throat. Two heads turned to stare, one dark, one light and golden. William came up from the bed, fury on his face. He seemed undecided what to do but his stance had silenced her.

Jillian had never seen a man naked, neither at rest nor in this state. Her mouth fell open, her eyes moving over her husband. Her attention flickered to the young god with the golden hair. He was in like state and had lain back in the bed propped by the pillows. His expression seemed sympathetic but her attention was drawn back to her husband.

"Well, Jillian?" William's words dripped honey, acid honey. "Is this what you wanted to see?" His eyes flicked over her attire. The light from the open doorway made the sheer gown transparent. His erection was fast diminishing.

She shook her head, not understanding. "I didn't know – you -."

"What, Jillian? What don't you know? That a man can love another man? It's quite possible; in fact, it's the best of two worlds."

He paused, but his temper had started to boil once again. "You know better than to come here uninvited. Go, cover yourself." He nodded toward her door.

She shook her head again. "Cover myself?" She looked down at her own trembling body, tears beginning to form. "Am I indecent to want my husband? Don't you want a child, an heir? Am I so ugly?" Now the tears were falling in truth.

Still naked, William caught her shoulders, gritting his teeth. "Stop it! You are beautiful and you know it. You are the best of my collection."

"Collection? I'm art to you? That's all? Not even your whore?" Her voice rose in hysteria and he shook her until she quieted. When her legs gave way he picked her up and carried her into her bedroom, kicking the door closed behind him.

He dropped her onto the bed but did not join her. He stared down at her, her cheeks streaked with tears, her mouth pouting. He smiled. She was adorable. He just had no desire whatsoever for her, for any woman.

"Won't the help wonder why you don't share my bed? Why there was no blood on the wedding sheets?" Her chin trembled in defiance.

He chuckled. "Gossip has it that I had your maidenhead before marriage – on that fateful night. Was it one of the St.James' or the Marquis? And I don't give a damn what the servants think." He removed her remaining slipper and dropped it to the floor. "On dit serves its purpose and I married you so I must have been the guilty party, hmm?" He admired her full lip, ran a thumb along the pout.

"You'll live with it, my spoiled darling. Now go to sleep like a good girl." He turned on his heel, but turned back to her.

"Any man in London will be delighted to share your bed. You have my permission as long as you're discreet. Just be damn sure you don't bear a bastard. My brother's children will inherit. That agreement was determined years ago."

Jillian stared at the closed door. This time she heard the key turn. How ignorant she was, how truly ignorant, and how alone. She heard laughter from the other room, quickly smothered.

She closed her eyes, seeing again the lean body of her husband then the slender youth of his bedmate. Neither of them particularly appealed to her. Did all men look like that beneath all those layers of clothes?

Unasked, Stephen's muscular torso came to mind; the feel of his rough hands on her breasts, shifting across her throat. She rememberd the hard length pressed against her belly, the muscles in his thighs. Her breath caught and her eyes flew open. No, no they were not all alike. Even his chest, when he'd opened his shirt – the dusting of dark curls beneath her hands – she sobbed and rolled over into the pillows.

But Stephen didn't want her and it was too late now anyway. The conversation she'd overheard made more sense now. Geoffrey didn't want her either. William must have offered her to her brother-in-law, offered her as though she were a plaything, a favour to be bartered; and he'd refused.

"Mama, oh, Mama, why aren't you here when I need you?" Her choked words were buried against the satin comforter. The childish need overwhealmed her. She'd never confided in her mother but now she needed to be told what to do. Just this once, she might do it. Was it too late?

CHAPTER FIFTEEN

Storm enjoyed taking his wife about Amsterdam. She'd never visited his brother, Jamie, since the main offices had moved from Marseille. Jamie's half-Dutch wife, Gabrielle, had inherited her father's shipping business and Jamie's share of their father's, Sharif's, enterprises made him a very wealthy merchant. The entire family was thriving, the better for leaving France.

Meghan had been fascinated with the ice-skating on the canals. She'd always loved cold weather and missed it where they'd lived in the south of France and then in Tuscany.

They spent a month getting to know their nieces and nephews again before hiring a coach to continue to the DuBois estate in France. Meghan chattered happily most of the way although her husband was often dozing. The fur robe about her lap and feet kept her cozy even in the drafty vehicle. Spring would be coming soon and she couldn't wait. She loved the snow, always had, but she was unused to it since they'd lived so long where it was warmer.

Meghan wondered what Storm's surprise was? He'd been so secretive about the entire purpose of this trip; not at all like him. She smiled as she watched him sleep. She was so lucky to have him; and so foolish to have run away in the beginning. Thank God he had persevered and made her his wife.

They'd had a letter from Margery before they left Holland. She thought she might be with child. She was very much in love with her new husband and he with her and she'd bubbled on and on. She hadn't mentioned her sister's ill-fated night of infamy but then it was possible she didn't know what had precipitated the quick marriage.

The girl had seemed surprised that Jillian had chosen a man twice her age. Her very words being, "I never thought Jillian cared more for money and power than she did for daring, handsome, young men."

Meghan leaned her head back against the squabs. Well, Jillian had been very subdued but had seemed pleased with the match. The Marquis would give her anything she could want and more. Several children under foot and the girl would grow up quickly. After all, most young ladies had dreams of a handsome knight sweeping her off her feet; yet she'd refused Stephen St .James' offer. She wouldn't even speak to the furious young man. The girl was trouble, always had been. The Marquis would settle her down, teach her the ways of the world.

Meghan smiled. She'd had her own tempting young man, hadn't she? She'd just been lucky enough to marry him.

....

They'd arrived near dusk at Comte DuBois' estate. They were expected and Michel, with his wife, Susana, were in residence. The evening was an early one due to the fatigue of traveling.

It was another day of renewing acquaintances, fashion talk for the ladies, and political discussions for the gentlemen, before Meghan was alone again with her husband. She'd begun to wonder if there was a purpose to this visit or if he's been homesick for old haunts.

She had decided to nap but before she could do more than close her chamber door Storm appeared. He was smiling broadly.

"I believe it's time, Kitten. Come with me for your tour of family history. I promise you it will not be boring." He took her arm and they strolled toward the gallery where family portraits were displayed. There was a cozy sitting room leading off of one side and a glassed conservatory filled with large green plants, flowers, and some herbs on the other. Both rooms were uncomfortably warm and droplets of moisture dripped from the domed ceiling of the conservatory onto the greenery below. The gallery itself was cool.

Storm stopped before each portrait, giving her the ancestor's name and what history he knew or thought she might find interesting. Meghan spotted a full-length oil of a beautiful woman with raven hair, dressed all in a deep blue-violet. Her eyes were the same shade of violet with thick curling lashes, her lips full and smiling.

"She seems so familiar. Your mother, Storm? The painting seems too old to be Anna but the resemblance is remarkable."

He chuckled. "The story behind this lady had best be told in yonder warm room. You'll be chilled out here before I'm done. Enough for now to say that she is my great-great-grandmother, Comte Andre DuBois' mother. Anna-Marie, or Anna as my mother is now known, caused quite a stir by her birth. She was so alike Andre's mother that she was accepted as a DuBois even though she was raised as another man's child. Come, let's go where it's warm."

They hurried to the small sitting room and Storm removed her shawl. "Such a beautiful woman. Your family makes me feel like an ugly duckling among swans."

"Nonsense. None of them have your wonderful flaming hair, Kitten, or your lovely creamy skin. And none of them have me." He kissed her neck, nibbling at her ear lobe, and she felt the old thrill that his touch always caused. "Now look." He cupped her chin and tilted her head to the mantel.

Another large portrait, another beautiful lady, this one more enchanting than beautiful, surveyed the room. Meghan caught her breath. "It is our Jillian, our very own Jillian." She turned into Storm's arms. "Who is she, Storm?"

"Angelise, as a young lady; before she married Andre DuBois. She was my grandmother, Anna's mother. Look at her eyes, those long lashes, thick and curling. She wears a blue-green gown here and her eyes are the same shade; changeable eyes, just like our daughter's."

Meghan stared. The lady, Angelise, seemed to be laughing at her. Her sensuous mouth, the lips parted to show even white teeth, invited a man's kiss, his wayward thoughts. Her hair was a pale brown, or the color of wheat with lighter streaks. Nothing special there, the color, and it was only a tiny bit darker than Jillian's.

Storm grinned, watching her. "And no dimple – it is not a prerequisite to being a DuBois." He kissed her neck again. "Now do you believe?" He held his breath as she turned to him.

She nibbled at her lower lip, glanced back at the image that could easily be her Jillian. "Why didn't you tell me?"

"I didn't know what was bothering you, why you hated your own daughter. I just tried to make it up to her and ended up spoiling her rotten. I'm sorry, Kitten."

"I didn't hate her. I feared her. From the day I saw those golden curls, so like his – and her eyes – you admit she can be stubborn and a bit wicked. The male sex can't keep their eyes off of her and you know she encourages it."

Storm laughed. "I admit nothing. She's my daughter and I'm a bit wicked myself. She's very like me, don't you think?" The old devilish gleam appeared in his golden eyes. "Let me show you just how wicked I can be." His mouth covered hers as he backed her to the soft sofa. They landed with a plop, his fingers tangling in her laces.

"You could help, you know. My fingers aren't as nimble as they once were." He looked down at the knotted mess he'd made.

Meghan laughed, reaching about him to tickle his ribs. "Does it matter? I love you just as you are." She shrugged the bodice lower, laces and all. "Make love to me, husband, show me how wicked you are." She straddled him, skirts about her thighs, and leaned down to allow his mouth to reach the tempting fruit.

The room was soon full of soft moans and giggling murmers. There were only embers when the couple rejoined the family for dinner. If they looked somewhat dishelved, well, this family was used to its own standards of wickedness.

……………………………………………………………

New Orleans was the topic of discussion in the next days. Storm was as honest with Michel as he could be without mentioning Meghan's rape. There was no way they would ever return to Louisiana.

"The ownership is safely in our hands once again but I would like to return it to you, Michel. We've waited for years but we have no desire, in light of what happened, to reside there again. I offered it back once before but you refused. Perhaps your children would like the property?"

Michel drummed on the desk. "I thought you'd change your mind. I did mention it to William and Marie however. He has more and more business with the American colonies. He likes it there, the freedom, the opportunities. Once this squabbling with England is over and things settle down he may be interested. At least it's still French."

"Marie likes to be queen bee, you know. She would be a leader of society there with her fair coloring and her pedigree. Then again, she might be bored; perhaps Charleston would be preferable. The trouble there is that their French population is mostly Huguenot." Michel laughed. "Still, that might very well work out. She has too much competition in Versailles; things change."

"I'll sign the papers over to you this trip, then. You mentioned that the family might reimburse me for part of the loss. I think I've convinced Meghan to give Montreal, in Quebec, a try. Andre is beginning to take over the reins of my interests here and in Italy. Jamie controls the business in Europe now and the whole of Quebec is thriving. We're planning a visit."

"I don't blame you. France could invite bankruptcy. Of course we'd back the colonies; that's no surprise. Anything to thumb our nose at England and the resentment is still strong over their treatment of our people in the Canadas. I'm afraid the cost is going to break our back. The price of maintaining an army here has increased and now there's the navy. Taxes for the people are being increased but it'll not help. Some have had the nerve to suggest the nobility should be taxed. Can you imagine?"

"Yes, I hear even the Marquis de Lafayette is contemplating fighting alongside the Americans. Do you know him?"

"Yes, he's rather young but I like the man. He's an idealist. I hear he's invested a lot of his own funds with Washington's rebels. His enthusiasm for liberal ideas does not seat well here at home. Even so, France would like to snub their noses at the British in any way possible." Michel spread his hands. "That American, Franklin, is all the rage just now; toadying to the Crown for favors."

Michel continued, "We need to stay out of this quarrel. I don't know what's to become of France if the King doesn't take homeland matters into his own hands. He cares not for the common people and they're the basis of his power. I speak treason but His Majesty doesn't seem to grasp the seriousness of the matter."

"I probably shouldn't say it but I'm glad I don't have direct responsibilities to the DuBois title or holdings. It's enough to be related and bask in your glory." Storm grinned.

With a laugh Michel crossed to peer out at the expansive grounds. Already several gardeners were hard at work. "Yes, well, I'm not so delighted myself. I rather enjoyed Louisiana. It was large enough and rich enough to support a family well. Now, with the children grown and gone their own ways -." He shrugged and faced Storm. "It may be that Susana and I would enjoy a brief retreat, a home away from these rising tensions. Let William take some responsibility here on the home-front."

………………………………………….....……………….…

Storm and Meghan returned to London only to miss their youngest daughter. It seemed that the Marquis had taken his new wife, along with several of his male friends, to his castle in Scotland.

Meghan sat down and wrote Jillian the longest letter she'd ever written anyone, pouring out her guilt at her past behavior, her love for her young daughter, and at least part of the explanation for her reasons. The rest could be said when they were face to face and was best not put to paper.

They extended an invitation for the couple's visit to Tuscany in the near future. This preceded the statement of their impending move to the province of Quebec. They would visit first in Marseille and then Storm's parents in Tuscany before leaving. Before the year was out they hoped to be settled in their new home.

CHAPTER SIXTEEN
Three Years Later

Jillian closed the door and crossed to the bed. At least it was comfortable. Her husband had been dead only a month when his brother and heir, George, had claimed what was rightfully his. The elder male of the family, now near ninety, still lived but wielded no power.

Matilde, George's wife, was older than her husband by some ten years but had brought him a nice settlement and an infant stepson to the marriage. Some said the boy, now grown, was actually of George's loins. There were no other offspring. The boy had been adopted by George while still an infant.

Jillian had never met the young man since the two brothers seldom interacted other than forced social occasions such as Jillian's wedding to William. If the nephew had been present then she did not remember him. At present, he was touring the continent. It was rumored he had somehow displeased his father.

Since moving in, the new mistress of the household was quick to assert her new authority. She had demanded

Jillian move from the family wing of the house to this older one. It was very near the servant quarters, little used, and in some disrepair.

William had been abed for two months before he died. The carriage accident had broken his back and his will to live. Jillian had been by his side day and night, at his request, until he passed away. With his mortality staring him in the face he seemed to realize that he cared for her even if he was not sexually attracted to her.

He'd worried about his brother's family and their opinion of Jillian. George and Matilde had all but moved in even before William's death and Jillian could do little to stop them. Over and over he'd warned her to be careful – of what she did not know. He'd been out of his head most of the time and George seemed to hover over his brother's bed. William had died clutching her hand. His last words were "no accident", which must have been the fever.

Now she waited for the maid to leave so she could retire. The fire was banked for the night. Though the weather was not cold this area of the house always seemed drafty and the fire was cheerful.

She hadn't loved William but he hadn't been cruel. As long as she did as he wished and allowed him to display her at social functions – as long as she did not enter his bedchamber – they got along very well.

The maid left, closing the door, and Jillian blew out the candle. Before she could climb into the high bed her door opened. The large man blocked the door for a moment, then stepped forward and closed it behind him.

Her brother-in-law held out a glass of wine to her as he crossed the polished floor. “I believe it’s time we got to know each other better, dear sister.”

Eyes wide, Jillian shook her head slightly. “You have no rights in this room, My Lord, and no welcome. I am tired. Please leave.”

Inside she was quivering. The new marquis had watched her like a hawk for weeks now. She had avoided being alone with him. The will was to be read in the morning and she had been trapped here until then. Perhaps she would be trapped here even after. Her chin lifted.

He put the glasses on the table. “I see you are ready for bed.” Hands behind his back, he began pacing. “You know, I know, have always known, what William was. He didn’t like women. When he married you I was worried for a while but he reassured me that the title, the inheritance, would be mine. He said nothing had changed.”

He stopped so close that his jacket brushed against her robe. “I believe nothing changed. Therefore, either you lied about the event that led to your wedding, or he married you for some other reason.” He caught her chin and tilted her face up to his.

Jillian went very still. Where was this leading? What did he want? Lord protect her, how did she fob him off?

“Did he like to watch? Hmm? Was that it?” He chuckled. “Or are you still a virgin and he wished to display your beauty – look but not touch? Hmm?” His long fingers stroked down her throat, then circled it, tightened for a moment before releasing her.

He stuck his tongue out at her, curling it, and she wanted to vomit. "There is one way to find out if you made a cuckold of your dear, departed, husband. And since you're to live at my largesse, it is my right to attend to the manner. Are you a virgin, my dear?"

"What was between my husband and myself is no business of yours, My Lord. Leave my room or I'll ring for the servants."

"Oh, but it is – my business. As your family I am now responsible for you, for your future."

Suddenly she was pressed back against the bed, his leg forced between hers. He would've kissed her but she turned her head, her hands shoving against him.

"Get off of me. Let go. I'll scream."

"You do that, darling. There's no one but you in this wing of the house." His hand kneaded her bottom, pulling her against him, arching her back. "Didn't William at least show you what to do?" His slobberly lips were all over her. "Shame on him. Send a little thing like you out into the world all innocent." He backed up, his fingers workiing on the buttons of his breeches. A look of pure terror was in her eyes but it didn't register with him.

In panic, Jillian twisted and managed to raise one leg. She kneed him in the groin as hard as she could, falling to the floor in the process. Panting, she crawled out of his reach as he doubled over, and grabbed the candlestick.

"Innocent I'm not and I'd as soon kill you as not. William warned me about you. I'll be better armed next time. Now get out of my room."

His hand cupping his throbbing member, he managed to straighten a bit. Teeth clenched, eyes narrowed, he glared at her.

"This isn't resolved, girl. You'll regret your attitude. I could've been gentle, you know."

He made a painful exit, leaving the door wide open. Jillian ran to it and slammed it shut. There was no key and she dragged a large chair across the room to place before it. Tomorrow she would find and load the little pearl-handled pistol William had given her. It was packed away with her trunks but she should be safe tonight.

She crawled into the bed and tried to sleep. Her heart was still pounding. Is that all she was worth? Where could she turn? Her parents were in Quebec. William had never allowed her to visit them even before they left Europe. They thought her marriage happy and successful.

Margery? It would cause trouble. She was well aware that her sister was jealous of her although she'd given her no reason to be. The will was to be read tomorrow. If luck was on her side perhaps William had left her enough to live somewhere else; she could manage in the country with only a small income.

Tears welled in her eyes. She hadn't been happy with William but she'd been safe. Whatever she did was overlooked as long as she didn't interfere with his lovers – those handsome young men that shared his bed.

When she finally slept it was to dream of her dark prince, her rescurer. Why was it he always took the form of Stephen St.James?

CHAPTER SEVENTEEN

George Shanksbury, the new Marquis, was fuming. The family attorney had reviewed his inheritance but insisted the widow be called before proceeding with the final details. His fingers drummed on the polished desk as they awaited Jillian.

In subdued black she still managed to look striking. Jillian paused in the doorway but entered when Mister Winston nodded to her, closing the door behind her. She glanced at her brother-in-law. His fingers stopped their drumming but his dark brows were drawn together in a deep frown as he observed her.

"It seems the will made certain provisions for you after all, sister dear. We awaited your arrival to determine just what this entails. After all, a woman alone, and so young - . I'm sure it's nothing I cannot handle for you."

The attorney cleared his throat, rattling the papers before him. "Well, now, My Lord, your brother did leave his widow enough to be self-sufficient, if that is what she wants. Just let me read here."

As his voice droned on it was hard for Jillian to keep the smile from her face. George, on the other hand, did nothing to hide his fury.

"What was William thinking? The lodging on Coxsbury Square may be small but it's valuable and too large for a single lady's residence. And monies to sustain it? For her life? From my estate?" Each utterance was separated by a gasp of disbelief. He muttered under his breath, "If nothing else, it should go to his - ."

He stopped in mid-sentence and Mister Winston managed to get a word into the one-sided conversation. He met Jillian's sparkling eyes. "The will also clearly states you have possession of all furnishings and contents of said dwelling, My Lady. The staff remains although you may fire or hire as you see fit."

George jumped to his feet, his palm slamming down on the desk. "I'll not have it. We'll be the laughing stock of the ton. Imagine my brother's widow not living under my care." He leaned over her. "You'll live here, Madam. You may lease the house out if you insist on keeping it."

Jillian's chin came up. She spoke to the older man and ignored George. "I wish to take possession as soon as possible, Sir. It depresses me to reside where my husband no longer is master. I would mourn his parting in peace and quiet. Would tomorrow be too soon? "

"That can be arranged, My Lady. I will send the keys to you this afternoon and notify the staff of your arrival." He gathered up the papers, not looking at the Marquis. "A copy of the will for My Lady will be made as soon as possible, My Lord. I believe this is yours. The original is in my safe at the firm."

He managed to keep his dignity as he left the room. He felt sorry for the new widow; such a fine looking woman to lose her husband so young. At least he had left her provided for and there was no way the new marquis could break the will.

In the silence that followed, George blocked Jillian's exit. His long fingers stroked her cheek. He made her nervous and that pleased him. He didn't like to share. There was no way he would support her with nothing in return.

"This isn't over, darling. Running away isn't the end of it."

He stepped back to allow her to leave then took the seat behind the desk and began to re-read the document. He would find a loophole. William had not had time to be that thorough on his deathbed.

……………………………………………....……………….....

Within a week Jillian was settled in her new home. Her brother-in-law had not spoken to her again since the reading of the will. His wife had been distantly pleasant. She was not allowed to take even her personal maid with her so all of her servants were new, or were those her late husband had acquired.

The house was in a good neighborhood although not so rich as the family dwelling. It was sturdy brick with large fireplaces and long, paned windows. The furnishings were expensive but she'd redone one bedroom for her own taste. It was obvious that William had used the master bedroom for his love trysts. She closed this room off and left it as it was for the time being. She'd been shocked at the paintings there and was too embarrassed to view the erotic couples much less call a buyer.

The other walls were filled with paintings and the rooms with glassed cabinets. Shelves contained figurines and ornate china from all over the world. Many of the artifacts depicted erotic scenes or were of some ancient gods. The basement was filled with crates only half unpacked. Junk! Jillian left them to lie where they were. She hadn't the heart at present to redo the household. After all, she had no callers.

One year before she could live again. One year of black for every stitch of clothing. One year before she had total control of her finances. She pinched her cheeks, looking in the mirror. She still looked pale. How was she to stand it? She'd sent a note to her sister but had received no answer. Custom dictated she only go out in public escorted and only to such things as a tea or a musical evening. She'd had no invitations. It had been three months.

She would have to take things into her own hands. She wrote Geoffrey requesting their escort to a play, to anything, explaining her perdicament.

Two days later Geoffrey called at her door, alone. Excited for the first time in weeks, she swept into the parlour. He was standing by the mantle, his red-gold hair handsome in the reflected sunlight. Her breath caught as he turned to face her.

His eyes swept the seductive figure of his sister-in-law. How did she manage it? Her black gown was sedate, plain, trimmed with black braid; her hair caught up in a loose coil at the nape of her neck. Loosened strands curled about her cheeks. Her face was pale but the lips were as full, as lush, as he remembered them. Her eyes were grey today, luminous behind the thick lashes. He held out his hand to her as she crossed the room.

"Geoffrey, oh Geoffrey, I'm so glad to see another human being." Instead of taking his hand she came into his arms, her head tucked beneath his chin.

Startled but charmed, his arms closed about her. The tender feelings returned with a vengeance; the remembered softness of her, the lushness of her mouth. He swallowed and gently pulled her away, looking down at her.

Eyes sparkling, she laughed up at him. "I've been in hell. There's no one to talk to, nowhere to go. I wrote Margery but she did not answer. My brother-in-law has seen to it I am not invited to anything where they will attend." She paused for breath, suddenly embarrassed.

He watched her slender fingers smooth the full skirts; her eyes on the floor while she regained her momentum. He smiled, catching her chin and tilting her face to him. He brushed a chaste kiss over her parted lips, noticing with satisfaction that her breath caught, her expression changed.

Jillian took a step backward. "My pardons for being so forward, Geoffrey. It's just that – that I'm so lonesome. Could you not entreat Margery to visit? Or perhaps the two of us could go shopping?"

He gnawed at a corner of his lip and she laughed. "My manners have suffered from disuse, I'm afraid. Here, I'll ring for cakes. Would you like something strong to drink or merely tea?"

He shook his head. "Nothing at all, thank you. I'm on my way to my fencing salon. You sounded desperate so I stopped by to see what you needed." He took a seat, crossing his long legs.

"If it's only company, I'll send Margery over tomorrow for shopping or whatever you ladies want to do. She needs to get over competing with you on every little thing. I've spoiled her, I'm afraid. She believes a husband need pay attention only to her."

He seemed about to say more, his eyes lingered on Jillian's mouth, remembering the taste of her. Color tinged her cheeks. The uncomfortable silence was broken only by the clock's ticking.

"I love my wife, Jillian. I didn't mean to say -." He leaned forward, balanced on his elbows.

"No, no, that's quite all right. I never meant – what you're thinking – I just need company. Forget I asked." Her face was beautiful with the flush of color.

They both rose at the same time, almost touching. He stepped away first. Jillian turned to the door to see him out.

"It's all right, Jillian. We're kin, after all. It's been months since you've been out in public. I'll take care of it." He followed her to the door, suddenly noticing his surroundings. "This place is most unusual. Margery will think she's in an art gallery – or a museum."

That night he'd broached the subject with his wife. Margery had blistered his ears but after a passionate night in his arms she had agreed. After all, Jillian was her sister. Geoffrey loved her and only her. She had nothing to worry about, did she?

The next few months Margery called a truce. She and her sister went riding, shopping, to a few quiet teas. Margery made sure her husband wasn't home then invited her sister over to play with the children during the afternoons. Now it had been near seven months since William's death.

....

It was midnight when he found it. George Shanksbury whooped with delight, banging his fist hard enough to make his whiskey glass jump and spill. That was it. That had to be it.

His sister-in-law, Jillian, was never mentioned by name in the will. The wording where the distribution was made repeatedly referenced 'my lawful wife'. Had she been lawfully William's wife? To be wed, under the law, the marriage must be consummated. Therein lay the key.

....

Rose waited nervously for her former mistress to appear. This house gave her the creeps, all those fancy vases and such. She jumped when the lady in black swept into the room and gave Jillian a quick curtsy.

"Why, Rose, whatever are you doing here?" Jillian stared at the girl. "They have not let you go, have they?"

"Oh, no, M'am. It's not that. It's just – I needed to talk – that is, I needed to tell you something. I hope you won't think me forward, M'am."

"Of course not. Please sit down, Rose."

When they were both settled Jillian waited for the girl to speak. Rose's hands trembled and she clenched her fists. Jillian had missed the little maid. Was she is some kind of trouble?

"I thought you should know. I overheard them talking last week. Then yesterday the master sent for me and asked for me to make a statement in front of a witness, Lionel, the butler, you know. I did what he asked, M'am, as best I could. I need the work, you understand."

"I know, Rose. Whatever it is, it's all right. Just what did he ask you to say?"

"It's about you, your wedding night and all. He's asked all the help if there was any signs of blood on the sheets that night, or the next, maybe – if you and the marquis was known to share a bed." Her words speeded up with her enbarrassment. "Or if we, any of us, ever saw any other gentleman exit your bedroom." She rolled her eyes, her face beet-red. "He even asked my brother, Ned, if any gentlemen had used the stables in the night, all secret-like."

Jillian's eyebrows had climbed in astonishment. She remembered Rose's older brother worked with the horses but did not know him on sight. What was George doing?

"He wanted to know if you were still a virgin, M'am, same as before you wed." Rose came to a rushing halt, twisting her hands.

"And what did everyone say, Rose? Do you know?" Jillian's voice was so soft Rose leaned forward to hear her.

"Only the truth as we know it. You never cheated on your husband. You were a good wife."

"And do you believe me to be a virgin still?"

"I don't rightly know, M'am. But I – none of us – ever saw stained sheets and we never saw him touch you like a man would, begging your pardon, M'am."

Jillian slowly nodded, thinking. "I suppose that's true. Well, you're only being honest. Thank you for coming to me. If you ever need employment or need anything, let me know." She stood and the girl jumped to her feet, eager to leave.

Jillian frowned as she thought it over. What was George up to? Had he found some new way to break the terms of the will? It had been seven months since William had died. Could he cause trouble forever?

She didn't have long to wait. Two days later Mr. Winston, the attorney, called upon her. He came right to the point.

"My Lady, I thought you should be forewarned. In my best interests I should keep quiet but my conscience will not allow it. I'm sure this is not a problem. William Shakesbury was very fond of you at the end and he wanted you to be secure in your finances. I tried to see to that when the will was re-written."

"There is a problem, Mr. Winston?"

"I'm not sure. I would think not; at least, one set to embarrass you only. It should not affect the will. It's only that the wording, for which I take the blame, is not entirely clear."

"What do you mean, not clear?" Her heart tightened. What did this have to do with her being a virgin or having affairs?

"It seems that the will states 'my lawfully wedded wife' throughout when referencing you, rather than referencing you by name. One is only lawfully wedded once the marriage is consummated." He cleared his throat. "I see that as no problem but the Marquis sees a loophole to be exploited."

Jillian had gone white as a sheet. So this is why the statements from the servants. She nibbled at the corner of her bottom lip.

"So, he wishes to prove whether or not the marriage was consummated?"

Mr. Winston nodded, his face even redder if possible. "If you were proved to still be a virgin the terms are void and the inheritance, all of it, would revert to him. I am so sorry, My Lady. It is all my fault."

She shook her head slowly, trying to understand the implications. "Any infidelity I might have had is not the question then? Only if I am still a virgin? And he will prove or disprove this how?" Her eyes fastened on the little man.

"He is even now preparing papers to be signed. He has a noted physician and a judge for witness. He will insist you are – umm – inspected – before said persons and himself – as to your state of – umm." His finger loosened his collar.

"That's quite all right, Mr. Winston, you need not continue. I understand the problem." She rose to her feet, dismissing him. "I will take care of it. Thank you for coming. This will be kept between just the two of us."

"Of course, My Lady." He hurried from the room to make his escape.

CHAPTER EIGHTEEN

Stephen St. James's endeavors were thriving. He should no longer be sailing his own vessel but managing his investments. He'd tried but never lasted longer than a few months in London before he took to the sea again. Already his net worth was equal to his father's estate, the estate Geoffrey would inherit, and growing.

His ships sailed from London, Amsterdam, Barbados, Marseille, and several ports in the American colonies. His flags changed according to circumstances. He'd established contacts in Baltimore, and Charleston but treaded on quicksand there until the conflict with the mother country was settled. The more he saw of the Americans, the more he admired them.

He'd begun as a privateer for England and had harrassed the shipping lanes from New York, Boston, and the Canadas where the Americans tried to break through. He still sailed under the privateer flag on occasion but only if ordered to a special assignment by the government.

His last assignment for the Crown had been to patrol the English coastline against that American pirate, John Paul Jones. He'd never sighted the man but a British presence made the populance feel safer.

Tonight he was once again in London and it was at the height of the season. He usually avoided the social events and any gathering that smacked of the ton. He'd run into his brother at his club earlier in the week and that had evolved into a long-overdue family visit.

Now he stood to the side of the dance floor watching the swirling guests. He smiled lazily at a portly gentleman's best efforts. The waltz was not an easy dance to conquer with a protruding belly. His own outfit tonight was black, elegant and well tailored, but distinct in its lack of color.

He'd been home for two weeks and was ready to sail again, restless as usual. The only thing that had stopped him was today's visit to his brother's family.

Geoffrey had been busy in the bedroom in the past years. Margery bloomed with the glow of happy motherhood, her two little ones about her skirts. He had his heir and a baby girl, the image of his wife.

He'd finally had to ask his brother about Jillian. Geoffrey had snorted and made some rude remark. Margery was not much kinder.

"She'll embarrass us all." She cut her eyes at her husband. "Jillian has put off mourning. It's been less than a year since William's death. It's just not decent. She has yet to be seen officially in public but all London will be whispering behind her back – and ours."

"It's all because of that brother-in-law of hers. He inherited the title, of course, and the estate – near all of it. His wife moved her to the old wing of that huge house, almost to the servant quarters. Even so, she was demure enough until he tried to take back the house and income William left to her." She turned to Stephen. "She was to have William's small house in town, with all its furnishings and other content, and enough to run it for the rest of her life – even if she remarries."

Geoffrey laughed. "William spent an increasing amount of time in that place. I wouldn't be surprised if he kept his – ." He glanced at his wife and shrugged. "Anyway, the new Marquis declared she should live with them and he would manage her finances himself; that she had not been William's wife long enough to deserve the lodging or her yearly stipend."

Margery laughed. "I would've liked to see Jillian's face when that was said. My sister has a temper though it may take a while to stir. Anyway, she packed up and moved to her new house soon after – but after she had proven her rights of possession."

Stephen frowned. "And this has decided her on the course to shock the ton?"

"Well, she seemed resigned to serve out her year of widowhood. She tricked me into escorting her shopping and to a few small teas- all sweet and innocent. Now - who knows what she wants? Another man?" Margery rolled her eyes. "She doesn't visit here often. I hadn't been summoned for a visit so last week I called upon her to see if she was all right. The dressmaker was there, that expensive French woman. Fabrics were everywhere, and in every shade – not a black or grey to be seen. She's ordered an entire new wardrobe."

Tongue in cheek, Gregory grinned at his brother. "So, perhaps she's shopping for more than gowns. William loved displaying her on his arm. Wait until you see her, baby brother. She's grown up. She'll not lack for suitors – of any kind."

Margery's mouth flattened in annoyance. "And she doesn't need you to add fuel to the fire. Remember, the ton has just now forgotten your involvement in that disgrace before she wed William. Stay away from her." With a flurry of skirts she left the room.

Stephen raised a dark brow. "The disgrace? She knows? I thought the culprits involved were only myself and the Marquis."

Gregory ran a hand through his golden hair. "I was a fool one night and confessed I was there. She doesn't know I had planned the trap. I wasn't that drunk, thank God. I think sometimes she watches my every move when I'm around Jillian though. Lord knows I love my wife and would never, never, - but – I'm careful."

Stephen chuckled. "Serves you right. Perhaps I should call upon the lady. After all, it's been three - four years. I must have been forgiven by now."

"I wouldn't if I were you. Just looking at her makes you want –" he glanced at the door –" want to pull her beneath you and taste all that fire." Geoffrey's face actually flushed. "I'm sounding like a raw youth, aren't I? But you'll see." He took a sip of his brandy. "Are you attending the ball tonight? It's possible Jillian will be there. She wouldn't dare ask for our escort but if she's wanting attention -." He laughed. "If she wishes to shock it will be the occasion for her first appearance."

Stephen nodded and started for the door. To his back he heard the murmered words, "She doesn't have any idea you're in town. You wouldn't stand a chance if she did. She still asks about you."

He turned with a smirk to his mouth. "Remember she chose the Marquis, not me. She knew what she wanted."

"That's debatable." Geoffrey stared into his brandy snifter, thinking of the expression on Jillian face when she'd married William.

……………………………………………..……….

Now Stephen scanned the room again. She wasn't present. Irritated, he started to leave. Then he saw her. Jillian had paused at the entrance to the ballroom, only a short distance from where Geoffrey stood with a group of men. Chin tilted up, lips slightly parted, she took a deep breath and descended the two wide steps. The floor cleared before her.

Her dress was perfection itself. A dark crimson taffeta, it rustled as she walked, announcing to the world her elegance. The bodice was low with black lace pretending to cover the tops of her breasts and forming small puffed sleeves. Amid all the peacocks she was the unique gem, the glowing sun in the pale rainbow of colors.

The cream of her perfect shoulders rose to the slim column of her unadorned throat. Dainty gold eardrops ending in a single pigeon blood ruby dangled from each ear. Her lips were full, sensuous, lush. Her hair, streaked with gold, tumbled from a simple coronet that held it in check, allowing stray strands to escape at random. She looked as if she'd been tumbled in bed and enjoyed every minute of it.

Every man in the room stared, their thoughts clearly written on their faces. Every woman in the room tensed. Unwanted, a silly smile broke across Stephen's face. Across the floor, conversation ceased. No one moved. A slight flush touched Jillian's high cheekbones and she nibbled at her lower lip as she stood there alone, defiant.

And then Geoffrey stepped forward to offer his hand. Her answering smile was brilliant. Conversation hummed again and the music for the next dance announced a minuet. Her hand upon his arm, she was led onto the floor.

Stephen leaned back against the doorframe to watch. It was then he noticed the three ladies to his left, their eyes glued to the pariah in crimson.

"It's not been a year since her dear husband passed away and just look at her. It's a disgrace."

"He gave her everything, took her everywhere. Why, he introduced her to court as though she were royalty herself."

"They say she's moved into that house he left her; wouldn't remain under the roof with the new Marquis like a decent woman should. Just look at the hussy."

"And the men – just watch the rakes – calculating, or taking bets, on which of them will be first to -."

"Shhh. Remember we're ladies." The brunette glanced in his direction and smiled sweetly.

They all turned to look again at Jillian dancing with her brother-in-law. Across from them stood Margery, a cup of punch in her hand. It was trembling and threatened to spill. Her face was pale against her flaming hair.

Stephen pushed away from the wall. He would intervene as soon as the dance ended and whisk Jillian to safer ground. He hadn't realized how much he'd wanted to see her but this siren was not the girl he'd left behind.

Nor was he the only man with like thought. Geoffrey bowed and left her at the far edge of the floor. She had already declined several offers to dance and the waltz was under way before Stephen managed to cross to her side, blocking her away from the approaching hoard.

"May I have the honour of this dance – for old times sake?"

Jillian lifted her hand, her fan dangling from her wrist. Ready for another polite refusal she looked up into the dark chocolate of his eyes. Her heart leaped into her throat, her lips parted in confusion. What was he doing here? And why tonight? On her first foray back into society? When they were all busily tearing her apart?

He brought her fingers to his lips for a light kiss. He felt her pull away and reversed his hold, enclosing her hand in his. His other hand circled her waist and he moved her in a swirl of taffeta onto the dance floor.

"I don't believe I answered you, Sir." Her words were like ice. But her eyes met his, eyes confused by the color she wore, eyes the color of a cat's, grey, rimmed with gold. They sizzled with emotion, denying the stiffness of her body.

Stephen allowed his thigh to brush hers through the fabric of her full skirt. Ah, too much encumbrance. He wanted more. They turned on the dance floor and he held her closer, too close to be proper. But then nothing about her tonight was proper.

Crushed against him, Jillian could feel the movement of each muscle as they moved together across the room. Unable to resist she began to relax and her lashes drifted downward, fanning her cheeks. He smelled so good; that unique smell only Stephen had. He felt so good, hard, and strong. Just like her dreams – her eyes flew open. Had his lips just brushed hers?

With a crooked grin he devoured her reaction. Only a touch, he'd dared no more, but heat had flared with that touch. She'd felt it too. He swallowed, attempting to think of some polite conversation but it was useless. The tip of that pink tongue flicked over where he'd kissed her and his guts tightened. That wasn't all that tightened. Innocent eyes widened as she felt his reaction pressed against her. He pulled her tight into his hips. Innocent, hell! There was no way that act could be true, not the way she looked, the way she fit against him.

And then the music stopped. The floor was clearing. He wanted to curse. He stood there like a dunce, losing his soul in her eyes. They were no longer alone.

They were surrounded, or rather she was surrounded, by gentlemen; all of them asking for a dance, offering to get her punch, pulling her away from him.

Stephen stood like a raw youth and let it happen. He hadn't been prepared for his own reaction to her. After all, it'd been near four years and she'd grown up, grown more beautiful, more enticing, more sensual. He didn't know her. He laughed at himself. Had he ever known her?

He watched as she handled her admirers, never once looking his way. Geoffrey had warned him, hadn't he? They would pounce on the beautiful widow now that she was out of mourning, a choice tidbit to be plucked. Whether for marriage or dalliance their suites were pressed. Assuredly they thought she had money, and she probably did. The Marquis had wanted her enough to trump his own offer, hadn't he?

Jaw clenched, he endured their attempted pawings. It wasn't the money and he knew it. It was her, every man's dream. He wanted to rescue her, to carry her away, but then she'd given him no encouragement, had she?

Jillian tried to keep her attention from wandering to Stephen. He was what she wanted, needed. Her blood still stirred from his touch, excitement centered where his manhood had pressed against her. If only he cared. The problem was she cared too much. She couldn't use him. She was afraid if she allowed it she would never get over him.

She smiled up at navy Captain Boyce Garrett as she opened her fan. His blond good looks were almost boyish. She remembered he was a good friend of Stephen's. The two were always in some scrape together when they were younger – or so Geoffrey had claimed. He wouldn't do for her purposes. What if he discussed her with Stephen? She would dance with him and that was all.

From the corner of his eye Stephen saw Margery's dismissal of her own husband, her angry stance as she followed her sister's activity. Irritated, he watched Jillian through two more dances. Disgusted with her and himself, he wandered into the room where a gambling hell had been set up for those gentlemen preferring cards.

As usual, his luck with cards had held. Bored, his mind still on the woman in red, he gathered his winnings and took his leave. As he entered the hall he caught a glimpse of crimson duck into an alcove down the columned corridor. Suddenly wide awake, he moved to follow.

She'd meant to hide away for a short respite before the late dinner was served. Perhaps she should leave now. Already two gentlemen had almost come to blows over who should escort her to dine. She'd had no idea what a stir she'd make as the merry widow. Always before, William had offered her protection of a sort. At least then the offers for dalliance had been descreet.

Her plan would never work. There were too many and she could trust none of them. She needed a man who would do the deed and keep his silence afterwards; a man she could find not too detestable. She would think on it. She had sown the seeds.

Her eyes closed, she laid her head back against the patterned wallpaper. A vision flashed before her. He would be perfect – and he would be leaving England. She could imagine his hands on her body, his sensuous mouth pleasuring her.

Her nose twitched at the perceived male scent and she smiled. Her imagination was running away with her. If she kept her eyes closed tight she could conjure up the handsome devilish face of Stephen St.James.

Strong hands closed over her shoulders, rough thumbs stroked the soft flesh. Her eyes flew wide. Her lips parted in question just before Stephen dipped his head and covered her mouth with his. His tongue slid against hers, tempting, teasing her to open wider. With a gasp, she succombed and he rewarded her, his lips and tongue setting her on fire. Her hand slid about his neck, encouraging him. He needed no words.

Oh, God, it had been so long! He was perfection. Her tongue mimicked his, dancing then withdrawing. She moaned as his fingers dipped into her bodice, roughing her taut nipple, squeezing the full breast. Her back arched into him, asking for more. His other hand slid the lace of her gown lower, off her shoulders, until he could feast his eyes.

Her head tilted back, offering herself to him as best she could. And he took, greedily, his mouth and hands moving over her hungrily. His erection centered between her hips, jutting into her belly and she felt the surge of moisture between her legs.

She heard another moan. Was that her? He looked up at her then dipped his head and pulled a nipple into his hot mouth. She almost cried out but his fingers played over her lips. She sucked on the fingertip that teased her, reveling in his reaction.

He turned her deeper into the alcove, half pulling the heavy velvet drape across the opening. His mind was no longer rational. It seemed all the years they'd been apart had disappeared. He wanted her now, or as near as he could have her, now.

Crumpling her skirt in one hand he followed the black silk stockings upward, his mouth loving her all the time. If they thought, either of them, this wouldn't happen. It had to happen. He wouldn't lose her again.

He'd make her accept him. She wanted it too; she hadn't stopped him.

Out of control, his hand closed over her wet mons, stroked the tangled curls. He caught his breath as her hands worked inside the buttons of his shirtfront, her fingers tweaking his flat nipples. Fire tightened his determination and he sank a finger deep into her satin heat.

She gasped, clutching at him, and he retreated, only to repeat his attack, slicking the pulsing flesh over and over. He massaged the swollen nub of her womanhood and she squirmed in his arms. Her hands fisted in his ruffled shirt. He kissed her deeply, bowed his head to her breast again, and sucked – just as his thumb pressed the nub and his fingers sank deep.

Jillian felt stars exploding behind her eyes. Never had she felt anything like this, never even imagined it. He was gently stroking between her legs now, his mouth moving over her throat, nibbling at her ear lobes. Her thighs quivered, her entire body trembled, as she pressed against him.

Stephen chuckled, biting her throat where her pulse pounded. "You're still a hot little witch, just like I always said. If you need a man in your bed, I'm here. Just ask." He dropped her skirts, the taffeta's swish announcing their presense if anyone was near. He didn't care.

Catching her hand, he forced it to encircle his cock. Her eyes opened wide, her soft lips parted. He wanted those lips around him but not here – no, not here. He kissed her again, letting her feel the throbbing force of his need. That wide-eyed innocence act was working. His shaft hardened, lengthened. With a groan he pushed into her hand. "I want you, Jillian. I've always wanted you. Just say the word, now, tonight, and we'll finish this."

Bewildered, Jillian stared at him. She tightened her grasp about his manhood. He was so large! Not at all as she'd remembered her husband. How would he look naked? He was all muscle, big, long legs. She swallowed. Why couldn't it have been him? Why didn't she choose him? Tears swam in her eyes.

"Aw, Sweet, one doesn't cry when one's just met heaven. Or is it you're wanting more?" He cocked a dark brow at her. "This isn't the place you know." He cupped her breast in one large hand sighing. "Beautiful." He dipped his head and licked around the dark point, blew his breath against the moisture, watching it pull tight for him.

The sudden staccato of a lady's heels froze them; only the shrill voice was worse than the sudden rush of cool air as the velvet drape was jerked wide. Close on Margery's heels followed Geoffrey but he was too late to stop the attack.

"You whore. Sister or not, you're a wicked slut. First my husband and now his brother. Shame on you. How many men does it take, how many?"

Margery's fingers burrowed into Jillian's hair and pulled. Curls spilled everywhere. Her eyes lit on the lowered lace, the flushed flesh barely covered. She reached for Jillian's bodice but caught the lace sleeve instead. It tore, taking much of the gown's covering lace with it.

Stephen pushed between the women. Jillian's spread hand held the bodice in place but little was left of it.

With the taffeta pushed low, the black corset pushed her breasts upward and they spilled over in abundant display. Like lush cream, topped with cherries, they nestled in the folds of crimson taffeta. Geoffrey stopped in mid-stride, his mouth gone dry.

Stephen barely managed not to bury his face where it had so recently been. Time seemed to stop. Both men ogled, lost in their own fantasy for a split second, unable to help themselves. Then Margery laughed, shaking her head, near hysteria. Geoffrey came to life.

Behind her, he caught his wife before she could do more damage. Managing to hold her about the waist he clamped his palm over her mouth. He was bitten for his efforts. Margery did quieten but her eyes spit fire.

At sight of her sister, Jillian had jerked her hand away from Stephen's erection but it was prominently displayed against his tight breeches, the tip defined by a damp stain. She followed Geoffrey's gaze there and her cheeks reddened to match her kiss-swollen lips.

Stephen's hands caressed Jillian's shoulders, managing to pull the lace and taffeta back into place just as several men appeared in the hallway, drawn by the disturbance.

"This is all my fault. I followed the lady and pressed my affections – if you can forgive me -." He raised her hand, kissing Jillian's fingertips.

She stared at Stephen, her hand trembling in his. She saw the sarcastic smirk on Geoffrey's face, the fury on her sister's. Stephen was watching her, waiting for his next cue.

The three guests hovered within view but moved no closer. Jillian glanced down at her scattered hairpins.

Then she felt Stephen's fingers in her hair, spreading the curls to frame her face. Gratitude washed over her. He bent to retrieve several jeweled pins and placed them in her palm, closing her fingers about them.

"I believe I prefer your hair loose after all, My Lady. It suits with the crimson, don't you agree, gentlemen?" He turned to stare haughtily at the intruders.

With a nervous nod they retreated, shaking their heads. Stephen had a dangerous reputation with the sword. Not a one of them would risk offending him.

Geoffrey nodded to his brother and sister-in-law. "Until later; we should talk." He moved away to call their carriage. He kept a firm hand on his wife's waist.

Alone once more, Jillian smoothed her skirt. It had caught up on one side to display a black lace petticoat. She moistened her lips, trying to gain her composure. Stephen watched her actions, his body racing with raw desire. His fingers itched to feel again the silk of her thigh, the tiny crimson rosettes that knotted about her garters. Nostrils flared as they noted the musk of her arousal; he dipped his head for another kiss but she turned her head.

"I – I made a mistake, Stephen. I can't do this. I'm sorry." Side-stepping him, she would've left but he caught her arm.

"I'll see you home."

She shook her head. "You're leaving soon, sailing?"

"Yes, but we need to discuss what just happened. You obviously need something I can give. I'll be careful next time. You won't be compromised." His mouth curved upward in that charming crooked smile the ladies loved.

His head dipped closer and he saw her lower lip tremble. He hovered close enough that she could feel the warm brush of his breath. He was still so hard he was aching and he knew she wanted him too. He could sense the surrender as she swayed toward him.

Her breath caught as his lips covered hers, his tongue slid within to tease. A tear slid down one cheek, then another. She felt him draw back.

"What's this?" His words were as soft as a caress yet carried an edge. He kissed the damp streaks, holding her chin with his fingertips. He tamped down his annoyance. Surely she wouldn't renege now. The gentleman in him won out though and his words were contrite.

"I'm not worth tears, my wicked sweet. If you want to go home alone, so be it. Another time, then. I'll call for your carriage."

CHAPTER NINETEEN

She hadn't contacted him this morning. She knew he was leaving soon. He'd be damned if he'd beg. Stephen sulked as he finished up his affairs in London. He'd be sailing in two days. He'd been so sure she would chase after him after the way they'd parted. My God, but she was breathless in that crimson – heated a man's blood to boiling.

Still, the least he could do was say goodbye. Somehow his direction had carried him to her neighborhood. It was now almost twelve, early for a visit considering the prior night. He knocked before he changed his mind.

The heavy door opened to the stern face of a dignified butler. The man's tone did not fit his words and Stephen frowned.

"Madam is not at home? I find that impossible to believe. Perhaps I'll just wait -." He'd gotten no further when a crash sounded from upstairs.

The butler looked frightened. He turned to look over his shoulder and Stephen pushed his way into the entrance hall. Another crash and a masculine voice was followed by a woman's scream.

Stephen bounded for the stairs, knocking the butler aside. The man caught at his coat, jabbering.

"Hurry, Sir, please hurry." As Stephen flew up the stairs he added, "Second door, second door on the right."

Stephen flung the door wide to a scene of chaos. Jillian was on the bed, her only clothing a nightrail. The cotton gown was twisted about her hips and rucked up to display long legs, one of which was secured to the bedpost. A flustered young man wearing the Marquis' livery was trying to wrap a stocking about her other ankle, pulling it toward the opposite bedpost. Her wrists were tied to the headboard, her hair in wild disarray.

At the foot of the bed stood the Marquis and two older men. All watched the proceedings solemnly although Shakesbury's mouth carried a definite smile as he watched the lady's struggles. A dainty table lay overturned and cupped shards of a shattered pitcher caught the sunlight in pools of water.

All but the younger man turned to stare at Stephen. For a split second Jillian ceased her protest and her leg was fastened tight. She pulled against the restraits, her movements somehow erotic.

"You disgusting slime. You coward, you -." She suddenly felt Stephen's presence and the words died.

"What the bloody hell is going on?" He advanced into the room, his short sword already drawn.

George surveyed the intruder with disdain. "The blacksheep of the St.James family, I believe? We haven't met. I'm the Marquis of Rathwild, George Shakesbury."

His voice was a drawl of disrespect as he looked down his long nose at Stephen.

"I know who you are. What are you doing here; molesting a lone woman?" The tip of Stephen's sword had moved upward in attack position.

Shakesbury's hands rose as he took a step backward. No one else moved. "We have the right here, St.James. I have with me Dr. Fritzsimmon and Magistrate Stratton as witnesses. We are about to prove this woman's virginity. No one will be hurt. She brings her current perdicament on herself."

"Stephen -." Jillian's voice broke in, pleading. "Make them go away."

The magistrate cleared his throat. "The late Marquis' will seemed to leave a rather large bequest to the lady here but there is a problem. We believe that part is void and this residence, etc., should in fact revert to George Shakesbury."

"What?" Stephen frowned but didn't lower his sword. From the corner of his eye he could see Jillian struggling to free herself, all in vain. "What has that got to do with your presence here? With your assault?"

Shakesbury spoke up. "There is no mention of this woman by name in the final will. The reference is to 'my lawful wedded wife'. She is such only if the marriage was consummated." His lips twisted in a satisfied smirk. "I know my brother's quirks, his preferences, his abilities, so to speak. There was no consummation and therefore no marriage. Our good Dr. Fritzsimmon is here to prove that fact, before witnesses."

He turned to the doctor, ignoring the stunned intruder. "Proceed when you're ready."

His face flushed with color, the grey-bearded man stepped to the foot of the bed. The other men lost interest in Stephen as he slid the soft gown upward.

"Noooo!" Jillian's scream broke the silence.

Shamed, Stephen came back to his senses. "Get out! Now! If the lady says she was truly William's wife then it is so." He stepped aside to allow their escape but only the young man scooted toward the door.

"We're unarmed, St.James, but you haven't heard the last of this. I have the law on my side. We have statements from the servants, from William's special 'friends'. She's nothing but William's pretty ornament as far as his estate is concerned." He glared at Jillian. "I'll be back."

The intruders took their leave. As the Marquis passed the butler his lip curled. "You are as good as fired. It's only a matter of time."

Stephen stood where he was until he heard the outside door close firmly behind them then he closed the bedroom door and sheathed his sword. He stared at the vision spreadeagled on the bed and Geoffrey's words came back to haunt him. 'Spread out like a feast, just for me.'

To disguise his inward groan he busied himself with unbuckling his sword and removing his jacket, folding it, and placing it over a chair. At last he turned back to the fantasy spread on the sea-green covers.

Jillian hadn't uttered a sound. Now her voice caught in a soft sob. "He'll be back, but thank you."

"Are you all right? Did they hurt you?" He withdrew the knife he always carried from his boot, preparing to cut the binding from her ankle.

"Only my dignity – and don't ruin that, please. They used my silk hose. Couldn't you just unknot it?" She tried to lean upward and the soft cotton pooled between her legs slid to one side.

Stephen swallowed at the fleeting glimpse of tight curls. Unaware of his hammering heart, she lay back. He sheathed the knife and concentrated on the hose about her ankle. One freed, he moved to the other, not daring to meet her eyes. This one was tighter. He was too aware of her slim ankle, his position between her legs.

Frustrated, he moved to the side of the bed and sat upon it, taking her foot onto his lap as he worked on the knotted silk. Once freed, he massaged the arch of her foot, the calf of her leg. She felt so good, so soft. Then she wiggled her toes and he released her as though burned.

Jillian waited impatiently for him to free her wrists. They were tied together and lifted over her head rather than to the posts. The bed was unusually wide. She had confiscated the large one from the master bedroom and reworked it to suit herself.

Stephen couldn't reach her hands. Gingerly he knelt on the bed, leaning over her. Somehow his knee slid between her legs, his upper thigh rubbing against the vee of her legs. He felt her reaction, the shudder that ran through her. He should stop, use the knife, end this. He did not.

Jillian felt his heat spread through her like a touch of fire. All the desire of last night's disaster returned with a vengeance. Her hips shifted to rub against where he lay.

His muscles tensed but he stayed where he was, moving slightly as he worked on the knotted stockings.

Her mouth was almost against his throat and she could see his rapid pulse. Why didn't he kiss her? She wanted him to kiss her. She raised her head and he looked down, his mouth hovering over hers.

Stephen lost his concentration. Drat the stockings anyway. He could make love to her right here, right now. He rather liked her wrists being tied, her being restrained under him. He felt his erection harden even more. He moved against her, heavy with need, and she made a soft mewing sound. Her eyes were closed but her lips were parted.

He dipped his head and slanted his mouth across hers. His tongue slipped inside, enjoying the devil's dance against hers. Hunger shot through him and his cock lengthened, uncomfortable in the tight breeches. He forgot about her wrists. His hands moved downward, over her firm breasts. He lifted his head to look at her.

Her pupils were dilated, dreamy. She moistened those soft lips and he took her mouth again, his hands kneading one breast. She twisted against him, unable to free her hands. Open-mouthed, he covered her breast and sucked through the thin gown. Jillian arched into him, like a kitten begging for attention. Nipping, roughing her nipple until it stood taut and proud he moved to do like to the other.

He felt her legs spread under his assault and came partially to his senses. He reached down to cup her mons. She was slick and hot. He sat back on his haunches. She watched him warily, her mouth sulky.

"Did William consummate the marriage?" His voice came out rough and gravelly but he couldn't help it.

She shook her head, her lower lip trembling.

"And during that marriage?" Was he trying to justify what he was about to do? The questions tumbled unwanted from his mouth.

"Does he have witnesses that state you only slept with others then? Exactly what does he have to prove?" Oh, God, his cock was aching. He cupped her, his fingers slipping back and forth in her wet heat. She smelled of musk, of female arousal, and some softer, sweeter scent. Her whole body trembled now.

She shook her head again, spreading the glory of her hair wider on the pillows. "No, no, I did not break my wedding vows. William liked young men. He never came to my bed. Never." She looked angry.

Geoffrey's handsome face loomed before him. Stephen closed his eyes but it was still there. So, she had given his brother her virginity and not known a man since? Pity, pity when she was so full of passion. What a waste. His nostrils flared as his thumb tortured the swollen seat of her pleasure and watched the play of emotions across her face.

"You've never been tempted? Not once?" What was wrong with him? He was torturing himself. She wasn't his. His fingers stilled and her small teeth caught at the corner of her full lip in annoyance.

"A long time ago, perhaps; when I was too young to know better." Long lashes fanned her cheeks for a moment and then she met his eyes again. "And last night."

He rewarded her by pushing a finger deep, his thumb moving hard pressuring the heated center of her. Her fists closed, nails biting into her palms, as her hips lifted, begging.

He backed from the bed, pulling his boots off as he moved. He pulled his shirt over his head, running one hand through his long hair. He struggled with decency and lost. She hadn't objected so far, had she? And no matter what the good Marquis thought he knew she was no virgin.

"You know even if it's been years, a maidenhead does not grow back." He could still hear his brother's words after that day at the lake; the bemused expression in the blue eyes as he described the girl that had let him have his way on the sun-warmed rocks.

He was staring down at her with the strangest expression on his face. Jillian frowned. Whatever was he talking about?

"If you want me to leave tell me now before it's too late."

She watched the play of muscles across his chest as he moved to position himself over her. Her heart gave a lurch. If only he loved her – but she knew better. He would solve her problem, take her virginity, but he would sail away. She wanted to grasp those biceps, dig her nails into his back while he sank deep inside her. She wanted to know what it was like to know a man – this man. She twisted her bound wrists, one brow raised in question.

He chuckled. "I guess you've missed your chance." He deftly released her hands from the bindings, refuting his earlier trouble. His muscles rippled as her hands kneaded his shoulders; his knee pushed her legs apart and he settled his hips between the vee of those white thighs.

If nothing else, Stephen was an unselfish lover. He would give her pleasure before he took his. He began to kiss her again, softly, and again, more possessively. He nibbled at her earlobe, whispering in her ear, "You'll be tight after so long but I won't hurt you. It won't be like that first time."

Jillian stilled. She pushed at his broad shoulders and he lifted up on his elbows to look down at her. His heavy shaft, still bound by his breeches, pushed against her thigh.

"There was no first time. I told you. I've never lain with a man."

He pulled back as though slapped, sitting on his haunches. "Never? I find that hard to believe. Your behavior last night, oh lady in red, was anything but innocent. Every man in that room wanted to spread your delectable legs. You invited it – and me. A few more minutes and I'd have taken you right there."

He ran the side of his hand between her legs. She was slick and swollen with need. "This has not the feel of sweet innocence. Do you want it or not?" He hadn't meant to lose his temper but his libido was raging and she had efficiently stopped him with her words.

Her face heated, she shifted her hips. Tears trembled on her thick lashes. "I have to lose my virginity, don't you see? Last night I meant to chose the man, the means, but I lost my nerve. And then you were there, in the alcove, and it was so easy. You wouldn't tell anyone I was a virgin. You were leaving in mere days. If only Margery hadn't interrupted - ."

She stroked her palms over his chest, lingering on the taut nipples, and absorbed his reaction, the ripple of his muscles. "So, yes, yes, I want it now."

He stared down at her, torn between what his body wanted and what his mind was telling him. He slid from the bed, searching for his boots. Barely able to function, he jammed his feet in the boots so hard his toes hurt. Forcing himself to take his time he pulled his shirt slowly over his head. He wouldn't take her like some hired stud, he wouldn't.

He forced a smile to his lips. He busied his hands with tucking his shirt in. They itched to knead her breasts; those lovely breasts that still peaked for him against the dampened cloth of her gown. She crawled forward to curl at the foot of the bed, closer to him. With every movement he wanted her more. He wanted to wrap his arms around her, comfort her, protect her. And she thought of him only as a means to keep her inheritance.

A pillow fell to the floor. Stephen stooped to pick it up, then slung it against the window, causing her to jump. He turned back to her, his hands on his hips.

"This is no way for your first time. It should be done with finesse." He watched her expression change from fear to one of delight. Oh, if only that delight was for him. His head cocked to one side, he flashed her that crooked grin. "You should have told me I would be your first. A man always likes to be first. I am honored."

She slid from the bed and ran to him, throwing her arms about him. Standing on tiptoes, she pulled his head down to reach his lips. Her kiss was pure joy, a mere brush of her lips, of her body, before she released him. She backed a step or two, her hands behind her back, her head down.

He cupped her chin. "Explain Geoffrey. Now. Then, we'll see -."

She shrugged, her lips pouted. "You knew about the lake, about Geoffrey and me. I thought you knew all. He kissed me, touched me as no one ever had before or since – except you – but that is all. He expected me to meet him that next morning but I did not. By then I knew he was my sister's betrothed."

Clear green eyes met his. "You see, I spied on him that night from the balcony. And I danced with you." At this admission, she couldn't keep the mischief from her eyes. "I was supposed to be sick in my bed – to please Mother. She never liked it when I interferred with Margery's beaus. I had run away from the school, the convent, where she'd sent me. She always said I was a little bit wicked but Father spoiled me whenever he could. He said once Margery was settled he would take me to London and Paris. But I had to stay away from Geoffrey."

Stephen's heart was beating much too fast. He was a man grown. What was the matter with him? He was happy, happy; that was it. His brother had not touched her, not in any way that mattered. He could claim her – except – he was nothing to her. He forced his eyes from those full lips to her narrowed eyes. She was watching him with suspicion.

"So, will you do it? I won't be much trouble, Stephen. I won't cry out or anything. In fact, I rather believe I will like it." Her face had flushed rosy and she nibbled on her lower lip.

She looked adorable. He scooped her into his embrace and gave her a light kiss, picked her up, and deposited her upon the bed.

"Your wish is my command, fair lady. But you must follow my instructions. I will call for you at seven tonight."

She looked dismayed. "Tonight? But, where are we going? Here is – um, perfect."

He shook his head. "Would you like the maid to view evidence of your lost maidenhood?" He crossed to the armoire and flung it open. "And you will wear something just for me, something not too daring, sweet, rather – a man likes to do the seducing." He selected a turquoise gown with a cream froth of lace at the neckline and held it out for her. "This will do."

He kissed her fingertips, ignoring the temptation to suck at her index finger. It was all he could do to leave. His cock was raging with enthusiasm, his imagination was worse. "Until tonight, Jillian."

He was no sooner gone than her maid peeped about the door. She surveyed the room, the broken crockery, the overturned furniture; her eyes wide.

"My Lady, are you all right? When the gentleman didn't leave with the others we didn't know what to do."

"Quite all right, Dolly. Do get someone to clean this up and bring hot water for a bath and I'm ready for a light lunch and -." Jillian paused for breath. She had to calm down or she would not last until seven. Was it Stephen or what would happen tonight? It was one and the same, wasn't it? She shook her head, causing the little maid to glance over her shoulder at her. No, no, it wasn't. The man didn't care for her. He was only doing her a favor. Didn't everyone say that a man enjoyed the act for itself? It made no difference who the female was; she could be anyone.

Her nails bit into her palms. She didn't want him to do it with anyone else – not those women that eyed him as though he were a platter of beef – not a paid courtesan – not the fresh chit who would claim him someday for a husband. He was hers – for as long as she could keep him.

CHAPTER TWENTY

Stephen watched her descend the long stairs. The soft flow of her skirts seemed to change from blue to green. The flouce of cream lace at her throat and wrists only made her seem more dainty, like a delicate doll. Her petticoats were cream as were her silk stockings. His eyes slid up from her slim ankles to her enticing waist to the demure bodice of her gown. No trace of the flamboyant lady in crimson peeked through.

But then she extended her hand to him. He took it to his lips, kissing her fingers, turning it to caress her inner wrist with his moist mouth. Her pulse was beating much too fast. He straightened and all resemblance to innocent appearance vanished.

Jillian's green eyes smoldered. Her mouth begged for attention, her lips pursed in an excited smile of anticipation. He gave her hand a gentle tug and she stepped down the one remaining stair.

"You are beautiful, My Lady." He lowered his voice, his words for her ears only, "I wish now I had planned to show you to the world before I devoured you."

She laughed, the sound like music. "The name is Jillian, Sir. You really should not be so formal, considering -."She touched the tip of her tongue to her upper lip then pushed them into a pout. His guts did a flip.

Was it possible the girl didn't know how she affected a man? Tonight should be interesting. Stephen ignored the butler and leaned closer, whispering, "Do that again and we won't make it to our destination."

Her eyes widened, the picture of innocence. "Then we should hurry, Sir." Her eyes were still twinkling as she looked back at her butler. He was smiling but quickly wiped the expression from his face. Goodness, did he know what was going on?

Stephen settled into the closed carriage beside her, his thigh pressing against hers. The night was clear and pleasant, the sky already full of stars. She sat quietly, her fingers laced together. What had he planned?

He opened a small basket on the opposite seat and removed one glass and a bottle of wine. "I thought you might like some refreshment. Our ride may take an hour."

She watched as he poured a liberal amount of the liquid. The basket also contained bunches of fat grapes. She obediently opened her mouth as he fed her the first sweet fruit. Her lips closed over the tip of his finger and she could feel his heat. He leaned closer, followed with another grape, then kissed her as her teeth sank into the sweet pulp. The taste of it, of him, mingled with the magic of the night.

He raised his head, drank from the wine, and brought the glass to her lips. She obediently drank and the ritual continued. She began to feel relaxed, her body heated, her senses attuned to his instructions. By the time he'd set aside the wine she was craving the taste of it, the taste of him, sweet, intoxicating.

He set her back against the cushions, leaning away from her. She felt the lost and would have moved closer but he held her away. His knuckles stroked down her cheek and he toyed with a curl of her hair, tugging it until it loosened and tumbled to her shoulder. He twirled it about his hand, pulling her to him, watching her. And still he did not kiss her again.

Jillian wanted to scream at him. She needed him to kiss her. Her lips pouted unconsciously and he smiled. With his other hand he traced the outline of her nipples where they pressed against the soft fabric of her gown. They tightened, beginning to ache. She felt the length of his muscular thigh crowd against hers and a sigh escaped, quickly bitten back. Was he going to torment her? Couldn't he just get on with this? She opened her mouth to ask when his lips descended, stopping all protest.

A kiss like none she'd known – tender, devouring, becoming more engulfing with each moment. Her fingers burrowed into the hair at his nape to hold him to her, to savor each morsel.

She barely felt him lift her into his lap but immediately knew he was not unaffected by their play. His arousal was firm, pushing between her legs, centering just where she was beginning to ache. She wiggled, settling him where she wanted him. Even through their clothes she felt him jerk against her, his breathing heavier, his mouth not relinquishing hers but becoming more demanding.

They were slowing. He released her lips and set her back onto the seat with a rueful smile.

"We're here. How time flies." He opened the door and stepped down, offering his hand to her.

Salt air; they were at the sea – but not at the London docks. She was staring up at the silhouette of a tall ship.

"Welcome to my home, Jillian." He lifted her into the small boat pulled onto the pebbly shore and began to row.

Once aboard he gave directions to one of his crew then led her to his cabin. Lanterns gave a soft glow, swaying to the gentle movement of the ship. A silver candlelabra graced the table where a feast was laid out for them. The captain's cabin was elaborate since Stephen spent most of his time aboard. There were shelves of books and the bed was large, not a bunk as was more common for shipboard. She noticed the covers were turned back and plump feather pillows were piled high. There were crimson rose petals scattered across the sheets. She stared at them, her cheeks coloring.

Stephen followed her glance. He tipped her chin up and brushed a kiss across her lips. "I think we should eat first; cook has worked hard." When she didn't meet his eyes, he questioned, "Jillian?"

She felt as though she would shatter if he didn't take her into his arms at that very moment but she managed to look away, to look at the table. "Of course." Never mind that her voice sounded breathless.

She waited while he seated her and helped her plate. Suddenly she was hungry. There were oysters, roasted duck, potatoes, small green peas, and candied pears.

A covered basket contained hot yeast rolls. Her quest forgotten, she closed her eyes in appreciation as the first oyster slid down her throat.

"Pierre does one proud. He's French but don't tell anyone. They do know how to prepare food. Makes English cooking appear a poor cousin." Stephen enjoyed his food, knowing they had the night and he did not intend to rush her initiation.

Once the table was cleared he asked her if she would like a tour of the ship. Tense again, Jillian almost declined. Perhaps this was a mistake. Perhaps he didn't want her at all and wanted to delay what he'd promised to do.

Above decks there was a light breeze and a sweet aroma of some blooming shrub reached them from shore. Standing close beside him, she lifted her head to take a deep breath. His hand cupped her face, stroked down her throat. His head dipped to kiss, then suck, where her pulse beat. Like a fire re-plentished, the heat rekindled in them both; became an inferno.

He pulled her into his arms, his shaft heavy with need. Her hips cradled him, moved sinuously against him. It was natural to her, this need, this desperate want. It was something she had done without, had thought she could live without. His hand kneaded her breast, roughing the tip, and it swelled to fill his hand, pushing tight against the modest gown.

Stephen absorbed the kittenish mews she made as he prepared her. It was all he could do to slow down. He'd sworn to himself he would do this right. He'd not expected his own reaction to overwhelm him. His body raged to possess, to imprint her with his own image.

It was an unusual emotion for him, spiking his desire, coiling deep in his gut.

He could stand it no longer. He swept her into his arms and carried her to his cabin. He noticed his first mate tracking their progress. Huh! His crew could go to hell. Since when was it their business if he made a fool of himself, anyway? He kicked the door closed behind him.

Immediately his fingers began to undo the tiny buttons down her back. As the dress peeled away, his lips followed the naked softness. Jillian's hands were also busy but without much success. He'd removed his jacket earlier and his shirt was open at the neck. Now her fingers fumbled with the shirtail until she'd pulled it free of his breeches but she couldn't get it over his head.

He paused long enough in her disrobing to pull off the offending shirt, sat and jerked off the soft leather boots. Jillian had stepped from her petticoats and stood, centered, in the poof of material. She looked like a flower rising from the petals. Her corset was cream with blue ribbons and little rosebuds. He grinned crookedly, desire raging, and rose to kiss the mounded breasts pushed upward for his delight.

His fingers nimbly unlaced her and caught the bounty of her breasts in both hands, bending to kiss and suckle the tips. She gasped, leaning back to thrust them out. His hand dropped to cup her bottom, massaging, holding her in place to rub against his throbbing shaft. As she moved, he lowered the lace of her chemise and she was naked before him.

Somehow they managed to separate long enough to unfasten his breeches and for him to remove them. He wore nothing beneath and his manhood sprang free. He vaguely wondered if he'd made a mistake, going too fast for her innocence.

Her eyes were enormous as she stared at his manhood. She backed a step, moistened her lips, uncertainty showing in her expression. He was huge, his shaft reaching almost to his waist. The dark dusting of hair that she'd loved on his broad chest continued downward, pointing the way to that so-male member. He was magnificent! She'd only seen one other man nude, and him only half-erect. William had not been anything like this.

Jillian's vivid green eyes met the molten heat of Stephen's brown. "How can I? How can it, it -?" She took a step backward but his muscular arm wrapped around her waist, dragging her to him.

"Don't think about it. Feel, don't think." His mouth descended on hers as he lifted her beneath her knees and carried her to his bed. He came down between her legs, his hand covering her wet mons, his fingers already stroking.

His mouth teased hers, growing more and more demanding until she relaxed beneath him, twisting and panting. Then, holding her wrists to either side of her head his tongue and teeth brought her breasts to aching peaks while he rubbed against her wet curls with his length.

"Please, Stephen, please." Her voice trembled as she thrust her hips against him.

He released her hands to grasp her bottom, lifting her, spreading her. When he began to breach her she sighed and wrapped her legs about him.

"Not yet, Sweet, not yet." He thrust until he felt the barrier, forced himself to wait, kissed her again. His tongue thrust deep, again and again, hypnotizing her with his desire, with his rhythm. He absorbed her moans, felt her body push against his but he retreated beyond her reach until she was frantic.

He lifted his head and looked at her beautiful face. "Open your eyes, Jillian. Look at me."

It was the last coherent words she heard. A deep thrust and Stephen was buried deep within her. Her eyes widened, her mouth pursed into a silent cry, and then she was biting her lip, mewing her delight, as he began to move. But a little pain – so little – and followed by such wonder.

Her nails dug into his broad shoulders as he rode her. She picked up his rhythm, striving to feel everything he gave her, to please him in turn. So full! He filled her completely! She had been empty without him and never even known. This was what life was all about. She laughed in delight, tightening her muscles about his shaft again and again so that he wouldn't stop.

Stephen almost lost it. The little vixen was milking him with her tight sheath, the pulses pleasuring him beyond anything he'd ever known. Remembering he'd meant to make this memorable for her he concentrated on withholding his own pleasure.

Not since his own initiation into sexual slavery had he desired a woman with such intensity. He closed his mind to memories. He'd not used his 'lessons' since that time but now he would. Three shallow thrusts followed by a deep one; then five shallow and yet a deeper one; again, seven shallow thrusts and a long, deep one. He shifted his position higher to offer her more pressure. Her body anticipated the thrusts this time and he could feel the pulsing of her sheath begin. When he again performed with nine shallow he pushed as deep as possible on the next one – to touch her womb - and felt her explosion as she shattered beneath him, all cries and heat. He followed her into heaven, gasping and collasping onto the satin of her body.

It was worth the torture of his memories. Her sweet abandonment, her body's surrender to him, his own weakness in paradise – he'd do it again; but only for her. He rested his forehead against the softness of her hair, gasping for breath.

Jillian thrilled at the sensation of his possession. She felt his hot seed fill her, spreading, seeking her own. She wiggled her hips one last time as he lay atop her, centering him deeper, claiming him as she could.

Exhausted, their bodies covered in a sheen of perspiration, they lay twisted in the sheets. Jillian liked the heavy feel of his body although she could barely breath. He still filled her and she lay very still. Her breath tickled his ear and at last he stirred.

His mind was numb, his body sated. A virgin, by God; one would never have known but for the initial thrust. She was all fire, all passion, and a match for him as no other had ever been. He moved slightly and felt her kiss his ear. He raised his head, took some of the weight from her by balancing on his elbows.

One dark brow raised, he met her grey-green eyes. They were full of laughter. “Well? The deed is done.” He wanted to kiss her, hold her to him forever, but her expression was one of amusement and he didn’t quite know how to take it.

Jillian nibbled at her lower lip to keep from laughing. She didn’t know what was so funny. He just made her so happy; having sex with him filled her with delight. His thick dark hair and liquid brown eyes made her happy. His puzzled expression made her happy.

Reality returned. Stephen eased from her and rolled over. Oh, God, he’d not pulled out. He stared in consternation at the slightly bloodied evidence of his excess between her legs. He exited the bed and returned with a damp cloth.

“I’m sorry. I should have taken care not to -.” He thrust the cloth at her and returned to the basin to wash.

Jillian washed, moved away from the bloodied spot on the sheet. Suddently embarrassed, she reached for her chemise and pulled it over her head. It was done, over. He would leave her now and she would be alone again. The laughter faded. She became aware of the soreness; soreness in places she hadn’t known she had.

Stephen was pulling on his clothes, his back to her. She began to dress. Neither of them said a word.

Clothed, she followed him to the open deck. The night had cooled, or perhaps, they had cooled. The trip back to her townhouse was subdued although they sat close, the length of their thighs touching, her hand clasped in his.

They stood looking up at her doorway. Had they really made love just a short time ago? Jillian wanted him to stay but couldn't find the words to ask. She pasted a smile on her face instead.

"I hope I wasn't too much trouble. I don't have a basis for comparison but I think you're a very good lover." She tucked her head as color brushed her cheeks. "I am well pleased. Thank you, Stephen."

Was she blushing? After the way they'd made love? Stephen tried to better see her face but the moon slid behind a cloud just then. That was it? She wanted nothing more to do with him. She'd gotten what she wanted and he was dismissed like a servant. Annoyance stiffened his jaw.

"There may be a problem, Jillian. I didn't mean for it to finish just as it did. I may have gotten you with child." He waited for her to say something but she did not. "If that should happen contact Geoffrey or my trading office and they will reach me. I will, of course, do the correct thing. The child will not be born a bastard."

He sounded like an ass and he knew it. What had possessed him to propose marriage in that way when what he wanted to do was drop to one knee and ask for her hand in marriage right now? He watched her face. But she would burst into laughter if he did any such thing. She had what she wanted, didn't she?

Jillian blinked. Had she heard him correctly? He'd marry her if he'd made her pregnant? Do the right thing – where had she heard that before? All the hurt from their early encounter came back, the pain of his forced proposal then, the marriage she'd chosen instead, his disappearance.

She drew herself up to her full height. "Don't feel obligated in any way, Stephen. You did what I asked you to do. I'm sure I can handle the consequences if there are any."

He touched her arm, his head dipped toward hers. He'd meant to kiss her goodbye but the stiffness of her stance changed his mind. He nodded instead. "Well, goodnight, then. Thank you for a most enjoyable evening." His crooked smile was forced.

Just then the door was opened by the butler who had been awaiting his mistress' return. Jillian glanced up at him then climbed the stairs. She didn't want him to see the tears hovering on her lashes.

It was near midnight but the clubs would still be open, the gambling hells thriving. Stephen turned and gave directions for one more stop. If he were lucky he would find his prey at the club and his duty would be complete.

……………………………………………....…………………....

George Shanksbury was at cards. He'd been losing but only a bit so was in a good mood. When he looked up at the newcomer his mood decidedly changed.

The tall, dark, man was expensively dressed but did not carry the air of the ton. Stephen leaned across the table.

"Should I sit in or may I have a word with you, Shanksbury?"

Frowning, the Marquis folded his cards face down and rose to his feet. "This hand can take a break, gentlemen, eh?" He led the way toward the private wing of the next room.

Seated in facing leather chairs, the two men accepted the proffered drinks from a server before speaking. Stephen sat relaxed, his long legs crossed at the ankles, his dark eyes staring into the fire. George sat upright, his elbows on his knees, waiting.

"I've just had a most enjoyable evening with a lady we both know. I thought you might be interested since what I have to say would save you a lot of trouble and legal expense." Stephen waited for him to bite at the lure.

George took another sip of brandy. He swirled the liquid, staring into it, frowning. "I assume you mean my sister-in-law, Jillian."

"Um, yes, the Lady Jillian. We enjoyed supper and the evening aboard my ship. She's good company." He leaned forward. "I just wanted you to know there is no way the lady is a virgin. Your theatrics will prove nothing. It was a false assumption on your part."

He stood, enjoying the Marquis' shocked expression. "Oh, and she will have my protection in the future. I may be out of the country but I have connections." He nodded as he turned his back. "Enjoy your evening."

George Shanksbury's face was mottled with fury. He flung the brandy into the fire causing several heads to turn in his direction. There was nothing he could do. The scroundrel had bedded her, no doubt, but who could prove it hadn't been his brother? The inheritance was hers. He'd lost.

CHAPTER TWENTY-ONE

Jillian stared into the cheval mirror, her breasts cupped in both hands. They were larger. It was not her imagination. And her nipples were larger, darker. Her fingers caressed the tips and her whole body quivered. They were definitely more sensitive to touch. Even the brush against her dress seemed to make them ache.

"Why doesn't he come back? Didn't our night together mean anything to him?" She lightly pinched a nipple and tears formed in her wide eyes. "Damn him! Did I have to propose to him?"

She turned from the mirror and reached for her chemise. She'd heard no word from Stephen. It'd been three months. Now she was sure she was carrying his child. Send word, he'd said; as if she would.

"Poor little darling. Your daddy doesn't want either of us." Her hand splayed over her still flat tummy. "Well, I will love you enough for both of us – so much – I will love you so much. Damn him." She burst into tears.

Why was she always crying lately? Perhaps it was the pregnancy but she felt quite well otherwise. She 'd posted the letters to her grandmother Anna the day before. They were either in Marseille or their villa in Tuscany; she didn't know which. A letter to both was sent saying she would visit for a while.

She hadn't seen her paternal grandparents in years but they'd always loved her. On childhood visits Grandfather Sharif had allowed her to sail with him and climb high into the rigging where she could see forever. He'd even taught her a little bit of his own language. It'd been a game. She'd pretend she was a princess of Arabia and only they could communicate. After all, her grandfather had once been Prince Sharif, had he not?

She'd considered every angle and this was the only way to have and keep Stephen's child. She would pretend a marriage, her second husband's death, the birth of the baby, all while she was away. She was packed and had booked passage to Marseille before she wrote the letter to Geoffrey and Margery. She'd paid the servants and expenses in advance for a year and her affairs were in the hands of her attorney. Still, someone in the family needed to know where she was.

……………………………………………....…………………....

Stephen bowed as he left the Admiralty. Drat the luck. He'd only just gotten back and been summoned. He held a packet to be delivered with as much speed as possible to the consulate in Naples. He'd have to sail before he'd had time to attend to courting Jillian.

He ran one hand through his hair before seating his hat. Not that she would allow his attendance in all probability. Well, it'd just have to wait until after this mission. They would sail on the tide.

……………………………………….………………..

Margery opened the folded letter and, without reading it, marched into her husband's study with it. Geoffrey was seated behind the wide desk, going through estate accounts. He looked up, wary of her expression.

"She addressed this to the both of us at least. The little hussy wants attendance for something again, I suppose." She waved the paper and dropped it on his desk. "Well? Read it for the both of us."

Geoffrey managed not to smile. His wife, although well-educated, was disinclined to read or otherwise use her brain if she could avoid it. That had been one of the many fascinations of her sister. How the two could grow up so different – he glanced at the signature.

"It is from Jillian. I suppose you already know that." He quirked a brow at his fiery wife. Her face was pale against her auburn hair but her cheeks were flushed in anger. "You're beautiful when you're upset, you know." He rose and circled the desk to take her shoulders.

A quick kiss to sweeten her temper always worked and it did now. She softened against him, her blue eyes shining with love, anger forgotten temporarily.

"I love you, Geoffrey. It's just that Jillian – she unsettles me. You always look at her differently and she has no morals. She cannot be trusted in the same room with a man." Margery pouted but lifted her lips to receive another kiss.

Geoffrey obliged, lingering in his attention. He stood back at last and retrieved the letter, motioning for them to sit on the wide sofa.

"You know she means no harm. The girl seems to attract attention. With the exception of Stephen she has never been too forward. That one night -." He knew he'd made a mistake the moment the words left his mouth.

Margery shook her head angrily, dislodging a wisp of a curl. "That night! I am still living down that night! Sister to the 'lady in red', the talk of the ton, the tart every male in London discusses! They say her house is always full of flowers or some such – sent by the rakes of the ton in hope of a chance to bed her."

Geoffrey wanted to retort, to ask her how she would know such a thing but he thought better of it. He bit his lip to keep silent and forced his face into a serious scrowl. He looked down at the paper he held in his hand and cleared his throat. A quick perusal then he began to read aloud.

"I thought it best that I visit our paternal grandparents for some months. Since I am not certain whether they are currently in Marseille or Tuscany I will stop off first in Marseille then proceed as necessary. The household affairs have been taken care of well in advance. I only write to you so you will be aware of my whereabouts.

Margery, I again apologize for any discomfort I may have caused you. I had my reasons, good reasons, that made my behavior that night necessary. At least, I thought so at the time. The problem has since been resolved.

Geoffrey, if you have contact with Stephen, do give him my regards. He was always ready to help a friend in need. You might tell him my health is good as always."

It was signed simply, 'Jillian'.

Geoffrey frowned at the last wording. "Stephen, help a friend in need? What a strange thing for her to say."

Margery no longer seemed angry but thoughtful. "I don't think help was the thing your brother had in mind the last time he saw her." She shrugged.

Her French mannerisms seemed to come through when she relaxed so Geoffrey took this as a good sign. He stood, folding the letter. "I'll just keep this in the desk for Stephen when he visits next. It's strange she mentioned him. Perhaps there's something there we don't know. Whatever it is, it's no concern of ours."

His wife snuggled beneath his arm. "I'm glad she's gone. Talk will die down and things will be normal again." She didn't notice Geoffrey's frown as he stared out of the window.

……………………………………………………………………

Several streets over, another man stared out at the busy street. George Shanksbury puffed out his chest as he rocked back and forth, his long-fingered hands clasped behind his back. He spoke to no one in particular and only the room absorbed his musings.

"So, she has flown the coop. I wonder what her reasons? She has everything she wanted, all legally tied into a bundle."

His hired man had just left. Paid to watch his sister-in-law for weeks the scab had finally earned his money.

Now all George had to do was wait until his planning paid off. He knew her destination, the vessel on which she sailed. He wished he could see her face when she realized she would not be returning to England. Whatever her reason for leaving she had fallen into his trap. His man was even now questioning her maid for information.

CHAPTER TWENTY-TWO

It was a beautiful day, with clear, skudding white clouds. The sea was a deep turquoise, the color richer as they left behind the bustling port of Marseille.

It had taken only a messenger sent to the Omar home there to determine her grandparents were in Tuscany. She had changed ships that same day. The mate on her vessel had recommended the smaller but swift craft that would anchor off the coast long enough for her to disembark near Anna and Sharif's villa.

Jillian was the only passenger although there was cargo aplenty. She hung over the railing wishing she could someday sail on one of Stephan St.James' ships, standing beside him, touching him, belonging. She paid no attention to the sail on the horizon that steadily gained on them although the deck hummed with increased activity.

"Madame, please to go below. There may be trouble. Yon approaching vessel does not show colors." The young man sent to direct her was excited but polite. His

French was heavily accented and she wondered what nationality he was.

Fascinated, Jillian watched the distance between the vessels decrease. Someone yelled at her and she tore her eyes away and started below. There was a loud boom as a shot was fired across their bow, followed by much shouting.

The acrid smell of gunpowder tickled her nose. She dug into her luggage until she found her pearl-handled pistol and strapped it to her thigh. Hidden by her full skirts, it might save her life even if it was small and good for only one shot. She waited, listening to the sounds above.

The door to the small cabin burst open. The man who entered grinned when he saw her and motioned for her to follow him. Jillian stood her ground, shaking her head.

With exasperation he grabbed her arm and dragged her after him to the deck. He whistled and the men who had boarded disengaged, leaping back to their own vessel. Jillian fought as the hefty giant caught her waist and swung with her to the higher deck. Rough hands pulled her aboard. The man saluted the captain of her ship and began shouting orders in some strange language. The ships pulled apart. Jillian was left standing alone on deck, bewildered.

After a few minutes, minutes that seemed like hours, she realized she had been the prize, the reason for the intrusion. Now she was being ignored as the ship gained speed, the sails snapping in the wind. She began to pick out words, words she had not heard in years. They were speaking in Arabic with a mixture of Greek thrown in. Pirates. What would pirates want with her?

………………………………………....………………....

They were hugging the coast of Italy; or she thought it was Italy. No one spoke to her but she was aware that they watched her. At last she was brought before the giant again, the captain, she presumed. He spoke to her in French, welcoming her aboard. She was taken below, to his cabin. It was large and richly furnished. One section was curtained off and she could hear rustling behind the hangings as though another person watched.

He plopped down among large, plush, cushions. One hand waved as he sighed. The curtain was pulled aside and a woman emerged, her eyes downcast.

"See, I told you there was no reason to be jealous, Shira. She is business only." His large hand waved in Jillian's direction. He spoke in Arabic and Jillian gave no indication that she understood him. Actuallly only part of his words caught her ear. She had forgotten much.

The woman glared at Jillian with slanted eyes. Her skin was flawless, her figure perfection. She wore some sort of soft material that emphasized the outlines of her body without defining it. She was not young, perhaps in her thirties, but her beauty transcended age.

The man looked at her with hooded eyes but affection was there. He held out his arms and she sank to her knees before him. He kissed the top of her head then turned to the stunned Jillian who still stood.

"Shira is my favourite, the mother of my first born. She will instruct you. You will listen and obey or feel my hand." This was spoken in French.

Jillian finally found her voice. "Why am I here? Why was I taken? I demand you take me to my grandfather, Sharif Omar, in Tuscany. He was at one time a prince in your land and he has immunity -."

She got no further. The man jumped to his feet, near toppling Shira to the floor. He stopped before Jillian, his face thrust into hers. His lips were drawn back in a snarl. She couldn't help it; she shrank before him.

"It does not concern your grandfather, this business of ours. You now belong to me; to do with as I please. You will obey without question." His eyes raked her. "Begin by disrobing. No woman of beauty would be seen in such rags. Western females have no taste; covering their very assets in private, then displaying them before strange men at their social gatherings."

When Jillian just stood there, her mouth agape, he grasped the neckline of her modest gown and yanked. It ripped to the waist. He grunted and motioned toward the curtain. Jillian ran. She was followed, more sedately, by a smirking Shira.

There was nothing to be done. She undressed behind the curtain, always aware that her captor was just beyond in the cabin. The woman, Shira, chattered to him in rapid speech – too rapid for Jillian to understand. He laughed, at her expense, she was sure. The corset, stockings, and slippers were discarded along with her torn gown, petticoat, and chemise. The woman clucked as she removed the tiny pistol from Jillian's thigh. She made some comment to her master and laughed. It was handed around the curtain into his possession.

The swinging lamp was lit and, after much chattering, a pitcher of hot water appeared. Shira pointed to the basin, demanding she wash. Embarrassed, Jillian balked, shaking her head, asking the woman to leave. Apparently Shira spoke little French and Jillian did not wish them to know she could understand them so no headway was gained.

She heard a guffaw and the curtain was pulled aside by their master. He surveyed her nakedness without apparent interest. Then pointing to the basin he informed her that she smelled of western decay.

He had returned to his seat on the cushions, out of view. It had not occurred to Jillian that the women's outlines were cast in detail against the pulled hanging. Periodically his gruff voice issued instructions. Apparently Shira was to bathe her as she stood. If she objected he would do it himself. Appalled, Jillian allowed the woman to bathe her. Her face scarlet as the soft hands washed her intimate parts, she closed her eyes. Several times she heard her tormentor laugh aloud and she gritted her teeth, irritation growing. Shira was very thorough.

The ordeal over, she was given sandals and a soft cream tunic to wear. It was embroidered with pale shafts of wheat at the edges and split up the sides almost to her hips. She did feel relaxed and clean. Shira had oiled her skin, rubbing it in everywhere. A faint sweet scent hovered in the cabin. All she wanted to do was sleep but anger still boiled.

He clapped his hands and the curtain was drawn aside. Shira presented her handiwork, turning Jillian to face him. A smile touched his lips and he nodded, congratulating his woman as though she had created Jillian from nothing.

Jillian's temper flared. She was someone in her own right. How dare he pretend she was no one. She crossed the soft carpet to stand before his crossed legs and glared down at him, hands on hips.

"What do you think you are? I'm worth more to you than some plaything. How soon are you sending to London for my ransom? I'll give you the names and addresses and you will have your money quickly. Or you can contact my grandfather. I'm wealthy in my own right. I demand you begin to treat me as -."

She got no further. With a wave of dismissal to Shira he pulled Jillian down into his lap. Laughing at her sturggles he turned her over his knees, raised his broad hand, and spanked her – hard. Then again and again, until tears appeared in her eyes and she quit struggling. With that, his rough hand began to massage her throbbing bottom, his voice gentle, his words French.

"You will obey me without question in the future. You will not be ransomed. I have been paid handsomely to see that you disappear and disappear you will. You will no longer have a forture back in your country. I will not have my Shira jealous so I will not, myself, keep you. So – you will be sold at market when I decide how better to increase the profit. You are not virgin, so I was told, but you are beautiful, well made. With the proper skills you would bring a good price. You will learn." His hand came down once again, hard, on her bottom. "Your first lesson. Many a man enjoys a female pressed into him as he invokes pain. I do not, myself, adhere to this but you should know the female is expected to pretend it excites her even if it does not. He will take you afterwards." She could feel his shaft, stiff and pushing against her as he punished her. He may not adhere to this pain thing but obviously it did have its effect on him.

Tears stung her eyes as he lifted her to her feet. "Enough. There are more pleasant lessons to be learned. There are men trained to teach these skills but for now Shira will begin." He ran his hands down her sides, resting them on the curve of her hips. "A man could be enchanted with those eyes. You are quite charming with tears on your lashes."

He looked up. Shira was standing just inside the curtain, her eyes sad. He smiled at her. "Do not worry, Sweeting. She is for profit only. No knife in the ribs, no poison in the fruit, eh?"

He turned Jillian and spanked her bottom as he pushed her toward his woman. Jillian's lower lip trembled in pain. She'd never be able to sit again. And to think a man actually liked this – and would want to make love afterwards! She shuddered.

Shira gave her no time alone. It seemed every moment the woman intructed her, touching, poking, murmering soft words. Only half her speech was understood by Jillian but the gestures began to make sense and when they did not, Shira shocked her by demonstrating. Her captor appeared periodically, questioning her progress. Once he stood before them as Shira demonstrated how he wished to be touched. Jillian's face burned but she was fascinated and absolved the lessons for future reference.

She was allowed freedom of the ship as long as she wore the covering garment above decks. So it was that when they dropped anchor off the coast of Naples she recognized their port. She scanned the other ships for the British or French flags. There were several but none nearby.

She had discovered a chest below with flags from many countries, probably from captured ships. Now she devised a plan. The nearest vessel with British insignia was not a man-o-war but it would have to do. With her heart in her throat she went below. She waited until Shira took her usual nap then stole the British flag from the chest and secreted it beneath her loose robe. She stepped out onto the open deck and moved to the base of the highest mast. Looking over her shoulder she dropped the covering garment to the deck and began to climb.

There were shouts as she was spotted, laughter, than angry yells. She scrambled upward in the rigging putting all of her childhood skills to use. Below she could see two sailors coming after her.

She was near the top when she shook the British flag out, flapping it in the wind, her legs wrapped into the ropes for balance. She tied it off and began waving her arms, screaming for help. Even if no one could hear her perhaps she could attract attention. She thought she saw the sun glint from a spyglass on the British ship but she wasn't sure.

One of the men had her ankle now. The other had cut the flag loose and it fluttered to the deck far below. She clung to the rigging, kicking out at the sailor and he cursed, pulling her roughly by her leg until her fingers loosened. He forced her against the ropes with his body while he slapped her open-handed until she was still. Out of breath they glared at each other.

He pointed down then gestured out to sea and motioned as though he would throw her overboard. Then he began to descend, one step at a time, forcing her to mimic his actions. When they reached the deck she was near sobbing with relief. She'd been in danger much more in his hands than alone.

The drama was being observed by the British ship's first mate. He watched in amazement as the female climbed the rigging like a veteran with the sailors in pursuit. Then he called his captain, handing over the glass.

"There, Stephen, just look at that!" The man was so excited he forgot to use his friend's title.

Stephen St.James focused on the woman just before she reached the pinnacle. He grinned. The wind whipped her clothing about her long, shapely legs as she climbed. Blowing strands of long hair the color of wheat disguised her face.

"By God, she climbs like a monkey!" He laughed aloud. Then he lowered the spyglass to watch the pursuing sailors. "What the hell is going on?"

The British flag blew free in the wind; the woman waving and signaling. His entire crew was watching the drama now and although they couldn't hear her they could tell she was screaming. Unable to help they watched as she was overtaken and returned below.

Stephen frowned as he trained the glass on her back. She was forced to the deck on her knees before the ship's commander. The man buried his hand in her long hair and dragged her to her feet again but someone pointed to the British ship and he moved to block their view.

Every muscle in Stephen's body tensed. That moment had been enough. Jillian! Impossible! It couldn't be. She was safe in London. His glass glued to the small figure, he watched as the girl was taken below decks. He was silently cursing.

His men looked to him. "Do something, Captain." The words were not spoken but seemed to hang in the air. The low murmur ceased as Stephen snapped the spyglass closed. He turned to his first mate.

"Get the men back to work. Lower the boat as ordered. I have instructions to deliver these papers as soon as I docked and that must come first." Stephen noted his mate's disapproval. "Send Harvey to scrounge for information on yonder ship. When I return, we'll see what, if anything, can be done."

As he stepped down into the longboat he called back to his first-mate, above, "You all know a captain is law aboard his own ship. The one yonder sails under a Greek flag - which is to say it is probably Turkish. We'll see."

CHAPTER TWENTY-THREE

Jalal al Mustafh shoved Jillian into the cabin. He should have been angry but his show of anger was feigned. What a woman; what courage! He kept the scrowl in place until the door closed behind them. He dismissed Shira with a wave and closed her out also. He turned to face the defiant female, her breathing still labored, her face flushed with both the excitement and the slaps endured at the sailor's hand. He smacked his lips then burst out laughing.

Jillian stared in fascination. Was the man mad? She had tried to summon help, had done her best to ruin his plans for her, and he was laughing? Barefoot, she stood her ground, waiting for doom to descend..

Catching his breath, Jalal shook his head at her. "What am I to do? You have the courage of a warrior, the sense of a flea, the body of a goddess." He pulled a small whip from his waist. "I should punish you until you beg to be allowed to please me."

He snapped the whip in the air beside her, once, twice. She didn't move a hair, merely lifted her chin in defiance. He licked his thick lips and replaced the whip at his waist, still amused.

"A shame you would cause trouble with Shira, a true shame." He caught her wrist and pulled her behind him to a windowless cabin down the way. "Perhaps confinement will be a better punishment. Think on your disobedience."

Jillian heard the bolt slid into place. Her courage left her and she flattened herself against the wall. There was no light, no porthole, no furnishings so far as she could tell. So small a place – she'd always hated to be shut into little rooms. She'd once been trapped in a storage room when the door had shut by accident. That had been years ago but it still gave her chills. She felt around the walls. There was only the one way out. She shuddered and sank to the floor.

Hours later he slid the bolt and let her out. It was morning. She'd been in there forever. Her hands were hurting from beating on the door.

Jalal looked down at the defeated bundle on the floor. She sat with her knees curled up, her head buried in her lap. He'd heard her pounding during the night. He'd waited until dawn. She must learn who was the master here. His heart wept at her tear-streaked face when he lifted her to her feet.

"Are you hungry?" His voice was gruff. He stood aside as she exited the tiny cabin and took a deep breath. He'd never enjoyed a punishment less in his life. He had to get rid of her before he did something he would regret.

He left her in Shira's care. Shira looked at him oddly but said nothing. She glared at the girl.

"Eat first." She pointed to a tray of fruit and bread and cheese. "Today we will teach you to dance." She made several sensuous moves and repeated, "Dance, you understand?" Dumbly, Jillian nodded. Jalal left them.

He returned at mid-afternoon to find Shira wringing her hands. She chattered so rapidly he barely followed her then placed his hand on the girl's belly. Her voice had developed a whine but she looked very satisfied. Jalal was shocked.

"You are sure, Woman? You do not make this up?" He splayed his hand wide over her stomach, stared at the large nipples visible beneath the thin tunic, and cursed.

Jillian stood very still. Why was he so angry? She knew the woman had just told him she was carrying a child but what difference did that make? Shira had been watching her closely for days and it was a matter of time only before the woman had known.

He caught her breast and twisted the nipple with cruelty. Jillian cried out and he gritted his teeth, glaring down at her. "Why? Why didn't you tell me you were breeding, English?"

Tears stung her eyes. "What difference does it make? You didn't ask. The baby is mine."

"Yours. Humph. You have just decreased in value by half. What man desires to bed a whore carrying another man's bastard? You will have to get rid of it." He punctuated his statement by jabbing his finger repeatedly into her belly.

"Nooooo!" Jillian fell to her knees, hugging his legs. "Oh, please. I will do whatever you ask only allow me to keep this child. Please, oh, please."

Angry both by the emotion she evoked and at her pregnancy, Jalal shoved her aside and strode from the room. There had to be a way to sell her before she was showing. Then it was her new master's problem. She was to be sold into slavery, to disappear, that was the bargain he'd made. It would be so but no one had said he could not make an additional profit. Now that profit was decreasing with each day he delayed.

He didn't notice Shira's satisfied smirk. Nor did he hear the words spoken to his captive after his departure.

"So, you thought to replace me, did you? He will sell you quickly now and to one he doesn't know. You will not go to a life of plenty, of luxury. He will not keep a bastard nor its mother." She slapped Jillian across the face hard. "You thought to entice him with a show of courage. Too bad, English."

Jillian stared at the woman. She would not fight back. It would do no good. The woman was jealous and might yet poison her. She had heard of such things among the women in eastern households.

CHAPTER TWENTY-FOUR

Stephen had been trapped all day in town. The information his man had collected proved to be both good and bad. The ship in question was indeed Turkish but sailed under a Greek flag. She was accompanied by two smaller ships, anchored to either side. They were well known as pirates and no one tangled with them. The captain was Jalal al Mustafh.

Jalal. Could it be the same - his tormentor of years ago? Stephen's forehead broke out in a cold sweat. He'd seldom sailed this far east since his escape. If not for direct orders from the British government he would not now be anywhere near Naples or that part of the Mediterranean.

It wasn't that he was a coward. He'd been no more that a youth just turned seventeen at the time. He'd been in the British Navy; aboard his ship when it'd been captured offshore from Greece. They'd been blown off course by a sudden storm and were probably in Turkish waters.

Every man aboard had been slaughtered except for the two higher-ranking officers surviving the attack, and himself – a pretty boy, they'd called him. Notice was sent, through the diplomat at Naples, for ransom. Their captain was immediately freed, his family having contacts in that country. The other officer, Gerald Sherbourne, was no more than twenty-two. He had a young wife at home. They'd been married only three months before he'd sailed.

Stephen closed the door of his cabin and crossed to the whiskey decanter. He polished off the glass and refilled it. Ridiculous. He was a man grown. He looked at his shaking hand, emptied it, and slammed the glass down.

"It was Jillian; no mistake. How the hell she got here - ." He scrowled, his dark eyebrows near touching. Now he was talkiing to himself. He shrugged his shoulders to relax them. He'd have to go after her. He poured another whiskey and sat down to think.

He could see Jalal's amused eyes as he'd left them, Gerald and himself, in that hell-hole back in the mountains. To what purpose? Just plain cruelty; it had to be. He'd not thought of it in years and didn't want to now but that night, that fateful night, kept repeating in his mind's eye. He wiped the back of his hand across his forehead.

The tribesmen or bandits or whatever they were had been in charge of seeing that the two British subjects did not escape until ransom payment was made. Jalal would return for them at that time.

There were women with the bandits but no children. They seemed to come into the camp from nearby to satisfy the men's urges. They appeared to ply their trade with enjoyment and were curious about the two prisoners.

Watched closely, Stephen and Gerald were restrained at night. They had no idea where they were. They'd been brought here by horseback, blindfolded, and had ridden for several days. It was god-forsaken country, parched for water except for a stream that ran through the camp. The twenty or so hosts split into two bands and periodically one band would disappear into the hills returning with booty from some raid or robbery. They were rough and coarse people.

Seated, secured to iron stakes with their hands behind their backs, each night became a hell in itself. Then the visits began.

Stephen had nodded off to sleep when he felt his trousers being loosened. His head jerked up. The woman was the one he'd seen eyeing him during the evening meal. She was gypsy in appearance with long black hair and full breasts. She put one finger to his mouth to quiet him and smiled.

Her hand reached inside his trousers, fondling. Stephen tensed, shaking his head at her, but her strokes were more than he could handle. He was no virgin but he'd always been in control and his knowledge was limited.

She laughed softly, leaned forward and kissed him. Her tongue plunged into his throat as she teased his manhood. Unable to help himself, Stephen's hips thrust forward as she worked faster. Then it stopped, her hand stopped, her tongue retreated. He stared at her, mouth agape.

She toyed with the drawstring of her blouse, pulling until her breasts fell free. She caught Stephen's head, bringing it forward until his face nestled between her bounty, chuckling at his gasping. His head turned to lick at a nipple and she helped him, thrusting it into his mouth.

Tormented, he took what she offered. He was going to disgrace himself if this didn't stop. He tilted his head back, retreating. She smiled into his eyes and crept forward, lifting her skirts as she did so.

She straddled him. When she descended he was buried deep in her sheath. She sighed and began moving. Her moans awoke Gerald who taristed to see what was happening. Stephen was too far gone to care. He filled her as she rose and descended on his prick, getting her own pleasure before allowing his. Behind him, Stephen could hear Gerald cursing at him but he couldn't stop. How could he with that hot puss surrounding him – working - . He came with a force unlike any of the tame trysts he'd known and his body shook with shame as she bit his neck, sucking at his lips, as she rocked back and forth in his lap. He cursed but it did no good. He was exhausted and helpless as she stood up, straightening her skirts.

The act repeated itself every night thereafter. Only her approach varied, her method. By now he was addicted to her. Whatever she wanted he gave. When she turned her rounded bottom to him, helping him to twist so he could take her from behind, he did so. When she stood over him with her skirt raised and forced his mouth to her wet mons, he appeased her; his mouth filling her with pleasure, following her lead as she showed him what she wanted. She spoke a smattering of Greek, Arabic, and Italian and he understood enough. Afterwards she took him however he wanted. And she was good, very good, at what she did.

On occasion she brought another girl with her. The two of them would share him. Guilt. Sin. This was never going to stop. She was going to swivel with him until he died of it – he was certain. Shamed and unable to cease his craving he endured Gerald's disgust. They no longer spoke civilly to each other.

It had been weeks, long nights filled with craving, long days filled with torment wherever the bandits could find it. Then one night the second band returned with an entire caravan of stolen goods. There was much celebration, a bonfire, music, dancing. The men began discussing the prisoners. It was decided they needed amusement.

Gerald was the first to be taken into the circle before the bonfire. He was stripped naked. Stephen could hear the loud laughter and see shadows but not what was happening. Five of the camp women came out of the shadows and stepped into the firelight. The men hollered and clapped. He had leaned much of the language by now, it had been over two months, but could make no sense of the laughing and coarse joking.

The men quieted, watching whatever was going on. Dread gnawed at Stephen's stomach. He yelled to them, asking them to take him, free Gerald. He sometimes felt years older than his fellow Brit. What were they doing? He heard laughter, ribald remarks, and finally silence.

The silence was followed by a blood-curdling scream; Gerald's scream. Oh, God, what had they done?

Moments passed. He smelled roasting meat. Two men appeared from the fireside, half-carrying, half-dragging Gerald between them. They were followed by a woman with his clothes.

He was dropped beside Stephen, no longer restrained, his head bowed onto his chest. He smelled of vomit. Blood smeared his thighs. He groaned and turned onto his back.

Stephen tried to lean over him. "What happened? What did they do to you? Gerald, Gerald, speak to me."

Gerald's eyes fluttered open, then quickly closed. He reached between his legs and retched, turning into the dust.

Stephen followed the gesture. His balls were gone. They'd castrated him. He was no longer a man. He felt bile rising in his throat. His voice wouldn't come.

"They cut me and cooked – roasted – ." His voice cracked. "A part of me – they ate -." He vomited again, then passed out.

"Oh, God, oh, God, oh, God." Stephen couldn't seem to say anything more. He was still trembling from anger and perhaps fear when they came for him.

He was marched before the bonfire, before the leering faces. One man stood, his bloodied knife catching the firelight. Stephen forced back his fear. He would not let this happen. He had his whole life ahead of him. He was ordered to strip and unbuttoned his shirt, flinging it to the ground. There he stopped. Hands on hips, he circled the squatting men, strutting. He snarled at them, hoping his words in their own language were making sense.

"Cowards! You ruin a man for your own amusement, nothing more. You are cowards; afraid to fight; afraid to match a British subject. I challenge you. Choose your trial. Give me the chance you did not give my countryman. I can do anything you can do – better."

They laughed, joking among themselves. The leader stood, motioning for the knife to be put away. He strutted about the circle of his cronies, making low remarks that Stephen couldn't catch. A broad grin split his leathery face. He beat his chest with a balled fist, then waving his arm at the group of women. He held up five fingers. Everyone laughed. Stephen was lost. He had no idea what he'd said.

Five of the women stood, entering the circle of light. They included his nightly paramour. All were smiling broadly, several swinging their hips, eyeing the new victim.

The challenged leader turned to Stephen, slowing his speech. He thumped his chest, gesturing to the women. "I can take – satisfy – all five women in one night – in one hour – one by one. All five!" He laughed and grabbed his cock. The men roared.

He pointed to Stephen. "You first." Coarse laughter almost drowned out his next declaration. "Fail and we serve your balls with the stew." He said something to the women and they lay down in a row, lifting their skirts.

Stephen swallowed. There was no mistake. He'd understood what the challenge was. They were insane, savages. The gypsy woman caught his eye. She raised one brow in question and pursed her lips, smiling. She was propped on one elbow, unlike the others.

He started to kneel but was stopped, pulled upright. With disgust he shed his trousers and small clothes. He had no boots. They had been taken to prevent escape. His maleness hung limp. The quiet didn't help. It was the end. He was going to be a eunuch.

His gypsy wiggled her finger to call him to her side. He dropped to his knees beside her, well, between her legs, and leaned forward. She cupped the back of his head and pulled him down for a long kiss. Her lips moved to his ear. The words were barely audible.

"Forget them. Think on me, on our nights. There is no one here, my fine stud, no one but us." She moved against him, raising her hips, and felt the first stirring of his hardening. " Remember my lessons. Take me last. I will pretend if necessary. Next to me – she loves a man's mouth on her sex. The one after you can please with your fingers alone. From there -." Her tongue dipped into his ear and she laughed low in her chest. Her fingers had been working all the while.

Stephen felt the stirring, the hardening. He kissed her deep, his own tongue thrusting, his courage, his excitement, growing. He locked out any thoughts of his audience. He loved women, always had. Modesty and desperation were forced away as he noted the attributes of the five females lined up for his enjoyment. That's what it was, a feast. He had to think of it as a feast. He closed his mind to the noises, the lewd jests, that surrounded him.

They laughed when he abandoned the gypsy but when his strokes and kisses for the second in line were followed by the pleasuring of his mouth and tongue against her sex they applauded and when the third succombed in moans to his fingers and kisses they leaned forward, some standing, for a better view.

The next one was small, a mere girl, but she licked her lips and pursed her mouth, reaching for his cock. He shifted to allow her to pleasure him and it almost was his undoing. He pushed her away in time, plunging his fingers into her dripping cunt until she screamed her content. He managed to regain his own control before turning to the next challenge.

He turned her onto her stomach, pulled her back onto her knees, her buttocks against his loins. He covered her petite body with his, stroking, teasing her hanging breasts, his shaft moving between her legs but not entering her until she shattered with need and his plunging fingers finished her surrender. He bit the back of her neck as she shivered her completion, her quavering moan near a scream.

His attention moved back to his gypsy. He sank between her soft thighs and pulled her legs onto his shoulders. He looked deep into her liquid eyes with a smile. Now he took his time. His nerves were stretched thin but she was the last, his final hope. Would she betray him? Night after night he'd been her love slave. Now it was his turn.

He entered her but an inch, barely breeching the swollen flesh – again and again. It was evident that she was already excited from the others. She wriggled her hips, attempting to get closer, to end the challenge. He laughed and she pouted. He lowered her legs, pullling her blouse open, and suckled the peaked nipples, She moaned, twisting beneath him.

His finger stroked her hot sex and she cursed. Her dark eyes flashed a warning. Her mouth formed the word "Now" as she thrust upward. He spread her legs, sat back on his heels, enjoying her spread before him. He'd forgotten his audience. There was only this female, this woman who had tortured him night after night.

"Damn you." Her words brought him back to reality.

He entered her in a forceful plunge, buried deep, withdrew. Again and again he filled her, nostrils flaring. One hand caught a breast, his rough thumb scraping across the sensitive nipple. His mouth took hers and he pumped into her with gathering force. She shattered and he followed. He collasped atop her.

Silence, then laughing, clapping. Stephen stumbled to his feet, grinning. The gypsy still lay with her legs spread but she was smiling, licking her swollen lips. Several of the men clapped him on the back in congratulation.

Their leader did not look pleased but he also congratulated Stephen. Another man stepped into the circle. Big and brawny, twice Stephen's size, he'd not been among the clapping men. The men grew silent, watchful.

The man put an arm around Stephen's shoulder. He said something unintelligible to the Brit but the others understood. They backed away. The man bound Stephen's wrists behind his back. With one giant hand on Stephen's nape, he tried to force the young man to his knees. In shock at this new challenge, Stephen balked.

"I won the challenge! I won! " His words were met by a gruff laugh.

"And so you win the prize. You are still a man. But tonight you are my woman." He kicked Stephen's legs from under him. Covering the young man's body with his own he dropped his pantaloons, the hard length of him stroking between Stephen's buttocks.

Stephen screamed in anger and frustration as the huge man raped him. Pain shot through him as he was taken again and again until finally the giant found completion. Only then did he notice the sound of horses.

The bandits fell back as Jalal rode into the firelight followed by a group of his men. His sword was unsheathed and he rode straight for the kneeling men. Stephen's tormentor withdrew just before Jalal's sword severed his head. Men and women shattered, screaming. Stephen rolled to his side in the dirt, his knees drawn up. His teeth drew blood as he bit his lower lip to choke back tears of shame.

Jalal wiped his blade clean, cut through the cords binding Stephen's wrists, touched the young man's shoulder.

"Your price is paid. We ride at dawn."

Without looking at anyone Stephen got to his feet, gathered his clothing and strode to the stream. One of the bandits brought his purloined boots and placed them on the stream bank. Silence reigned as he washed and, still wet, donned his clothing.

He held his head high as he braved the gauntlet of rough men. His chief tormentor, their leader, stood with arms akimbo, watching his progress. Stephen stopped before the man. With all his strength he drove his balled fist into his gut.

There were gruff coughs to hide amusement as their leader doubled over and fell to his knees. Jalal held out his arm and motioned that Stephen should follow him.

"Come, Whelp. Time to eat."

It was in the night that his companion Gerald committed suicide. Stephen even now felt the shame of that night and blamed Jalal for what had happened. It had taken years to banish the nightmares.

He'd been in Jalal's custody for weeks after the night of horror before he'd been released. Jalal could see no wrong in their being left in the care of the bandits. They had orders not to kill the prisoners but that was all. He had never condoned men who liked other men and the scene that had greeted him on his return was enough to trigger the man's death.

The full tale of the night's amusements had been told about the campfire that night, much to Stephen's chagrin. Jalal slapped him on the back, congratulating him on his abilities and stamina. The tale had made a legend of him, young as he was.

And it had ruined him for women for quite some time. He'd not wanted to see another female naked, not wanted to feast on her lovely body, for several years. They were all conniving and sex-crazed in his young eyes. It's taken his brother, Geoffrey, to retrain his inborn love of all things female – well, that and his natural needs. Coaxed nights in an elite brothel, special companions, and soon he was back to normal – better than normal.

His expertise matched or surpassed his brother's and by the time he was twenty-one all of London's beautiful women were sighing over him. None of them had meant a thing to him other than pleasure – until Jillian. But then he'd thought Jillian was taken. He'd been so sure his brother had enjoyed her charms; and he'd been wrong.

Now she was here – in the hands of his worst enemy. How could this have happened?

CHAPTER TWENTY-FIVE

It was twilight when the longboat approached. Bristling with arms, the men waited for Jalal's instructions. Words were shouted back and forth and suddenly their captain gave a shouted greeting and leaned over the railing.

"Will wonders never cease! I thought never to see you again, Whelp!" His huge hand covered Stephen's as he hauled him onto the deck. He stood back and surveyed the younger man. "You've grown, filled out." He thumped Stephen's back with enough strength to knock over a weaker man.

Stephen held his own, answering in kind. "Heard you were at anchor. We had a packet to deliver in Naples then we're away. I also heard you had women aboard."

Jalal's laugh was genuine. "Now I know your true reason for this visit. Did you witness the female monkey in the rigging yesterday?" He gestured. "Your ship?"

"Aye, it is and I did. None of my business but any puss who can wiggle up rigging like that should be seen to, eh?"

Jalal became thoughtful. This might solve all his problems and turn a nice profit too. "Your reputation with women is still undisputed. Prove your stamina and seal the legend. She's worthy of you."

Stephen shook his head. "I'm out of practice. Just wanted to see you before I sailed. I don't come much to these parts. Brought you a present." He handed Jalal a velvet bag tied with gold tasseled cord. "I picked this up in Venice for a special occasion."

They'd reached the cabin and Jalal opened the cord as he entered. The beauty of the ornate mandolin widened his eyes. Inlaid mother-of-pearl on the neck and ornate wood inlays gleamed in the lamp light. Jalal stroked the instrument with gentle fingers for such large hands. His eyes met Stephen's and he nodded his thanks.

They supped together, sprawled on the plush cushions, served by a veiled Shira. The younger female was nowhere in sight. The water pipe was brought out and Stephen declined but at his host's insistance the sweet fragrance soon filled the room. It'd been a long time and Stephen succombed to the pleasure before he was aware. The mead had been laced with a tonic also and he was becoming aroused as he watched Shira hovering over them. He frowned. The woman was veiled. What was the matter with him? This is not the reason he'd come.

His host dismissed the woman with several soft instructions. She dimmed the lamps on leaving. Stephen sat on the cushions facing Jalal. Behind Jalal was the pulled curtain. It was well lit from behind so that the silhouette of the veiled Shira was plainly distinguished as she dropped her veils. Stephen sat up straighter as another female appeared behind the curtain and began disrobing.

Jalal continued talking of old times but Stephen was having a hard time concentrating on the conversation. Shira poured water into a basin and proceeded to sponge the other female, slowly, intimately. She was then patted dry.

Jalal watched Stephen's nostrils flare as the scent of sweet oil was poured into Shari's hands. He smiled lazily when the younger man shifted, the better to see. He knew the light had been turned down but that a bronzed mirror was placed so that the girl's body was reflected for his guest to view. Her face would be in shadow but every stroke of Shari's hands over the girl's nude body would be visible. And every stroke would stoke Stephen's libido. He knew.

The girl preened under the administration of the older woman's knowing hands. Stephen caught his breath as Shirai disappeared into the adjoining cabin. The other female was dressing in some gossamer outfit. He stared, no longer catching Jalal's words.

A snap of his host's fingers and the curtain was pulled open. The girl stepped into the semi-darkened cabin. She wore a short bolero, fastened by a single button. The bolero barely came to the bottom of her breasts. Her trousers were sheer, bloused, and caught in at the slim ankles. Her feet were bare. She had been shown of pubic hair in the Eastern manner and as she moved slowly to stand before him Stephen could see that the trousers were open at the vee of her legs for a man's convenience.

His cock throbbed, hardening, so heavy it seemed like an iron bar. He shifted to a more upright position.

It put his face closer to her invitation and perspiration broke out on his forehead. Vaguely he was aware of his host's rising.

"I'll leave you to enjoy the rest of the evening. Don't prove me wrong. Your mead tonight will increase even a pitiful man's stamina."

Stephen wet his lips. He rose to his knees on the cushions and pulled her toward him, burying his face against her mons. She quivered in his hands and meshed her fingers in his hair, pulling it loose from the leather queue.

Jillian moaned as his mouth moved against her, his tongue darting into her swollen lips. Shira had seen to it that she was aroused even though she had fought it and now – now she was as needy as this man. He stroked, lapping at her, his hands kneading her buttocks. His short beard tickled as well as tantalized as his mouth moved over her. When he began to tease the rigid nub of pleasure she almost fell but then he thrust with his tongue again and again ending by sucking as one finger entered her in short jabs. She bit her lip to keep from screaming as stars burst everywhere. She would have fallen but he was clasping her as he suckled and she pleaded for him to stop as she came again, hot juices flooding his greedy mouth.

He grunted in contentment and lowered her to the cushions, pulling off the trousers as he did so. He kissed and tongued her naval, then moved up to her breasts. He pushed the bolero aside, finally finding the tiny button to throw it wide. His mouth fastened over one fat nipple and he sucked, his hand kneading the other breast.

She arched into his mouth, trying to get closer, twisting in delight as he used her. His teeth raked and nibbled while he shed his own clothes as he could. At last he moved to her mouth and she tasted her own honey on his lips before he teased her tongue, her lips, her throat. Vaguely she was aware that their bodies had moved nearer to the one lamp still burning but she didn't open her eyes.

He was heaven and she never wanted him to stop. Jalal had sworn that if she did not seduce this man, did not please him in every way, he would get rid of the child she carried. She had agreed; anything to keep Stephen's baby. Guilt had eaten at her as she had allowed Shira to entice the man with her display. Now, heaven help her, she no longer cared.

She squirmed, trying to entice him to take her, to bury himself deep where she ached. He shook his head, burying against her throat, his tongue doing wonderful things to her.

Neither of them were aware that Shira had entered the room and extinguished the lamp. She didn't want to risk the man's noticing the slight rounding of the girl's belly. Not until she was rid of her.

Jillian felt rather than saw his hand drop to his shaft. What was he doing? Why didn't he take her?

She didn't know he was having doubts that he should complete the act. Some vague problem lodged in his brain, some reason not to take this woman. Jillian – that was it – Jillian. It wouldn't be right. He grasped his throbbing cock. Was this Jillian?

And then he realized she had spread his legs and was kneeling there. Her hands pushed his aside. His sharp intake of breath told her she was doing something right She moistened her lips and covered the slick tip of him. Her fingers circled the hard shaft at the base while her other hand cupped the rounds that made him a man. He groaned as she took him further into her hot mouth, her tongue dancing over the length of the extended veins on the underside. She squeezed and worked the balls gently while her circled fingers twisted his shaft. Stephen surrendered helplessly to the seduction. He thrust; panting, pulling her upward with a growl in his throat.

His mouth covered hers as he rolled her beneath him and thrust deep. The thrusts never stopped but she met each with her own, both of them frantic, as heat rose and time stood still. With a roaring in his ears, he filled her with white heat, ramming it deeper until he had no energy left and he collasped over her.

He felt her soft lips nuzzle against his neck and he rolled to the side, still holding her tight, so he wouldn't crush her with his weight. And he slept.

Jillian smiled, nibbling at her lips. She didn't know how but it was a miracle. This man was perfect, even better than Stephen. But the beard – she wished he was clean-shaven like her Stephen. Even so, it wouldn't be so bad to belong to him and the baby – the baby would be safe. She drifted to sleep in his arms.

Near morning she awoke to his prodding. Her hips were pressed back against his groin and as her eyes fluttered open his shaft buried deep in her, thrusting to meet her womb. She gasped at the new sensation and wiggled to get a better position. He chuckled and pressed a hand against her damp mons to allow deeper pentration.

His fingers worked where their bodies met as he pumped. He nibbled at the back of her neck and as he swelled to completion he sank his teeth there. She saw stars exploding as he bit and sucked, his cock pumping, filling her. His arm wrapped around her, squeezing her breasts. She screamed as she came, her sheath rippling about him.

He chuckled, releasing her neck, sucking the bite mark. He nibbled at her earlobe. She couldn't get her breath. She managed to turn ever so little in his direction and choked.

Dawn light was filtering into the multi-paned windows. The handsome face that hovered over her was that of Stephen St.James; bearded, yes, but still St.James.

He cocked an eyebrow at her and gave her that crooked grin of his. He shook his head, shushing her with silent lips. His dishelveled hair curled over one eye and his lips looked as swollen as hers felt. He lowered his lips to her ear and whispered a warning.

"Do not say anything, not a word. They must not know we are acquainted; that we've ever met. I do not know your name, remember?"

She stared, her mind in a stupor. "But – but -."

He kissed her, distracting any thought she might have had. His mouth against hers, he murmered, "You're very good, you know. I don't know when I've enjoyed a woman quite so much."

He managed to dodge her slap and caught her wrist. "Uh-ah. If you want to escape this ship you are as obedient as you were last night, remember?"

His eyes glinted dangerously. He was not happy with her behavior. She had not known who he was until that moment. With whom had she been practicing her talents? Angry and confused by the turn of events he left their love-nest and proceeded to pull on his clothes.

Jillian glanced around. Who knewby whom or how they were watched? She stretched, aware that Stephen watched with enjoyment. Nibbling at her lower lip she gathered what passed for her clothing. She strolled toward the curtained area, trailing the garments behind her. The swaying of her naked hips was pure wickedness. He'd tricked her. Let him be in torment.

She hadn't known it was he, her lover. Would he know? Could she pretend she'd recognized him even in the dim light? She looked coyly over her shoulder. He was watching her with narrowed eyes, his hands on his hips.

He walked to the outside door and left the cabin. Jillian stamped her foot. At the noise, Shira stuck her head around the door. Nasty woman; she was all smiles.

Both men returned within a half-hour. The women had been banished from the quarters while the men talked. Stephen was willing to negotiate with Jalal but did not wish to seem too eager. He waited for an opening. Jalal poured the strong Turkish cofee into tiny cups, passing one to Stephen.

"You appear well sated, hmm? A good bedding is a good ending for the evening, eh?" Jalal leaned forward, elbows on his crossed legs.

Stephen was having a harder time being comfortable on the cushions. It had been years since he'd foregone the relative comfort of a chair - until the prior evening. He shrugged, rolling his shoulders.

"My companion was an unexpected delight. It was she that led you a chase in the rigging, hmmm? Such moves -."

Jalal nodded, his eyes hooded. "Very talented. My pleasure to attend to your needs in every way. Today, perhaps, there is something else you desire?"

Stephen kept his face blank. Damn the man. Could he not give an opening? He sipped the thick liquid, saying nothing.

He wasn't taking the bait. Jalal tried again. "Your bedmate is to be sold on the market when I return to home port." When Stephen met his eyes but didn't reply, he continued, "My Shira does not like sharing me with new females."

"Umm. Well, then, if you have a price set perhaps we can do business. We didn't waste time talking last night. She is British, did you say?"

"I didn't but yes, she is a little British. Speaks fluent French and Italian, learns fast what is expected of her. She cannot be returned to England however. That is part of the agreement when I obtained her."

"Oh?" Stephen's eyebrows shot up. "Rather an odd arrangement. There's a reason, I suppose?"

Jalal shrugged, putting the tiny cup down, spreading his hands. "There's always a reason. It cost me nothing to agree. You used her. She is worth the decision, don't you think?" He smiled, his yellow teeth flashing. "Of course, a new purchaser might not know of this agreement. It would add to the price paid however – in case there is trouble later."

The men haggled for a quarter hour. In the next cabin both women listened with close attention. Jillian understood only a few words but understood Stephen was negotiating to buy her from the pirate.

Shira was pleased. She would rid her man of temptation. She cut her eyes at the girl. The captain would not be gentle to a slave. Western men did not know how to savor the favors of a concubine. They only respected a woman if she was a wife. She gloated to herself. Flaunt herself before her Jalal, would she? She hoped the captain beat her every day.

There was a curt order from Jalal and both women entered his cabin. The men were standing. As instructed, Shira pushed the girl forward. She had dressed her in the soft tunic once again. The girl's peaked nipples showed dark against the cream fabric and Shira smirked at the British captain's expression as his eyes fastened there before moving on to her partly exposed legs.

Jillian kept her eyes downcast but she could feel the men's attention, their estimation of her worth. She straightened her shoulders and met Stephen's liquid eyes. They were so hot she almost moaned. Her heart beat faster, an ache began deep in her belly. How had she not known it was he? How? Her lips parted, her tongue flicked over the lower fullness.

Stephen knew it was a mistake to look at her the moment he did it. Jalal read his every thought as though he had spoken. His numb mind heard the pirate's low chuckle and he tore his eyes from Jillian.

"The price has just doubled." Black eyes smiled maliciously into brown. "She is ripe for market."

Stephen's nostrils flared in irritation. His jaw clenched. "We have an agreement."

"Double – to be paid in gold."

"You know I don't keep that much aboard ship. My credit is good. There are deposits in Naples -."

"Gold. You have friends in the city. I'm sure you can arrange a loan even on short notice." Jalal turned his back – motioning for Shira to take her away. "I will be in port only until dawn tomorrow."

Stephen gritted his teeth. The expression on Jillian's face was a knife to his heart as she was led away.

"I will return before then."

....

Shira was irritated. Not only would the girl bring more gold than she was worth but perhaps she would not even be sold to the British captain. Her hand slapped Jillian's face leaving a white print. She glared at the girl as she saw tears, cursing at her. At last slowiing her speech, switching to broken French, she snarled, "You will entice him to buy you or you will be my slave. Mine. I will see to it. Not my Jalal's but mine. You will serve me as long as I let you live. Disobey me and I will see you die a slow death. You will grow afraid to eat for fear of my power." Again her hand connected.

Jillian almost hit back but no, it was not a smart thing to do. She took the punishment. It wouldn't be much longer and she would be out of this hell. She dropped her hands to her sides. She objected only when Shira's hand spread over her belly. Her eyes widened.

"No, please. I will do whatever you say." She bowed her head in submission as her clothes fell to the floor. The baby must not be harmed.

Shira's eyes narrowed. "You will do as I say. When he returns you will smell of your sex. He will think of nothing but you, of owning a concubine, of spreading your legs. He will not balk at the price."

Sweet oil was massaged into her body. The soft hands lingered on her breasts, turning her to massage her buttocks, and then back to soothe her belly, her thighs, and higher. Fingers almost fed her desire but it was a promise only as she was readied for the man who would own her.

Jillian writhed as sinful waves of pleasure filled her. She was unaware of Jalal's observation until he spoke. His voice was like gravel.

"Enough, woman. She doesn't understand half of what you say. Cease or I may take advantage of your ministrations."

Shira jumped, her hands leaving the girl's thighs. She hadn't known he was there. She had begun to enjoy her work too much. She bit her lip and smiled up at him. He lifted her from her kneeling position and stroked her cheek. He was hard as a rock.

With a last glance at the girl he led Shira to his cabin and took his pleasure. He would have no trouble in his quarters. Soon, soon he would rid himself of the pregnant female.

CHAPTER TWENTY-SIX

The sun was appearing over the bright blue of the sea when Stephen arrived at the docks. It had taken visits to everyone he knew to gather enough in coin. He blinked, his mouth open in astonishment. "The damn fool is leaving! I have the gold and he is sailing!"

He swore as the pirate's sails unfurled. With a curse he jumped into the long boat waiting for him. There was no way he could reach Jalal before he was in the open sea. He joined the sailors at the oars. They pulled for his own ship.

Jalal watched the figure on the docks, waving, yelling. He threw back his head and laughed. He would sell the woman but why not enjoy it first? He had lacked true amusement for a long time. He slacked back on the sails a bit. He didn't want to get too far away before he was caught.

……………………………………………....…………………....

Stephen's ship was ready to hoist anchor when he climbed aboard. They had been watching and were ready but not happy at the ensuring events. The pirate was heading for Sicily or perhaps the Greek isles. His two cohorts were trailing behind. They stood the distinct risk of a trap.

He signaled immediately and Jalal's ship slacked speed although they still veered toward the east. Stephen had had little sleep and his temper was showing. His jaw tense, his hands behind his back and legs spread, he snapped orders at his officers. His first mate and friend hurried to see them accomplished. The distance shortened as the morning headed for noon.

It was late afternoon when he came within hailing distance. They were on the leeward side of a small island. Stephen's crew was armed and ready for battle without being told. The two smaller pirate ships, if that is what they were, had fallen further behind and poised no immediate danger. The boat was lowered and Stephen's men pulled for the other ship. He'd changed into fresh clothes but had eaten only some hot gruel and tea. He was not amused. His stomach churned. His mind filled with dread of captivity, fear and pain long buried. He didn't like this.

Jalal was waiting for him at the railing. His dark face split into a smile as his prey climbed aboard. Immediately he turned and strode to his cabin. Stephen followed, his teeth clenched. Vivid memories of his captivity, his shame, washed over him. Was he trapped here? Had he allowed his prick to lead him to a fate he considered worse than death? Cold perspiration broke out on his forehead as he descended the steps.

Jillian was standing there, clad in the same tunic. This time she wore some undergarment that disguished her form and full pantaloons of the same soft fabric. Dark crimson sandals of tooled leather were the only spot of color other than the soft honey of her hair. It had been brushed straight down her back and glistened in the brilliant shaft of sunlight where she stood. The light scent of spice and female, especially female, hovered about her. Like a bolt of lightning he hardened, wanting her.

His eyes fastened on her full lips and they parted. He met her eyes, drowned in them. He tore his attention away, back to Jalal. The man held a rolled paper. He set about anchoring it with various objects on the table.

"You have the gold?"

"That was the agreement, was it not?" Stephen plunked the bags upon the table. "Perhaps you owe me a fee in return. I was there at sunrise. You -." He bit his lip to keep from cursing.

Jalal merely smiled. He picked up the gold, weighing it in his hands. "I did not wait. But then, I could not. As I explained, I sailed at sunrise. I have a passenger, a holy man. He needed to return home – to this island – on this day." Jalal waved his hand toward the open windows. He returned his attention to the business at hand. He called out an order.

A burly sailor brought in a brazer in a sand-filled basin. Within was a small branding iron, the tip already red hot. Stephen frowned, puzzled.

"Sign the paper and then we will complete the sale." Jalal waited while Stephen wrote his name with a florish. He could not read the script although he spoke the language. He reseated the pen, sanding the paper.

Jillian was motioned forward by Jalal. He held her upper arm and motioned for the sailor to proceed. The hot smell of metal intensified as the iron was lifted from the glowing coals.

"No! Don't let them do this!" She shrank away at the same time that Stephen's hand caught the man's wrist.

"What the hell are you doing? Branding? She is my property now."

Jalal's fingers tightened about her arm. "Not quite. My original agreement was to see that she disappeared. I agreed that she would never again set foot in England as a free woman. What better way than to see she carries the brand of a slave? My promise is complete."

"That promise no longer is yours to keep. She belongs to me."

"Not without proof. Either she bears the mark or - - ." He spread his hands, his smile oily. "You could wed her. She would then be tied to you for life, would she not? Under our eastern laws she could not divorce you although you could free yourself if you so decided – and sell her at that time." He watched the emotions scatter over Stephen's face. "She would not be a free woman. The bargain is met."

He looked at the girl's pleading stance. She hadn't understood a word of what was said. His voice was cajoling now.

"She would not need to know. Let her think she is your concubine, your slave. Easier to rid yourself of her later." Jalal grinned. How he enjoyed the gullibility of the British. The man he called Welph would obviously do anything to obtain this female – as though they were not all alike. He only favored his Shira through long habit.

Stephen's fingers caressed Jillian's cheek, cupped her chin. In French he spoke to reassure her, "I won't let this happen. Be still."

Shira had been watching and listening. The soft words angered her. The girl would be cared for, perhaps actually loved. It wasn't fair. She moved to get their attention.

"She's carrying a bastard. She's breeding. Do you want to marry with a whore? " She grimaced with pain as Jalal slapped her. "She's a slave. That's all she is." She dropped in a heap to the floor as Jalal again raised his hand but her eyes flashed defiance.

Stephen felt as though it were him that'd been struck. He met Jillian's eyes in disbelief. He switched to French. "Is this true? You carry a child?"

Her eyes widened at the sudden accusation. A meek 'yes' was all that she uttered. She could not say more in front of these people.

He turned on Jalal. "I thought you said you had not sampled her." Stephen's voice had dropped to a dangerous level.

Jalal's hand rested on the hilt of his dagger. "I have not. But she is breeding – very early in her time."

"We don't even know who the father is." Shira got in one last retort before she scooted behind the curtain to hide.

Stephen felt sick to his stomach. At last, at last he'd found the woman he wanted – even one he would wed – and she had betrayed him, lied to him. He stared at the bags of gold, at the burning coals, then back to the paper he'd signed.

"What did I sign? She belongs to me now? Both she and the child?"

Jalal nodded. "If you complete the sale with the brand of slavery – or the other." The smile had left his face . "Either way the gold is mine by default. It was agreed."

"Yes, it was agreed." He pulled Jillian to his side, tucked her against him. She belonged there no manner what she'd done. He looked down at her upturned face and ran his thumb over her lower lip. She had no idea what had transpired other than her admission of guilt.

He saw tears on her dark lashes and brushed them away. "Make arrangements for the marriage. There's no need for the branding."

Jalal rubbed his hands together, his glee obvious. "Yes, yes, I will get the holy man. He is still aboard ship. He can witness both the sale and the marriage so it is final and complete. There will be an extra charge, you understand, for the ceremony."

Jillilan stood as directed a step behind Stephen. The bearded man in the full robes spoke on and on, finally leaning toward Stephen. When Stephen answered the question he continued droning. At last he acknowledged her presense with a nod. He stooped down to the low table and wrote an addendum to the document then signed with a flourish.

Not understanding a word, Jillian did think this appeared to be a ceremony of sorts. She plucked at Stephen's sleeve.

"Was this some sort of marriage?" Her heart was pounding with hope but she remembered her role enough that she spoke in French. She didn't notice Jalal's amused expression.

Stephen frowned down at her, shaking his head. "It finalizes your fealty to me, umm, my ownership. It makes the branding unnecessary. Now be still." He would have laughed at the pout this produced if he hadn't been so angry at her behavior, her lack of morals, the fact that she carried another man's child.

He scooped up two of the gold coins and gave them to the holy man. Jalal didn't object.

The day's amusement had been worth the cost and his arrogant former prisoner was about to lead a changed life. He wished he could see the two of them when her belly became large, when St.James's bewitchment became jealousy. Would he sell her east? Would he admit he had just wed her? Would he curse this day?

He laughed and slapped Stephen on the back. "If you ever have need of me, Whelp, I can be reached through Naples."

Stephen nodded; silently swearing he'd never again venture as far east again. He was going back to civilization.

CHAPTER TWENTY-SEVEN

Relief that they were almost on the open sea; relief that they'd not had to fight their way out; emotions tugged at him as the sails filled. Stephen stood beside the wheel reveling in the scents of the land-blown flowers and spices. His hair blew free from its usual containment and he took a deep breath, his head tilted back.

Jillian watched, clinging to the rail further along the deck. Free! She was free! She smiled at Stephen St.James in delight although he didn't see her. He looked so handsome. It was amazing she'd not recognized him that night although he now sported a short beard. She giggled, then covered her mouth quickly. It had tickled – tickled all her special places – slightly curly and soft it was like sleek fur. She wondered if he would shave it off now that they were again heading for England.

He felt her and turned. What was he to do with her? Even knowing what he did he still wanted her in his bed. His eyes fell to her breasts and thighs outlined as the wind pressed the soft fabric against her. Did her belly have a slight round? Why had he not noticed that night? He'd been seduced by her tricks, by that scene in the mirror before, so randy he would have fucked his own - . He cut off such thoughts and turned away, his jaw tightened. He still wanted her, damn it. Just the thought of her in his arms made his blood run hot.

Jillian frowned. He was angry still. Was it the baby? When did she dare tell him he was the father? And would he even believe her now? Perhaps, after all, she should just go to her grandmother's as she had planned.

Stephen picked up the spyglass, his back to her. She was his wife now, for better or for worse, whether she knew it or not. He'd wait to tell her, see if it was working out. If the baby proved to be black or Arab he'd banish her and she'd never know. He remembered the pirates, all races, all misfits, that manned Jalal's ship. How many? Dear lord, how many had had her? She hadn't learned those tricks with one man. He swore at the reaction his musings brought, the wave of desire, and snapped the glass shut.

…………………………………………....……………….....

Their first evening alone came too soon. Facing him over the food-laden table Jillian took a morsel of bread and dipped it into the savory sauce before popping it into her mouth.

"I see you still have your French chief aboard." She licked her finger as Shira had taught her in order to be seductive. Catching her mistake she quickly picked up a napkiin with her other hand but it was too late. Stephen's eyes were fastened on the guilty finger. Molden brown eyes slowly lifted to hers and narrowed.

He cleared his throat but his voice was like gravel. "When, Jillian? When did you realize it was me?" He tried to sound pleasant but his tone wouldn't cooperate. "Or are you always so delightful in your beddings?"

Her face flushed and she lost her appetite. "When we awoke, when I first saw you in the light – but it was not as you think - it wasn't."

He didn't allow her to continue. His guts had knotted tighter with her expected answer. "Well, you are good at what you do, extraordinary, in fact. I don't know when I've been so sated." He forked a potato, forced it past his lips, chewed slowly. "Quite a difference from your first time with me in London."

Jillian felt the stirring of anger. He didn't know what it was like to have no control over one's actions. She'd had to protect the baby, his baby. She nibbled on her lower lip, cutting her eyes up at him. And he had been so forceful, so handsome, those muscles -. She felt desire flood her body at the memories. She was sinful, wasn't she? But he wouldn't get away with giving her all the blame.

"I suppose you are that lusty with every female that falls into your arms? You held nothing back. And did you know it was me? Of course not." Her breathing had somehow become labored. Heat curled in the pit of her stomach.

He grinned, suddenly relaxed. "From the moment I saw you climbing the rigging like a runaway monkey I knew it was you. What were you thinking?" Somehow he was standing, his napkin falling to the floor. He took her by the shoulders, pulling her to her feet, shaking her slightly. "You could have been killed. If you'd fallen."

His mouth covered hers, crushing her lips until she allowed him entry. With a sigh her arms wound about his neck, her fingers burrowing into his thick hair. His hand caught her bottom, bringing her into his hips as his mouth continued their loveplay.

He was so hard he throbbed to strip her and bury himself, standing as they were. She rubbed against him and he groaned. His hand caressed the globe of her breast, his thumb roughing the peaked nipple. His head lowered to her neck, nipping, sucking, licking.

Her tongue darted into his ear, swirled, and he jerked in response. Soft words whispered, "I seduced you to protect the baby. If not you, someone else. They would have taken it, killed him. I was ordered, taught, to seduce -."

She got no further. He froze, putting her from him. Hell fire! The baby again. His smoldering eyes glared at her, his libido still raging. He closed his eyes, willed for self-control. He turned on his heel and left the cabin, the door slamming shut.

Jillian stood where he'd left her. She'd been going to tell him, tell him the child was his, that she would have done anything to protect what he'd given her. Tears rolled down her cheeks unnoticed. Stephen wanted only her body, not her, and certainly not the new life she carried. Why did it hurt so much?

"I love him. Why didn't I know when he first took me in his arms? Why?" That night in England seemed so far away, the night of innocence.

Stephen stood watch, relieving the man on duty. His empty stomach wasn't the only thing causing him discomfort as he attempted to banish Jillian from his thoughts. When the anger began to lessen his musings turned soft, back to their first night together.

Would he'd had enough sense to claim her for himself then. So she hadn't encouraged him, so what? Women never knew what was good for them, what they really wanted. He slapped his open palm against the railing. She was his now, damn it, and he'd have her if he wanted her. She was already breeding so what difference did it make?

His shift over, he returned to his cabin quietly. His mouth tipped upward at the low light she'd left burning for him. She'd be asleep but he knew just how to awaken her. Anticipation curled in his belly as he thought of lying in her arms.

He removed his sword, boots and stockings, and began to pull his shirt over his head as he moved toward the darkened bed. He frowned. She wasn't there. It was turned back but the sheets were uncrumpled. Then he saw her.

Curled upon the padded window seat, she had donned the light shift given her by Jalal's woman. Her feet were bare, her hair loose and curling over one bare shoulder where the neckline gapped open. She was fast asleep.

He stood looking down at her for a long while, devouring every detail. He touched her cheek with a fingertip, drawing a line downward to cup her chin. She didn't awaken although her lips parted a little. Tenderness swamped him, drowned the aggression he'd intended. He scooped her into his arms and carried her to the bed, depositing her gently, tucking her feet into the covers.

He finished undressing and lay down beside her, pulling her back into his hard body. Her soft buttocks pressed against his hardened shaft and he bit back a groan as she wiggled, shifting closer without waking. His arm curved about her and he tucked her head beneath his chin as he attempted to find sleep.

She awoke to the scent of him, the memory, the imprint of his holding her. She sat up. There was no one there. Early sunlight slanted through the windows where she'd gone to sleep. He'd come, he'd slept beside her. Jillian's mouth curved into a smile that exploded into delight.

"He does care. He was here." She jumped from the bed and stretched, dancing circles about the table in her happiness. Now, if only she had something else to wear, something English, so his thoughts wouldn't center on that night on Jalal's ship. But it was not to be.

Dressed, she hurried up to the deck. There he was – arms akimbo, staring out to sea – so handsome it hurt to look at him. He turned and met her eyes. For a moment she hesitated.

Stephen drank her in. She was like a sweet poison in his blood. Just to see her was to want her. And the others? Had the other men felt the same way? She had stopped and was watching him. Was she afraid of him? He smiled crookedly and she again moved toward him.

"Good morning." She wet her lips as she looked up at him. She would be shy, reserved, today. That would convince him she was not a hoyden. That was what he wanted, wasn't it? She caught at her tunic as it billowed out in a gust of wind displaying her shapely leg. She hadn't worn the pantaloons today and already regretted it.

He watched her tongue flick over her full lower lip, the small white teeth catch at the corner. His eyes fell to the slender leg she exposed. Anger flared. She was trying to seduce him again, was she? Put him at a disadvantage? Ignoring his watching men, he reached for her and pulled her hard against him. With a soft growl in his throat he cupped her head and covered her mouth with his.

Jillian's hands came up of their own accord, pushing against the muscular chest. How dare he? In front of his crew? What would they think?

His mouth was hard at first, possessive, his tongue forcing entry, sliding along the seam of her lips. She sighed as his hand moved her into his hips. Sighing, her mouth opened, her tongue duelled with his.

At her surrender he released her, a half-smile upon his sensuous lips. Triump reflected sparks in his molden eyes as they slid from hers to seduce her mouth with their touch. She caught her breath so she could speak.

"Do you think you can manhandle me in front of your crew, Sir?" Her words were coming in little gasps. Her heart was hammering in her chest.

His crooked smile appeared again. "I can do whatever I wish with you. You're bought and paid for, remember? To them or to that document you're no Englishwoman."

Before the angry retort could reach her lips he pulled her into his arms again and took possession of her mouth. His other hand caressed her peaked nipple through the soft fabric of the tunic.

The nearest crewmen turned away as she moaned softly. None of their business what their captain chose to do with his slave. Maybe she was once English but he'd bought her, hadn't he? They knew how things worked in this part of the world.

Stephen ended the show of loveplay when he felt her trembling. His fingers were buried in her long hair and he held her head still as he looked deep into the grey-green eyes. He felt some guilt but not enough to let her go. She would learn he was the only man for her, no more teasing, no more seductive glances at other men.

He leaned down to her ear, flicking his tongue into its whorls. She jerked and clutched at his shirt front. His voice whispered in a deep rasp, "You belong to me. Remember that. You will ache for me and no one else, ever."

He released her so suddenly she would have fallen if she had not had her hands fisted in his shirtfront. He caught her wrist and took her below, scooping her up and depositing her in a heap on the bed.

Breathing hard he stared down at her. Her eyes were wide with fright but as he watched her expression changed. She caressed her lip with the tip of a pink tongue, her legs parting ever so little in invitation. No! She would not dictate his use of her. He turned abruptly and left the cabin, slamming the door behind him. His temper was barely held and his sex throbbed with need for her. He leaned his head against the door, his eyes closed. His balled fist crashed against the closed door before he again ascended to the deck.

She was driving him crazy. She was his if he wanted her – but he didn't want her like this – forced. No, he wanted her as she'd been in London, innocent and full of curiosity. He wanted her love.

Jillian lay where he'd left her, spread-eagled on the bed. She'd wanted him as much or more than he had wanted her but she'd fought him just the same. He must never know how much she loved him. Somehow she had to make him love her back.

She'd make him need her, crave her. Every time he looked at her or took her she would teach him anew what it was like to be seduced. Her lessons as Jalal's slave would not be wasted. Stephen would not ever get enough of her. And someday – someday – he would love her. Only then would she tell him the baby she carried was his, that they'd never been another man. How long to nightfall? He'd be back.

………………………………………...……………….…

But he'd returned only to sleep and that late at night when she could no longer hold her eyes open. The days passed.

Ports were visited as supplies were replenished, postings exchanged. At last they passed the Italian coast.

Men scrambled to furl the sails. They were near to Marseille. Already Stephen had refused to allow her to disembark in Tuscany at her grandparents. He hadn't even answered, merely grunted and stalked off. Now he approached and she ran moist hands down her sides, pasting a smile on her face.

"Will you leave me here, Stephen? I can stay at the townhouse until they return from Tuscany. They're never away for longer than six months and it's been -."

He shook his head. "You will not be leaving the ship." His jaw clenched. He had avoided asking her, not wanting to know what mischief had led to her capture. "It's time you told me why you were so far from England. How you came to be on Jalal's ship?"

Jillian's chin lifted defiantly. Why hadn't he allowed her to tell him before now? He'd ended every quest for conversation either by stalking off or with a devouring kiss, a kiss that left her wanting.

"I intended spending a year or so with my grandparents in Marseille. They're usually here but I arrived just shortly after my letter and they had gone to the villa in Tuscany. So I left some of my baggage in their house in the city and hired a small boat to take me down the coast. The sloop was captured by that pirate. You know the rest, I suppose."

"It would seem the capture, the taking of yourself, was a planned event; set in motion by someone in London. Someone wishes you to disappear and I need to find the owner of that small boat. He took you straight into Jalal's arms."

Her grey-green eyes widened as she stared at him. "Surely not! Why would anyone want me gone? I only told the servants and my factor – he because he was to pay the expenses for the household until I returned. I did write Geoffrey and Margery a letter which I posted when I left. I simply told them I was going on holiday."

"And your brother-in-law? Did he know?"

She shook her head. "I hadn't seen him in some time and anyway, I would never tell him anything of my affairs."

Stephen realized he was holding his breath and forced himself to breathe normally. "And your reason for this sudden holiday? Did you suddenly find the amusements of London dull? I would think that after I had dispensed with your virginity your opportunities for amusement -."

His head snapped to the side as her palm caught him. White fingerprints stood out in stark relief against his sculptured cheek. He had shaved his beard only that morning and now regretted it. His eyes narrowed.

"My apologies, Madam." He turned on his heel and shouted an order to two sailors before returning to her side.

"I was pregnant. I left London because I was pregnant."

Stephen's gut twisted. The father was British? Was it possible? But when – how long ago did she leave? His eyes dropped to the small round of her belly. The breeze molded the soft fabric against her. She was definitely increasing. His eyes strayed upward. Her breasts were larger. He knew that – fuller, with plush nipples. Hadn't he enjoyed those nipples – pressed against him as she slept? The slightest brush against them and she responded with soft moans. He licked his lips, his shaft hardened.

Simmering fire shot upward to meet her eyes but her long lashes masked her expression. His hand circled her upper arm and he pulled her against him. Hidden between them one hand moved over her belly. Wonder filled his heart but he didn't dare hope yet. She hadn't been true to him. She couldn't have. Her new expertise in the bed had to be learned at the hands of a master – or many teachers. His chest hurt; his heart seemed to swell with grief – or sorrow – or an increasing anger.

"You're hurting me."

His fingers dropped away from her arm. His face was ashen. He leaned down until his lips near brushed hers, his breathe fanning her face. He almost choked on his words, almost cried the question.

"Is the baby mine?"

Jillian felt herself drawn into those molten chocolate eyes. Why did he doubt it? Didn't he know? Couldn't he tell she loved him? She leaned forward a fraction, brushing soft lips against his and he made a noise deep in his throat. Her tongue ran along the seam of his lips and they opened, devouring her. She moved her hips against him, felt him increase, harden more. She tried to form the words to tell him as she pulled back. She didn't want it to be here in front of all his men. Her lower lip trembled with emotion.

"Jillian?" This time the question was a plea, a croak. When she didn't immediately answer he growled, "Damn you! Damn you to hell!" He turned before she could respond and stalked away. His heart was breaking, torn by his shattered hope.

Tears hovered on her dark lashes. Why? Why hadn't she just blurted it out? What was the matter with her?

She had to step out of the way. Sails were being furled, orders snapped. Men were running to see the ship to dock. Stephen took his place at the helm, his emotions seething.

Jillian wanted to go to him, to fix what she'd ruined by her silence. She didn't dare. Fury was written on his face and his crew was all around. It was best she leave, best for both of them. Tonight she'd slip from the ship. He'd never been to her grandparents' house here. It was very private. She'd wait there until Anna and Sharif returned from Tuscany. He'd be glad to be rid of her.

……………………………………………....………………....

He'd found an old salt from the ship that had taken Jillian from London. The man insisted on his innocence but was ready enough to repeat that night's happenings. He'd heard things, yes, he had.

Stephen mulled over the new bit of information. There had definitely been plans laid and paid for to dispose of the lady passenger. Their own mate had suggested the sloop she took to transport her to the coast of Tuscany. He'd been found later with a knife in his back.

Stephen suspected Jillian's brother-in-law. The Marquis wanted her declared dead for some reason. He would bet on it. He stared into his mug. He'd been in the tavern for several hours. He should've left after he'd supped but he dreaded going back to the ship, to his cabin.

He traced the deep grooves in the wooden table with one finger. Night after night lying beside her, wanting her. He was an idiot, that he was. She was his for the taking, wasn't she? He'd had too much to drink, that was all. He pushed to his feet and out into the dark cobbled street.

Tall masts stood outlined against the sky. The harbor was several streets away. The night air helped clear his head but he kept one hand on his sword hilt. These narrow steets were dangerous.

He heard running footsteps headed his way; a woman or youth, followed by two heavy-set seamen. Their heavy boots clattered on the paving stones as they yelled ribald remarks at their victim. One of them caught her – it was a her – and straddled her as he pulled at her clothing. She screamed, clawing at his face.

The moon came from behind the clouds and Jillian's pale hair spilled into view as her cap came off. Stephen had already drawn his sword but now it was personal. He advanced on the two with a bellow. The bearded man threw Jillian to his partner and drew a sword from his sash, diving at Stephen.

Stephen staggered back at the sheer weight of him but parried the blow. From the corner of his eye he saw Jillian struggling with the taller man. He laughed as he held her feet off the ground, his arms wrapped around her as he held her as a shield.

Damn the drink! Stephen's head was spinning. He backed until his shoulder hit a wall, dropped low, and brought his blade upward. The sailor yelped as the steel bit into his left thigh. He stumbled, swinging at Stephen's head. Stephen dodged, still a little dizzy, and went down on his knee.

He heard Jillian scream but she sounded far away. Then his opponent staggered, staring at his limp right arm. Blood gushed forth and his weapon dropped with a clatter. There were running footsteps. The watch was coming.

Jillian stood over him with the tall attacker's long knife in both hands. She was breathing hard.

Stephen squinted up at her, a lop-sided grin on his face. "Did you kill him?"

"Nooo." Her voice was a wail. She was shaking all over. The knife dropped at Stephen's feet.

He took her in his arms, dizziness giving over to anger. "We've got to get out of here before the watch comes." He caught her hand and pulled her at a run, darting down street after street, into the city.

He stopped before a sturdy building where they could hear laughing and music from within. He pressed her shoulders to the wall, leaning into her so she could not squirm away.

"What the hell were you doing in town – and after dark? I gave strict orders you were to stay aboard. You could've been killed."

He could feel every soft inch of her. Now, now he would have her. Mayhap it was the drink but he'd waited long enough. She was disobedient and he would take her. He rubbed his erection against her as he waited for her answerr.

Her lower lip pouted. She didn't back away from his pressure but molded herself to him. Her head tipped back to look into his eyes. "I was leaving. I was going to my grandparents. You don't want me and you wouldn't give me permission if I asked you."

"Don't want you? Don't want you?" His sex hardened as his mind centered on just how much he wanted her. His nostrils flared and his mouth covered hers, his tongue pushing within.

The door opened and a well-dressed man emerged. He glanced in their direction then proceeded in the other direction. Stephen released all but her hand. He knocked on the door and it was opened by a smiling brunette.

"Stephen St.James, as I live and breathe! Come in, come in. It's been too long." She noticed Jillian then and looked her up and down. "Bringing your own now? Are my girls not satisfying?"

"Now you know better than that, Lilli. This is not my usual problem. Just for tonight I need a room, a good room. I'll still pay the full price." He kissed her on her full lips with a smack.

Laughing, the woman kissed him back. She glanced at Jillian once more, then led the way through an elaborate room to some stairs. "Last door down the hall, but it'll cost you."

He nodded his thanks, pressed coins into Lilli's hand, and pulled Jillian after him up the stairs. Eyes wide, she tried to take in everything she saw. Several beautiful women, half-dressed, occupied the lower room. Gentlemen were caressing them, drinking, laughing. One sat across a stout man's lap as his hand slid up and down her naked thigh.

The door closed behind them and she was facing Stephen. His face was a mask of – what? Anger? Lust? She felt her own response pool between her legs and backed from him but he caught her arms at the elbows and lowered his mouth to hers.

She pushed at his hard chest. Not like this – not in a bordello – she wouldn't have it. Her eyes flew open to meet his smouldering expression and she couln't speak. He began to unfasten the over-tunic she still wore, pushing it from her shoulders. It fell to the floor. The soft top went next and she wore only the pantaloons, caught at her ankles.

Jillian stared at him, hypnotized, as he lifted her in his arms. His mouth found a breast and he sucked. She arched, clinging. He smiled and carried her to the wide bed.

Unhurried he removed her sandals, leaned in once again to nip at her breasts until she tried to squirm away from him. He smiled, standing to remove his sword, jacket and shirt. His boots sounded loudly on the polished floor as he continued to strip. Jillian swallowed nervously. Would he rape her or seduce her? He was still angry, that was evident.

Stephen pulled the twisted ties from the bed hangings. He straddled her body with his knees as he caught her wrists together, fastening them to the headboard. Smiling he backed down, pulling her pantaloons off as he did so. He stared at her now naked body.

Jillian clamped her mouth shut in defiance. She would not plead, would not beg; whatever he had planned. She watched as he wiped his forehead with one arm, blinking as though to clear his head. He was half-drunk, that was all. This was not the Stephen she knew. She lay perfectly still.

He smiled crookedly. One dark lock fell over his eye. Her heart went weak. He looked so naughty, so adorable, so wild. He pulled the throng from his hair, releasing the rest to lie almost on his shoulders. He leaned over and licked at her navel, kissing and nipping the undersides of her breasts, his knees once again straddling her legs.

The door opened. He moved to take a bowl from the girl who stood there but she had stepped inside and closed the door. She was smiling, her chest thrust out, her mons emphazied by each step she took as she moved to rub against Stephen. Her hair was pale blond, her eyes a sky blue, her breasts huge and tipped with rouged nipples.

"I brought up the whipped cream, Stephen. You always like that." She sat it on the little table beside the bed and looked down at the stricken Jillian, her eyes missing nothing. "Not ready yet, hmmm? Want me to stay? You know how you enjoy the trois -."

Stephen caught her shoulder, turning her toward the door. "Not this time, Evie. Just the two of us tonight. She's new to this."

Evie ran her hands over Stephen's cock, squeezing. "Well, you know I can help that. I'm a good teacher. Between us you'll -."

They'd reached the door. "No thanks, Sweetheart, another time." He closed a coin in her hand and gently pushed her through the door. This time he turned the key.

He crossed back to Jillian. Her eyes were wide, disbelieving, her lips parted, her cheeks flushed. He grinned and began unfastening his pants.

"So you're not ready? You will be, sweet Jillian. You will beg me to take you before the night it out. Beg me."

Her mind wouldn't focus. She stared at his magnificent body. His chest and shoulders rippled with muscle as did his thighs. Dark dustings of curly hair defined his chest and marched downward to cluster in a mass of curls. His manhood stood from the dark mass, erect, thick and strong. Her eyes traveled back up his body, remembering the feel of his pulse where she'd nuzzled his throat. Their eyes met.

His were amused, laughing at her. She bit her lip in anger. How dare he? And he obviously was a customer here -.

"That girl – that woman – what is it she would have done? Why did she stare at me like that?" Her nipples had tightened to hard peaks and her cunt was full and aching. She was angry and annoyed with her own body.

Stephen chuckled as he crawled into bed, bringing the bowl of cream with him. He again straddled her legs between his but then nudged them apart with one knee. She twisted, pulling at her tied wrists, but only succeeded in inflaming both herself and him more.

He dipped a long finger into the whipped cream and pressed it against her lips. Her mouth opened, her tongue sucked the offensive finger. His shaft jerked and he caught his breath. Again, the finger dipped. Cream painted the pouting nipples, circles the full breasts, trailed downward to pool in the shallow navel. He leaned forward to kiss her, his mouth now tasting of cream.

There was no way for her to resist. He painted her belly, the creases of her legs, down her thighs, never touching where she ached, where she wanted his touch. Holding his body away from hers he began at her throat and moved downward, his tongue licking, his mouth savoring, nipping, as he devoured the cream.

Jillian's legs parted to give him access but he didn't seem to want it. He just wanted to torment her. She moaned as his mouth devoured her thighs, moving higher and higher. His large hands cupped her bottom and lifted her as he observed her need. He massaged where his hands held before releasing her.

Fingers dipped in cream slid between the swollen labia. It was still cool and teasing to her hot body. Again and again – a quick touch. Jillian whimpered. His head dipped and his tongue lapped at the cream. Her heels dug into the sheets but he held her in place as he played. She bit her lip to keep from screaming as the throbs of need took her. She would not beg; she would not She would outlast him.

One finger tapped at her swollen nub, her hips raised to ease the sweet torture of cool cream dripping from the intrusion. At last he bent his head. His tongue plunged deep and she gasped, her hips twisting. Almost there, she was almost there. He stopped. His head lifted and he surveyed her. Her body quivered, begging in its own language. She blinked rapidly, her lips trembling.

"Ask me, Jillian. Tell me what you want. Beg and I will give it to you. I will always give you your heart's desire." He watched the emotions flicker across her face. He brushed lightly against her swollen breasts and she moaned, thrusting upward to touch him more. Still, she said nothing.

"Talk to me then, sweet Jillian. Tell me why you couldn't wait for me to come back to London. How many men have you taken between these beautiful legs?" His hand cupped her and she almost climaxed – almost but not quite. "How many did it take to satisfy you before you were caught and had to run away?" His jaw clenched. "Who taught you to seduce a man? The tricks that drive a man wild? Who, dammit?"

His sex lay heavy on her thigh. He moved to press against her labia, weeping with readiness. Jillian caught her breath but a sob escaped. His penis jerked in reaction.He barely heard her soft surrender, the words that escaped her swollen lips.

He was beyond control. He leaned forward and took her mouth, his tongue filling her, as his shaft pushed deep to touch her womb. He felt her shatter as he entered her, her sheath pulsing about his sex, her entire body convulsing as he rode her. He pumped, his seed exploding deep to claim her. He felt her shatter again and lost all thought as he joined her. At last he collasped, his body heavy upon hers.

"Damn the other men. Damn them all." He nuzzled against her throat until his heart slowed. Without lifting his weight he reached up and freed her wrists.

She lay for a moment then her arms encircled his shoulders. Her face buried in his thick hair and she clung to him. She was floating in the aftermast of heaven. He was heavy and she didn't care. She liked the weight of him, the possession of him, her own surrender. She smiled and nuzzled his ear.

"There were never any others, never. Only you, Stephen. This child is yours."

He became very still. His head lifted and he drank in the truth in her grey-green eyes. "For truth? For truth, Jillian?" He kissed her ear, the tip of her nose, her throat. He had begun to soften and slip from her body. He would have rolled from her but she locked her heels over his legs and held him there.

"Jalel's woman was my instructor. I was being trained to enhance some man's harem. I never lay with another man. The only other man I ever tried to seduce, the only one I wanted, turned out to be you, yourself." Her laughter filled his senses. "I think fate was laughing at me then."

He pulled from her arms and rolled to lie beside her, propped on one elbow. His body was so sated, so satisfied, that he could barely think. He'd never felt like this during or after sex before. Only Jillian could bring him to his knees. He ran his fingertips over her brow, down her cheek.

"Did I hurt you?"

She shook her head. "If I hadn't been so stubborn -." She reached up and kissed the corner of his sensuous mouth. "But then it was so good – this feeling of your wanting me, my wanting you."

Stephen bit his lip. It had almost tumbled out; the words he feared to speak. He loved her, every inch of her. Even if the child had not been his he would have loved her. He knew that now. But she couldn't know; not until she loved him did he dare tell her. Would she ever love him after all he'd done to her? When would he dare tell her she was his legal wife? Would she hate him for the trick he had played? She had not mentioned him with the word love, only want, only need. They were not the same. He would wait.

CHAPTER TWENTY-EIGHT

London. The fog rolled like a shroud to hide its secrets, allowing an occasional glimpse, like a tear to enhance both its beauty and its stench.

Stephen had been in the city for hours and Jillian was worried. He had insisted she stay aboard and out of sight. Whoever wanted her to disappear was here and might have a watch on the docks.

She nibbled at her lower lip and then bit down in disgust. Her tongue flicked at the drop of blood she'd caused. Why had she allowed him to take the lead? It was her problem, wasn't it? He was behaving like a husband. From the narrow stairs where she sat she watched the two men left to see that she stayed put. Stephen had taken no chances this time.

"Humph. He's probably in a brothel somewhere." She spoke aloud, feeling sorry for herself. Since their wild love-making in Marseille he'd not touched her again except to brush her lips with his on occasion.

"I should never have told him the baby was his," she muttered. Now, it seemed, he was worried that he'd cause some harm if he made love to her. Dratted man. She cupped her tender breasts, rubbing a thumb over the sensitive nipples. She wanted him. How could he be so stubborn? It wasn't as though she'd asked him to marry her. She closed her eyes, wishing the comforting hands were his.

Stephen was busy with a woman but not in the carnal sense. After delivering the packets and letters he'd gone straight to his brother's house. Geoffrey was absent, on a hunting trip with friends. Margery was delighted for his company and immediately included him with the evening's guests for the elaborate dinner she had planned. Still the same size as his brother, he bathed and changed into borrowed finery. One of the guests, with his wife, was George Shanksbury, Jillian's brother-in-law. He couldn't have asked for a better opportunity to approach the man.

If the Marquis was surprised to see Stephen he covered it well. He nodded but did not speak and crossed the room to kiss his hostess' hand. "I see you've found a replacement for your husband while he's away. I didn't realize your brother-in-law was in the country." His pale eyes met Margery's as one brow rose, waiting for an explanation.

Margery smiled, not noticing the undercurrent between the two men. "He just docked last night. He's been in Naples, on government business. You do know each other, I believe?"

"Quite, my dear. Naples, you say?" He turned to Stephen. "Any news in that part of the world worth mentioning? I've never been there but I understand many Englishmen find it fascinating – all those available women, masked balls, and such." He ignored the blush spreading on Margery's fair face.

Before Stephen could answer he continued, "Didn't I hear the area was the start of all your troubles? Something about pirates, ransom, slavery – something like that? You know how the ton does love gossip. I suppose what you endured was exaggerated but then –" His words hung in the hushed room.

Stephen's jaw tensed. One fist balled to keep from striking out at the man. Word had gotten around about his youthful ordeal at the hands of pirates but no one mentioned it in polite society. Surely Geoffrey hadn't told even his wife although he knew about the disgrace, the rape. The British officer who'd paid his ransom had known all the details and although he appeared shocked Stephen doubted he'd kept the scandalous secret.

"I make it a point to ignore whatever passes as truth when on dit. And I wasn't in Naples long this time. We did have a run-in with an old acquaintance though, a pirate named Jalal. Would you know him?"

George's eyes flashed a warning but his facial expression was bland. "I've never been anywhere in Italy except for Venice. Now, that's a beautiful city."

"Marseille? Surely you've visited that port on your way." His brown eyes had darkened to almost black and they bored into the frozen blue of the Marquis.

George shrugged and turned to his hostess with a seductive smile. "Why are we discussing some distant city when we have the cream of the ton before our eyes? And the husband is away? May I escort you into dinner, My Lady?" His eyes dipped to Margery's lips, to her low bodice, and back. His mouth pursed with an air-blown kiss.

Margery looked startled, then laughed, and took his arm. "Certainly, my Lord. I would be honored. I'm sure Stephen would be delighted to seat your wife."

Stephen forced himself to relax. The other guests showed no sign of what lay behind the old gossip and what did it manner now, anyway? It was over, done. Shanksbury had accomplished his purpose, if he had one. He was distracted by the old memories, still raw after so many years. Only one good was derived from the conversation. Now Shanksbury knew he'd been in the area where Jillian had been taken. Did the man know Jalal's name? Was he guilty of selling his own kin into slavery? If so, for what reason?

He waited until the soup was finished and the next course passed. The ladies on both sides of him flirted outrageously and he answered in kind to keep them both happy. His devilish good looks always assured him attention by the fairer sex. He cut a thick slice of venison and centered his gaze on Shanksbury.

"Have you news of your sister? I thought I saw her on my travels but it couldn't have been so." The question was directed to Margery but his eyes remained on Shanksbury. The man's fork clattered to his plate. He covered the lapse quickly and sipped from his wine glass.

Margery leaned forward to answer. "We had a letter some while back. She sent it only after she'd left, the dratted girl. She's spending a year with the Omar-DuBois', our grandparents. You may remember they live in Tuscany, a beautiful villa with olive trees and grape vines. We haven't heard from her since." She sighed. "It's a shame you didn't stop by and see her when you were so close. Jillian may be a bit naughty at times and we've had our differences but -." She slathered butter on a roll.

"You know, Stephen, she was rather taken with you." She glanced around the table but even George Shanksbury seemed to be otherwise occupied. She lowered her voice. "I shouldn't have lost my temper with her. What if she doesn't come back? I have the strangest feeling."

Stephen noticed the twitch in George's cheek. He finished chewing then put his fork down and took Margery's soft hand in his. "She'll be back. I'll see to it. You never know where my ship will take me."

He met the cold eyes across the table as he released her fingers. "Have you heard from her? Perhaps family matters? I did understand all the legalities of her inheritance were taken care of before I left."

"I know nothing of her circumstances. We were not on the best of terms, as you know. I didn't even know she'd left the country until I heard her house was shut up for the season." He motioned at his wife. "On dit, you know. Isn't that so, my dear? She wasn't at home to your last visit?"

Margery frowned as she looked between the Marquis and his wife. "My Lord, I didn't know you were on speaking terms with my sister at all. I mean, after her behavior – and the house -." She stopped in mid-sentence, her face reddening. She covered her mouth with her napkin. "Oh, I am so sorry. Perhaps a bit more wine, James." She motioned to the hovering servant.

Stephen laughed. Everyone turned to stare at him. He raised his glass. "A toast to family squabbles. May the solution be as innocent as it seems."

The tic in Shanksbury's jaw was noticiable as he raised his glass. General conversation began again and the hum of casual flirtation and gossip relaxed the guests. With the Marguies' departure, the party broke up early.

…………………………………………...………………...

The morning was spent in arranging funds to be paid out in Naples to cover the purchase money for his 'wife'. His fortune was such that even so large a sum barely made a dent but he wished to keep his creditors and friends solvent.

His next stop was at Jillian's house on the square. The door was answered by a petite red-haired maid. She bobbed her head but then began immediately to dismiss him.

"The mistress is not at home, Sir. She is on an extended trip to the continent."

The door began to close but Stephen's hand held it in place. "I am a close friend of Lady Jillian Shanksbury. I know she is in Tuscany. However, I would like to come in and speak with the housekeeper for a short while."

She stared at him, shook her head. The mass of red curls threatened to escape her ruffled mobcap. "The housekeeper is not here at present, Sir. The staff is very small while My Lady is away."

"Nevertheless, I will come in." Stephen pushed pass the girl and strode toward the parlour. She followed, her hands wringing in her apron.

"It's only me, Sir. No one else is home now." She almost bumped into his back he stopped so suddenly. Her bright eyes fastened on his lovely eyes, slid over his broad shoulders. He smiled as she smiled back. Lord, but the gentleman was handsome.

"Your name, Miss?" He had leaned down to her level and she caught her breath.

"Mavis, Sir, Mavis Collins." She sighed as he took her hand and patted it.

"Well, Mavis, I only wanted to speak with someone in the house, someone who would know. Could we sit for a moment?"

"Know what, Sir?" Her wide eyes gazed at him in obvious fascination. A lord did not talk to a maid like this that she knew of – not ever. Dumbly she followed him further into the room and sat on the edge of a cushioned chair. He had taken a seat across from her.

"Tell me, Mavis, has anyone else called upon your mistress? I understand she had few visitors while she was in residence."

"Well, no one except the solicitor who pays the bills and he was to see Mrs. Berkley, the housekeeper, you know." She rearranged her skirts, her eyes on his polished boots. "There was a rather odd man in a suit but he was no gentleman. Mrs. Berkley had to call the yardman to get rid of him. He kept saying the Marquis sent him and Mrs. Berkley was awfully angry. Don't know what he wanted but there was a lot of shouting and shoving before he left. I did hear him say he needed to list the inventory, whatever that is."

"And did he, indeed, get an inventory – a listing of the contents of the house? From Mrs. Berkley, perhaps?"

"Oh, no, Sir. He did not." Her head shook vehemently. "In fact, she's had the yardman sleeping in the house since that day – for protection, you know."

Stephen stood up. "Well, I'll see someone from my staff is sent to help with that until your mistress returns. He'll have a note from St .James, Ltd. as introduction and his salary will be paid by me. Will you inform Mrs. Berkley of this arrangement?"

He turned at the door with a last glance around the overstuffed room. Why hadn't Jillian gotten rid of some of this junk? He almost knocked a bust of some Roman from its pedestal as he turned. "Oh, and Lady Shanksbury may be away longer than first thought. I'll see her solicitor is informed of the arrangements. Your positions are secure so there's no worry for the staff. Do not allow strangers inside the house without either her permission or mine. Here's my card and thank you, Mavis, for your help."

He leaned close to her ear. "For your knowledge only – but you may tell your Mrs. Berkley – I am your mistress' fiance."

He left the girl staring after him, her mouth agape, as he hurried to his next stop. Word would get around whether it was believed or not. Now, arrangements must be made to protect the house and its staff and pay its upkeep until such time Jillian returned.

He'd spent the night at Margery's and it was late the next evening before Stephen headed back to his ship. Why was Shanksbury so interested in Jillian's house?

Or its contents? Was it pure malice or something else? Malice, he decided. The man couldn't stand the idea of being bested on the inheritance – and he'd had a thing for his sister-in-law too.

He'd filed the papers, including the Arabic document, for verifying his marriage to Jillian but they awaited the final seals. With her supposedly out of the country a proxy was used as stand-in at the civil ceremony. Jillian need never know unless, or until, he released the documents. His solicitor would take care of that. He smiled to himself. His son, or daughter, would bear his name. And if things worked out between them - .Who said one could not have one's cake and eat it too?

He was humming to himself as he ducked under the low threshold of his cabin. Jillian jumped to her feet. She was enticing in the near-sheer Egyptian cotton chemise, its neckline left open to draw his attention. She neared him and tipped her face up for the expected kiss and he obliged.

She didn't know how hard it was to back away with only a kiss. He still was not sure he believed her about the parenthood of her child. It was all just too neat a package and she had yet to say she loved or or even cared for him. He trailed a finger down her jaw, down her throat, until it opened the placket of the flimsy garment. His mouth watered to take her offerings with his lips, tease her until she begged once again. He swallowed as she swayed toward him and dropped his hand to her curved belly instead and smiled.

"And how is our son?" His hand splayed wide, circling gently.

Jillian backed away in annoyance. “Is that all you can think about? Do you not ever think about me? Where have you been? I’ve been so bored – and worried – yes, worried a little bit about you.” Her lower lip pouted

Stephen laughed, rubbing his thumb over her lip. He dipped his head and sucked it into his mouth, then kissed her thoroughly as her reward for worrying about him. He felt her pulse flutter and released her. Why, why wouldn’t she admit she loved him? Did she, indeed?

“I was at Margery’s – and I had business to attend to. It took longer than I thought.”

He sat and began removing his boots. “I thought you’d be asleep.”

She stomped her foot in vexation. “Asleep? I was waiting for you.” Tears hovered on her lashes and she turned away so he couldn’t see. She wouldn’t give him the satisfaction of knowing how worried she’d been.

“No need. I can always find a warm bed.” He cut laughing eyes at her back. If she was angry enough might she allow her true feelings to show?

“I’ll just bet you can. And her name isn’t Margery, either.” Desire, or pure lust, overtook her and she hugged her arms close. “Damn you, Stephen St.James, do you think - .” She broke off. She would not give him the satisfaction of knowing she wanted him to bed her, only her, that she ached for his touch, that she was hopelessly in love with him.

Puzzled, she flounced to the bed and crawled in, forgetting to be ladylike. She pulled the covers up to her waist and turned her back to him.

He grinned at the display in her haste to withdraw from the battle. That sweet, rounded, bottom nestled against his groin each night causing him near pain.

The grin faded. Was he torturing himself for nothing? Was she a lier or was she not? Everything pointed to someone else fathering her child, one of many. She'd been gone from England long enough for a month's dalliance and he didn't know how far along her pregnancy was. She was small, the rounding of her belly still slight. His guts tightened into a knot. Damn if he'd claim her as a wife if –. She'd seduced him, damn it! She'd not known it was he on Jalal's ship and she'd held nothing back, nothing. He felt the almost instant erection at the memory of her hot mouth suckling him.

If the child was his he would know when he held him; he just would. Time enough to claim her, to tell her, either she was a wife or a slave. To be assured, he would free her if the latter. Though legal still, slavery was not something he would ever condone – but she didn't know that, did she?

Frowning, he crawled into bed and pulled her back against his hard shaft. He thought she moaned as it nudged against her but the noise she made was so faint he wasn't sure. He pushed between her legs then settled her beneath his chin as his eyes closed.

Jillian didn't find sleep so easily. He was driving her mad. She could feel his heavy male sex pressing between her legs. How could he do that and not take her? She ached for him, her nether curls wept for him. She screwed her eyes closed and clenched her jaw. He shifted, obviously asleep.

Damn him. Her hand raised her chemise until her fingers could find the slickness he'd caused. Hot and wet, her fingers slipped inside, her thumb circled the swollen nub. Again and again, as she imagined it was Stephen that pleasured her. At last she gasped against his circling arm and her body shivered, then relaxed, as release came. In his sleep he'd pumped once against her as though in protest. It had sent her over the top. She sighed and closed her eyes.

CHAPTER TWENTY-NINE

Stephen's eyes flew open. Attuned to the normal noises aboard ship he'd slept soundly until now. That had been a muffled thud – what? The three stairs descending to his cabin creaked once.

Still naked, Stephen whirled to the side of the bed, searching for his trousers. The damn things weren't within reach. He pulled Jillian up and onto the floor beside him, his hand covering her mouth.

"Be quiet. Get down behind me." He shoved her to the floor into the darker corner as the door opened a crack. All hell broke loose within the silence.

Soft thuds followed silver streaks as knives sank into the bed where they'd been only seconds before. The wielder of death stood to the side of the door, a slight figure. Moonlight reflected on his remaining blade, larger than the others.

Stephen dove for the legs, yelling for help. His first mate should be sleeping in the next cabin; if he were on board at all. Still groggy with sleep, Jillian made no sound but curled into the corner at the foot of the bed.

All she heard now was cursing, men grunting, blows connecting with sickening effects.

Stephen had the attacker down, his body astride the slighter figure, and was demanding who had sent him. The cabin smelled of sweat and fear. Without his knives the man was no danger. His back to the door, Stephen didn't see the second man enter. It all happened so fast. The blow meant for his head hit his shoulder instead as he shifted at the slight noise. He rolled away just as the cudgel swung again.

Jillian screamed. Stephen had his hands full with the giant. The man was twice his weight and all muscle. Where the hell were his crewmen? His hands closed on his short sword where it'd been knocked to the floor. With a leap he slashed upward and it buried to the hilt in the man's belly.

Stephen's head was ringing from the last blow, blood running into his eyes. He staggered and looked around for Jillian just as two of his men stormed into the cabin.

Oh, God! The man who'd attacked with the knives had her by the throat and was squeezing the life out of her. No wonder she'd not made another sound. Without thought Stephen's blade flew through the air to bury itself between the man's shoulder blades. He fell forward, blood gushing across the floor. The side of his face was a scared mess where her nails had raked him.

He rushed to Jillian. She wasn't breathing. Her eyes were closed. He gathered her in his arms, rocking her, his fingers brushing the curling locks from her temples.

"Don't leave me, Sweetheart. Stay with me. I love you, Jillian. I love you. Forgive me." His voice cracked. He'd lost her. Tears burned his eyelids.

He didn't hear the uproar above decks for a long while. A twist of smoke caused him to raise his head. Fire on board! Once again a thinking man he cleared the bed of the embedded knives. He lifted Jillian into his arms and placed her on the bed. He could hear shouts now and running feet but the smoke was no worse.

He started for the door. He'd not let her burn at least. Then he heard a soft moan. She was breathing! He returned to her side, cupping her head with his hand, his face breaking into pure happiness.

Her eyes fluttered open. She tried to speak but only succeeded in a croak. Her throat was bruised and raw. There was a lump on her cheek which was already turning dark.

Jillian was trying to smile at him. Yes, she definitely was trying. Stephen's face broke into a lopsided grin. He swallowed, his own throat dry. "Don't try to talk just yet, Sweetheart. It's all right. They won't hurt you anymore."

Her hand brushed his hard thigh – the only part of him she could reach. Her lips curved upward and her eyes actually twinkled. "Clothes - on." The words were faint and slurred.

Stephen looked down. He was still nude in all his glory. He laughed. The world was good. She was alive, he was alive, and all his parts were there. He found his trousers and donned them, stomped into his boots.

"I'll be right back. Everything is all right now. Just rest. I'll get a doctor." He broke into a run as he climbed the short stairs to the deck.

The fire was out and had caused little harm. His first mate was back and had taken over. Billy's body, that of the boy on watch last night, was stretched out on deck and covered with a sheet. The young man hadn't stood a chance. The knife throw had severed his jugular. That would've been the thud that had awakened him.

Stephen sat impatiently as the doctor put stitches in his scalp. Jillian had been examined and judged all right except for some bad bruises and a very sore throat. The cabin floor had been scoured to rid it of the stench of blood.

"Shame one of them wasn't taken alive but there was no choice. They meant to kill us in our sleep. Was only Jillian the target or am I getting too close to the guilty party?" Stephen had explained part of the situation to his first mate, John Bates. He didn't yet want his brother to know Jillian was with him. Geoffrey couldn't keep his mouth shut and Margery was not to be trusted.

John cleared his throat. "We found flint and oil-soaked rags around the deck. There must have been a third man but he only had time to light a few or maybe they wanted to be sure of their own escape before the blaze was too fierce. They meant to burn the entire ship after the deed. This won't be the end of it. I've doubled the watch and with seasoned men this time – if that's all right with you."

"Of course. You're the only one I've confided in, John. I think the Marquis is the guilty party but there's no way to prove it. Why would anyone go to so much trouble over his sister-in-law's inheritance? How much is pride worth to a man like George Shanksbury?"

"How much is the lady worth to you, Captain? I mean no offense but we've been friends since boyhood and you've never cared one way or another for one particular female. Wouldn't it be easier to put her in her sister's hands – eh, your brother's?"

Stephen didn't answer for a moment. "You think her still a concubine to me, a mistress, hmm? Not so. I'm afraid I fell for the lady almost the first time I laid eyes on her. At the time I thought she 'd been claimed by someone else but that didn't prove to be so."

Tongue in cheek, he grinned crookedly at his friend. "This is true confession time, it seems." He shrugged. "I waited too late to state my case. Then she showed up aboard that pirate ship. What are the chances, hmm?"

John clasped him on the shoulder. "So, what are you going to do about it? I'll help any way I can." He knew the captain's lady was breeding but thought best not to mention it. Whose child was it? It couldn't be St.James', now could it?

....

Gill St.James, Stephen's father, stood beside him in Jillian's townhouse. Only recently returned from their country estate, he'd insisted on seeing the property for himself. He had yet to be told of his son's new bride although he suspected something was afoot. It wasn't often Stephen asked his advice.

Mavis had again been the only help on the premises. She let the gentlemen in and disappeared into the back of the house. Gill circled the front parlor with a frown, occasionally lifting a figurine or other object and peering at the bottom. He moved his inspection across to the library, closely followed by Stephen.

Everything was immaculate and smelled of polish and wax. Still, every room was cluttered with bric-a-brac or excess paintings. Gill frowned, his hands clasped behind his back. He had unconsciously adopted the stance when he'd first inheritated the English title denied him in his youth. It made him feel more British. After all, they weren't that fond of his French upbringing by his stepfather.

"You say there's more of the same in crates in the basement?" He turned to peer at his son, an image of himself.

"Yes, Sir, and the master suite is filled with erotica."

"And this lady, Margery's sister, has lived here for months without packing it away. Hmm – decrees bad habits or pure laziness. Perhaps she likes her deceased husband's tastes?" His mouth crooked into a half-smile.

Stephen shook his head. "I do not think so, Sir. She simply didn't care. She had few callers and wished to be independent, away from her brother-in-law."

"Yes, well, George Shanksbury is a firm believer in his own magnificence. I can imagine, now that he has the title, he is an over-bearing ass."

Gill led the way up the stairs. "Shall we inspect the master bedroom? Even I have heard of the art employed there. I believe William was known to give rather wild parties in his youth in this house; not that I was on his guest list."

They entered the master's suite and paused. Stephen's eyes twinkled, waiting for his father to notice the long mirror hidden in the canopy over the bed. Instead, Gill walked straight to the wall facing the foot of the bed and stared at the erotic painting there. It depicted two men and a buxom woman in a tangle of limbs draped upon an oversize bed.

"Dear God! I wondered what had become of this. It once hung in a very private collection – I won't say whose – and just disappeared – sold, so they say, but no one knew to whom. It's worth a fortune." His eyes scanned the other paintings in the room. "Is its mate here also? I've never seen it but reportedly there is one – more explicit than this one, the sexes male only. I understand George kept it for his eyes only."

"I haven't inspected the contents that closely. There is an attic and a basement, both full of crates. It could be there."

Gill turned slowly, inspecting the room again. He shook his head. "I believe your mystery is solved. George may have inheritated the title and estates but I would bet most of the money is tied up in this house." He watched his son carefully. "You say Jillian Shanksbury inherited the house, monies to run it, and its entire contents?"

Stephen nodded. "The will stated it so. At the end it seems William was actually fond of her. George tried every trick he could to break it but was unsuccessful."

"And where is the lady now?" Gill's voice had become stern.

Stephen swallowed. "Aboard my ship, in my care."

Gill's brow peaked. "And why is that? What is your interest? You asked me here to survey the house and its contents but there is something else, is there not?"

Before Stephen could answer Gill continued his musings. "She is the younger sister of Margery, the uncontrollable sister. The one you made a fool of yourself over before she married William Shanksbury – that one?"

Stephen opened his mouth but nothing came out. He was thinking fast but not fast enough. He should have had a good explanation before he consulted his father.

"Didn't I also hear a rumor that Geoffrey was enamored of the girl before his marriage to Margery? Yes, and that gossip after William's death; something about a courtesan's red dress while she should have been still in mourning. And she's aboard your ship, is she? And in your bed, I'm guessing?" Gill's voice was harsh.

Stephen tried to remember he was no boy. His stern father had been young once too. Had he never been in love? He opened the connecting door to Jillian's bedroom, a light, airy, room. It was tastefully decorated in pale greens and blues with simple furnishings. He stepped inside as though it would center his answers. His father followed him.

He gestured around the feminine space. "This is Jillian, Sir. Not the sinful master suite, not the over-stuffed parlor, not the gossip that tickles the palettes of the ton. She's beautiful, inside and out. I'm thinking she would make a fine wife." Anger tinged his tone.

Gill simply stared at his son. When had he grown up so? This man did not sound like his wild offspring. His sinful mouth, identical to Stephen's, curved upward. "So? When do I meet her again? I barely remember a young girl with gold hair and mischievious eyes."

Stephen's breath expelled in a whoosh. He burst out laughing. His father extended his hand but Stephen clasped him tightly instead, much to his own surprise. After a moment they broke apart, self-conscious at their display.

"We, umm, I thought it prudent for her to remain on board. I had thought it safer until last night's incident. Also, Geoffrey and Margery do not know she's in town - which might be for the best. The sisters don't get along well of late."

Amused, Gill sucked at his lower lip. "Yes, well, I do remember some remarks from my daughter-in-law. If I didn't know Geoffrey loved her dearly I'd think she was jealous of her sister." He picked up his hat and headed for the door. "I'll just accompany you back to the ship then."

"There's no need, Sir. Jillian still bears bruises from last night and will not be pleased to receive company. I'll bring her 'round to your place in a few days time."

He was too late. His father was already giving the driver directions to the docks. Reluctantly Stephen climbed in beside him. All hell was going to break loose. How was he going to explain? He could only hope whatever she was wearing would disguise her condition.

…………………………………………....……………….....

The day was unusually sunny for this time of year. A light breeze blew through the cabin where Jillian had opened every available window. She was wearing the pale rose gown she'd just finished. It was full to allow for her increasing girth but caught up with dark ribbon of green beneath her breasts. The short, puffed, sleeves and wide neckline was cool and set off her lovely arms and slender throat. Her neck still bore dark bruises from the attack but her voice was back almost to normal. Her hair was pulled upward and fell in a cascade of blond curls from the green ribbon that held it. She had on only one petticoat, a soft ruffle of palest pink that gave the gown a lighter color. She hoped Stephen liked the outfit. She thought she looked unusually pretty.

The men's voices startled her. Stephen had someone with him. She waited, pretending to look out the open window, until he entered. The door opened and she turned, her eyes wide in recognition.

Good lord! The girl had grown into a most beautiful woman – and she was carrying Stephen's child. Gill St.James stopped so short that Stephen bumped into him. Then his manners returned. He crossed the room and took her hand, lifting it to his mouth. As he brushed her fingertips with his lips, he again surveyed the beauty of his son's lady.

"I believe we've met before, Lady Shanksbury. You are looking even lovelier than I remember." His eyes dropped to her rounded form as his irritation at the situation won out. "And very prolific."

Jillian's face blushed with color. She wet her lips but said nothing, her eyes flying to Stephen's. How could he bring his father here without warning? Her temper flared but she managed to smile, her hand splaying over her belly.

"You have not had the banns read as yet, Stephen?" His voice was a whip cutting the air.

His jaw clenched, Stephen met his father's narrowed eyes with like expression. "There's some discussion we need to have in private, Sir. Jillian – Lady Shanksbury – and I have not decided to -."

"Why the bloody hell not?" His father's voice interrupted him. "My apologies, my Lady, for the language. This escapade of my son's is not – well, is beyond -."

"My Lord, I do not wish to marry your son – that is to say, to force him to – there are circumstances that you do not know." Jillian's temper was beginning to show. "I have had one very bad marriage and I will not be forced into another one. I have enough to be independent -."

"Independent? Oh, I would say extremely independent. You are a very wealthy woman. Were you aware of that?" Gill glared at her, then at Stephen.

Stephen cleared his throat. "Jillian, we, uh, I asked my father to have a look at your townhouse and its contents today. I thought he might spot something we didn't, some reason for George Shanksbury's treachery."

One brow flew upward. "Oh? And did he?" It was all Jillian could do not to scream at them both. Marry indeed. He would hate her if he were forced to be her husband.

"The contents, all those paintings and figurines that you despise, are worth a probable fortune." Stephen was clearly unhappy. His expression was as neutral as he could manage but she could see the turmoil behind his dark eyes.

His father had calmed down. He paced the cabin, his eyes flickering between the couple. "I have business to attend. Perhaps tomorrow you will call on me, Stephen, before noon." It was not a request. He bowed slighlty to Jillian, turned on his heel, and took his leave.

Stephen waited until the door closed before approaching her. She was stiff in his arms but that didn't last long. He knew well how to soften her mood. He brushed his lips down her throat, across her chin, captured her lips before she could turn her head away from his advance. With a sigh she relaxed against him and he threaded his fingers through her hair, dislodging the green ribbon. He buried his face in the gold of her curls, letting their fragrance soothe him.

He sighed. She was wealthy now. She wouldn't want him. He had money, a lot of money, and investments all over Europe and the Americas. Still, he hadn't exactly been honest with her, had he?

When she realized she was married to him she would hate him. It no longer mattered whose child she carried. In his father's eyes it was a St.James. He, himself, had given the baby his name by completing the paperwork. All the civil ceremony lacked was for the papers to be filed. Did he want to do that now, under the new rules? A widow, alone, rescued, was susceptable to his charms. A wealthy widow might not wish his name, child or no child. And he'd not told her, had he?

Stephen groaned as her full breasts rubbed his chest. She was still behaving as though she was his concubine, his to control. Had she not understaood what his father had just told her? Was it possible she didn't care?

Jillian's eyes glimmered with unshed tears as Stephen worked his magic. All it took was a touch here, a touch there, and she was his. Did he not know? Now, what damage would his father do to their fragile hold on each other? She moaned as his hands caught her rounded bottom and lifted her fully into his hips. He was careful not to press her too close, careful of the baby. She caught his hair and pulled his head down so her lips could reach his. He would break her heart yet and there was nothing she could do about it.

As usual, he backed from her after the initial seductive fondling. She wanted to scream but she pretended it was nothing to her, his tantalizing kisses. She smiled, catching her skirts to display her new garment. She was proud of her new skill.

"Do you like it? I worked hard to finish it for your return." Lips parted slightly, she awaited his answer. She didn't care what he said, just so he didn't immediately leave again.

Perplexed at the gown's importance, Stephen surveyed it. His gaze rose to her mouth. What he really wanted was to crush those soft lips to his again, tumble her into bed - . "The color suits you. You look beautiful and tempting, like a fruit ready to be plucked." Not the words he'd meant to say. He needed her to love him, to need him, not be seduced.

Jillian beamed, nibbling at her lower lip. "Good. Then you're forgiven for bringing your father here unannounced. Do you think he'll keep my secret? I left London to save my reputation, you know."

Stephen shrugged. "Of course. He's a man of many secrets. He may be the picture of dignity now but I've heard tales. I don't doubt he has many skeletons of his own, albeit old ones. Tomorrow I'll face him better prepared."

……………………………………….....………………....

Stephen had begun to relax. The meeting with his father was going well. He'd managed to explain how Jillian, Lady Shanksbury, had felt she had to take desperate measures and worn the crimson gown to the ball, breaking her mourning. The terms of the will, her brother-in-law's imminent forced proving of her marriage's consumation, his own participation in the deflowering, all had been explained in brief. His father had not uttered a word, his fingers steepled as he listened, a frown or a smile tugging at his features on occasion. Stephen paused. He was not prepared to go further.

Gill grinned, tongue in cheek. "I trust you ravished the maiden with finesse? After all, a lady's first time may set her pattern for life."

Annoyed, Stephen snapped, "It's not a subject for discussion." He met his father's amused eyes and relaxed. "The lady in question was well pleased, the setting romantic, the gentleman knowledgeable." He conquered the laughter that threatened to surface.

"Good, good; then what more is there to say? Apparently the coupling was fruitfull. Marry the lady."

Stephen turned from the window alcove where he'd taken temporary sanctuary. "It's not that simple. The child may not be mine. Anyway, we're already married under Muslim law but she is not aware of it. Jillian does not seek marriage – at least, not to me."

His father leaned forward, his elbows on his knees. "Why not? What did you do to her?"

"I'm not a child to be admonished," Stephen growled. "I bought her, that's what. She was to be sold as a slave into the concubine market. She seduced me as much as -. she's well trained, believe me. I'll give her that. It's a long story." He hadn't meant to say as much. He dismissed it with a rude gesture and crossed to pour himself a brandy. His hand was actually shaking and his father's eyes bored into his back.

Gill stood. His voice lowered two levels at least. "You bought her? Explain yourself."

Stephen turned to face him and downed the brandy 'way too fast. He almost choked but managed to set the glass down. "Legally I own her. I know slavery is frowned upon in this part of the world but it is legal. She cost me a damn fortune." He shook his head to clear it. "That's not the problem. I'd never enforce such a thing." He plopped into a chair, his head down, caught between his hands.

"Her owner would have branded her as chattel. I can still smell the hot iron. The fool insisted he'd made a bargain that she would no longer be a free woman and he would keep that bargain. Someone here in England had paid hansomely to see she disappear. I agreed to wed her as well as pay to stop the branding. Voila. If she is my wife, my responsibility, she is no longer a free woman – at least legally. Jalal had fulfilled his bargain."

"And she doesn't know?" Gill couldn't believe the mess his son had gotten himself into.

"Well, she knows I paid to purchase her." He shifted uncomfortably in the chair. "And she fulfills her part of the bargain."

"Fulfills - ?" Gill swore under his breath. "Just what is that supposed to mean?" His stance was battle-ready. "No son of mine -."

Stephen jumped to his feet. "Sir – it's my life, my woman. I processed the papers in London when I arrived. She doesn't know. She's my wife legally but she'll never accept that now. She no longer needs me – or won't once this child is born. She's wealthy, damn it!"

The sudden silence was broken only by the ticking of a clock somewhere near. Gill poured them both a brandy, handing a snifter to Stephen. He cleared his throat.

"Do you want her for your wife?"

Stephen ran his fingers through his hair. "More than anything in my life. I do believe I'm foolishly in love. Anyway, it's legal now even if she doesn't know." He swirled the brandy, sipped.

His father sat, motioning for him to do the same. He leaned back, his long legs crossed at the ankles. "Did you ever know the story of your older sister, Lily?"

Stephen frowned, wondering what the connection was. He remembered Lily although no one mentioned her now. She'd married a French nobleman and disappeared. She'd been years older than himself and he'd hardly known her. He nodded.

"Lily was quite dark skinned, straight, aquiline nose. I always thought she had beautiful black eyes; and her hair – so straight and as dark as midnight. She always felt she did not belong. It led to many of her troubles." Gill hesitated, lost in some sad memory. "I trust she is happy now."

"We – I – accepted Lily as my child all those years. Your mother had mixed feelings and I often wondered if she loved the girl. You see, my Catherine was taken to wife by one of those Indians in America. They were considered savages but he loved her in his own way and I was jealous of that fact. It took me months to find her after her capture and she was bearing his child when we married."

Stephen stared at his father. He'd never heard this story, no one in the family had. "I didn't know, Sir." He felt humbled.

Gill cleared his throat. "Well, I just wanted you to know, a child can be loved whether it is yours or not. The decision is with you. I do not know why you think she may have lain with others but in the end if you love her it will not matter; enough said." He rose in dismissal. He finished the brandy, setting the snifter down.

Stephen rose also. "I, um, talked with Jillian after you left. She would like you, or myself, to sell some of the artwork and deposit the money for her – possibly beginning with that painting in the master suite."

Gill grinned. "Good choice. I'll see to it. You know, I have some good friends in Barbados. Weren't your original plans to continue with your privateer career against America?"

"I did want to do that. The money is good. It's legal and the shipping lanes are full of traffic; American, French, and some Spanish – all within reach. This insurrection has become a full-fledged war while I was busy in Naples. The naval office would like help with a blockade but I prefer to work alone, I think. Why did you mention Barbados? They're not involved that I know of although they have close ties to the Carolinas."

"Come into the library and let's review some maps. I think I have your solution. And if you haven't already,

I'd file those marriage documents. The child needs a name. The two of you can work out your feelings later."

CHAPTER THIRTY

The voyage had been a lesson in denial. It was hard to say who was more frustrated, Jillian or Stephen. He watched her whenever he thought she wasn't looking; his eyes hungry. He kept busy but the nights were still there, the shared cabin, the necessary closeness.

It wouldn't do to have a woman, even a pregnant one, aboard a ship with so many men without the understanding that she belonged to him. He proclaimed his ownership when they occasioned to be together on deck, running his fingers down her cheek, cupping her chin as his lips brushed her throat, or perhaps his arm slung carelessly about her hips as he escorted her below.

Little did she know that his touching burned him, that each small intimacy was a small torture when he had declared to himself he would abstain until the child was born, until she could choose without so much emotion what she would do with her future.

He'd told her only that his father had friends in Barbados and she would be welcome there until after the baby was born or longer if she liked. That way she would be safe from the enemy in London and safe from gossip. He would use the ensuring time to further his own interests along the coast of the Americas. His father was looking into the problem in London.

He'd already made one fortune as a privateer. The Spanish galleons were ripe for taking and heavy with gold and other treasure. The English crown's share was a small price to pay for legitimacy. If a French ship was captured along the way so much the better; an upstart of an American – the government was even more pleased.

Jillian closed her eyes as his dark head ducked to brush her cheek with his, his lips causing her breath to catch. Oh, God, did he know what he did to her? Didn't he care? Her teeth caught at her lower lip to stop its quiver. Only a little – if she turned her head only a little his mouth would touch her lips. She ached with wanting him. Every nerve in her body seemed to be tuned to his touch. It wasn't fair.

Stephen raised his head and grinned at her pouting lip. Her eyes shot fire at him. So, she was angry at him now. Good. Perhaps she wouldn't brush those magnificent breasts against him tonight in passing or one of the other multiple things she continuously did to torment him. He looked out to sea and took in a deep breath of sea air to clear her scent from his nostrils. They'd be in Barbados within days and he could get his mind back to business.

"Sail to starboard!" The shout caused a stir aboard as all turned to view the distant ship. "Two, three, sails to starboard!"

Stephen swore under his breath and reached for the spyglass. Two days before they'd taken a French ship. His crew was split and his first mate was now aboard the captured vessel and it well on the way to port as captured spoils. They were still licking their wounds. Now was not the time for another confrontation.

"Get below, Jillian, and stay there." He'd already turned again to view the rapidly gaining vessels. Perhaps they were British but he didn't think so. Privateers? No, they flew the flag of the American colonies.

"Damn the luck." What were they doing so far south? Would they attack? Sometimes they hadn't the powder and avoided a fight but this time he knew he looked like easy prey. Short of manpower, wounded men aboard, and outnumbered; he didn't care for the odds. He gave the order to tack on more sail but it was too late. They were upon him.

"Battle stations! Ready to fire!" Stephen swung to position and their cannon boomed. The rebel's ship shuddered as she took the shots but she managed to return fire. She was lower in the water than the British vessel and the damage was near the waterline. Sharpshooters in the rigging aimed relentless fire down on deck as they drew close. These rebels weren't short of powder. Stephen cursed, shouting orders above the confusion as the second ship closed.

Jillian heard the crunch of wood against wood as the two ships paralleled. Grappling hooks grasped with sickening thuds as the ships' shudders ceased. Metal clanged on metal, screams, the stench of powder and blood sickened her. She held her belly, crooning to the little being within that all was well.

But all was not well. Men were dying on the decks above. She shoved aside the large trunk and crawled behind it, covered by a quilt. In her shaking hand she held one of Stephen's pistols, primed and ready.

It was quieter now. Was it over? The ships were still attached. Someone had come into the cabin, overturning chairs, breaking the pitcher and bowl, rifling through the large box on Stephen's desk. Then they were gone.

She crept out from her hiding place and straightened her clothing. It was eerily silent but for one voice above decks. What was he saying? Something about a hanging? Her heart near stopped its beating. She silently ascended the stairs and peeped out. Their backs were to her.

A keg was centered on the deck. On it stood Stephen, his arms bound behind him. Around his neck was a noose. His always immaculate shirt was ripped nearly off and blood had darkened what was left to rust, his dark hair was matted with blood at his temple. His full lower lip was cut and swollen. A single lock of hair fell over his forehead in defiance of the rope at his throat. She'd never seen him look so beautiful.

The victor was, indeed, speaking. The man, this American, had sandy brown hair and no decent uniform but a mixture of clothing. They seemed to know each other.

"You have deprived me of one ship, taken my crew, and my means of living. I swore last year that if I ever laid eyes upon you again you'd hang for it. No letter from His Majesty gives you the right to prey on my ships." Hands on hips, the rebel glared at his prisoner.

Stephen's head came up, the rope scraping his throat. "We have the right to suppress rebellion. Your colonies have reduced your rights to naught. No one knows what you want – least of all, yourselves. If we knew your grieviences perhaps we would be more sympathetic. Now you'd make yourself worth less than a common pirate, a criminal, by this act." He jerked as the whip wielded by another sailor caught his back. It almost cost him his balance and a tightening of the noose.

The rebel captain growled at the seaman and the whip was coiled and laid down. "Unfortunate, that, my apologies. Our belief in freedom sometimes is a deterrent to discipline."

Jillian felt the whip's lash as though it had been her and not Stephen that it caught. Anger filled her. They would not kill him. He was the father of her child and he was hers. She glanced to the sides of the doorway. All eyes were on the coming hanging. She stepped quickly out.

Captain Andrew Brandon tensed as he felt the muzzle pressed into the base of his neck. He registered astoinshment on the faces of his men, the growing grin on the face of his captive. Slowly, he raised his arms above his head.

"Order them to remove the noose."

The voice was that of a female. He relaxed, his arms dropping a bit. The muzzle pressed harder.

"I wouldn't try anything. It only takes one shot and I'm very good." Jillian's voice was low but firm. Inside she trembled but her hand was steady.

"I'll bet you are, Sweetheart." Andrew's voice drawled as he started to turn. Immediately he felt the prick of a knife in his side. Damn the bitch. She had a knife as well. "Remove the rope. Aid our friend down."

Stephen took a deep breath. Jillian's expression was unreadable. They weren't out of this yet. His arms still bound, he gave the rebel a little bow of his head.

"I'd like you to meet my wife, Captain, the Lady Jillian St.James." He didn't know who was more startled, the Captain or Jillian. His eyes met hers. Her face flushed with a charming color but she said nothing.

"Wife? You'd bring a wife on a voyage of pilfering?" Andrew whirled as he spoke, surprising Jillian. The gun and knife were easy to remove from her grasp. He looked between the two of them. She was very pregnant. Perhaps he'd been wrong. Perhaps the Brit had not been on the prowl.

Stephen thought fast. All his men were prisoners, as was he. Jillian's safety was at stake as well.

"I was taking her to Barbados to stay with friends. I'd intended joining your fight as soon as she was safely tucked away. Times do change you know, and so do loyalties."

Andrew was skeptical. One brow raised, he surveyed the faces of the captured crew. "I didn't see any lowering of the British flag."

"You didn't exactly give me a chance. We took a French ship two days ago. My crew was split, exhausted. And I'm not saying I'm friends to the Frenchies as well. I'll only go so far. You, though, you could use some help. Your coast is full of British ships. What better way to pass than to fly the flag? I needed to get my wife to safety – and I didn't expect Americans this far south."

Andrew considered. He took in Jillian's appearance. She looked like a lady, not some doxy, but she was dressed simply. He had an idea. He took Jillian's arm and tugged her to the railing. One of his officers held her there. He watched Stephen's eyes narrow dangerously as the man tensed.

"I will make you a pact, St.James. You will fight with us, aboard your own ship. I'll pad out the crew with my men. Your wife will go with me as a hostage until your duty is satisfied. Any diviation from your patriotism and she will reside in prison – one of ours."

Stephen lunged at the man but was pulled to a halt by his captors. His head throbbed, his gut wrenched with fury. "Damn you, man. She's done you no harm. She's almost to term. I've given my word."

One of Stephen's own crewmen cackled. "Aye, his word, but would he care? He bought the woman off a Barbary pirate. She ain't his wife."

If looks could kill the man would be gutted on the spot. Nostrils flared as Stephen met Captain Andrew's steady gaze.

"It's true I paid the ransom – the purchase price – for my lady. She was to be sold into degradation. However, the papers declaring ownership also made her my wife under Muslim law." He switched his eyes to Jillian, trying to communicate, willing her to silence. "In London the papers were filed and the marriage made legal under English law. She is my wife and she carries my child." He saw a single tear trickle down her cheek and his heart caught. Would she refuse to acknowledge the marriage? Would she refuse him altogether? He took a step toward her but was jerked back.

Andrew looked from one to the other. The lady hadn't taken her eyes from St.James. A slow smile cracked his sun-bronzed face. Wife or no, the man cared for the woman - and deeply. It would serve.

"My decision stands. She comes with me." He motioned to his officer and Jillian was bundled across to his ship. He ignored his prisoner's outcry to the woman.

"I'll find you, Jillian. I'll come for you – when this is over - ."

The captain turned to St.James. "Release him." He waited while the ropes were undone. The woman stood aboad his ship's deck now, gazing back at them.

Stephen growled deep in his throat. He took a menancing step in the rebel captain's direction. "If you harm one hair on her head I'll hunt you down, you and yours. I'll do my duty. See you do yours. She's near birthing -." His voice cracked. She was watching him intently but her expression was unreadable.

Andrew nodded. "She'll come to no harm. I've a sister, Amy, near Charleston. I'll leave word there as to her whereabouts – in case something happens to me."

Andrew motioned to the crewman who'd been so outspoken against his own captain. "Put him in chains. The hold is good enough for such disloyalty."

"She's nothing but a ship's whore, I tell you. Fled London 'cause she was breeding – right into that pirate's arms. St.James can't be trusted for the likes of her. You're making a mistake." The seaman lunged for the rail. "Let me work your ship. I won't sail for a fool."

"Seize him." Captain Andrew positioned himself before St.James who was trying his best to get at the man. "I'd not believe the likes of him against your word even if you are a pirate." He nodded at the seaman. "Take him below."

The man cursed, pleading for mercy, as he was dragged off. “He’s yours to do with as you see fit. Your lady is safe as long as your word stands.”

CHAPTER THIRTY-ONE

Stephen's ship, along with the other two American owned ships, was dispatched to the Boston area. There they hoped to prevent the British troops trapped in the city from receiving reinforcements and supplies from the sea. The British navy was formidible but American privateers could be like stinging hornets, attacking and disappearing, fighting with undisciplined and unpredictable enthusiasm.

Winter was soon upon them and the northern storms made life at sea miserable. It was worse in Boston. The British had taken to tearing down old houses for fuel. Smallpox was rampant. And just so near were the ragtag American forces, short of fuel, bored, but forever watching. Both sides waited.

Captain Andrew Brandon remained near the southern coast. There must be a way to deposit his prisoner in Charleston at his sister's. Then he would join in the haphazard blockade.

Disgusted, Andrew watched the boiling sky; a late tropical storm by the looks of it. Black clouds hung over the churning sea, their color tinged with odd shades of greens and gold. The sun was setting and they'd not make port before it hit.

He sent word to his guest to stay below, preferably in the bed where it was soft. He called every able-bodied man topside. They were in for a long night.

…………………………………………...………………....

Jillian thought the ship would sink. She'd been in storms but never anything like this. No matter her determination to remain on the bed she was thrown about like a cork.

She'd never see Stephen again, never tell him she loved him. Tears filled her eyes and she angrily dashed them away. Then the pains started. Clutching the bedpost she prayed the baby would wait. But the pains became worse and she looked about frantically for padding for the bed, for a knife to cut the cord, for – what? What did one do?

She was reaching for a basin when a wild bucking of the ship sent her sliding across the floor. Her head hit the bulkhead and she knew no more.

The sea finally calmed. Andrew decided to check on his guest. She was probably frantic. He knocked and when there was no answer he opened the cabin door.

Dear God! She was lying in the floor, a quilt knotted in one fist, her knees drawn up to her chin. He lifted her and took her to the bed. There was a large lump on her head but no other damage.

Jillian moaned and opened her eyes. The captain's worried face hovered over her. "The baby – it's time, I think." She caught his strong hand as another pain hit her. He turned a good shade paler but brushed her hair back with his other hand.

"It's too early. It will wait. We'll be in port soon. We've been blown off course but -." He frowned as she squeezed his hand again. "I'll get MacIntosh – ship's surgeon." He pried her fingers loose and fled.

Reality hit him. MacIntosh had a broken right arm suffered in last night's storm. Still, he dragged the man to the cabin.

The old man surveyed his patient. "It's your time, M'am, rightly so." He smiled at his captain. "Been a while since I've been asked to assist a birth. Even so, can't do much with this arm. You're goin' to have to do it, Andrew."

As Andrew shook his head the old man started giving him a list of what was needed. Periodically he patted Jillian's cheek to soothe her. Jillian would have laughed but the pains were coming faster and she couldn't quite manage it. She noted that Andrew had mastered his trepidations and was bucking up to the job at hand though. That made her feel better.

Now morning sunlight streamed through the open window. The day was clear after the storm, washed of sin, her mother used to say. Jillian's hair clung damply to her temples in the close air. How long did it take to have a baby, anyway? She closed her eyes once more, her long lashes stark on her pale cheeks, and held onto the captain's firm hand. The old man was feeling beneath the quilt and nodding.

She gazed into the face bending over her. "Whatever happens, Captain, thank you for trying."

He smiled and pressed the cool cloth to her forehead. “Andrew, call me Andrew. After all, we’ve gotten to know each other quite well.” He raised her fingertips to his mouth, kissing them gently. Somehow it seemed appropriate.

MacIntosh cleared his throat. “Time you took over here, Captain.” He watched Jillian’s determined grimace as her eyes squeezed shut once more. “The head’s crowning. Here, Sir.” He moved aside.

With a look of awe, Andrew felt the small body slid into his hands. He laughed. He’d never imagined anything like it. His expression was that of a small boy who’d caught his first fish. His tousled hair framed his face and the crinkles at the corners of his eyes seemed more relaxed. He met Jillian’s smiling eyes knowing he should be embarrassed. Then the doc was giving orders again and he bent to the task at hand.

A loud wail rent the air as he held the baby aloft. He grinned from ear to ear. “You have a son, My Lady, a beautiful son.” He took a deep breath to keep from whooping.

He and the doc together cleaned the child with sweet oil and wrapped him in a soft cloth. Ever so gentle, he placed the boy in his mother’s arms. He watched her grey eyes soften as she kissed the downy cheek. She was so beautiful. Perhaps all women were beautiful at this moment. His heart swelled with tenderness. Quickly he looked away and rose to his feet.

He flung the door open and called to the seamen without, “It’s a boy! Mother and child are well!” There was an outcry of good wishes. They’d all been waiting, as proud as new papas.

He returned to her side. "And what will you name him, Mistress?" He reached out to allow the tiny fist to curl about his long finger.

"I think you may call me Jillian after what we've shared, don't you, Sir?" She nibbled on her lip as she noted his fond caress of the child. "I think he should be called Stephen Andrew St.James, after the two men who've mattered most in his life. What think you?" She cut her eyes up to his.

"I think I would be indeed honored. I hope he will be pleased to have two ship captains related in his naming." He beamed in delight.

…………………………………………....…………………....

She'd been up and about in two days. After all, being the only woman aboard was awkward enough without requiring assistance with everything. Her mother would've been shocked as it was.

She dozed in the chair as she nursed her son. The breeze carried fresh air and sunshine into the cabin and his rosebud mouth had lulled her into a daze. She was unaware of the door opening or of the man standing there.

Captain Andrew closed the door softly and simply stood, absolving the domestic scene before him. The baby sucked occasionally at her full breast but both seemed to be sleeping. Sunlight turned her hair to gold where it spread about her shoulders. The child's tiny fist was caught in one long strand as though reaching for an anchor. He stirred, realeasing her tit and, nuzzling, fell back asleep.

Andrew's breath caught, his chest tightened. He wanted to go to them, encompass them in his arms, bury his face between her breasts, kiss her full lips. The urge was so intense he had to force himself to be still. Was he in love with Jillian? Another man's wife? He shook his head to clear the thoughts and she stirred.

Sleepy grey-green eyes focused on him and those sensuous lips curved into a smile. She wore a pale green gown today, at the moment unbuttoned to allow the baby sustenance. She glanced downward, moved the baby lower, and attempted to button her bodice with her free hand.

He hadn't meant to – hadn't thought – but somehow he was there, kneeling before her, his fingers fastening the buttons. The feel of her soft skin where his fingers had brushed against her sent chills up his arm. He realized what he'd done when her lips parted as though to chastise him, her hand brushing at his; but she said nothing.

He looked up into those turbulent eyes, noticed the pink now flushing her cheeks, but could offer no excuse for his behavior. Still, their hands touched. He leaned closer, the desire to kiss her burning in him.

The baby awoke, squirming, stretching. Almost with relief, Andrew rose to his feet. He tore his eyes from her full lips, focused on the child. His voice was like gravel when he finally spoke.

"I'll see to a wet nurse as soon as you're in Charleston. Amy, my sister, will know someone."

Jillian came to life. What had he just said? He'd almost kissed her. She was sure. And now he was giving her orders?

"I will nurse him myself. This isn't London where it's considered poor taste and I am your hostage, am I not? Not a lady of the ton anymore."

His jaw clenched stubbornly. "You are, indeed, under my direction and in St.James' absense, I will see to it that you do not damage your – um – assets. A lady need not risk her figure when a substitute is easily affordable."

Her face flamed. She shifted the baby to the crib at her side and stood up. A little shaky still, she swayed a bit at the sudden movement.

Andrew's hands steadied her immediately. They stood thus, niether withdrawing, until his mouth crooked upward into a smile. "Do you really wish to fight with me, My Lady? You'll lose. I am as your husband until he reappears on the scene and you will obey me in this."

Unable to help himself, his eyes dropped to the overflowing bodice of her gown. "And God help me if he doesn't return." He forced his hands to his sides, took a step back. "Forgive me - ." He hesitated but she said nothing, her eyes melting his senses with their intensity. He fled the cabin.

Jillian nibbled on her lower lip, a small frown marring her forehead. The captain was an imposing man, a more than handsome man, and he was on the verge of becoming a problem. She would admit she felt an attraction to him but he was not Stephen. He had held her hand, soothed her belly during labor, even performed the actual delivery as the so-called doctor spewed directions. He'd seen her at her worst – all of her. Why his simple touch now caused so much emotion was confusing. She wanted his comfort, strength, his maleness; but she loved Stephen. Tears welled in her eyes. Why couldn't life be simple?

……………………………………………………….

At last they'd docked in a cove near the city. There were British ships in the harbour and Andrew was taking no chances with the woman and baby aboard. He sent spies into town for news and to hire a wagon for transport.

By the next day Jillian and the baby were safe at his sister's house near the market. He'd given Amy only enough information to know that Jillian was to be protected but kept there until his return – even if it meant by force. One of his men was left at the house in case there was any doubt of her status. He would serve as both protection and jailor as needed.

Amy, a widow, was ten years Andrew's senior. Her sandy hair was speckled with grey and tiny freckles danced across the bridge of her nose. Her husband had left her well enough off and she was content with her lot – or thought she was until Jillian came. Andrew had been in such a hurry to leave. What was she to think?

One glimpse of little Andy and she was in love. Why had God not given her children? She took him from Jillian's arms, cooing to him, touching his tiny nose. "Oh, you're just like your dada, aren't you, little man?" She looked up to see the blush spreading over her guest's face. Confused, she patted Jillian's arm. Perhaps they were not yet wed?

"I'm so sorry, dear. I'm sure my brother will do right by you when he comes back. The war and all - - but I saw the way he looks at you."

Jillian's breath caught in her throat, choking her. She thought - . She shook her head, reaching for her son.

"He's not – Andrew's not – "

"But his name is Andrew?" Amy looked puzzled.

"His name is Stephen Andrew. My husband is Stephen St.James. Your brother, umm, was present when I gave birth and I named him - ."

She got no further. Amy hugged her to her bountiful breast causing little Andy to wail. "I'm so embarrassed. Please let's start over. I just assumed – Andrew didn't really say -." And her brother was smitten with this lady if ever she saw it. She shook her head. There would be trouble before this was over.

"Let me show you upstairs. You can have the front room. It's Andrew's when he's here but it's the largest and you'll have the morning sun." She hurried toward the stairs to cover her embarrassment.

Days turned into weeks. Jillian was restless once her strength returned in full. There was no word from either of the men. The house had a high walled garden that was quite lovely and she spent hours there. Her silent protector did not wish her to go into the city but he was not always present and at last she talked Amy into taking her to the market with her. The many booths were busy and ladies followed by black servants twined their way through the narrow aisles.

Amy stopped to wave at a petite blond. The girl was so pretty she appeared fragile. Dressed all in pale blue she was more like a butterfly than a flesh and blood being as she crossed to their side.

"Sally Burton, I'd like you to meet my house guest, Jillian St.James." Amy turned to Jillian. "Sally has had her hat set for Andrew for a year now but he doesn't stay in port long enough to notice."

Sally's tinkle of laughter reminded Jillian of a princess in a fairy tale. She stared at the girl. So, she wanted Andrew, did she? A smile curled her full lips. Perhaps Sally would solve her problem. The girl appeared too inexperienced to handle a man like the captain but she could change that if she got the chance. A man like Andrew needed more substance to hold his interest.

"Why don't you come by for a visit? I'm sure Amy will be thrilled and I would love to get to know you. I don't have many friends here." Well, none, actually, but that was about to change.

Amy looked startled but smiled and nodded. What was the girl up to; - a new way to escape back to her husband? By now she'd wormed the whole story out of Jillian and did not quite approve of her brother's tactics. Still, she was not about to allow the girl too much freedom.

There were no more forays into the city. Amy did not wish to go against her brother's instructions. If the girl needed to be kept in the house that is what she should do. It was hard enough to refuse Sally's offers of an occasional outing. She should never have taken Jillian to the market. Even with the baby in the house, mightn't the girl escape? She was a hostage, wasn't she? And she couldn't confide in Sally Burton whose parents had fled to England.

……………………………………………...………………....

The day was dreary with clouds scudding across the sky. Amy had developed a fever and a racking cough in the night. She insisted she was fine but Jillian wasn't so sure. She remembered seeing an apothecary shop two blocks over; close enough to justify her trip for medicine. She was so sick and tired of the house. It was the perfect excuse to escape for a little while.

Jillian donned her oldest dress and pulled a shawl over her shoulders. She borrowed one of Amy's bonnets to cover her braided hair. There; one look in the mirror was all that was needed. No one would recognize her and she'd be right back. Amy wouldn't be angry if she returned with the medicine. She slipped out of the garden gate and into the street.

The shop had been easy to find and she was almost home. Every breath of fresh air was dear, even if there was little sunshine today. Suddenly her path was blocked by a man in uniform, his red jacket declaring him British. She kept her eyes down and stepped aside but he followed her maneuver. Damn!

She tilted her head back to look up at him. It was a mistake. He smiled with a toothy grin and gave her a small bow.

"Where to, Mistress? I could buy ye a mug o'ale or maybe a ribbon? Just for a little company – what'd you say?"

Oh, Lord, she'd not dressed well enough to discourage such a situation. She nibbled on the corner of her lip, shaking her head, and tried to step around him.

His face reddened, he reached for her shoulders. Her bonnet fell off and the shawl joined it in the dust of the street. Her hand resounded against his cheek but he only laughed and lowered his head. Good grief, was the idiot going to kiss her? Furious, Jillian kicked him in the shin.

"Now, what'd ye do that for? All I want is a bit of company? You colonials think you're too good for His Majesty's men, do you?" His hand caught her bottom, squeezing, as he again lowered his head.

Jillian was considering murder when a horse butted against the man as its owner dismounted. She looked up into blue, blue, eyes – eyes that were only a shade lighter than his jacket. The handsome face of Captain Boyce Garrett, his blond hair and uniform impeccable, gazed at her in shock.

He barked an order at the soldier who hastily backed away. When he turned to Jillian again his expression was one of disbelief. It had to be her, the "Crimson Lady", as he and his besotted fellows had called her. The drab dress did nothing to enhance her lovely breasts but he knew their beauty. Hadn't they caused him hours of discomfort after that dance? And hadn't gossip connected her to his friend, Stephen St.James?

He lost his manners. His gaze fastened on her luscious mouth. "What the hell are you doing here? Are you in trouble? Is St.James with you?"

Jillian panicked. He knew her. She stooped to retrieve her shawl to gain time but he reached for the bonnet, brushing it off, running his fingers around the ruching before handing it back to her.

Her expression frozen she met his eyes, one brow raised in question. "Thank you so much, Sir. I don't know what I would've done without your help. My baby – my little boy - was ill and I only went to the apothecary for a bit of medicine. Everything is fine now. Thank you again." She took the bonnet. At that moment her pinned braids chose to loosen and part of her hair spilled down.

His fingers reached to touch the cascade, his expression unreadable. She backed away. If they knew Stephen fought for the colonials he would be hanged. Her heart pounded against her chest. She didn't dare confide in this man, friend or no friend. He was British Navy, wasn't he? What if Stephen attacked his ship by accident? She forced the thought away. She had to get rid of him.

"Please, Sir, I do not know you." She pulled the lock of hair from his grasp. "Thank you again but I must be going." She turned and walked away as quickly as she dared.

He stood in the middle of the road watching her. She could feel his eyes on her back. She didn't dare enter the house and walked past it and around the next corner before ducking through an opening in a wall

"Never again," she muttered to herself. "I'll not chance it ever again." The house no longer seemed a prison but a refuge.

CHAPTER THIRTY-TWO

The baby had been moved to the upstairs nursery. After all, it had been crowded in the bedroom with his cradle and now he was in a small bed. How fast they grew. He was walking a bit and Jillian wanted to weep every time she pictured the miniature Stephen. So like his father, with soft brown eyes, his dark hair threatened to curl but only remained unruly rather than curly.

She talked to little Andy about his father – away at sea. She wanted him to know his dada when he appeared – if he ever did.

Tonight, like so many others, she was restless. She rose from bed and, without pulling on her robe, stepped out onto the verandah. The long porch ran the length of the house, allowing access from all the bedrooms. It was beautiful in the light of the full moon, peaceful. The heavy scents of hundreds of blossoms drifted into the night air. Jillian leaned against the railing, half-asleep, making a wish upon the twinkling star so far above the trees. She wished her Stephen would come for her, that she could feel his arms around her once again.

Perhaps he'd marry her when she presented their son. He had pretended, hadn't he? The lovable scoundrel – she cupped her breasts imaging it was his hands there, and sighed.

....

Capt. Andrew Brandon slipped through the alley door and into the silent house, stopping only long enough to remove his boots. It wouldn't do to wake his sister and the household this late at night. He'd surprise her in the morning.

His spying mission had taken longer than he'd planned. He needed to be back to the inlet and aboard ship in time for the tide but he could get a night's sleep first.

At the top of the stairs he turned to his old chamber and closed the door behind him. He didn't light a candle; didn't need to with moonlight spilling across the floor. He shed his cutlass, jacket, and shirt and stretched. Lord, it was good to be on firm ground for a little while at least. He pulled his socks off and began to unbutton the loose trousers he wore at sea.

Something blocked the moonlight from the open verandah doors. In distinct outline he recognized the woman who'd filled his dreams for the past months. She'd come to him! She must've heard his entrance. His heart pounding he swiftly closed the distance between them, stopping so close his bare chest brushed her thin chemise.

"Jillian." Her name was a throaty whisper just before he lowered his head and took her lips. So soft, full, and sweet; he ran his tongue along their seam until she opened for him with a little sigh. He didn't notice the hesitation of her response but he knew when she softened against his hard body, allowed him to pull her between his spread legs. His mouth devoured her, his hands roaming, her breasts crushed against him. Between kisses she'd murmered her lover's name – Stephen – but he ignored the whisper, pulling her into the dark room, pressing her against the wall.

Her fantasy worked his magic, taking her breath away. Stephen, no, it wasn't Stephen. She'd first thought he'd returned. Even his kiss – it'd been so long. Her fantasies had distorted the memories. Even as she realized the man pleasuring her was Andrew her nature betrayed her. She wanted, needed, the feel of a virile man. She melted into his strength, not thinking, only feeling.

Vaguely she was aware that his hand cupped her; that she was already wet with desire. It should have shamed her. She should push him away. But then his fingers slipped between the swollen lips, his fingers pushed deep, and she was quite lost.

Jillian's moans shattered any remaining doubts in Andrew's mind. She wanted him. She was hot and enticing; her body writhing against his maleness. He couldn't wait much longer.

His hand pulled the chemise downward allowing it to puddle about her ankles. He dipped his head to take a pouting nipple into his mouth, nipping, scrapping the tender tip with his teeth. He raised his head. Her eyes were closed. He ravished her mouth again, his hand once again between her legs. Too fast – too soon – his other hand closed about her thigh, raising it over his hip as he backed her against the wall.

Cupping her round bottom he lifted her just enough to plow deep with a single thrust. Dear God, she was like hot satin. He swallowed her gasp, his mouth open as his tongue mimicked the action of his shaft. Again – and again – he pumped into heaven as he shifted her hips for deeper penetration.

Her head was flung back allowing him access to her slendar throat as he filled her with white heat. He buried his teeth against the pulse in her neck, sucking, licking, before taking her lower lip into his mouth. He felt every tremor as she climaxed, her nails digging into his bare shoulders.

They stood, if one could call it standing, pressed together against the wall for support. Both of them drained, slick with perspiration. At last he lowered her leg but he didn't back away. Her head had fallen forward into the crook of his neck. Idly he ran his fingers through her hair, kissing her temple. Slowly, slowly, their breathing returned to normal.

She gave a soft laugh; her fingers playing with the curls of his chest hair, her face still hidden. He caught her chin and raised her face to kiss her swollen lips softly. She gave him a little push and he stepped back then took her hand and led her to the bed. He lifted her into the plump mattress and followed her down.

She rolled away from him but he wouldn't let her escape. One strong arm pulled her against him, her buttocks snug against his groin. She stiffened slightly but he didn't relax his grip about her waist.

"Talk to me. There's nothing to feel guilty about, Jillian. You're not wed; I know all about the sham he tried to pull."

"This shouldn't have happened. I was dreaming of him and then you were there. Why were you in my room anyway?"

Andrew's soothing hand ceased moving. "Your room? You came to me, Jilly. I always sleep in this room when I'm in town."

Her words were almost smothered by her pillow. "Amy gave me this room. This is my bedchamber." She was silent for a moment but half-turned toward him. "You thought - ?"

His mouth covered hers stopping any excuse she might have had. He turned her toward him, ravishing her lips, snuggling her body into his, until she ceased struggling and surrendered. Then he raised his head and looked smugly down at her.

"Discussion ended. We both enjoyed it and you know it. You're the best lay I've ever had." He was hardening again and rubbed her against him so she'd know it. "You may have just pretended you thought it was him but this time -."

Jillian couldn't help it; her breath quickened, her pulse raced, she laughed as her hips reacted to the weight of him, arching upward. His broad hand cupped her bottom and ground her tighter. He groaned into her ear, his tongue darting deep as his erection surged.

She shivered as need again swirled over her. She tried to contain the moan but it escaped as his hand closed over a breast. She moved her head from side to side to negate her actions. Too late; he was over her, the smooth tip breaching her slick curls. In surrender her legs spread and he slid inside. She sighed in contentment as his hips began to move and she matched his rhythm.

There was no excuse. They'd lain, exhausted, spoon fashion, for the rest of the night. Now dawn was breaking and they had to remedy their actions – or at least she had to. She'd barely drifted off to sleep, worrying, guilt-ridden, her body satiated for the first time in over a year.

Andrew ran his hand down the curve of her back. She didn't stir. He had to go. If he didn't make it appear he'd slept in the guest chamber – the one he'd thought was hers – he would face his sister's wrath and ruin Jillian's reputation. He leaned over her to kiss her cheek but somehow his shaft slipped between her bent knees. He grinned.

How would it be to be married to a woman like Jillian? Would he have a constant hard-on? He shifted his hips forward but she didn't awaken. How long would it be before he could see her again? He moved her leg and pushed into her wet heat, pulling her hips back against him. Out and then deep again; he shifted her almost to her knees before she sleepily opened her eyes. She shifted to accommodate him as he caught her breasts in both hands and spread her legs with his knee.

She mewed softly as he filled her, his balls slapping against her buttocks. So good, every touch of her was good. He waited until he felt her sheath pulse with a shivering climax before he allowed his own completion. He dug his fingers into her soft butt to push deep before he slid out. His hand slapped her bottom as she collasped onto the bed. Her protest brought a smile to his lips but he'd already rolled from the bed.

Working against the spreading light he gathered his clothing. Jillian watched his nude body, the muscles rippling. So alike they were – her two men. One dark, one lighter, but built much alike and both so big, so male. She tried to think of something to say; something to dismiss the sins of the night.

"You know I will wait for him. This never happened." She nibbled at her lip, her eyes shadowed, her mouth swollen from his kisses.

Andrew turned from pullling on his trousers, his gaze searing her. "This did happen. If I have a choice it will happen again. Have you even heard from him?"

Her temper was beginning to build, both at him and at what she'd done. "Heard from him? How can I? Have you even told him where I am? Andrew, please, listen to me. I should not have – we both should -."

His laugh was hollow, false. He came to stand beside the bed, looking down at her. "Yea, well we should not have but we did. And I am damn glad. Wait for him if you must but know that I want you. At least promise me you will tell him about tonight – some version of it. Promise me. Then come running to me when he leaves you. I'll be waiting."

Her lip trembled. "I'll tell him. He'll love me anyway." Her fingers splayed over her belly. "What if I'm - ."

"Pregnant? Then you're mine. I win." Andrew turned to the door but with his hand on the knob, looked back. "And, unlike some I know, I'll make an honest woman of you."

He was gone. She heard soft footsteps as he moved down the hallway. She prayed he made it to the bedroom before the maids were upstairs. Lord, but every part of her body ached. She lay back down, pulling the covers up to her chin. Oh, but the ache was a satisfying one.

Would Stephen forgive her? She didn't have to be that honest with him, did she? Just explain that she and Andrew had – had – what? Oh, why hadn't Stephen truly married her? It would've made a difference. She would be his wife, a loyal wife. She'd know he loved her and wanted her for always. A guilty tear rolled down her cheek. Oh, she was so tired and so lonely. She needed Stephen. Please, God, let him forgive her. It would never happen again; even if she had to wait two more years – ten - forever. All she needed was for him to want her, to take her to wife.

Dawn came fast. Andrew appeared in his doorway to order hot water at the first sounds of scurrying servants. He'd had little sleep but there was a smile on his face that wouldn't disappear.

She was everything he'd dreamed. The tales told him by St.James' mate held true. She was free with her passion and knew how to please a man – and this was only their first night together. Did he love her? He doubted there was such a thing as love but he cared for her and he'd see she wanted for nothing. He'd have her moaning his name only before he was through. No female trained in the East could deny the craving for sex for long if the tales were true. She was the tantalizing example. He'd had enough of perfect, obedient, dull, ladies.

He cocked his head to listen to noises from the end of the hall. His namesake was awake. Pulling on a shirt he padded down the polished hallway to the nursery.

He found it hard to separate the child and the mother. Both were so full of life. He held the little boy in his arms; shame his eyes were the chocolate brown of his father. The child pulled at his hair and Andrew grinned. "Say Papa – Papa." When the boy responded as bid, he laughed aloud and kissed the smooth cheek.

Jillian had slept until mid-morning. She was exhausted. When she awoke she ordered a bath and took her time with her toilet. What would she say when she saw him this morning? She peered into the mirror. Her lips were still swollen from his kisses and the love mark on her neck was reddened. Frowning, she asked the maid to change the bed linens even though they'd been changed only the day before. She ignored the peculiar look she received in return.

At least she was downstairs in time for a light luncheon. Amy was at the small table the family used, alone. She looked up as Jillian entered and took a seat. Amy's face was a mass of smiles.

"Guess what? Andrew was here last night. It'd been so long since I'd seen him. I wanted to wake you to say hello but he wouldn't allow it. He spent quite a while upstairs with little Andy – said the child called him 'Papa'. Isn't that sweet?"

Jillian felt a chill chase through her. "Papa? Surely he corrected Andy. He probably thinks any strange man is his papa."

Amy looked at her with a puzzled frown, a piece of buttered roll held suspended in one hand. "Why, what does it matter? He's confused is all; and it tickled Andrew. Umm, he said to tell you goodbye." She took a small bite of the hot roll.

"He's gone? Without -." She stopped. Why should it matter? Amy certainly didn't need to know she'd spent the night in his arms. She rubbed her neck – she'd tied a grosgrain ribbon there to cover the mark – and blushed. She dropped her hand. Amy was staring at her.

Amy licked the melted butter from her lip with a dainty gesture. She took in Jillian's appearance, the slipped ribbon, the overly-full lips. Just when had her brother come home?

She put the remaining bread down. She stood, coming around the table until she stood over the girl in her care. Her fingers touched the love-bite on Jillian's neck that was revealed by the slipped ribbon.

"What has my brother done, Jillian?"

Her voice trembled with the rush of emotions. "I thought he was Stephen. And then I knew he was not. Still I -."

When the long-lashed eyes filled with tears, she took the girl in her arms, hugging her against her ample bosom.

Patting Jillian's head, Amy waited for the tears to slow. In the silence that followed she once more took her seat across from the girl. She deliberately cut slices of ham and pushed some onto both plates. She met Jillian's eyes across the table.

"And do you still wish it to be Stephen that comes to your bed or has Andrew supplanted him?" Her expression was unreadable.

Jillian shook her head, concentrating on cutting the meat into the tiniest of pieces. “I wanted it to be Stephen. I miss him so. I love him so. But I don’t know how he feels about me.” She shrugged and laid the knife aside. “And Andrew? It was a mistake. He thought I’d come to him; I was in his old room, you know. But then we both knew it was only an excuse. I wanted him. He made me want him; and it was so easy.”

She took a long swallow of the strong coffee – no one drank tea just now. “I’m ashamed to say I – .“ She looked up into Amy’s eyes. “How can Stephen come for me if he doesn’t know where I am? Andrew promised, he promised.” She caught her lower lip between small white teeth. “And I promised I would tell him when he came – about what happened between us.”

Amy’s cup clattered as she sat it down. “Are you sure that’s wise? Men can be extremely possessive. If it’s Stephen you want then perhaps it’s best to say nothing. Surely my brother is enough of a gentleman to keep his mouth shut.”

Jillian shook her head. “He insists he will have me one way or another – and he seems sure that I will have no other choice once Stephen knows. Perhaps he’s right. My behavior is enough to confuse anyone.” She twiddled with her spoon. “Andrew is handsome, a good man. I buried the knowledge that he wasn’t Stephen. I needed him, his strength, his passion – I didn’t think; he forced me but after the first time I wanted it to happen – I more than wanted it – I craved more. I’m as guilty as he is.” She hung her head, her voice low. “Yet I love Stephen.”

Amy's fingers drummed on the table. First time? After the first time? Good lord. "Perhaps there's a way to distract Andrew. He's always gotten his way but he's never done anything so despicable. He pursues the unusual, excitement. Do you remember Sally Burton?"

…………………………………………...………………....

So it was that Sally was invited to the house for long afternoons. Her parents in London and only an elderly aunt for a chaperon, the girl was bored and more than eager for new company.

It was soon evident that Amy had been correct. The lovely slip of a girl was innocent of men but her head was filled with daydreams of Capt.Andrew Brandon. Her rosebud lips in a pout, her pale blond hair pulled up in a cascade of curls, she sank down onto the sofa across from Jillian. Her fingers self-consciously spread the skirts of her pale blue dress until it fell to a perfect sweep to the floor. Only the tips of her slippers were in sight beneath the yards of fabric.

Jillian leaned forward. "You see? Again you are worried about presenting the perfect picture; men don't want perfection. Better a small glimpse of petticoat, a silk stocking with the embroidered flowers leading upward from your ankle." Her smile was genuine as she plucked at the girl's hem, lifting it ever so little. "See? Much better. When you sit, catch the skirt mid-way down and it will cause the distraction to happen."

Sally laughed. She had a lovely laugh, soft and flirtatious even when there were only the two of them.

She leaned over the silver tray of little cakes on the low table. Her dainty fingers fluttered to cover the gapping gathers at her bodice but she caught the shake of Jillian's head and lowered her hand. She took a deep breath, lifted the tray, and offered a sweet to her hostess. The view was just what a gentleman would prefer.

Jillian smiled and nodded. "You're a good student. When it comes naturally, without thought, it will be fun."

The lessons progressed. At first no mention was made of the dashing sea captain. Sally drank in the advice on fashion, on flirtation, on conversation. When the subjects were exhausted the topics turned to spicier fare.

It took courage for Jillian to admit some of the things she'd done in the bedroom. It was not the usual topic for the ears of an unmarried lady. Still, the girl thought her to be a happily married woman. She gave Stephen, the missing husband, credit for teaching her how to entice and please a man. This information was passed along with much whispering and giggling on Sally's part. At first there was the admonition never to indulge in any of these antics unless blessed by marriage. Soon, however, the warnings took second place and Jillian could see the unfulfilled desires kindled behind those pure, blue, eyes. Would she be able to entice Andrew? To hold his interest?

"I wouldn't want you to be seduced, ravished, by some handsome lout – even Capt. Andrew – so be careful what you do." Jillian had just described in intimate detail the delights of returning a kiss. "The idea is to promise, not to give, until he has declared himself." Yes, she thought, if only I'd done just that.

Camaraderie between the two grew. Jillian had never had a female friend. She felt years older but was only Sally's senior by several years. She was having misgivings as she viewed her pupil in her new wardrobe. The girl's sensuous nature was displayed but ladylike, her mannerisms perfect for the game. Already she was the object of many local gentlemen's attention. Sally was delighted but withheld her favors. She was waiting for Andrew's return.

....

Jillian had enjoyed the days and weeks as Sally's accomplice. She needed to pass the time and to keep her mind off of the night with Andrew. She reviewed over and over her explanation to Stephen – her plea for forgiveness. With Andrew's attention on Sally – if their scheme worked – perhaps it freed her from having to confess?

She shook her head as she paced her room. No, she must be honest at least to a degree. Perhaps Stephen wouldn't care – perhaps she was worried for nothing. She closed her eyes, hugging herself. She wanted, oh, she wanted; his arms around her, his caress in her hair, his strong lips on hers. Why had she ever allowed Andrew to - ? She gritted her teeth. It had been so long!

She didn't even know if he would ask her to marry him. She thought once again of the lie he'd told aboard ship so they would treat her like a lady – a wife. Her eyes misted. If only it were true. But he'd not mentioned it before, had he?

Perhaps she should not have tutored Sally. Perhaps she would need Andrew as a protector, a husband. He was certainly willing. Had he sent Stephen to certain death? Is that why he'd not returned?

No, not Andrew; if Stephen didn't come back she would return to London. With a son, even her sister would not think she was a cause for jealousy. The St.James family would protect her from whoever had been trying to kill her. Little Andy was over a year old now. How long did she have to wait?

She and Amy read the news and listened to the gossip whenever there was word, which wasn't often. The Continentals were not giving up but neither were the British. Goods were sometimes hard to come by since more and more local-owned ships were being boarded, their cargo confiscated, their crews pressed into the British service. And now Charleston seemed overrun by Tory sympathizers. Redcoats were seen everywhere and arguments broke out in the taverns and in the streets. A militia was being formed - it was said by those who had nothing to lose but a hot head.

"Oh, Stephen, I miss you so." Her head on her arms, she allowed the tears to come. What did it manner if her eyes were reddened tomorrow? Who was there to care?

CHAPTER THIRTY-THREE

Stephen was still captain, master, of his vessel. Most of his men were Americans; his own crew having been absorbed into Captain Brandon's ship. Still, once his word was given he was committed as far as he was concerned. Jillian's safety came first but he had always admired the stubborn pride of the American colonists. His business ventures had done well there. Never would he have gotten caught up with politics, profit aside, if it had not been orders from his government.

Their travel northward was uneventful except for worsening weather. A week into the journey he sent for the shackled seaman to be brought before him. The man's name was O'Shields and he had signed on in London two days before they'd sailed.

Haggard and fearing for his life now, the man was eager enough to answer questions. He knew the odds were in favor of his being tossed into the sea.

"Are you in the habit of disputing your captain's word when your only knowledge is gossip? What did you think to gain? My death?" Stephen turned again to face him. "Or was it my wife's demise you sought?" He played with the blade of his knife as he spoke.

O'Shields' eyes fastened on the knife. "Guess I just wanted to be noticed – singled out, so to speak. Thought I might get picked for the Yank's crew, y'know." He'd had little to eat and been kept in total darkness. His nerves were stretched thin and if he was going to die he might as well say his piece. His eyes blinked in the bright light, irritated and itching.

"Not good enough. Your accent comes and goes – a bit of the East End, a bit of – where?" Stephen stepped close, the blade under the bound man's chin. "Why did you sign on board?" His boot stepped on the man's foot.

The seaman's beady eyes narrowed. "Weren't none of your business why. You pay, I work. I don't have to like working for your kind – keeping a woman aboard. And every one o' your crew knew she's a slave. They was there when you bought her right out of that harem. Needn't blame me if I thought the Yank might favor a bit of sharing."

Stephen backhanded him across the face. The man showed no reaction other than the snap of his head to one side. "You knew she was pregnant before she left London. How?" His face was so close he could smell the man's stale breath.

"Need I repeat the question? I'd as soon toss you into the sea as not. Save your scurvy hide and answer the question." His strong fingers tightened about the man's throat.

Choking, the man met Stephen's eyes and nodded best he could. The pressure lessened on his windpipe.

"I do investigations; paid well for it, too. The nob that employed me wanted her watched. If any harm was to come to her he'd pay extra. I wouldn't have hurt her meself, you understand." He twisted his neck but it felt no better.

"Of course not." Stephen's voice dripped sarcasm. "This nob's name?"

"He's a Marquis or something. Never gave me a name, exactly. Big man, house over on Covert Square; he wears a small beard."

"George Shanksbury by any chance? My wife's uncle?"

The expression on the man's face was answer enough. Stephen swore under his breath. "Did he give any reason for this mission? Any hint of a reason?"

The wily seaman shook his head but his shoulders straightened somewhat. Perhaps he could deal here.

"I could find out – if we was to return to London. I could tell him she disappeared into the colonies as a prisoner of the rebels."

Stephen said nothing. "Do you always do your dirty work without any conscience? Without knowledge of the people involved?" His dark eyes bored through the culprit.

His prisoner couldn't help but shiver. "Don't usually need to know. The Marquis – he did say something about she would ruin his family name. I think he wanted a painting or something she'd inherited." His beady eyes were unblinking once again. "Yes, that's what he said. If she were dead or gone for good he would have it. That's all I know, I swear it."

Stephen sent the man below again but he was fed and he would have a lantern but it kept well outside his reach. He was lying about how much he knew but Jillian's brother-in-law was the culprit just as he'd thought. But to go to so much trouble and expense? It had to be more than jealousy over her inheritance or her ignoring his authority. How had the man known she was pregnant? There must have been a spy in the house, a maid perhaps. And what was it that he was afraid of? What did Jillian have that he wanted so badly?

He penned his findings in a long letter to his father though when it could be posted to London he didn't have any idea. His contact with British shipping was definitely not friendly at the moment.

………………………………………….....………………....

Four miserable months later and the ships were to be sent south again. Stephen thanked his lucky stars. Enough of those confounded New England winters. He'd done his share of damage to British shipping and been heartily commended for it. There was word the British were leaving the area for the Carolinas again but stragglers still lurked in the waters.

In the past months he'd changed loyalties without realizing when it'd happened. He'd always be British but these brave men, from all walks of life, fighting for what they believed was right – well, it was hard not to admire them.

He'd been invited ashore for a meeting with their commander, a General George Washington, after his ship had taken a supply ship right out from under

English noses. He'd never been more impressed. The man was a natural leader, tall, demanding obedience with his mere presense. His army of rag-tag civilians was filled out with not near enough experienced officers. The turnover due to short enlistments kept their ranks churning and still they persisted against the best-trained and best provisioned army in the world. It was to be admired. They were tired and, lord, he was tired, bone weary.

He closed his eyes and pictured Jillian's face. He'd had no word from her but he knew where Andrew Brandon's ship was patrolling. It was time the man trusted him with her whereabouts. He'd beat it out of him if necessary. Did he have a son or a daughter? The child would be walking before he saw him or her if he wasn't careful. Pray God they were both all right. Women died in childbirth. What if Jillian had died? He shook off the feeling. No, he'd know if she were dead. He could feel her with him yet.

He was jerked back to the present by a shouted warning of sails on the horizon. Two British vessels were soon identified, one a man-'o-war, too large for his slate. He couldn't take both nor could he outrun them but by damn he'd not surrender without a fight.

……………………………………………....……………….…

Hours later Stephen St.James stood before Captain Boyce Garrett of the British Navy. Managing not to sway in exhaustion, he longed to wipe the trail of blood that tickled his temple as it made its way downward. His jacket was torn, his pants bloodstained, his wrists bound behind him. His bloodshot eyes met those of his captor. A half-smile touched his split lip. They were alone in the cabin.

"Been a long time, Boyce."

Hands clasped behind his back, one blond brow quirked upward, Garrett observed his prisoner. "Still up to school-boy pranks, huh, Stephen? What the bloody hell are you doing? Don't you know we're at war with these rebellious colonies?" Capt. Garrett paced the length of his table and back before he looked at his old school chum's face again. "I suppose you have an explanation why you attacked a ship belonging to the British Navy?"

Stephen straightened as best he could. "Can't say that I do, Captain. Seems I got swept into this thing and before I knew it -." He shrugged.

"You know all surviving hands are to be sent to England to the prison ships until this affair is settled." He cleared his throat. "It is said very few actually survive the journey across and less are likely to live until hostilities are settled. You've committed suicide, old friend."

"Don't suppose Papa will buy me out of this one, huh?" Stephen attempted a laugh but his lip split more and he licked at the cut.

The two men stared at each other for several minutes, both remembering shared escapades of two young lads in easier days. At last Boyce broke the silence. "Do you still swim?" When Stephen looked puzzled at the question, he continued, "Remember we used to swim in the river. You always beat me across. I couldn't manage the strong current."

Stephen nodded. "I still swim when I can. The coastal waters around the islands, further south, are pleasant." He grinned in spite of his hurt mouth. "All bets are that I can still beat you."

There was a knock on the thick door. Captain Garrett met his prisoner's weary eyes as the seaman entered. "This is not the man I knew in England; same name, different man. Take him below but tend to his wounds. As captain of a captured vessel he is to watched but is due extra rations. Keep him separate from the other prisoners." He shouldn't have made any explanation to a mere seaman but Garrett wanted no inkling of his connection to the prisoner.

Should he have mentioned his chance meeting with the lovely Lady Jillian Shanksbury? Drab or no, it was the Marquis' widow he'd seen in Charleston. He should put both of them under arrest. He should. She'd spoken of a child – a lie or was it true? Is that why she'd disappeared?

He turned his back on Stephen as he was hustled from the cabin. He was staring at a large map pinned to the bulkhead; a map showing the coast of the American colonies. Their orders were to sail south. They could offload the prisoners at their next rendevous with a returning ship. A vague idea was forming. It might work. If not, then heaven help Stephen St.James - and his lady.

No longer bound but surviving in complete dark Stephen shoved the stale bread into the broth and chewed slowly. Double rations? He'd hate to see what his crew subsisted on. His stomach growled in complaint. He blinked at the faint light shimmering through his barred door. It was getting closer.

The lantern blinded him for a moment but he was able to recognize his once friend's voice. The guard moved away and they were alone. Garrett stood over him and Stephen forced his stiff body to straighten.

"There's not much time. Tomorrow we meet the Lady Fair. She'll take on the prisoners and sail immediately for London. We'll be within reach of the coastal islands off the southern Carolinas. The weather is fair. Think you can reach land – you've strength for the swim?" Garrett peered at him in the semi-dark.

Stephen's grimy face split into a grin. "I'll wager you fifty pounds – to be paid at White's when next I see you."

Garrett returned the grin, reaching out to grasp his shoulder. "Taken. I'll do what I can. You'll have to go overboard when you see the chance but I'll keep them from shooting. I'll anchor as close to land as I dare. May God be with you – whatever you've gotten yourself into."

He turned to go, the lantern in his hand. "I saw an old friend of ours in Charleston, the widow Jillian Shakesbury." He watched the flash of pain flicker across St.James's face. "She was dressed as though in disguise, colonial drab, but it was she. She pretended she didn't know me but the look on her face -."

"Where? Where was she exactly? Did she have a – anyone – with her?" Stephen's heart was pounding. So, he had hidden her in the port city. He should've known. Had Capt. Brandon mentioned a sister? Perhaps she lived in Charleston.

"She was alone, and skittish as a young colt. It was near Bedon's Alley and she mentioned she'd been to an apothecary shop – something about medicine for her baby – a son, I believe."

"A son? I have a son?" Stephen grabbed his old friend about the shoulders, thumping him on the back.

"So that's how it is?" Garrett managed to speak amid the thumps. "I'd guessed as much. Whose idea was joining the colonials?"

"It was an accident. I'll explain when I see you at White's, old man. A son – thank God she's all right." Stephen ran his hands through his hair. He hadn't realized how worried he'd been.

"Boyce – hate to ask more but there was a letter, to my father, in my desk. If you have it could you see he gets it? It has nothing to do with this war, I so swear."

Garrett nodded his consent. "Your personal possessions are in my cabin including your papers. I'll send it with my dispatches."

The next day was overcast but the sea was calm. Stephen was among the first to be taken above decks so his eyes had time to adjust to the light. Confusion reined as the prisoners milled about. They began to climb down to the boat for the transfer to the Lady Fair.

From the corner of his eye Stephen saw Capt. Garrett step closer. His boot crushed down on a large prisoner's naked foot. The man cursed, jostling into the man next to him who shoved back. The seaman in the process of climbing onto the rope ladder lost his grip and fell. The British crewmen attending them shouted orders to restore order, leaning over the rail to see where the luckless man had landed.

Stephen stepped backward into the space cleared by his cohort. With a run to the opposite side and a swandive he was clear of the ship. Cool water closed over his head. He felt the excitement take him as he struck out with powerful strokes.

Above, two soldiers sighted rifles on the escapee. Passengers themselves, they'd kept their equipment by their sides. Capt. Garrett was quick to knock the barrels aside.

"Don't waste your powder. He'll not get far." He forced his attention back to the others, praying they'd obey, praying Stephen's old prowess in the water would be enough.

....

The lure of the sandy beach drew him. His shoulders ached, the calves of both legs jerked at the unaccustomed exercise. Several times he attempted to touch bottom before his toes dug into sand. Thank God. With a final struggle he forced his tired body onto the tiny open stretch of land and rolled into the reedy growth out of sight. He raised his head. The ships were still there but no one was coming after him. He grimaced as he watched them. The irony of it; the Lady Fair was his own Tempest, now repaired and carrying the British flag once again.

When he awoke the sun was setting. How could he have slept? The horizon was deserted but he could see another island in the near distance and yet another. Could he be near Charleston? Garrett had said he was on the Carolina shores. He staggered erect and began to explore his domain.

Around the bend there was a small dock, now deserted. Several dinghies were overturned on the sand and a small sailboat was anchored nearby in the water. He looked inland, and decided to follow the path. Half a mile or so the tangled trees cleared. A ramshackle house with a wide rustic porch stood in the clearing. Several small cabins spread out behind the main house. There were lights in one room of the house and he headed for that. He hoped they didn't shoot on sight.

A dog barked before he'd gone far. Stephen stopped to hold out his hand and the animal nuzzled into his fingers. Together they walked onto the porch just as the door opened.

"Well, I'll be." The white-haired old man took in the apparition that had appeared before him. An old musket was cradled in one arm. "Escaped have ye? Which side?" He looked Stephen up and down.

Stephen grinned. The old fellow didn't look very dangerous but one never could tell. "Depends on where I am. Could you spare some supper? I'd be much obliged." He idly patted the hound's head.

The old man called to someone over his shoulder and stepped back to allow Stephen entry. A young black girl scurried out the back door as he entered. He stopped just inside, waiting.

The house was clean; the walls white-washed. The furniture was worn but had once been expensive. A woven rug covered part of the pine floor. His host led the way to the lighted room where an elaborate pewter candelabra was aglow on the spread table. Several dishes, still steaming, made Stephen's mouth water.

"Help yourself. Name's Kirkland, Clem Kirkland." He took his seat again and continued eating.

Mouth watering, Stephen helped himself to venison stew, hot rolls, butter, and potatoes. "I'm Captain Stephen St.James, originally from London. Politics undecided, but I just escaped being a prisoner of the British Navy." He sighed as the hot savory stew settled in his stomach.

His host just grunted and shoveled another spoonful of stew into his mouth. The hound had joined them, lying across Stephen's feet under the table.

The meal continued in silence. When both men had eaten their fill they pushed back from the table. Kirkland nodded toward the porch. "Care for a smoke?"

He stood and Stephen followed him outside where the old man settled into a rocking chair. Stephen sat on the steps. He took the proffered tobacco then passed it back to his host. Blue smoke curled into the night. Mosquitoes buzzed about his ear and he swatted at the air. The old man chuckled.

"Wife died two years ago. Don't go into town much now. Don't care 'bout this disagreement. She drank tea, liked fancy things. I don't care where you come from or where you're going. Care to sleep here tonight, you're welcome." With an effort, he rose to his feet. "I'm for turning in 'fore the 'squitoes eat us."

Stephen nodded his assent. "Thanks. I'll be on my way in the morning if it's possible."

He was too tired to think of any hidden danger. The old man appeared to be alone except for some servants, probably slaves, in the cabins. What would be, would be.

He dreamed of Jillian; Jillian welcoming him with a small baby in her arms. He woke up hard and sweating beneath the netting. His hand covered his erection as he pictured her hot mouth pleasuring him. Was she wanting him? Did he invade her dreams as she did his? Did she awaken slick with need? Oh, God, she was a craving in his blood.

…………………………………………....…………………....

It'd taken almost a week but he was in the city. Ignoring the stares he made for the old warehouse that served as an office when his company had transacted business here. He stepped inside and blinked. There were no goods stacked to the rafters, no sounds of busy loading. Somewhere a drip splashed onto rock with an annoying repetition.

He crossed to the closed doors on his right. It was mid-morning but the light here was augmented with a lamp on the old desk. His back to the door a stoop-shouldered young man was packing papers into crates.

"Hello, Jamison." Stephen's voice echoed in the near-empty space causing the worker to start and turn, dropping his handful of documents.

"Oh, oh, Mr. St.James, Sir – no one expected to see you. Again, I mean no one expected to see you so soon, again." His voice quavered into a stutter. He gathered the dropped papers into a little pile.

Stephen's dark eyebrow peaked in question. "Really? And whose instructions have been followed as to my commodities?" He looked back over his shoulder at the empty warehouse. "Where are they?"

"Gone. They're gone, Sir. The British have taken them. But they left receipts to be collected later. We could do nothing to stop it, Sir. If you hadn't been British they'd not have given even the receipts."

Tongue in cheek, Stephen grunted his answer. The receipts were worthless. He'd have been better off to have donated the goods. But then, he'd not been here. If they'd known he'd fought with the colonials would they have fired the warehouse? No, probably not. That would endanger the entire city. He surveyed the cramped room.

"Are my personal belongings still intact?" He'd always kept a few clothes including evening wear at each location just in case it was needed.

"Oh yes, Sir. I personally saw to it." His expression spoke volumes as he took in his employer's appearance. "I'll have them delivered wherever you wish, Sir."

Two hours later, bathed and dressed, Stephen St.James again felt like a member of the human race, the British nobility, the king of his domain. Now all he had to do was locate his wife; and do some explaining.

His first stop was at a goldsmith's where he ordered a simple gold band, one wide enough to engrave with their entwined names and a note of his love within. Since the man had to obtain usuable gold locally or the ring itself from England it might be a while before it was available. Law was strict on local craftsmen and now circumstances made it more difficult.

Neverlheless, Stephen paid in full and instructed the man to keep the ring until he retrieved it. He did, however, give him Jillian's full name should something happen to him. When they returned to London he'd see to more appropriate jewelry, a ring splendid enough for his lady wife.

He'd learned Capt. Andrew Brandon's sister's name at the goldsmith but the man wasn't sure where she resided. He began visiting the apothecary shops; there were several. The one nearest Bedon's Alley gave him the address.

The house was of brick with tall windows open to catch the breeze. It was on a corner and he walked past the front door to the elaborate wrought iron gate set into the garden wall. A gnarled oak tree of gigantic proportions spread over the wall and shaded the cobbled street. On one low limb a rope swing, one like he remembered from his childhood in England, moved gently back and forth. And in the swing was Jillian St.James, her toe touching the flower-petaled ground ever so often.

He stared; a smile touched his lips and sank into his heart. One hand on the gate, he cleared his throat. She looked up. A light breeze stirred a shower of flower petals across the path, pink petals landing in her hair, caressing her cheek as they fell.

He didn't know how they got there but they were in each other's arms, laughing, their hands full of each other. His mouth caught hers, brushing gently then demanding as he pulled her tighter between his hips. The soft fabric of her dress was as nothing. She stood on tiptoe, her arms about his neck, her fingers threaded in his hair.

At last he broke the kiss, holding her from him enough to look at her. The neckline of her dress was askrew, her arms still about his neck, her full breasts pressed close. He dipped his head and kissed where her pulse raced, nibbled the lobe of one ear. His hand weighed one breast, roughing the tip until it pebbled for him. She laughed in delight, her hands dropping to slip under his jacket, spreading over his chest in circles. His manhood responded with instant hardening.

"Much more, darling, and we'll disgrace our hostess." In response he felt the lightest touch of her fingers against his swollen shaft. A groan escaped. "Damn polite society. I need you - now. Is there somewhere?" He looked over the little garden as though there might be a hidden escape.

The garden was larger than it had first appeared, rounding back into a deep section to the side of the house. Near the back wall was a gazebo, roofed. Trellises covered in tiny budded climbing roses shaded the inside. He pulled her in that direction, hoping against hope it would be secluded.

Inside were benches secured to the outside braces. Laughing, he drew her with him to the fartherest one where the pale flowers hung low. No words were spoken; none were needed. Removing his jacket he lay her down upon it and covered her with his hard body as his hand snaked beneath her skirts. His mouth ravaged hers, his tongue tasting her sweetness. Her small hand cupped him and squeezed gently and he lifted his head, his eyes closed, to catch his breath. When his head again lowered he nuzzled into her bodice, his teeth catching the taut nipple found there.

He twisted then suckled as she squirmed under him. Her hand closed on his erection, rubbing until he was almost mad. He removed her hand, trying to unfasten his pants before it was too late. Her hips arched to meet him, her skirts bunched high.

He relinquished the unfastening to her fingers. His turned to feel the slick heat between her legs, slipping two fingers within. She dug her heels against the bench, trembling, as his tongue matched the actions of those long fingers.

He felt her spasms begin and he retreated, forcing his trousers open so he could spring free. A moment and he was buried deep between her legs, his long craving punishing them both as he pumped his life-blood into her. She came in a burst of light that took her strength, pulsing about him, sucking him deeper. His heaven was immediate, devouring, possessing. If he never lived past this moment, it was enough. He collasped upon her soft body, exhausted.

Her legs spread, her skirts twisted about him, she licked his neck, kissing him as he lay heavy. He was back. Her love was back. She nuzzled into his perspiring throat and sighed with happiness.

A noise from the house awakened him. Good lord, but he'd fallen asleep. So content, so sated, his body pressing down on her softness. He raised up on his elbows and looked down into her laughing eyes. One of his hands was still cupped about her pale breast.

"It might be wise if we -." Her soft voice trailed off and he heard the female again calling her name. He leaned down and licked the tip of the exposed breast, watching it pebble hard, grinning, before he pulled the bodice up to cover it.

His hand cupped the underside of her exposed knee, ran lightly up her thigh to squeeze her buttock. Slowly he slid from her body, adjusting his trousers, still crouched between her legs.

Jillian smiled saucily at him, her tongue touching her upper lip. His shaft hardened again with a jolt. "Damn temptress." His words were muttered with a crooked smile. He left her skirts up until he was decent, pushing her hands away when she half-heartedly tried to adjust them. Then he leaned over and kissed her belly, running his tongue into her navel. He laughed softly as she quivered at his touch.

"Do you know how long I've seen you just so in my dreams?" His voice vibrated against her tummy and she returned his laugh.

He lifted her to a sitting position and just as her skirts dropped to at least a presentable position Amy stepped into view. She stopped immediately, her mouth a round 'o'. She took a step backward.

"Oh, I am so sorry." She half turned to go then turned back. "You must be Stephen St.James. I hope you're Stephen St.James." Her hand covered her mouth and she ran for the house.

"Well, so much for dignity." Stephen brushed the petals that still clung from Jillian's hair. "I take it nothing shocks the lady."

"Ummm." That was all Jillian could get out. She cuddled under his arm as they stood. Her knees felt weak. He was stroking her head as though she were a kitten. She turned wide blue-green eyes up to him.

"I love you, Stephen. No matter what has happened or what is to happen, I love you."

One eyebrow raised, he leaned down and kissed her nose, then brushed her lips with his. "Perhaps I should go in for a formal introduction." Her words were what he'd longed for but did she mean it? His brother always said a woman lied as easily as spoke the truth after she'd been thoroughly loved – her mind dwelling on sex, not the soul.

Her fingers curled within his large hand and he felt a lump in his throat. She was everything he'd ever wanted and she was his. He'd take what love she was willing to give. It was time to confess he'd secretly forced her hand. She was his wife and had been since London. If the money bothered her it was hers to do with as she liked. He'd not touch it.

Amy almost succeeded in keeping a straight face as Jillian introduced Stephen. Tiny pink petals kept falling to the floor as the girl's fingers twiddled with her hair. Her cheeks were still pink and her lips plump. Amy's attention was drawn to the man at her side.

Tall, dark, and not altogether handsome St.James was striking. He and her brother were of a size but this man was more muscular. Immaculately dressed he still did not seem at ease in the tailored coat and trousers. He needs a gold earring and a pirate's sword, she thought. His eyes were warm chocolate as they seemed to memorize Jillian's face. Even a fool would know they'd just made love.

Jillian had stopped chattering. What had she said, asked? Amy smiled up at the tall stranger. "Perhaps you'd like something to drink? Then again, perhaps you'd like to be alone for a while. I'll just go and see -." She hurried from the room.

Jillian and Stephen looked at each other and laughed. There was so much to say neither knew where to start. Jillian knew she had to tell him about Andrew but not now, oh surely, not so soon. The baby – he needed to know he had a son. Both of them began to speak at once. Stephen's deep voice won out.

"That day when you were taken, when I said you were my wife – it was, is, true. I was waiting to tell you until the child was born, until I was sure the problem in London was solved and you were safe. I wanted you to make the choice, to be my wife, or not." He ran his hand through his hair as was his habit. At her frown, he stroked his fingers down her cheek, a slight smile on his lips.

"It was the money, your money. You are now a very wealthy woman in your own right. You should have had a choice and I didn't give you one. But I won't touch your money; it's yours. I've more than enough for us and -."

The slight flare of her nostrils should have warned him. Her voice had lost its softness. "Money? For some reason you think I am wealthy and independent and would not wish to wed you?"

The smile widened to his crooked grin, the grin no woman could resist – usually. "Of course it's too late now, darling. We're married."

"Married? How can we be married? You've never even asked me. First you made sure I was your chattel, your slave under Eastern law, then you 'freed' me but then I was carrying your child. And still you neglected to wed me properly. I waited and waited for you to say – to say that -." Her voice quavered and she blinked back tears as anger faded.

His arms were around her in a flash. He kissed her with tender care, her pouting lips, her eyelids, her nose, before holding her head against his chest. His hand stroked her hair.

"I love you, Jillian. I'd loved you so long and I wasn't sure you'd accept. The ceremony, the one that made you my slave actually made you my wife under Eastern law. When we arrived in London I had the papers filed and arranged our civil marriage by proxy since they thought you were out of the country."

When she said nothing he dropped to one knee, amusement once again flickering in his eyes. "Will you marry me, my lovely?" He brought her fingers to his lips, nuzzling each in turn.

She couldn't help it. Her laughter pealed across the room as she pulled him to his feet. "How can I if you're already my lord and master?" Her arms circled his broad chest as she hugged him.

"That's a 'yes'?" He tipped her chin up just as Amy reappeared. Without looking at their hostess he said, "I do believe we're engaged to be married. Now, that's a relief. Congratulations are in order."

"Well, a toast then." Amy crossed to the decanters, mumbling, "At least the boy will have a father."

"Oh, your son, how could I forget, you have this beautiful little boy and he looks just like you. Come, Andy's upstairs." Jillian took his hand starting for the stairs.

"Andy?" The name did not fit his image of his heir. "You named him Andy?" He'd stopped at the first step.

"Well, actually it's Stephen Andrew but we've been calling him Andy. After all, Andrew delivered him and -." She stopped at the look on her husband's face.

"He did what?"

Jillian's face tinged with color. "Andrew was there when he was born. There was no one else. There'd been a storm. We were still at sea." Her voice failed her. "I know it wasn't proper but sometimes -."

"Andrew Brandon saw you – was as good as intimate with you - ." His voice became a sputter. He looked from Jillian to the dark hallway at the head of the stairs. "And you named my son Andrew."

She shook her head as dread filled her. "It wasn't like that. Please, Stephen, try to understand. I might have died." Her hand squeezed his. "We can call him Stephen if you like. It's not yet official. I was waiting for you before -." She tugged but he didn't move. Oh, God, this wasn't happening. And now she didn't dare tell him about that one night. He'd never forgive her.

Suddenly the front door opened, slamming against the wall. An out of breath Andrew filled the entire doorframe. His gaze fastened on the couple frozen on the stairs, he took a deep breath and stepped within, closing the door behind him.

His sister, Amy, was still in the parlour. Delighted to see her brother she had almost run to greet him. Then she saw his expression and halted. She looked from Andrew's face to Stephen's and back again.

Andrew fought to keep his face blank. Jillian was still here. He hadn't taken her away. He still had a chance. Something inside of him relaxed.

"I thought it was you. I saw your ship in the harbour - Beaufort, escorted by a British warship. It's taking on provisions. Hell, what side are you on, anyway?" His mouth was a snarl as he glared at St.James.

Stephen loosed Jillian's hand as his fingers dropped to where his sword usually hung; but he was unarmed. He grimaced in disgust. This man had endangered everything he wanted from life and he was unarmed. His hands fisted. His expression must have been warning enough for suddenly petite Amy was between the men, her arms outstretched.

"Please, please both of you. Not in my house."

Jillian had descended to stand beside him and was clasping his sleeve. He forced his fists to relax and patted her hand but never took his eyes from his nemesis.

"I've fulfilled my promise to you. For the past year I've fought on the side of you Continentals, you Americans. You know damn well that's the truth." He harrumphed. "I've even begun to agree with your principles, some of them."

"Then explain the British flag flying there, the escort of limeys, the damn confiscation of stores -." Andrew got no further.

"Are you sure it's the Tempest anchored? I lost her some weeks ago to the British. If I'm not mistaken, her cargo at the moment consists of my crewmen taken prisoner, bound for the prison hulks."

Excitement was beginning to take him. Could he free his men – claim his ship? Speed was of the essence.

Andrew's eyes narrowed. He knew of Stephen's exploits against British shipping. The man was no liar; if anything was a hero. His eyes cut to Jillian. Had she told him? They'd been arguing when he'd burst through the door. He willed her to look at him but she would not. Separate them, he had to separate them again.

Hands out-turned, Andrew allowed a smile. "All right, so I know for a fact you've fought them well, more than well. I've had reports of the damage you've done. You can explain later what happened aboard the Tempest and how you happen to be here. Right now, with my help, we can intercept her if the warship leaves her side. I doubt she'll have so important an escort once she's out of port."

"Agreed." Stephen couldn't keep the grin from his face. He felt Jillian's fingers tighten about his arm but ignored her. "They'll be heading north to load more prisoners, I think. There were near a thousand taken after the Brooklyn, New York fiasco."

"What are we waiting for? Two of us are anchored in the cove out of sight. We'll have to get ahead of her to intercept. Are you with us?"

"I need to get my things – change - at the Lion's Inn." Stephen was already down the stairs, his hand on the door. "Meet me there."

Jillian came to life. He hadn't even seen his son. They had been arguing. She had so much to tell him. Her voice failed her but she ran to him and flung herself into his arms. Her head burrowed into his chest.

Stephen's smile was tender but his thoughts were already on what must be done. He stroked her hair, tipped her chin up, and kissed her soft lips. "Take care of our son. I've committed to this cause. I'll be back as soon as I can." He released her and hurried away.

Stunned, She watched him stride down the street. She whirled on Andrew who still stood in the hallway, a broad grin on his handsome face.

"You – you did that on purpose." She was so angry she sputtered, her chest heaving.

His eyes dropped to the lovely shape of her breasts as they rose and fell, moved up to the kiss swollen mouth. At last his clear eyes met hers.

"I see he lost no time in staking his claim once again. You told him about us, didn't you? But of course you did. You were arguing when I entered."

Jillian's hand caught the side of his handsome face. He didn't change expressions, just drew her into his arms, lowered his head and kissed her hard. She kicked him in the shins and he released her, laughing.

"For old times sakes, darling. So you don't forget me." He backed to the door, watching her. Lord, but she was a fiery one, a temptation to a man's soul. And he would have her if he could but he wanted her to want him, not St.James. Competition was the excitement that stoked his existence.

Jillian had stepped backwards until she felt the wall for support. Her eyes were wide with disbelief. "I'm his wife, Andrew, his wife. It's true. Tell me you're not leading him to his death. Promise me you'll bring him back to me. Promise."

The smile left his face. Perhaps he was mistaken in her feelings. Tears hovered on her lashes. His jaw clenched. He glanced over at his sister, who had not said a word, and then back at Jillian.

"I promise. I'll at least bring him back."

Andrew was gone. He'd closed the door so softly she wasn't sure. She crossed to lean against it, her hands pressed to the hard wood, her head bowed. She barely noticed Amy's arms about her as she turned into the consoling embrace.

CHAPTER THIRTY-FOUR
Late 1776

The day was humid, the sun broiling. There was no wind to fill the sails but the two ships waited for their prey anyway, their spyglasses on the horizon. Two days in this heat, tempers flaring, waiting.

At last a man had been sent into town for news. He reported back quickly. The warship was homeward bound as soon as the winds were favorable. The Tempest, now also outside the harbour, was thought to be sailing north. It was as they'd guessed. They were all at the mercy of the weather.

Stephen stood with one leg propped against a keg, his eyes on the distant clouds. Even they showed no intent of movement. He nodded as Andrew took up position beside him. So far the two men had avoided each other as much as possible.

"I should thank you for the care you took at my son's birth. Circumstances being what they were I'm sure you did what was necessary." Stephen's jaw clenched at his own forced words.

Amused, Andrew merely grunted. He wanted, nay, needed to drive a wedge between this man and the woman he wanted for himself. He thought back, picturing her with the infant at her breast. His pulse quickened, his nostrils flared, as amusement became resentment. Why should St.James have her?

"I did my best. A man doesn't realize what a woman goes through birthing his child until he is forced to watch. Her hand grasping mine as the pains came and went, her moans as I wiped her brow with a cool cloth, the absolute miracle when the babe slid into my hands -."

Stephen had tensed all over. His left hand curled about the rope so hard his short nails bit into his palm. "There was no midwife, no doctor, there?" There seemed to be a red haze over his eyes. He blinked and shook his head to dispense it.

"We were at sea. There'd been a terrific storm just the night before. Our surgeon who would have served as midwife had an injured arm and could only give advice. It went well. You have a brave lady."

He needed to take a deep breath, and another, and another. It couldn't be helped. They had both survived, mother and child. What did it matter in the long run if this man had knowledge of his wife that only he should have? But then the fool's tale continued.

"I almost hated to arrive in Charleston. Mind you, it's distracting enough to have a woman aboard ship. Nursing mothers are a common sight but when one views the scene and you are directly involved – the little one that you held in your own hands taking sustenance there in your quarters – his tiny fingers spread against the cream of - well -."

He got no further. Stephen's fist connected with the hard jaw, sprawling Andrew flat on his back. Up at once, he tackled the man he'd been torturing with words only, eager for blood.

The bored crew quickly converged on the two antagonists. They began to take bets as the two men fought. Andrew's nose was bleeding, probably broken, both men had a blackened eye. Stephen's lip was split and blood trailed down his neck. He grunted as a hard fist crunched into his ribs and he doubled over only to head-butt his opponent. Barrels of supplies tied down on deck were torn loose as the two of them fell into the ropes.

A cut over Stephen's eye was blinding him. He pounded a fist into his rival's stomach and grinned as Andrew fell, ignoring the pain as his lip split further. Not for long, his legs yanked from under him, his head hit the deck and he saw stars. Rolling away from Andrew's well-aimed foot he caught it and twisted. Down he came.

The crew was getting worried. After all, one of these men was their current captain and the other had been captain over many of them. They seemed determined to kill each other. Both were barely able to stand and still they swung, the blows thudding, punishing.

Few noticed that a wind had risen. The empty sails snapped as they filled, the ship strained at the anchor. Hallelulah, they were in business again. With a scramble the men dispersed, even without orders, to lift anchor and direct the ship to the position for interception.

Staggering to their feet, Andrew and Stephen swayed a bit before getting their balance. Grinning, Andrew's first mate handed him a bucket of water, clapped him on the back, and took the wheel. He used part of it, over his head, handing the balance to his opponent.

Stephen shook his shaggy head slinging water in all directions. He squinted through a half-closed eye at the bleeding man before him. He took out his hankerchief and handed it to Andrew, motioning to the man's nose.

"Better get that straightened or you'll look like a dock hand. 'Twould be a shame to ruin so handsome a face." He swiped at the blood on his mouth. "Think you broke a couple of ribs." He coughed. "Damn, that hurts."

Andrew swayed and Stephen grasped his arm in support. Andrew steadied, his tongue licking at a swollen lip. He nodded at the peace offered. Grey eyes met brown in resignation and amusement. The fight was gone out of them. They turned to duty. The British would be on the move

Later they heard that Clinton had attacked Fort Sullivan at Charleston and been rebuffed. Clinton had rejoined with Howe to the north. Washington was on the run but digging in as he went. The Redcoats were reportedly headed for Philadelphia. Franklin was in France negotiating for aid. And winter was setting in.

It would be a long struggle.

CHAPTER THIRTY-FIVE

Christmas had come and gone. Provisions were tight in Charleston but the British were gone again. News said Washington had escaped New York and had won a battle there against the Hessians. No one knew what to believe.

Amy climbed the stairs to the nursery to find Jillian. She paused at the door as she watched Andy playing ball with his mother. They had tried to call him Stephen, or little Stephen, but it just didn't work. And so he was Andy, or Andrew. Mayhap the men had made peace.

She tapped the letter against her hand and Jillian looked up. Everything about her lit up with a smile as she rose to her feet and reached for the note.

"It's from him – Stephen – your papa, sweeting." She patted the little boy on the head. "He misses us and he loves us and - ." Her voice trailed off as she read. Her fist crumpled the single sheet of paper and she ran from the room.

Amy looked at the nanny, then stooped to comfort the wailing boy. “Mama will be back. Nanny will bring you some cookies.” She rose to find Jillian.

She was in her room, pacing back and forth before the long windows. Outside the rain beat against the panes, blown inward over the verandah. The droplets matched the tears streaming down Jillian’s face.

“I have no way to tell him, Amy. No way to let him know he’s to be a father again.” Her hand flew to her rounded belly. “He’s off to England, he and Andrew. They freed the prisoners on his ship and he’s captain again. They’ve decided to harrass shipping off the English coast, try to free more prisoners before they die aboard those prison hulks there.”

She turned on Amy in fury. “Why? Why couldn’t he have come here first? I need him too. I need him.” She sank to the floor, sobbing.

Amy dropped down beside her, wrapping her arms about the shaking shoulders. “He feels he must do this. He loves you. He’ll be back, don’t you worry.”

“But he doesn’t even know about the baby and – and – that I love him more than life. I don’t want him to die.” She took a deep breath trying to stop the tears.

“Andrew will bring him back safe and sound. He made a promise to you and he always keeps his promises.” Amy wiped Jillian’s eyes and nose with her handkerchief. She hoped that wasn’t a lie. Her brother was unpredictable when it came to Jillian. She didn’t know him anymore. She felt iin her heart Andrew had forced this decision somehow.

……………………………………………...…………………....

Only two weeks later there was a knock at the door. The goldsmith, a slim man with half-glasses on his nose, had a package for a Mistress Jillian St.James. He was shown into the parlour.

Both Jillian and Amy greeted their visitor, full of curiosity. They offered refreshment but the little man shook his head nervously.

"I must be going. I've decided to take ship for London. Business has not been good and I will not be returning. I have been closing down my shop."

The two women looked at each other. What did this have to do with them? Amy spoke first. "Is there something you wish us to do, Sir?"

"Oh, no, Mistress. It's just that I was supposed to hold this –umm – package for Mistress St.James until the captain's return but now, you see, well I thought I had better bring it to you in person, M'am."

He extended a small box to Jillian. "It's paid for and I'm sure you will find it to your liking. He was very particular about the wording. I couldn't work it until I found enough gold so it took a while to finish. And then when he didn't come back -. I must be going. Ladies." With a small bow he scurried around them and out the front door.

Jillian stared at the small offering as though it would bite her. Slowly she sat down and removed the lid. The most beautiful gold ring she'd ever seen was inside. Her lower lip quivered as she lifted it to slid on her finger; a perfect fit.

"He said it had wording. It's so wide, how unusual" Amy was almost rocking on her toes she was so excited. She sat down beside Jillian.

The ring was carefully removed and held up to the light. ‘I’ve loved you from our first waltz – Stephen’. Her smile turned into delighted laughter as she replaced the ring on her finger. She was loved; she always had been. She raised the ring to her lips. She could wait now; she would wait forever.

CHAPTER THIRTY-SIX

Where had the time gone? Jillian cupped her daughter's curly head in one hand as she rocked her. Stephanie had her mother's light hair, almost golden, and eyes the color of a summer day. Her thick lashes lowered and the rosebud mouth mimicked her mother's pout as she observed her brother. She was the darling of the house and everyone knew it.

Stephanie squirmed to get down and Jillian lowered her to the floor. Now two years of age, the little girl tried to follow her brother everywhere. Andrew, sturdy and tall for his tender years, watched her with solemn brown eyes before taking her hand.

"You have to mind me if you come outside. Until Papa comes home you do what I say." He gave her a tug and they headed for the garden door.

Jillian's heart tightened at the words. Until Papa comes home – would they see Stephen before they were all grown up? He'd sent money and letters and his love. Andrew had written Amy more of the happenings than had Stephen.

He'd shown no sign in his letters that he'd received hers but then she hadn't expected he would. She'd written in care of his London office and he'd probably not dared go there.

The war with England seemed to be going well for now. France was an ally. Ben Franklin had been, and was still, extremely instrumental in gaining their help. He was so popular there it was said even the ladies' chamber pots were enameled with his portrait. She grinned at the thought. Sometimes she missed the naughtiness of society, just wanted to do something shocking, something a little bit wicked. She had turned into a dull colonial and she didn't like it.

....

Stephen was in London. At wits end for news he'd chanced flying under the British flag. He'd gone first to his shipping firm's office, knowing his father had seen to its status as neutral. There he'd found Jillian's letters. It'd taken a hour to devour them, then re-read every word more slowly.

He had a daughter! A golden blond with blue eyes named for him. He laughed aloud, closing his eyes and picturing the dark-haired little boy holding her hand. He was going back to America. Enough was enough. He hadn't even seen his son and now he was blessed with a little girl. He couldn't wipe the grin off his face as he folded the letters and tied them into a packet.

Jillian had gotten the ring. She loved him still. She missed him. Oh, please, God, let her still love him when he returned. His heart thumping he leapt upon his horse and headed for his father's house.

Gill St.James had just finished dressing to go out when his wayward son was announced. Plans cancelled; he retired with Stephen to the study to exchange news, thumps on the back, and toasts to the newest members of his family.

"I heard some wild tales of privateers freeing American prisoners a while back. Did you have a hand in the venture?"

"Yes, Sir, Andrew Brandon and I together. Guess we represented the American Navy though, not privateers. Managed to do a bit of damage along the coastal waterways also. France has been more than a friend when we needed to refurbish after a fight or take on vittles. They tell the British Navy one thing then allow us access behind their back." He grinned at his father. "I think this war is coming to an end, thank God."

His father nodded. "So do I although not many here would admit to that view. When there's time I'd like to know how you've ended up siding with the colonials – Americans. I'm sure you had your reasons. I did receive one letter from you but the explanation was vague." He turned his glass carefully where it sat on the desk. "But for now I have important news for you, concerning Jillian."

Stephen leaned forward. "Did you catch Shanksbury, the villain? He must have lost touch with Jillian's whereabouts by now. There's been no trouble that I know of in Charleston; at least she hasn't mentioned any."

With fingers steepled, Gill studied his son. "After you left I worked with the contents of the house, inventoried each work of art, each portrait, as requested.

The excess, especially the erotica, was to be sold as Jillian requested. I had several dealers' help and some rather significant bids on the items. The painting in the master bedroom was the first to be sold and I removed it myself."

"As I took it from the wall, it slipped. In catching it, my fingers pushed against the carving surrounding it. The damn thing, a section of the wall, moved – rotated, so to speak. There before me was another painting, a portrait of a young man. He was all but nude, a striking pose, the blue eyes meeting yours in invitation."

"What in the world? Was the model someone you recognized? Why would William hide it away like that?" Stephen leaned forward in excitement.

Gill shook his head. "I don't know. The young man was very blond and looked familiar yet I don't recognize him. It's stored upstairs if you'd like to take a look. William must have cared a great deal about the painting, or the young man. He could rest in his bed and it would have been directly at the foot, in his line of vision, if turned correctly."

"Anyway, I did not show it to anyone else and it has been covered since. Probably it has something to do with our mystery but I'll be deuced if I know what."

"Shanksbury himself came by to see me shortly after that. He said he'd heard we were selling some of the artifacts and might like to bid on some of them. I was non-committal, said a few were already sold and gave him the names. He did check with the buyers but I understand he made no offers on the articles. I've heard no more from him."

....

Stephen stared at the painting. He lifted a cloth and held it to hide the body so he could concentrate on the handsome, almost feminine, face.

"You know, I've seen him somewhere before but I cannot place him. I would bet he was one of William's young lovers. That would explain the placement of the portrait. I doubt if it has anything to do with why Shanksbury wants Jillian removed from England. Perhaps that's pure spite."

His father shrugged and covered the portrait, sliding it into its hiding place once again. "Are you bringing her home? If so, I would suggest we spread the word that you are wed ahead of time. Let all the ton know. The gossip will die its own death before your arrival. Also, it may bring Shanksbury back into play where we can watch him. Is it Jillian or the contents of the house he fears?"

CHAPTER THIRTY-SEVEN- Late 1780

She'd seen the ships docking. All morning she'd hoped it was they, her two men. Surely now Stephen and Andrew would come home. The British were defeated, weren't they? At least gossip said they'd all packed up and gone home. Charleston was jubilant. They'd seen the last of them sailing away in May. Loyalists, most leaving their belongings, had sailed with them to England.

"He's here!" Jillian rounded the corner from the garden and flew through the glass doors just as Andrew entered the room. She stopped before colliding with him, collecting her wits. Her summer frock was low cut with small puff sleeves, the neck and waist edged in ribbon. Her hair was tied back and up to leave her neck free in the heat but strands had escaped and flew about her face. Excitement tinged her cheeks with color.

Wide grey eyes stared at him in dismay, then lowered demurely to hide her expression. Her shoulders sagged.

Andrew wanted to catch her in his arms; lord, how he wanted to feel her against him. It had been months since they'd slipped into any town, years since they'd had a decent night's sleep beneath a roof. But it was not he she wished to see and he knew it. He forced the smile to remain on his face.

"Don't dispair, Mistress. He's here." He stepped aside as Stephen entered behind him.

"Oh!" Jillian ran into her husband's arms. "Oh, thank God. Oh, I've missed you so." She was covering Stephen's face with kisses and they were both laughing.

At last Stephen held her still and crushed her mouth with his, claiming a savage kiss. His hand cupped her bottom, pressing her close. They were lost to Andrew's presence as they devoured each other.

Andrew cleared his throat and Amy, who had just entered the room, actually giggled like a girl. Jillian stepped back, gazing up at her husband, memorizing every detail, every change. Her fingers brushed through his dark hair, trailed down his chiseled cheek.

"I believe you've given me a daughter and a son, My Lady. I have yet to meet them. Where -?" He looked around with an amused grin, one brow raised.

Jillian took his hand, laughing. "Come." She led the way up the stairs to the nursery, chattering all the way.

Amy watched her brother's face as his eyes followed them. "It's well that's he's back. It would not have worked, you know."

Andrew turned a bland expression on her. "What would not?"Accepting her kiss of welcome, he followed her into the parlour and sprawled on the sofa.

Amy poured him a brandy and placed it before him. She followed his eyes as he again looked toward the stairs. She made an exasperated noise, slapping at her brother's arm, as he started to rise.

She lowered her voice. "Give them some time alone. She's not yours." When he relaxed back onto the sofa she sighed. "Sally Burton did not follow her family back to England, you know. Methinks she was waiting for a special someone to come home. She still lives at the big house; they haven't confiscated it. She shops at the market every week on this same day, with a servant. If you hurry you could see her, perhaps arrange something. You'd like her now."

His mouth turned up in amusement. "Is she as perfect as ever? Do you not know why Jillian fascinates every man who lays eyes on her? She's wicked – inside she knows how to create havoc with a man – just knowing she was trained for a man's bed – the way she moves – all unconscious of her curves - ." He stopped. "I shouldn't be talking to my sister this way. I've been away too long. My apologies." He glanced up the stairway again.

Amy supressed an outright laugh. "A good husband can teach a woman what she needs to know to please. I may be a widow but I remember. Will was happy with my few talents. Also, Sally and Jillian have become friends. They've had long chats."

Amy watched the stairs. "You should not burn for what you cannot have. He is back. She is happy with that. They are married and have a family. Let it be."

Andrew's nostrils flared. "Married, hmmph. He admitted he tricked her into said marriage. Still, she seems to prefer him. I will leave it at that. Anyway, he's a good man to have by your side in a fight." He kissed his sister's freckled nose. "I guess it'll do no harm to visit Sally. She's a pretty little thing as well as I can remember." He looked toward the stairs once again. "They're takiing a long time. Perhaps -."

He shrugged and sank back to the sofa as his sister caught his arm.

Upstairs, Stephen had indeed enticed his wife into his arms once again. His mouth ravaged hers as his hands roamed over her softness. He'd backed her against the wall at the top of the stairs. Pulling her sweet bottom against him he groaned when her legs parted to cradle him with her hips.

His eyes met hers, melting with heat, unfocased. "Where? Your room?" He murmered against her lips, "Which room is yours?"

Jillian couldn't catch her breath but glanced to the front chamber. He gathered her into his arms and deposited her on the bed there before she was able to speak.

Frantic, they tore at their offending clothes, all the while touching, caressing. When he entered her she was already so wet with need she shattered about him, her body arching, as his mouth caught her cries. He followed into that world of wonder with such explosive force he thought he'd died. Still panting, arching to get closer, her sheath pulsed around him as she came once again. Laughing softly, Stephen kissed her deeply.

"I don't think I'll live long with you as wife but I'll die the happiest of men." His crooked grin was interrupted when she bit his lip, her tongue salving the hurt. "I'm hardening again. We'd best save this for later or they'll wonder what's happened to us."

Jillian giggled, her tongue playing havoc with his senses. "They'll know." But she wiggled from under him, dizzy with sex and happiness.

……………………………………………....…………………....

Andrew walked close to the stairs as he heard footsteps descending. Jillian came into view, her dainty ankles kicking up ruffles with each step. She looked dishelved, her cheeks rosy, her lips bruised. Her face was all smiles.

"I didn't mean to ignore you, Andrew. I was just so excited to see Stephen. Do forgive me – and thank you for bringing him back." Jillian leaned over the banister to greet Andrew, her hand extended to him.

He took her fingers in his, brushing his lips across them. His view at that moment caused his breath to catch, his manhood to push for escape against the restraining trousers. How could she be so tempting – so unthinkingly wicked? The beauty of that slim throat, her shoulders, the twin globes nestled in soft gathers. Every breath she took was suddenly torture. He almost groaned, his throat dry. She was still speaking. What had she said?

As though in a dream he noticed Stephen descending behind her, the small girl sitting on the crook of one arm, his hand enclosing his son's. Unaware of the scenario playing out below him he studied his son as he murmered softly to his daughter.

Andrew wanted to escape before his condition embarrassed everyone. Why had he come with Stephen to the house? He should've remained aboard ship. Now his sister had convinced him to drop by the market today, hadn't she? Sally Burton would be there - sweet, beautiful, perfect, Sally. He wanted Jillian, wild, beautiful, wicked, Jillian. Damn Stephen St.James for surviving the rebellion – the war – whatever the hell it was.

His expression must have reflected some of his thoughts for suddenly Amy caught her brother's arm and pushed him toward the door. "You'll be late for your 'chance' meeting." She stretched on tiptoes to whisper into his ear. "Don't worry. All women, beneath that sweetness and fluff, are a little bit wicked."

Andrew's chortle filled the air as he sauntered down the path to the gate. So they were friends, were they? Had Jillian taught Sally how to be naughty? He couldn't wait to find out. Onward to the next challenge.

CHAPTER THIRTY-EIGHT
London 1781

The ball was given by the Earl of Montclair in honor of the new Duke of Glenburke, Lord George Shanksbury. The old duke had died the previous year and the title and holdings were now in his possession. The entire ton was invited, anyone who was anyone. Even the newly arrived blacksheep, Stephen St.James and his disgraceful wife were included. After all, she had been the new duke's sister-in-law. Giles St.James had made sure they received an invitation.

It was their first foray into society since their arrival and the St.James' unexpected appearance brought a hush to the room upon their announced entrance. Women brought their fans up, the better to peer over them at their rival for attention. The men, married and unmarried alike, observed Jillian St.James with obvious discretion. Would she or would she not? One had heard her husband was a jealous man but arrangements could always be made.

Two of the more notorious rakes were overheard in a discussion of her charms, and a comparison to the younger 'lady in crimson', notorious in ton gossip from a few years prior.

Lord Shanksbury stilled at her appearance. He hadn't heard she was invited or he would have made certain arrangements. His eyes flickered to the far side of the room where his stepson, his son now, stood with a group of young men. He motioned to get his attention and Philip crossed to his side.

"You didn't tell me she was in town."

"I don't know everything, Father. Besides, it's been years. There's no need to worry." Philip's blue eyes twinkled as he met his father's stern ones. "She'll like me. You'll see."

"I should have left you on the continent until I had the matter taken care of. With luck she would have remained in that God forsaken country they call America." George turned his back to the room. "Try to stay away from her."

Philip merely smiled and strolled in the direction of the new arrivals. He could almost hear his father's teeth grinding behind him. He reached the St.James and executed a bow.

"Cousin Jillian, I believe. I'm the new marquis, heir to my father, George Shanksbury." He raised her proffered fingertips to his lips and brushed them with a kiss, his blue eyes sparkling. "Philip Shanksbury, at your service."

Jillian smiled at the handsome young man. He was probably only a bit younger than she. The lights of hundreds of candles seemed to shine from his golden hair. She turned to her husband to introduce him but Stephen had turned to another group and was deeply involved in conversation.

"I don't believe we've ever met but I was at your wedding - to my Uncle William. You were a lovely bride and he was very proud of you."

Jillian couldn't remember him but then she didn't remember much about her first wedding. She'd been so unhappy yet filled with hope. It hadn't worked out.

A cotillion began and Philip asked her to dance. Glancing at her husband, who nodded, she accepted. Once on the floor she had to concentrate on the intricate steps. It had been a few years since she'd gone to a ball.

Light conversation passed back and forth as the dance permitted. But whenever she met Philip's eyes it was as though she was touched with a shadow of something unpleasant, some memory, something. She frowned.

"Am I making you unhappy, My Lady? It was never my intention. I would always cherish your happiness if it were up to me." He smiled at her, giving her fingers a slight squeeze.

What a strange thing to say. She answered him politely, assuring him she was having a lovely evening. When he led her to her husband's side as the dance finished she introduced him and he departed. She looked after him in confusion. It had been a strange conversation.

She danced the waltzes with her husband, the other dances each with a different man. They seemed to cluster about her in droves but Stephen seemed amused so she decided to enjoy it. Even so, he stayed nearby for most of the evening although he did his duty, dancing with a number of ladies. He was as much in demand as she but more able to excuse himself from participation.

Her father-in-law had brought her punch. Gill took her arm, leading her to the open doors and onto the terrace.

"I saw you dancing with a blond young man I haven't met. He's Shanksbury's adopted son, I'm told. How well did you know him?"

"I didn't before tonight. He's a strange young man. He's been traveling on the continent for a few years it seems. He says he remembers me from my wedding to William but I don't recall seeing him there. Of course, I was not too aware of the guests that day."

"You don't remember seeing him at William's estates, in the house, at any time?" Gill waited for a reaction, watching her face. He was guessing but would not put the idea into her head unless - .

"I don't think so." Jillian shook her head. "But when we were dancing and I met his eyes it seemed to fill me with melancholy. Foolish, isn't it? He's so nice and quite good-looking."

In the library, behind closed doors, Philip was having his ears blistered by his father.

"You think you know everything, do you? What if she remembers? Everything I've worked to bury will be common gossip."

"You mean everything Mother worked for, don't you? If she were still alive the lovely Jillian would not be here; a shame."

The elder Shanksbury's face turned a mottled red. "Do not speak to me like that, you young pup! Everything was done for you, everything! You have not the sense of a toad!" He wiped his perspiring face with a lace handerchief and tucked it back into his sleeve.

Calmer now, he continued, "You've breached the family gap now so you might as well make use of it. See if you can find out if they will reside in London; if they will be selling the house. The elder St.James has been selling off some of the contents for her but only one of the paintings has gone - that monstrosity of erotica."

"So, they haven't found it yet." Philip tapped his pursed lips with a slender fingertip. "Perhaps they won't." He frowned. "Oh, by the way, I understand the head stableman, Ned, is quite ill. You wouldn't have anything to do with that, would you, Sir?"

His father glared at him without answering. "Some things are best left to nature. Your mother never trusted the man."

"Is that a confession?"

"Humph!" With that said, George Shanksbury straightened his gold-threaded vest and exited the room.

……………………………………………...………………....

Jillian and Stephen settled into a routine of sorts in the following days. They resided at his father's townhouse, with the children. The nursery there was always maintained for guests or visiting relatives and the house was large.

In the evenings they attended suppers, the theater, musicales, or various entertainments. The couple's notoriety served to increase their popularity. No attempts were made on Jillian's life but she was not allowed to go out without a strong male escort.

Jillian's inherited house was being refurbished and was full of painters and decorators. She was constantly in and out, observing or changing something. No decision had been made but it probably would be leased once it was again decent.

The various artifacts that were left and the remaining paintings that were not wanted would be displayed in the lower rooms before the final furnishings were in place. They would give a viewing with refreshments so the artwork could be seen for purchase.

It had been Jillian's idea; not quite the thing to do for one of the ton, but she no longer cared what they thought. They made no secret of being in trade and this alone separated them from the old order.

She and Stephen were planning to buy a small country estate and his father and brother were scouring the countryside for suitable property. They'd had enough of London. When Stephen was there on business or they wished to attend some function they could stay at the family townhouse, as now. The old house made her sad and she did not wish to live in it although it would be a good investment for the future.

Stephen's shipping business was thriving. His reputation seemed to have survived the American strife although it was known that he'd favored their independence. Few knew just how much a role he'd played in the effort. London would always be his head office but he continued to do business with the fledgling country. His heart had a real stake there.

Gill and his lady, Catherine, settled into life with children underfoot once again. They'd never been the type to keep their own little ones exclusively in the nursery and now enjoyed Andrew and Stephanie's antics.

Only Stephen was still obsessed with the threat to Jillian. Was it still present? He wouldn't allow anything to happen to her after he'd found happiness. They'd not shown the blond Adonis' portrait to Jillian. His father had insisted to let it be unless there was trouble. He had his own theory but did not share it with his strong-willed son.

It was a lazy day and they'd had a late night. They'd been called to Jillian's house around midnight. Someone had gotten past the guard, broken in, and searched through the packing boxes. They'd not been caught nor was anything missing that they could tell. Sleeping late, the family had just finished a light lunch when an unusual visitor was shown into the back sitting room. Jillian joined her there.

The girl turned to face Jillian. She wore a neat but plain dress, that of an upper-class maid. Her hair was tucked into a mobcap. She was twisting her hands in her skirt.

"Rose? Is that you?" Jillian took a step forward to embrace her once maid, her arms outstretched. Younger than Jillian, the girl broke into nervous giggles as Jillian's arms folded about her.

"Oh, Mistress, I've missed you." She backed away as she was released. "I thought you'd never come home again."

"It's so good to see you, Rose. Is this a visit or are you out of work? Do you need a job? I could use a good maid, I could." She was one of the few friendly faces she'd known in William's household.

The girl bit her lip and shook her head, then followed with a nod. "I would like very much to work for you, M'am. Can I start just now? I can't go back there. I'm scared." Her chin quivered.

"Of course you can – but -. Why, whatever is the matter?" Jillian motioned for the girl to sit.

"You know my brother, Ned, was head stable master. Well, he got the promotion after you left. Anyway, he died, a week ago Friday. He's buried and all now but he wasn't sick that long and it wasn't right, his being sick. Ned, he was always real healthy. He was all I had in the world."

She looked down at her hands, knotted in her lap. "They'd have let me go after you left if it weren't for Ned. He had this secret. He told me when he was dying – said I was to come to you."

The two women were unaware of Stephen standing just outside the door. He'd followed his wife to tell her he'd be at his fencing practice. He'd stopped when he'd heard the conversation. He could see his wife lean forward, saying nothing, but taking the girl's hands in hers.

Rose's head dipped, her eyes on the floor. "He said you'd forgive him; you were a good woman. If it weren't him they'd of got someone else and let us both go." Tears had begun to roll down her rosy cheeks.

"It was the lord, Lord Shanksbury. Ned was supposed to 'cause the coach to come loose on that bad curve, throw the master out. He was supposed to die right off but he lingered forever, his back broken and all. I'm so sorry, M'am, so very sorry." She raised a tear-streaked face to Jillian. "You can change your mind if you don't want me."

Jillian sat very still, stunned by the tale. Stephen stepped into the room and Rose attempted to flee but he caught her wrist.

"You have the job, Rose, and our protection. Sit back down. Tell us who ordered this 'accident'?" He stood over her, intimidating but kind.

Rose tried to speak, stuttered some nonsense, snapped her mouth shut. She began again after looking at Jillian for reassurance.

"He said it were the lady, Mistress Matilda herself, what came to him. Paid him a handsome fee to do it and promised him she'd take care we both had jobs and him a promotion when it was done. Ned didn't have no choice, Sir, you see?" She straightened her shoulders. "And I'm a good maid, Sir."

"George Shanksbury, Lord Shanksbury, never approached your brother? Are you sure it was his wife?" Stephen was thinking fast. Matilda was dead now but Matilde's son – the son, Philip – was George's adopted heir.

Rose shook her head until her mobcap loosened. "No, My Lord, it were the lady. The new Lord don't like the horses much. He never came around the stables until lately; just before my Ned took ill. Ned thinks he put something in that half-bottle of whisky he left in the coach; told Ned he could have it, he did." Her nose twitched with resentment. "Ned always did like to take a swig." She clamped her mouth shut, offering no more.

Jaw clenched, Stephen met Jillian's eyes. "Have the housekeeper put her on staff. I need to talk with my father."

……………………………………….……………….

"So, George is cleaning up the loose ends, is he? 'Tis said the woman doted on the boy." Gill took a sip of the fine brandy Stephen had just offered. "And who is next, I wonder?" He and Stephen exchanged looks. "It's time we show Jillian the painting."

"Or perhaps not just yet, Sir. I have an idea." Stephen smiled but the smile did not reach his eyes.

……………………………………….……………….

The open viewing was a success. There had been notices in the museum and the university. Special invitations had been extended to art connoisseurs and interested members of the ton. The George Shanksbury and his son, Philip, were issued separate invitations to be sure each was received.

The painting of the handsome young man was prominently displayed in the front parlor on an easel. Stephen and his father roamed through the rooms keeping an eye on the guests. There were several hired Bow Street men for security also.

Jillian stood gazing at the prime display, a slight frown on her face. She'd seen him before, but where? The frame itself was worth a fortune. William must have favored this particular portrait. She glanced down the youth's torso. He had been portrayed nearly nude. Would it create a scandal or be deemed a work of art? He was very beautiful.

Something triggered in the back of her mind. The youth must be one of William's young lovers. That was it. That was why it was framed in such a special way. She turned to tell her husband and bumped into a broad chest.

"Philip Shanksbury? Oh, I, we weren't expecting you but I'm so glad you could drop by." Her eyes were even with his chin and the slight cleft there caught her attention as he broke into a broad smile. Without thought she turned back to the portrait. The chin, the blue eyes, the - . Her breath caught and her hand went to her throat as mermory flooded her senses.

Those eyes offering sympathy as he lay in William's bed, as her husband had berated her for her intrusion. His nude body displayed across the satin sheets. His shaft erect, nested in golden curls. And William, when she'd invaded his room – William's hard body covering the young man's.

"Oh, my God, it's you." Her words were a mere whisper but he'd heard her. His hand closed over her wrist with surprising strength. Still smiling, he tugged her in the direction of the side entrance to the garden.

Once out of sight he forced her against the brick of the wall, his face an inch from hers. He was no longer smiling. His body threatened to crush her, taking her breath.

"We will wait here for my father. I am supposed to create a diversion. Do you have any suggestions how we might do that?" He was entirely too close. She wanted to call for help but that seemed foolish at the moment. After all, he wasn't exactly hurting her and the house was full of people.

"Why, Cousin? Why couldn't you let it alone? Why did you have to display my portrait for all to see? I was barely sixteen when that painting was done. Still, are you stupid enough to think everyone will not guess I was William's lover?"

Jillian's mouth moved but no sound came out. They stood so close her lips brushed against his face as his eyes locked with hers. One of his hands encircled her throat, slowly tightening but not strangling her. She couldn't cry out now. She tried to shake her head in denial of the display. She'd had no hand in it.

Inside, Stephen watched the crowded rooms for George Shanksbury. Philip was here but the trouble would come from the father. He saw his own father stroll through the front room, glancing at the protrait. It had a group of ladies about it, all smiles and giggling behind gloved hands. Had no one recognized the young man? And where was Jillian?

Jillian managed to pry her fingers between his so she could whisper. "I didn't mean to hurt you. I didn't know."

His knee jammed between hers, spreading her legs, throwing her off balance. "Didn't you?" He tightened the fingers at her throat. "Father wishes me to marry. Did you know that? Says I must like the ladies as well. In fact, I'm told I'm very pleasing to them. Would you like to see? While we wait?" His upper thigh began to move, pushing against her sex. His hand tightened once again about her throat, his mouth hovered over her parted lips.

"Mewling, disgusting things – women. So easy to manipulate." His knee lifted her, forcing her to ride him. He grinned against her mouth. "See? So easy. I can have you begging in moments. Are you wet yet? Would you give me what William could not stand to take?"

Tears hovered on her long lashes. She tried to escape but she was pressed hard against the brick, her arms caught between them.

"Shall I show you real delight? Here, in your garden, where one of your guests might venture to see? You may scream when I take you. That should qualify as a diversion, even for my father." His eyes were cold as blue ice; his expression no longer sane. "It's been a long time. I've done without, you see, to please my father. I've earned a bit of ass."

He turned her to face the wall, caught her wrists behind her. The coarse brick scraped her face as he pushed her face-down over the low railing leading to the flowerbeds. She made a croaking sound as air came back into her throat.

"That's it. Scream; scream for your husband. I'll be waiting. He caused this, shamed me." His voice had risen an octave. "If I can't gut him, he'll spend the rest of his life as a eunuch. Scream, damn you." His left hand tightened cruelly about her wrists.

Jillian clamped her mouth shut. Her hair had come loose and fell over her face, blinding her. She felt the cool air as her skirt and petticoats were lifted. Oh God, oh God. She twisted but his grasp was firm. She felt his knee separate her legs as she was leaned forward.

His right hand was fumbling with the opening of his breeches. She tried to kick backward but her feet couldn't touch the ground or him. Sobs tore at her throat as she felt his hand fondling her bottom, his hips fill the vee between her legs. Her eyes squeezed shut, she tensed for his rape.

Instead the weight lifted from her. Her husband, her Stephen, was there. He dragged Philip backward by his throat, his fist connecting with the trim jaw. Long-legged and in good shape, Philip was still unprepared. He landed against the far railing, bringing several pots filled with flowers down atop him. He recovered at once, shaking his blond hair from his eyes, glaring at Stephen. He saw Stephen turn to his wife, pulling her skirts down to hide her nakedness, lifting her to the terrace floor.

Philip's hand closed over the knife hidden in his boot. He'd learned much in France. When he stood, he let fly the deadly blade.

Stephen's distraction with Jillian was enough. He had considered the young man a fool but not dangerous. She called a warning just as the knife left Philip's hand. Too late; it buried itself in Stephen's back.

The Bow Street Runner shot at the same time. Philip crumpled, clutching his belly. Pandemonium broke out.

She didn't remember screaming, her throat raw. The garden was suddenly full of people. Jillian sank down beside her fallen husband. Gill St.James, not realizing his son was injured, searched for the missing Shanksbury in the farther rooms where he'd been standing. A doctor, present among the guests, pushed his way through to Stephen's side.

George Shanksbury had been in the parlour, glowering at the painting when the uproar had begun. He hadn't known his son was in the garden but he had asked for a diversion. In the confusion he managed to slash the protrait from its frame. Now, he tried to make his exit but was stopped by another Bow Street Runner. Gill was close behind. He was dragged onto the terrace to join the now-silent gathering.

....

Behind the painting there were love letters between William and the young Philip. One included a frightened message asking William to speak with his mother who'd just learned of the affair. It was dated a month before William's fatal accident.

Philip had been mortally wounded. Both men were turned over to the authorities. Enough evidence was there to convict the two of them of multiple crimes, if not murder. The Shanksbury family name was at an end.

....

Jillian wiped her husband's brow with a cool cloth. His chest was taped with linen bandages still but he was breathing easier. He opened his liquid brown eyes. They seemed to melt and darken as he looked at his wife.

"It's over." She brushed her lips across his. "I forgot to thank you for my rescue. I could never have faced you again in the marriage bed if he -." Her thick lashes fell to hide her eyes.

Stephen's smile was seductive, his old crooked one designed to make her forget. "Never is a long time. No man but me will touch you again. I'm very possessive. I so swear. And if it had happened - remember this – I love you, no matter what. The sin would not have been yours." He raised her hand to his mouth, kissing her knuckles.

Sin; there was that word again. She'd never told him about Andrew. The man was gone, meant nothing to her, but she had sworn she would tell Stephen. Guilt still ate at her. The time was never right.

She hesitated. "Stephen, you know I love you. I've loved you since forever. But I doubted you for a while there, in Charleston. I imagined you'd fabricated the tale of our marriage to smooth my way as a hostage. I didn't hear from you. It'd been over a year since you'd touched me. I thought you'd forgotten me. I was so lonely. I dreamed of you; imagined your kisses, your body taking mine. I ached for you."

His eyebrow rose to a peak. Where was this going? Her tongue played over her full bottom lip making him think of other things. He was only half listening. Then he caught Andrew's name. He frowned. She had stopped speaking. What had she said? Something about promising she'd tell him.

Her eyes glimmered with tears. She leaned over him and kissed him with tender care, then drew back. "If you do not want me I will understand" She swallowed. His eyes lingered on her slender throat. So beautiful; he imagined his lips there. "When our son was near a year old – it was late and I couldn't sleep – I thought it was you at first – that man in my bedchamber. I don't quite know how it happened -." A tear rolled down one cheek as she hung her head. It splashed onto his hand.

Stephen's fingers reached out to stop her lips. Nothing mattered anymore but his love for her, not even Andrew. "Shhh. No more, my darling. I am not a priest, nor a saint. I do not hear confessions. What is done is done, and past."

She fell into his arms without thought of his injury. He had to force himself not to stiffen as the pain in his back objected to her weight. Then they were smiling, their hearts beating as one, both attempting to feather kisses everywhere they could reach. He caught her nape and kissed her thoroughly, loving her, forgiving her anything, anything at all. He tipped her chin up so he could see her lovely eyes, eyes centered on him alone.

"What would life be without a little bit of wickedness, my love?"

THE END

Printed in the United States
42727LVS00001B/1-24